Christmas
Wishes

Katie Flynn

Christmas Wishes

arrow books

Published by Arrow Books in 2011

2 4 6 8 10 9 7 5 3

Copyright © Katie Flynn 2011

Katie Flynn has asserted her right under the Copyright, Designs
and Patents Act, 1988, to be identified as the author of this work.

First published in Great Britain in 2011 by
Arrow Books
The Random House Group Limited
20 Vauxhall Bridge Road, London, SW1V 2SA

www.randomhouse.co.uk

Addresses for companies within The Random House Group Limited can be found at:
www.randomhouse.co.uk/offices.htm

The Random House Group Limited Reg. No. 954009

A CIP catalogue record for this book
is available from the British Library

ISBN 978-0-0995-5053-2

The Random House Group Limited supports The Forest Stewardship Council (FSC®),
the leading international forest certification organisation. Our books carrying the FSC
label are printed on FSC® certified paper. FSC is the only forest certification scheme
endorsed by the leading environmental organisations, including Greenpeace. Our paper
procurement policy can be found at www.randomhouse.co.uk/environment

Typeset in Palatino by Palimpsest Book Production Limited,
Falkirk, Stirlingshire

Printed and bound by
CPI Group (UK) Ltd, Croydon, CR0 4YY

For Kath Arnott, who bore
patiently with the questions
and queries I hurled at
her husband; thanks, Kath.

Acknowledgements

My sincere thanks go to Roy Arnott, who did his best to unravel the mysteries of the Fire Service in the 1940s and 50s; the bits I got right are due to Roy, any mistakes I made are my own!

Chapter One

October 1945

When Miss Jensen came into her classroom, the Lawrence twins were fighting. Miss Jensen sighed, walked across to the desk and rapped sharply on it. The twins immediately broke apart, but whereas Joy beamed at the teacher, Gillian, though she also smiled, broke into speech. 'It weren't my fault, Miss Jensen,' she said defensively. 'Joy said she were goin' to sit next to Annie when we get aboard the Liverpool train the day after tomorrer, and *I* want to sit next to her. She's as much my pal as she is Joy's and I'm the eldest, so it should be up to me. Ain't that so, Miss?'

Miss Jensen sighed and rubbed the back of her neck; she suffered from occasional severe headaches and could feel one coming on, and her back twinged when she had to keep jumping to her feet. But she never let the children know; what good would it have done?

'Behave yourselves and stop squabbling,' she said crossly. The twins were identical, but the fact that Gillian had come into the world twenty minutes before her sister must be known to everyone, both in the school and in the small village to which the girls had been evacuated several years earlier. Most of the children had already gone home, but the families of the ones remaining had

1

elected to leave them with their foster-parents until the school half term, owing to a shortage of accommodation or, sadly, the death of one or both parents in the bombing. The twins' mother had been such a casualty, but their father had said he could cope once he had made arrangements with his relatives and employers. 'Sit down, both of you . . . no, not in a double desk; you'll only start squabbling again. Gillian, you share with Avril . . . and as I've told you a hundred times, we all know you're the elder and we don't care a bit!'

'Oh, but Miss . . .' the older twin began, only to be promptly squashed.

'Don't be ridiculous, Gillian. As I've just said, age doesn't come into it,' the teacher said sharply. 'And isn't this a little early to start claiming your place on the train? Remember, even though the war's over, many things, including rail travel, have not yet returned to normal. The journey back home may mean several changes, and many delays, so you could take turns sitting next to Annie, if you feel it is so important.'

Annie, a placid, plump and pink-cheeked fourteen-year-old – the twins were thirteen – twisted round in her seat to grin at her friends. 'I got two sides, haven't I? Joy could sit on me left and Gilly on me right. What's wrong wi' that, you two?'

'We can't . . .' and 'Don't call me Gilly,' the twins chorused, Gillian adding in a belligerent tone: 'It's always the same. My mam chose me a real beautiful name – of course when I popped into the world she didn't know ugly old Joy were comin' along behind – and if she'd wanted me to be called Gilly . . .'

Miss Jensen, sighing and feeling every one of her

sixty-six years, pointed out sharply that since the twins were identical Gillian could scarcely call her sister ugly, but Joy cut across her words. 'We can't sit one on each side of Annie because twins have to be together,' she explained kindly to the now seething teacher. 'Actually, I don't mind who I sit next to on the other side – though of course I'd rather it were Annie – since at the end of the journey we'll be back in our own home, with our own dad, and that's all that really matters.'

Miss Jensen clapped her hands smartly as the girls began to chatter and waited for silence before she spoke. When she did so, the children must have realised from her tone that she was in no mood to be trifled with, and both twins and Annie mumbled, 'Sorry, Miss,' before settling back in their seats, all three wearing expressions of meek obedience which an angel might have envied.

Miss Jensen cleared her throat. 'I know you're excited at the thought of returning to Liverpool after so long away,' she said, smiling a little, 'but this conversation is getting us nowhere and there's still work to be considered.' She turned her head to glance at the clock. 'I shall give you an essay to be done between now and tomorrow morning, so get out your homework books please.'

For a moment she wondered wildly what subject she could choose which would be interesting enough to put the thought of returning home out of the heads of her rebellious charges. It was not an easy choice, for the class now consisted of children of various ages who had remained behind after a good few of their classmates had returned to the city when the worst danger of bombing raids seemed to be over. The twins, Miss Jensen reflected now, were a case in point. After their mother had been killed in the May blitz their father, Alex Lawrence, who was sub-officer on Blue Watch at the fire station in Old Gadwall Street, had explained to both the teacher and the farmer's wife that with two nine-year-old girls on his hands he would not be able to give his whole mind to his job, which was an essential one in wartime. Both had agreed that he was doing the right thing.

In the four years since then, he had managed to visit them three times, and Miss Jensen thought that no man could have done more, for the journey was long and complicated. She had met Alex Lawrence once or twice and had liked him. He was a tall, well-built man with close-cropped light brown hair, and though not handsome he had a craggy and attractive countenance and an easy, pleasant manner. The teacher knew that he wrote weekly, because the twins were proud of his letters and showed them around. He illustrated them with tiny pictures which he thought might amuse them, and meticulously addressed such letters to each twin by turn, though he knew of course that they would read every word of every missive many times over, regardless of to whom the letters were addressed. No girls, Miss Jensen was convinced, could have had a better father, which was as well since the twins, though delightful in many ways, were not the easiest of children.

Now, faced with two rows of expectant faces, Miss Jensen thought quickly and came up with a subject she hoped would be within the capabilities of her ill-assorted class. 'First memories,' she said briskly. 'I want you to write an essay of at least two pages, in your best handwriting, telling me the very first thing you can remember. That should be possible for all of you, no matter what your age, and because we shan't be here much longer I shall dismiss the class as soon as you've had your dinner, which will give you a whole afternoon to complete the task. Any questions?'

Annie's hand waved and she jumped up and down in her seat. 'Shall we do it in pencil or ink, Miss?'

'In pencil, of course, since that will enable you to rub out spelling mistakes or grammatical errors,' Miss Jensen said, wishing she could have growled *In blood*, the way her old French teacher had answered that perpetually asked question. 'Any other questions?'

A hand belonging to eight-year-old Lizzie shot up. 'Please Miss, I don't 'member nothin' before the fire, and then all I 'member is this great big tall feller wi' a shiny 'at on 'is 'ead carryin' me down a ladder. But that weren't me first memory, 'cos I were quite big by then, but don't 'member a single fing afore that.'

'Then that is your first memory,' Miss Jensen was beginning when Gillian interrupted.

'I bet that were me dad, the feller wi' the shiny helmet,' she said importantly. Miss Jensen opened her mouth to tell her pupil to speak properly, the way she had been taught, then shut it again. In normal circumstances the twins spoke with very little accent, but now, thinking about going home to Liverpool, they seemed to drop into the dialect they had scarcely used for the past six years. 'He's saved a thousand kids, my dad.'

'Not a thousand,' Joy cut in, looking reproachfully at her sister. 'There ain't a thousand kids left in Liverpool because of the evacuation.' She twisted round to face the younger girl. 'Were it our dad, Lizzie? How old was you?'

'I dunno,' the child said vaguely. She was a small, mousy little girl, orphaned since the May blitz, and was apt to trail in the wake of the twins, attracted, Miss Jensen thought, by both their self-confidence and their pretty looks. However, it would not do to let the girls start chattering amongst themselves, so Miss Jensen rapped sharply on her desk once more.

'*Will* you be quiet!' she said crossly. 'Yes, Elizabeth, that's a very good first memory and I shall be awarding a small prize for the best essay, so remember to write with great care.'

Another hand waved; this time it was Suzanne. 'Miss, Miss, my first memory's real borin', not excitin' like Lizzie's. I 'member fallin' downstairs when I were a little bit of a thing, only I didn't know I were fallin', I thought the world had shook up and the house were turnin' over and over . . .'

'Wharrabout us, Miss?' Gillian interrupted. 'We's identical twins, so we's bound to remember the same things. But I don't want to have the same memory as our Joy. It's time I had somethin' of me own. Even me initials aren't really me own.'

Miss Jensen opened her mouth to reply, but Joy was before her. 'I bet our memories are different as anything,' she said indignantly. 'And of course your perishin' initials are your own, because I'm Joy Isabel Lawrence and you're Gillian Ianthe Lawrence. J I L and G I L are quite different.'

'Well, they sound the same,' insisted Gillian. 'When we get home, I'm goin' to ask our dad to let me have a different middle name. I want to be Gillian Bridget Lawrence, like our mam. I'd like to be called Bridget!'

'Well you shan't; it's our mam's name. Don't you dare

try to steal it,' Joy said, clearly forgetting her usual placidity at her twin's suggestion and growing pink with indignation. 'If our dad heard you say that, he'd give you a ding across the lug.'

'That's enough!' Miss Jensen said, her voice rising to something perilously akin to a shout. She descended from the dais on which her desk stood just as the dinner bell sounded and with one accord the class rose to its feet and surged towards the door. The twins would have followed, but by then Miss Jensen's temper was up and she grabbed a shoulder of each with a thin and bony hand, forcing them to remain seated. 'Joy Lawrence, I'm ashamed of you! What would your father say if he heard you speaking so coarsely? But because I know you and your sister – and the other children of course – are tremendously excited at the thought of going home, I won't give you the punishment you deserve.'

'Thank you ever so much, Miss,' the twins said in chorus, Joy adding: 'I dunno why we behaved so badly, and you're right about our dad: he likes us to talk proper.'

'Properly, you mean,' Gillian said reproachfully. 'Dad says our mam never talked Scouse.'

'As for you, Gillian,' Miss Jensen said, ignoring the interruption, 'you should be even more ashamed of yourself. Only ten minutes ago, you were reminding us that you were the older twin, and therefore more responsible. Now you're behaving like a five-year-old.'

Gillian cast her vividly blue eyes up to the teacher's face. 'I'm sorry, really I am, Miss Jensen, only sometimes it's no joke being a twin. Sometimes you just want to be yourself . . . oh, I can't explain; you'd have to be a twin as well to understand.'

7

'I understand a good deal more than you imagine,' Miss Jensen said grimly, pushing a strand of thin grey hair behind her ear. 'But I know how you two children have longed to go home to your father and the rest of the family, so just this once I'll let you off with a caution. I shall expect excellent behaviour throughout the journey back to Liverpool, however, or I shall be forced to tell Miss McCullough that you are troublemakers. I'm assuming that your father intends you to return to St Hilda's, which is a good school with an excellent reputation, and Miss McCullough, as headmistress, wants that reputation to remain untarnished. Will you give me your word that you'll behave properly from now on?'

The twins promised fervently to do exactly as they were told, and since, as a rule, they were bright and helpful pupils Miss Jensen dismissed them and returned to her desk as they scampered from the room.

It's always the bright ones who give the most trouble – and the most rewards – she reminded herself, tidying her desk and heading for the staffroom. I wonder what sort of essay I'll get tomorrow morning from those two little monkeys, though. One thing I'm sure of – despite Gillian's remarks, they will be completely different, because though the girls look alike their personalities are almost exact opposites.

For the first couple of miles on the way back to their foster home, which was a good distance from the village and the school, the twins squabbled. There was no malice in it, and Joy had known how it would be the moment the teacher had mentioned 'first memories'. Gillian had always vowed and declared that she remembered an incident which had happened when they were only a few days old. She said she had been lying in the old Moses basket when a long, weathered face had appeared before her. She said she had been frightened, had clutched at her twin, even as the strange woman – for it was a woman – spoke. 'Like as two peas in a pod,' the woman had declared in a creaky, odd sort of voice. 'Oh aye, Biddy my love, you've followed family tradition. As I say, them little 'uns is like as two peas in a pod, same as your cousin Liam's boys and his brother's wee girls.' She had bent even closer, her black, gypsy eyes gleaming. 'Sure an' ain't they the prettiest things,' she had cooed. 'Mind you give 'em pretty names.'

Joy herself could remember nothing of the occasion and was convinced that Gillian was remembering not her Irish grandmother's visit but their mother's description of that visit to their home in Liverpool. After all, a babe, only days old, could not possibly have understood words spoken in any language. It was tempting to confront Gillian with these facts but Joy, knowing how it would irritate her twin to have the story disbelieved, held her tongue. Instead, she said mildly, linking her arm with Gillian's: 'Are you goin' to tell how our Connemara gran came to visit us and left before we was two weeks old? Only if you do, you can be sure our first memories will be different as different.'

Gillian gave her sister's arm a squeeze. Joy thought the squeeze probably meant *Thanks for not scoffing*, but she continued to gaze enquiringly at the other girl. 'I dunno,' Gillian said vaguely. 'Perhaps I'll say my first memory was the day Mum and Dad took us to the seaside. We must have been three or four and what I remember most . . .'

'. . . is how astonished we were when the holes we dug filled up with water,' Joy said, remembering the incident perfectly. 'It seemed like magic, as though our little wooden spades had found a secret spring. And then there were ices and that pink cotton stuff which melted away when you got it into your mouth . . .'

Gillian snatched her arm away from Joy's and gave her a shove. 'That was *my* bleedin' memory!' she shrieked. 'Oh, I *knew* how it would be! Whatever I do, you simply have to copy me. Well, Joy Lawrence, that day out in Rhyl is going to be *my* first memory, so don't you dare try to pinch it!'

Joy giggled; she couldn't help it. Gillian's reactions were always the same, but as Daddy had said, she was just like a bottle of pop when you shake it up. It fizzes and froths, then gradually goes calm again. So she simply said: 'You're a twerp, Gillian; I was just remembering. I wouldn't dream of using the same rotten old memory as you. Anyway, it wouldn't be true. I *think* my very clearest memory is of evacuation day, and Mum pinning the labels on to our coats, reminding us that I was to wear a green ribbon to hold back my hair and you were to wear a red one. She said Miss Jensen had promised to see that we weren't parted, but she thought folk would be more eager to take us in if there were a way of telling one from t'other. I remember how our mum cried and kissed us, and reminded us to fill in our postcards and send them off as soon as we knew where we would be living. D'you think that would be okay?'

'It's better than mine,' Gillian said, her tone more

admiring than envious. 'Only I don't *think* it could possibly be your first memory, because we were what, seven or eight? And people of eight remember what happened when they were four or five, if you see what I mean.'

'Ye-es, but it's something I'll remember all my life, if I live to be a hundred, or even a thousand,' Joy said, after some thought. 'And Miss said we could choose . . . at least, I think that was what she meant. Anyway, that's the memory she'll get from me, and tomorrow's our last day in school . . . last day in the village, really . . . so if she don't like it she'll jolly well have to lump it.'

'I wonder how she feels, going back to Liverpool and St Hilda's after so long away,' Gillian said thoughtfully. 'Of course she's returned to Liverpool sometimes, in the school holidays, but she's always come back to us.' She looked sideways at her sister. 'But have you thought, Joy? We went to the baby class at St Hilda's because Mummy said a good grounding was important and we would get that there. But she also said that she and Daddy wouldn't be able to afford the fees for the senior school, the one you move to when you are eight, so I don't suppose we'll be going. I wouldn't dream of saying so to Miss J though, because she's a dear, really. In fact we've been really lucky, Joy, to have had her all the time we've been here. I'd have hated to have a new teacher every few months, like some kids have had.'

'Mm . . . hmm,' Joy said rather thickly through a mouthful of the little wild marabella plums which grew in the hedgerow. 'But do you know *why* she's stayed with us? It's because she's so old. She had retired in 1938, but came back into teaching when so many young ones – man teachers and lady teachers, I mean – left to join

11

the forces. I remember Mrs Dodman saying how she admired Miss Jensen for continuing to teach such a motley crew as our class. After all, she was a St Hilda's teacher and St Hilda's pupils are all clean, tidy little girls like us, smart as paint and clever as – as the Prime Minister, but she's had to cope with village kids and evacuees from other schools too. It can't have been easy.'

It was Gillian's turn to giggle. It had been dry for a week and the girls had been scuffing through the white dust and dead leaves which lined the lane. Both had mouths and chins purple with plum juice and their skimpy gingham dresses were faded, their cardigans patched. 'I wouldn't call us either smart or clean, and only one of us is clever, which is me,' she said, digging Joy in the ribs with a sharp elbow. 'Are you going to miss the country and the Dodmans, and our funny little bedroom crammed under the eaves, where we can watch the birds making nests in the thatch of a Sunday morning? I know I am.'

'I'll miss all of it, of course, especially the Dodmans,' Joy said thoughtfully. She ignored the remark about cleverness, because challenging it would have been point-less; Gillian was easily the brainier twin, though her claims to be the prettier Joy thought daft. Oh, Gillian's hair was a darker auburn and her freckles were less pronounced, and when they stood side by side Gillian was perhaps an inch the taller, but the differences were so slight that only when the girls were together were they ever commented upon.

Now, Gillian chuckled. 'Do you remember how the Dodmans hated us when we first arrived?' she asked. 'Mrs Dodman said she'd never had chick nor child of her own and didn't fancy sharing her home with a couple of kids from a big city, who would doubtless drive her demented in a week.'

Joy chuckled too. 'She tried to palm us off on the farmer, but Mrs Goody said that they were getting their land girls, so that didn't do poor Mrs Dodman much good. I don't know what they might have done to get rid of us if it hadn't been for Mr Dodman needing all the help he could get at lambing . . .' She sighed reminiscently. 'Many a time he told us that he was a shepherd, a master of his craft, and not a mere farm labourer. But of course he had to turn his hand to everything when the younger chaps were all called up.'

'When the land girls arrived, things were easier,' Gillian pointed out. 'They were wonderful once they'd learned what was expected of them, but at first half of them were scared of the animals and went into hysterics at the thought of assisting a sheep to give birth to her lambs. That was where we came in. We liked it all and did whatever we were told to help, so when things quietened down a bit and Mrs Goody offered to find us lodgings nearer the school, the Dodmans were horrified.'

'Yes, I remember it well,' Joy said. 'They pretended they were afraid they might get even worse evacuees than us, but the truth was, we fitted in pretty well. If you ask me, they're going to miss us like anything, though Mr Dodman pretends it will be nice to have the cottage to themselves.' She turned to her sister. 'Do you remember the house in Liverpool, Gillian? I think I do, though it's pretty hazy. Our bedroom was up a flight of quite steep little stairs and there was a long, low window. I remember if you pushed the window open as far as it would go, stuck your head out and looked to the right, you could see Daddy's fire station. I think there was a rug, with pink roses, and the floor was shiny boards, but I don't really remember the living room or the kitchen. And of course we've never seen the bath and lavvy that Dad's had put in the little boxroom, have we?'

'No, and won't it be grand to have a proper bath?' Gillian said dreamily. 'And we shan't need to use the jerry if we want to widdle in the night. Daddy thinks of everything, doesn't he?'

'He sure does; I mean to wash my hair every Friday night, like the girls in the magazine advertisements,' Joy said at once. 'Friday night's Amami night, that's what they say. But we're going to start a whole new life, aren't we, Gillian? No more country lanes, or walks through the woods collecting acorns for the pigs. No more ambling into the village when Mrs Dodman wants some shopping done. No more pond dipping or traipsing round the jumble sales looking for a dress to fit. I know you said Mrs Dodman sold our clothing coupons, but she fed us really well, so she was welcome to mine. Do you remember once, when we were eating that fruit cake, Mr Dodman said it weren't really fruit cake, it were the new serge skirt Mrs Dodman had had her eye on? They both cackled like anything, because I'm sure they thought we didn't know what they meant, but of course we did.'

Both girls chuckled at the memory, but when they reached the little path which led down through the trees to the Dodmans' cottage, Joy stopped and looked around her. 'It's rare beautiful though, ain't it, Gillian?' she said wistfully. 'I'm never sure whether I like spring or autumn best, but I think autumn's the loveliest. Look at the different-coloured leaves on the trees; the wild cherries red, the beeches gold, the chestnuts a lovely goldy green until they turn brown. And very soon the hedgerows will be scarlet with hips and haws . . . yes, I'm sure we'll miss the seasons because they don't happen in the city, do they? It'll just be roads and pavements and the good old Mersey . . .'

'Oh, but think of the shops!' Gillian breathed. 'I've missed the shops something terrible. When I told Daddy we missed them he said we weren't missing much. Half the shop windows were empty, he said, so it weren't too exciting, but now the war's well and truly over – even those horrible Japs have surrendered – I 'spect the shops will be crammed with good things. And the markets, of course.'

As she started walking once more Joy thought again of the hundreds of things she would miss, but reminded herself, brusquely, that living once more with their father would make up for everything. And when I'm grown up, I mean to marry a rich feller and have a farm of my own, she told herself. And Dad did promise that he'd bring us back to stay with the Dodmans for a couple of weeks every summer. That will be the best of both worlds.

Albert Dodman was hedging and ditching in the long meadow which ran alongside Millers Lane when he heard the twins approaching. Hastily, he ducked out of sight, though he was pretty sure they would be far too involved in some quarrel or other to so much as glance in his direction, and as soon as they had passed he resumed his labours. This hedge would be relaid before dark if he kept at it, but if he had allowed himself to be distracted by the twins heaven alone knew when the work would be done.

The thing was, though he had grumbled mightily when the girls had first been billeted on them, he had grown quite fond of the brats. He knew that had they spotted him they would have wanted to help, or at least to chat, reminding him of their imminent departure and asking him, for the hundredth time, if he wouldn't miss them like anything once they were gone. Naturally, he had always said that he'd prefer their space to their company, had scoffed at his wife's openly voiced regrets, had even gone so far as to tell the girls that all he would miss would be the weekly sum paid by the government to everyone fostering evacuees, but he thought that he had not fooled them for a moment. They were good kids, the pair of them; ripe for any mischief, of course, but always eager to help and bright, too. I never wanted young 'uns, Albert told himself now, skilfully bending a branch which wanted to grow upright into a horizontal position, but if I'd knowed what they could be like mebbe me and the missus might have took on one of her sister's kids after her feller was drowned, seeing as how we had none of our own.

Albert worked on steadily, trying not to think how empty the cottage was going to feel when the little room under the eaves no longer sheltered the twins. He had never climbed the ladder-like stair during their occupancy – his rheumatics forbade it – but his wife had told him that the kids kept the room in apple pie order, though at first she had objected to the ragged bunches of flowers and leaves, the badly blown birds' eggs and the other rubbish brought in and apparently highly regarded by two city kids.

But it would never do to brood, so Albert speeded up a little and by the time the light was fading the hedge alongside the lane was finished. He stood back. 'Neatish bit o' work,' he said beneath his breath in self-congratulation, for the hedge had been in sad need of relaying. 'Ah well, best be gettin' on home. Mother will have the kettle on the hob and the tea on the table by the time I get back.'

Despite the fact that they had never had children, he and his wife stuck to the old country habit of referring to one another as Mother and Father, and for the first time Albert realised how strange this was. Then he dismissed the matter from his mind and, gathering up his tools, set off for the farm, meeting one of the land girls as he entered the yard. He grunted a greeting but did not linger; this was likely the last evening the twins would have time for him, so best make the most of it.

Chapter Two

The crowing of the old cock who lived with his numerous wives at the farm which employed Mr Dodman woke Joy, as it had done every morning for the past half-dozen years. In the depths of winter it would still have been quite dark outside, and Joy would simply have rolled over and gone back to sleep, knowing that she would be woken in good time for school by Mr Dodman shuffling around in his bedroom on the ground floor and shouting at his wife to 'get the kettle a-boiling so I can have a warm wash as soon as I reach the kitchen'.

Today, however, was the last day in school and though she wondered, hopefully, if Miss Jensen might not mind late arrivals on such a day, she swung her feet out of bed, seeing without surprise that Gillian was doing exactly the same. There was enough light coming through the window to enable them to wash and dress without the candle, but she knew that Gillian would light it anyway. Her sister was finicky in her habits, brushing her hair vigorously before plaiting it and spending time making sure her clothes were neat and tidy and her person immaculate. Joy tried her best to follow her sister's example but the fact was that in this, as in so many ways, the twins were very different. Joy seldom thought about her looks and scarcely glanced at her reflection in the small mirror which stood on the chest of drawers, whereas Gillian, having ascertained that she had left no button unfastened, would dip a finger into the washing water and smooth down her eyebrows, an affectation which always made Joy giggle.

This morning, seeing Gillian doing this, she dug her twin in the ribs. 'What'll you do tomorrow when we have to be at the station at the crack of dawn, you conceited little pig?' she asked. 'We shan't have much time to spare, you know, 'cos we don't want to miss the perishin' train.'

Gillian whirled round, gave her sister a shove in the chest, and then let her eyes flick scornfully over her. 'I'll get up earlier, of course,' she announced. 'And you'll have to do the same, like it or not. It's your turn to carry the slop bucket. Did you use the jerry in the night? If so, you'd best empty it into the bucket and make sure that the lid's firmly fastened.'

'I didn't; I almost never do,' Joy said placidly. 'Oh, come on. Mrs Dodman's got the porridge on. I can smell it from here.'

The girls descended the stairs, Joy coming last, holding the slop bucket carefully away from her school dress. The cottage only had one upstairs bedroom – the one the girls occupied – and the Dodmans used the small room on the ground floor at the back. The rest of the cottage consisted of the large, quarry-tiled kitchen and a parlour so crammed with fancy furniture that there was scarcely room for anything else. Indeed, the Dodmans only used the room at Christmas and for the occasional party or meeting, for Mrs Dodman was a keen WI member and when her turn came round would not have dreamed of entertaining her fellow members in the kitchen.

Following their usual routine, Joy made straight for the kitchen door and headed through the windy grey morning towards the midden where she would empty the slops. Gillian, she knew, would be doing what Mrs Dodman called 'laying up', which merely meant setting the table for four persons, fetching the milk from the cold slab in the pantry, and standing a jar of the Dodmans' honey in the centre of the table.

As she re-entered the kitchen, Joy saw that her sister had also set out a large pat of dewy fresh butter and a jar of their hostess's homemade plum jam. Joy licked her lips. A large loaf of Mrs Dodman's bread stood ready for cutting and Mr Dodman was sitting in his old basket-weave chair by the fire, holding out a laden toasting fork and telling his wife that they must go easy on the honey, for in winter the beekeeper feeds the bees and not vice versa.

'As if I didn't know,' Mrs Dodman scoffed. She turned to the twins. 'Mr Goody up at the farm knows I'm a-goin' to pack up a li'l hamper for your daddy, so he's given me a few things . . .'

'Yes, yes, that's all very well,' Mr Dodman said quickly, and Joy guessed that he had seen how his wife's hand had gone to her cheek, surreptitiously wiping away a tear. 'Get a move on, girls; I've near on finished work in long meadow, but I'll walk wi' you that far, if you hurry yourselves. And as it's your last day in school, you'll mebbe come out early; if so, you'd best pop into the farmhouse and thank the master and mistress for the grub they've sent for you to tek home tomorrer.'

*　　*　　*

20

Because of the slow trickle of departing evacuees which had taken place since the Japanese had surrendered, Miss Jensen only had seven children to supervise on the journey back to Liverpool. They met, as arranged, on the platform, fifteen minutes before their train was due, the children huddling close to one another and each face surrounded by a halo of steaming breath, for it was cold so early in the morning. Despite the fact that they were going home, there were many signs of tears, and both Joy and Gillian had had to wash their faces a second time at the pump before leaving the cottage.

Mr Dodman had borrowed the pony and trap from his employer and he and his wife had driven the girls to the station, where they had helped them to carry their luggage on to the platform and had then hung about, Mrs Dodman full of inexpert but well-meant advice for young travellers and her spouse, gruff-voiced, reminding the twins of their promise to write and assuring them that should they come back to the cottage for a visit no one would be happier than he and Mother.

Earlier, Joy and Gillian had helped to clear away the breakfast things, each aware that this was a moment they would remember for the rest of their lives. They had often grumbled to each other that Mr Dodman was old and cross and Mrs Dodman demanding and stingy, but now they knew that they could not have had better people to take care of them. Mr Dodman's occasional grumpiness always had a good reason and his wife's insistence that waste, especially waste of food, was a sin, particularly in wartime, had its roots in the poverty they had known in the thirties and was never meanness. Indeed, she was the soul of generosity.

'Farmer and his wife have give you a bag o' apples and a batch of cream scones,' Mrs Dodman had announced, indicating the bags and parcels piled beside their suitcase with a jerk of her head. 'We've put in a loaf of my own bread, a jar of honey, another of plum jam, a pat of butter – you'm never been give margarine at *my* table – and a few little extras. I reckon your pa'll be glad of them, havin' two great girls to feed instead o' just hisself.'

'Never mind all that; they'll doubtless be havin' a bit of a snack as soon as they're settled in the train if they know there's food goin' beggin',' Mr Dodman had said hastily, and Joy had realised that he had once again been trying to deflect their attention from a tear rolling down his wife's weathered cheek.

'No, we shan't,' Gillian had begun indignantly before Mr Dodman had seized the bulging suitcase and the heaviest of the paper carriers, and bidden them somewhat curtly to follow him or they'd miss the blessed train and then where would they all be?

'In the suds,' Mrs Dodman had said rather thickly, and, as if it were a signal, both twins had begun to cry and Mr Dodman had to shout at them to 'git aboard the perishin' trap or we really will miss the train!'

Snivelling, the twins had helped to load the trap and then they had washed their tearstained faces at the pump, flung themselves at the Dodmans and given them ferocious hugs, and taken one last wild look around them at the cottage which had been their home for the past six years. Then they had climbed aboard the trap and tried to compose their features so that when they reached the station no one would guess at their distress.

Now, Mr Dodman cleared his throat and glanced around at the other adults who had accompanied the evacuees and were staring hopefully in the direction from which the train would come. 'Reckon it's time we left these young people to fend for theirselves,' he said gruffly. 'If I'm not back in the yard with his pony and trap by the time work starts, Mr Goody won't be best pleased.' He grinned at Miss Jensen. 'So Mother and meself will be off,' he finished, and before anyone could say anything he had seized his wife's arm and marched her out of the station, closely followed by the other foster-parents.

'Oh, but we didn't say goodbye properly . . .' Joy cried, but at that moment the train arrived and all was bustle and confusion. Some of the adults turned back but the Dodmans were already, Joy guessed, climbing into the trap, because when she and Gillian turned towards the booking hall through which they had gained access to the platform there was no sign of the old couple.

Miss Jensen began to pile the luggage aboard and the children, helping, were saved the embarrassment of a protracted farewell by the porter coming along the train, slamming doors and waving his flag. Goodbyes were shouted, and as the train began to move the twins leaned out of the window, knowing that the Dodmans would stop the trap for a last wave as the train picked up speed and thundered over the level crossing.

When the train rounded a bend so that the village was out of sight, Joy sniffed and rubbed her nose. She had always hated farewells, but she reminded herself, briskly, as she took the seat beside her sister that Dad had promised a return visit the following summer. It's not goodbye, she was thinking, when Miss Jensen, who had been rummaging in a large Gladstone bag, smiled around the carriage.

'How sensible you are, children; no tears or fuss,' she said approvingly. 'And I must remind you that you aren't saying goodbye to your good hosts, but merely au revoir, which is a French phrase meaning "see you again soon". And now, though I expect you have had breakfast, I've a little treat for each of you.' She produced from her bag a number of small chocolate bars, which she handed around before producing another bundle. 'I took the precaution of packing some old copies of the *Beano* and the *Dandy* in case you grew bored with watching the passing scene,' she said, offering them around, and the twins were soon absorbed, as were their companions.

It was not a corridor train, so they had the carriage to themselves for the first part of the journey. Joy realised that they should put the past behind them and look forward to the future. Oh, won't it be wonderful if Daddy really does meet the train, she thought; he said he'd try to do so but trains are hardly ever on time any more, so it might not be possible. She turned her head to look out of the window and saw the scarlet ball of the sun edging up over the horizon and gilding the fields and copses as they passed. Miss Jensen had warned them that it might be a trying journey, but Joy knew that so far as she and Gillian were concerned it was an adventure, and the crock of gold at the end of the rainbow was to have their own dear daddy back in their lives once more.

Joy settled back in her seat, refused the copy of the *Dandy* which Gillian was flourishing, and pressed her nose against the windowpane. Comics she could have in the city, but the beauty of the Devonshire countryside was a fleeting pleasure as the train hurried towards its next stop, and Joy settled down to watch.

Alex Lawrence awoke and, seeing sunshine through his bedroom window, thought it was that which made the day seem special. But as soon as he swung his legs out of bed he remembered. The twins were coming home at last, and how he wished he had his darling Bridget beside him, sharing his excitement at the thought of having their girls back with them again.

When everyone had known that war was imminent, he and Bridget had talked of the evacuation and decided, though only after much heart-searching, that the twins must go with the rest of their classmates. 'Look what the Huns did in Spain during the civil war,' Alex had reminded his wife. 'Bombing the big cities despite promises to do no such thing. Do you think they won't do the same here? Air power will be the thing this time, not trench warfare, and the children will be a good deal safer in the country than living cheek by jowl with one of the biggest ports in England. Biddy, my love, I know you hate the thought of sending them away, but it's for their own good – no, for their lives – and we mustn't let sentiment cloud our judgement.'

So Gillian and Joy, two little seven-year-olds, had been despatched in September '39 to a small village in the heart of the Devonshire countryside, and with no children reliant upon her Bridget had looked round for war work, and found it. Alex was a fireman at the big fire station just up the road from their house, and as soon as it was known that women were being recruited to run the control room Bridget had volunteered and been taken on. Alex and the other firemen worked shifts – three days on, then three nights on, then three days off – and so did the staff in Control. Alex loved his work and talked about it constantly at home, so Bridget had had a head start over the other workers, and had soon become a valuable member of what Alex always referred to as his 'family'.

When the May blitz had started, the firemen had been on call constantly. Alex and Bridget had barely met for the best part of a week, and Alex knew that Bridget had followed his Watch's call-outs in constant dread, for firemen were at the very forefront of the action. Shamingly, he thought now, it had never occurred to him that it might be Bridget who died, yet it had happened. The raid had been over, though the whole city had seemed to be ablaze, but when Alex had come off duty and made his way home it was to find Fred Brown, the Station Commander, awaiting him. 'Your missus was caught by the blast as she left Control,' the man had said roughly. 'They've taken her to the Stanley. You'll want to see her . . . I'll come wi' you, old feller.'

'Is she much hurt?' Alex had asked, his heart starting to beat overtime and a coldness invading his limbs. He had known the question to be a foolish one. The officer wouldn't have waited for him if it had been anything trivial. 'I'll come at once, of course. Is – is she . . .'

The man had taken his arm. 'She's gone, mate,' he had said gently. 'It was blast, so she looks peaceful; I reckon she didn't know a thing.'

The days that followed had been a nightmare and Alex's only consolation had been to work even harder than he had done before. He had arranged the funeral for a day when the twins could be present but when he had seen them, two tiny figures in makeshift black, clutching their teacher's hand whilst tears poured down their pale cheeks, he had regretted insisting that they come home. He had not wanted them to return to the house, even for a night, with all its memories of their mother and had accepted gratefully when his sister Serena and her husband had offered to take them in; two very subdued, sad little girls, strangely polite but anxious, Alex had realised, to escape from the terrible gloom which had enveloped, it had seemed, the whole of Liverpool.

The girls had been in Devonshire ever since, and Alex hoped that it had been long enough for them to forget the misery which had surrounded that visit. He knew they were bound to miss their mother and had intended, at first, to sell their small house and move. On one of his rare visits to the farm he had put the suggestion forward, only to have it indignantly refuted by both girls. 'We like to be near the fire station and we can scarcely remember the house anyway, so it won't make us think of Mummy more than anywhere else would,' Gillian had said. 'Please, please don't make us move again, Daddy. We know the neighbours and the shops and the park; why should we have to get used to somewhere different?'

So Alex had complied with their wishes, though he had had a bath and lavatory installed in the boxroom and repainted the kitchen and living room. He was glad now that he had not tried to move house, for every room in No. 77 held memories of Bridget and with the passage of time he had grown to value those memories, all happy ones. He was sure that the twins, too, if they remembered their lives before the war at all, would feel the same, for his Bridget had been a young woman, always smiling, with a great sense of humour.

Now, Alex left his bedroom and crossed to the bathroom, looking around him with pleasure, trying to see it as the twins would do. The bright blue linoleum matched the blue of the curtains at the window, and when he turned the tap and ignited the geyser hot water gushed into the hand basin. Alex grinned to himself; great to have hot water for shaving without the bother of boiling a kettle in the kitchen and carrying it upstairs. Of course the twins would not have to consider shaving, but at thirteen they probably considered themselves young ladies and would appreciate instant hot water.

Alex finished shaving and dressed in his best: a white shirt, a Fair Isle pullover and dark grey trousers. Then he headed for the stairs. In the kitchen he made himself toast and tea and ate and drank quickly, thinking about the day ahead.

Alex had been preparing for his daughters' return for weeks and would be off to the station to meet their train in half an hour. Now he stood, eyeing the kitchen table with considerable pleasure. He had been determined to greet his children with a wonderful celebration tea, but he was no cook and certainly would not have dared to use precious ingredients in an attempt to bake something fancy himself; for the past few years he had lived on fish and chips and shop-bought bread, cakes and pies.

To make today special, however, he had been prepared to go to any lengths and had sought help from Cyril Clarke's widow, a notable cook and a cheerful, energetic little woman. She had no children of her own, but she often babysat for young mothers who wanted a break from their offspring, and always asked after the twins when she and Alex met. Mrs Clarke lived in the end house of Alex's terrace, and despite the fact that before Cyril's death the two men had been good friends he did not know her very well, although he always stopped for a few words when he came across her, either going to the shops or exercising the fat, evil-tempered pug which she had taken on after its owner had been killed in the May blitz. The pug was named Dilly and though Mrs Clarke had never owned a dog before, and disliked pugs in general and Dilly in particular, she was too soft-hearted to let the animal be destroyed and now shared her home – and her rations – with the pop-eyed, irritable creature.

At work one day, a couple of weeks before the twins were due to come home, Alex had voiced his desire for some real home cooking so that his girls would have a grand homecoming and one of the young firemen had suggested that he should approach Mrs Clarke. 'She's a rare cook, and if you give her the flour and that she'll make whatever you want,' the young man had assured him. 'She's ever so nice, Mrs Clarke, honest to God she is. I reckon she'd be happy to help. My mam always calls her the good Samaritan because of the way she rescued that perishin' pug. You go round there, tell her what you want, and ask her what you're to buy.'

Alex had felt uneasy about asking such a big favour from someone he did not know well, but when he had seen a small box of chocolates in a shop window and found he had exactly the right number of coupons with which to purchase it, he decided fate was taking a hand. Armed with the chocolates he felt he could approach Mrs Clarke, so on his way back from the corner shop he had knocked on her front door.

It had only occurred to him that she might think the chocolates were a bribe when he heard footsteps approaching, and so embarrassed had he been by the realisation that she might be insulted by his offering that he had turned and walked away. He had been heading for his own home, hot-faced and feeling as guilty as though he really had been about to offer a bribe, when he had heard the patter of feet on the pavement behind him and felt a hand on his arm. He had swung round, meaning to explain that he had knocked on her door by mistake, but it had proved unnecessary. The little woman had broken into hasty speech. 'Oh, Mr Lawrence, I've been trying to catch you, but you're such a busy person! I remember how it was when my dear Cyril was alive, so I do understand that you've not much spare time, but a little bird told me . . .' she had looked coyly up at him, her rosy face growing even rosier, 'a little bird told me that your girls are coming home at the end of the week and I was wondering if you could do wi' a bit of a hand, like?'

Alex had drawn a deep, ecstatic breath; he had dreaded having to ask a favour and here she was, offering him help as a matter of course. He had let out his breath in a long whistle of relief. 'Phew! I meant to come and ask you if you might do some baking for me – I'd pay for it, of course – but it seemed a lot to ask, so I bought a box of chocolates, only after I'd knocked your door it occurred to me . . .'

'It occurred to you that I might think you were trying to pay me in advance,' Mrs Clarke had said, beaming up at him and taking the chocolates Alex was proffering. 'Thanks very much, Mr Lawrence. I shall enjoy these, if Dilly don't get at them first! I've a sweet tooth, so you needn't have been afraid I'd turn hoity-toity on you and refuse to accept them. However, anyone round here will tell you I'd be happy to help and ask no payment. I enjoy cooking almost as much as I enjoy eating, so you'll be doing me a favour, not vice versa. If you tell me what you want, I'll get the ingredients and bring you a bill so's you can see I've spent what I said I would. Now, will you come back to my house whilst we talk baking, or would you feel more at ease in your own place?' She had twinkled up at him. 'If you come to mine, I'll make you a cup of tea and you can sample my work, 'cos just before I come out I'd taken a batch of almond tarts out of the oven and stood 'em on the windowsill to cool. Course, I didn't use real ground almonds 'cos they're difficult to find, but almond essence does nearly as well. Folk tell me my almond tarts are good, but you must judge for yourself.'

Alex had gone back to the end house and for the first time in ages someone else made him a cup of tea, buttered a scone for him and then presented him with a pretty floral plate upon which reposed two delicious-looking almond tarts. 'This is prime,' he had said to his hostess as, cup in hand, she had sat down opposite him. He had looked around the kitchen, which was a replica of his own so far as size went but bore all the signs of loving care which his own, he knew ruefully, lacked. 'When Biddy was alive . . . but no use to look back. Only I suppose I've let things slide, what with the girls being away and myself more often at the fire station than not . . .'

Mrs Clarke had nodded sympathetically. 'I remember how it was when the war started. I worked in a factory making munitions, only after Cyril died I became allergic to some of the materials used in the factory and had to find another job, so I became a fire watcher. All I had to do was take up my position on one of the highest buildings around and report any fire whose location I could identify – I had this sort o' telephone thing, which you wound up by hand. So I did help in my own small way. And on the days when I wasn't fire watching I worked in the WI canteen, or went out on one of the vans, so's the fellers trying to dig out folks who had been buried in the rubble could have tea and a wad, as they used to say.' She had chuckled suddenly. 'Trust me to get off the subject and go rambling on! Where were we? What I was tryin' to say was that firemen don't have much of what you might call spare time. Why, even when you aren't on Watch you could be called in. So don't worry, Mr Lawrence, I'll be happy to do the shoppin' for you. Which shop are you registered with? Only I think I'll have to have your written permission to buy the stuff with your coupons.' She had leaned forward. 'What did you think of those almond tarts?'

For answer, Alex had held out the plate, clean as a whistle. 'I've not tasted anything so good for years,' he had said frankly. He had then bent down to pat the dog, who was investigating the quarry tiles around his boots, and had yelped sharply when Dilly had snarled and snapped at his fingers.

'Sorry, but it doesn't do to get between Dilly and her grub. She thought you were goin' to tidy away the crumbs before she'd had a chance to gobble 'em up,' Mrs Clarke had explained. 'Well? I take it you'd like me to do you a bake? I don't know if you're aware of it, but like many another I keep half a dozen hens in me back yard, so eggs won't be a problem. And I can lay me hands on a grosh of apples and plums at this time o' year. So what d'you say? Little individual fruit pies are nice . . .'

The discussion had become animated, and by the time Alex left a menu had been drawn up which had made his mouth water. He had asked what he could do to help and after eyeing him shrewdly for a moment, Mrs Clarke had suggested that he might buy some flowers with which to decorate both the kitchen table and the twins' bedroom. 'I expect you have a pretty tablecloth and a set of napkins,' she had said. 'When I was a girl, every one of us had what we called a bottom drawer where we stored away stuff for when we were wed. Your dear wife was clever with her needle; I remember her showin' me the most beautiful tablecloth, embroidered all round the edge with snowdrops, crocuses, primroses – oh, all the spring flowers you can think of. I'd put money on you having it still.'

'I'll find it,' Alex had promised. 'I've not seen it for years, but I'll find it before the girls come home.'

A knock on the door brought Alex back to the present and, with another quick glance at the table, he crossed the room and opened the door. The young daughter of another member of his Watch, Fred Finnigan, stood there, holding a bouquet of chrysanthemums, tawny, dark red and gold. As he opened the door, she pushed the flowers into his arms, her cheeks flushing a delicate pink as she did so. 'Hello, Mr Lawrence,' she said breathlessly. 'The flowers are from Dad's allotment. He thought as how you might like 'em to give a bit of colour . . .' She glanced sideways and saw the table and her eyes widened. 'Gosh, that looks just wonderful, but I see you've already got flowers.'

Alex took the chrysanthemums from her and laid them carefully on the Welsh dresser. 'Mine came from one of the stalls on Great Homer, and I'm afraid they're already looking rather sad,' he said untruthfully. 'I'll put them in the parlour window and use the ones your dad grew as a table centre. My, they're magnificent! Tell your father I'm most grateful and I'm sure the twins will be as well.' He hesitated, looking at the laden table, as was his uninvited guest. Knowing that she must seldom see such delicacies as those spread before her, he picked up a plate of tiny brightly coloured cakes and held it out. 'Help yourself to a couple,' he said.

'Gosh, thanks, Mr Lawrence,' the girl said, choosing with care. 'Where on earth did Mrs Clarke find crystal-lised lemon rind? Our mam was only sayin' yesterday that she'd not seen an orange or a lemon since 1939.'

Alex laughed and returned the plate to the table. 'I believe she used to make candy peel herself and store it in large sweetie jars,' he explained. 'She's a marvellous cook and no one could have a better neighbour.' He had closed the door when the girl entered, but now he opened it again and held it politely. 'Thank you for bringing the flowers, dear, and don't forget to tell your dad how grateful I am.' He looked at the chrysanthemums, their great heavy heads almost as big as household mops. 'I'm sure they're prizewinners, every one.'

The girl flushed brightly. 'They're grand, ain't they, Mr Lawrence?' she said shyly. 'And . . . me name's Irene.'

'That's a very pretty name, and you're a very sweet girl,' Alex said gravely and patted her cheek, noticing with some amusement how the touch of his fingers made her blush. 'Goodbye now, Irene, and thanks again.'

After he had closed the door, he wondered whether it had been wise to pat her cheek, even though it had only been the sort of fatherly caress one gives one's daughters; she was only a couple of years older than Gillian and Joy, but he scarcely knew her, even though her father was his second in command and a good friend. But there could be no harm in it, after all. Sighing, Alex dismissed the matter from his mind, picked up the chrysanthemums and gazed rather helplessly down at them. He knew he had no vase big enough to hold them, knew that if he did put them on the table they would look absurdly out of place. Now that he could look at them closely he realised that there were only four flowers, but they were so large that the best home for them would be on the parlour windowsill, where they could be admired by passers-by. He would have to put them in the largest jam jar he could find, though, which would look rather odd.

He was still pondering the problem when the clock above the cooker struck two. Cursing his forgetfulness, he headed for the stairs, for he had promised himself that he would be at the station promptly at two, though the children's train was not due until nearly four. But how dreadful if the train were early and he missed his girls!

He grabbed the chrysanthemums and ran water into the sink, plunging the stalks into it. Then he gave one last, proud look at the table, left the kitchen, locking the door firmly behind him, and set off towards Lime Street station.

Irene crossed the yard and went into the jigger, where her friend Lucy Biggins awaited her. As soon as they set eyes on one another they both began to giggle until Lucy, sobering up first, demanded to know what had happened.

'Oh, Lucy, I love him more than ever,' Irene said, linking her arm with her friend's. 'I give him the chrysanths – my, wouldn't our dad be livid if he knew it were me that took 'em – and Mr Lawrence were real pleased. He give me a couple o' little cakes with curls of candied peel on top.' She plunged a hand into the pocket of her skirt and produced them. 'I were goin' to keep 'em for ever, on me bedroom windowsill, so's when we're married I could show him the first gift he ever gave me, only . . .'

'. . . only they'd be green wi' mould and stinkin' after a week,' her friend said cruelly. 'Shall we eat 'em now or later?'

Irene looked regretfully at the pretty little cakes, but her mouth watered as she handed one to her pal. There would be other keepsakes, she told herself, licking a dusting of sugar from her lips. She meant to befriend the twins when they came home, for though she had left school the previous June – she was fifteen and working in a small grocery shop not far from St Hilda's – she was sure she would find opportunities to ingratiate herself with the younger girls.

Irene watched as Lucy devoured her own little cake in a couple of hungry bites, then seized her by the arm. 'He axed me in. The table were just splendid, Lu, all laid out on a fancy cloth with flowers an' everything. Why don't we go up to Lime Street station and see if we can meet the kids' train? Then we could walk home with 'em, and . . .' here wishful thinking took over, 'they might invite us in to share their grub, seein' as we'd provided them prize chrysanths.'

'And they might not,' Lucy said severely. 'Don't you go lettin' your imagination run away wi' you, Reenie Finnigan! It's awright to have a crush on a feller, even if he's old enough to be your father, but . . .'

'He is not! And I ain't, either,' Irene said, flushing hotly. 'Still, mebbe you're right. We could stroll up to the fire station, though. We might see Chalky; you're keen on him, ain't you?'

Lucy tossed her head. 'Chalky's okay,' she said with feigned indifference. 'But he won't be at the fire station, not if Mr Lawrence isn't on duty. They're in the same Watch, ain't they? I reckon we'd best walk up to your dad's allotment and think up some story of how we see'd someone nickin' his prize blooms.'

Reluctantly, Irene agreed, and the two girls, heads close and arms linked, made their way up the road in the direction of the allotments.

* * *

'Daddy, Daddy, Daddy! Hoi, Gillian, I won't bleedin' well carry the suitcase *and* all the perishin' bags! Oh, Miss Jensen, I weren't swearin', I never swear . . . Daddy, this is Miss Jensen, what's been our teacher . . .'

'Hey, hey, hey,' Alex said, staggering under the sudden weight as the twins hurled themselves into his arms, ignoring their luggage even when a fat old man walked into it and narrowly escaped a nasty fall. 'Why on earth are you trying to introduce me to your teacher, when I've known her for as long as you have, though of course not so well!'

'Sorry, forgot,' Joy muttered against Alex's coat. 'Oh, Daddy, it were the longest journey in the world, so it were, we thought we'd never arrive . . . Miss Jensen bought us railway cakes and cups o' tea when we'd ate our carry-out . . .'

'It were lovely sweet tea, wi' two saccharin tablets each,' Gillian added, swinging on Alex's arm. She turned to beam at the teacher. 'Thanks ever so much, Miss. Do you want to talk to our dad about school?'

Alex picked up the suitcase and the biggest of the bags, pretending to stagger under the weight, ordered the twins to follow him out to the taxi rank, then turned to Miss Jensen. 'Your headmistress wants me to come up to the school as soon as I've a spare moment,' he said. 'I'm off duty for the next three days . . . would tomorrow do?'

Miss Jensen said graciously that tomorrow would do very well, especially if he could manage to be at St Hilda's for ten o'clock or so, and they parted, Miss Jensen to see her remaining pupils to their homes and the Lawrence family to make for the taxi rank.

'Why do you have to go up to the school when we've only just arrived home, Daddy?' Joy said, rather reproachfully, as they settled into the taxi cab. 'I thought we'd do something nice, as you're not on Watch.'

Alex sighed. He had not wanted to raise the subject so soon; trust his daughters to home unerringly on to the one thing he wanted kept for later. 'Look, girls,' he said hopefully, 'I've got a surprise for you when we reach home . . .'

'I know why Miss wants to see our dad,' Gillian squeaked, clutching Alex's arm. 'Miss wants me to take the scholarship examination, and I can do that one day this week because St Hilda's has a whole week for half term, and not just a day like the other schools. She's sure I'll pass with flying colours – and she said Joy might as well try too, even though she's thick as porridge.'

'I am not!'

'You are!'

'Not!'

'Are!'

'Not!'

'Are!'

'Quiet!' Alex bellowed as he saw the taxi driver wince at the shrill voices so close to his ear. 'Yes, Miss Jensen wants you to sit the exam for a scholarship, which would mean your fees would be paid. Only she was afraid that if only one of you passed you'd not want to be separated – *no*, Gillian, let me finish – so you'd both have to go to the local school. So if that's how you feel . . .'

'No it isn't,' Gillian squeaked, tugging at Alex's coat sleeve. 'I'd love to go to a different school from Joy, so people wouldn't always be sayin' stupid things about us.' She lowered her voice, slipping easily into the broadest of Liverpool accents so that she sounded just like the woman who ran the corner shop. 'Can't tell one from t'other, can yer, chuck? Like as two . . .' She tailed off as the taxi drew up outside No. 77. 'Oh, Daddy, it looks so *small*! I thought it was quite a big house.'

'It looks small because when you last lived in it you were only seven and pretty small yourselves,' Alex pointed out. He paid the taxi driver whilst the twins heaved their luggage out on to the pavement, then unlocked the front door. The girls went inside, each clutching a variety of carrier bags, whilst Alex himself took the suitcase from the driver, thanked him again, and entered the house behind them.

The twins immediately rushed up the stairs and into their room, exclaiming with delight at the patchwork quilts, the pretty watercolours on the walls and the curtained-off alcove where they would presently hang their clothes. Then they bounded into the bathroom and Alex, who had followed them up with the suitcase, smiled with pleasure. He had expected enthusiasm over the bathroom, but had not realised how appreciatively his efforts in their bedroom would be greeted. He had bought the quilts from one of the stalls in Paddy's market, and the watercolours were the work of one of his colleagues at the fire station. He had hoped his girls would be pleased with their room and was delighted that they were clearly thrilled, as they were with the bathroom.

Like most firemen, Alex had a part-time job when his team was not on Watch. He worked as a porter at the fruit and vegetable market on Great Nelson Street, lugging heavy sacks of potatoes and so on from the delivery bays to the stalls. He wanted to keep both his jobs, because fire bobbies, as Liverpudlians called them, were not well paid. Now that the twins were home, he just hoped that they would be able to cope with his frequent absences from the house; time alone would tell. Nights might be difficult if the girls were nervous, but he thought it likelier that they would sleep soundly and only wake when the alarm clock shrilled.

'I'm going to put the kettle on,' he called over his shoulder as he descended the stairs. 'I know you used to drink milk, but now that you're thirteen I expect you'd like a cup of tea, so I'll get things ready whilst you wash your hands.' He opened the kitchen door, and when the twins appeared they stared open-mouthed, exclaiming over the wonderful spread on the table. 'Gosh,' Gillian breathed. 'Aren't you clever! It's like a wedding feast, isn't it, Joy? Oh, Daddy, did you make those lovely cakes and things yourself? But what are those chrysanths doing in the sink?'

'I got a neighbour to do some baking for me,' Alex said. He put his arms round his children's shoulders and gave them a squeeze. 'As for the flowers, I didn't have time to decide what to do with them before I had to leave to meet your train. I know, though – we'll put them on the windowsill in your room.'

Once they were seated and beginning to eat, Alex apologised to his daughters for agreeing to visit St Hilda's on their first full day home. 'But the school has the week off, so Miss McCullough and myself will be able to get down to brass tacks without interruptions. I'm afraid the visit won't be very exciting for the pair of you, though. You'll have to hang about until I'm ready to leave.'

'We think just being with you is exciting enough,' Gillian said at once. 'And oughtn't we to go to the secondary school on the corner to register Joy, as well? That's where she'll probably end up.' She dodged her twin's swipe, grinning from ear to ear.

'It depends on what sort of agreement I come to with Miss McCullough,' Alex said. 'In fact, rather than coming to St Hilda's with me, wouldn't you prefer to look up some of your old friends? I remember you used to go around with a girl called Fanny and another called Isabel – they were evacuated, but I'm sure they're back in the city by now . . .'

'And there was Johnny, and his brother Luke,' Joy broke in excitedly. 'And that awful boy with spiky hair and spots . . .'

'Oh, and the school on the corner's a mixed school, so boys go there as well as girls,' Gillian interrupted. 'You'd like that, wouldn't you, Joy? When we were evacuated and you found that Jacky Evans was being sent somewhere different, you cried for a week.'

'I did not!'

'You did, 'cos you said he were your best pal!'

'Didn't!'

'Did!'

'Didn't!'

Alex drew in a deep breath. 'Quiet, the pair of you! I will not have quarrelling, arguing or disagreeing making my home hideous. If you want to fight, then go up to your room and stay there until your tempers have cooled. I've gone to a lot of trouble to make your homecoming a happy one; can't you reward me by behaving like nice young ladies instead of hooligans?'

The twins stared at him. For a moment Alex regretted shouting, then decided that he had done the right thing when the twins hurled themselves into his arms, vowing and declaring that they would be good, that it was excitement which had caused them to argue, that they would not let him down by behaving badly.

'We're always kidding each other,' Gillian said, tears running down her cheeks. 'We don't mean a thing by it, do we, Joy? We'll be angels, so we will, isn't that so, Joy?'

Alex's lips twitched, but he managed to suppress the smile that lurked. 'I'm glad to hear it,' he said severely. 'Now, as soon as we finish eating, I think we ought to visit your grandma, just to let her know you're safely home.' He waited for objections, knowing that the twins disliked their grandmother and had always tried to get out of visiting her. Today, however, though they exchanged a furtive look, they both murmured politely that to see Grandma would be a rare treat, so it would. Alex smiled grimly. 'Best bib and tucker,' he said briskly. 'And we'll take her some trifle and a couple of sausage rolls – oh, you've eaten them all. Well, she can have a nice big slice of chocolate cake instead; her teeth like soft food.'

Up in their own room, changing into their navy blue Sunday dresses, white cardigans and white strap shoes, Gillian and Joy pulled faces at one another and groaned softly beneath their breath. 'She's as batty as a bat and she smells funny,' Joy whispered. 'In fact the only good thing about her is that she can't tell us apart.'

'Can't tell red from green either,' Gillian riposted. 'When we stayed with her for that weekend whilst Mummy and Daddy went off to a wedding in Scotland, you must have told her a dozen times and I told her a hundred that I was the red ribbon twin and you were the green one.'

Joy stifled a giggle. 'She kept calling us Bessie and Lil, what were Dad's cousins, I think. But we mustn't be too hard on her; she's our dad's mam after all!'

As soon as the twins had settled in, Alex called a meeting with his daughters. He had already told them that he intended to run his home life in the same way he ran Blue Watch. They would meet once a week, himself and his girls, and discuss how they were getting on and whether he needed to employ someone to work in the house and do the shopping, or whether the girls could manage.

'The first week is the most important one,' he had stressed. 'I know you helped Mrs Dodman with both shopping and keeping the cottage tidy, and I'm sure you can do simple cooking. You will have to agree between you who does what, but if I find the house being neglected, or milk turning sour because it's been left in the kitchen and not moved to the slate slab in the pantry, then I'm going to have to think again.'

So now the three of them were assembled in the kitchen, Joy and Gillian looking anxious and their father, Joy was pleased to notice, glancing round at the tidy room with an approving look. She began to say that the only thing they felt they needed was some simple cookery lessons, but Alex shushed her with a reproving frown. 'I call this meeting to order,' he said firmly. 'I will give a résumé of the past week whilst you sit quiet and don't interrupt. When I've finished, I shall ask one of you to explain the whys and wherefores; do you understand me?'

Rather overawed by their father's businesslike approach, Joy shot an anxious look at her twin. They had done their best because neither of them wanted their father to have to employ a woman to carry out tasks they were sure they could do themselves. They had worked harder than they had ever done in their lives before, but had it paid off?

It was easier now than it would be in the future, she realised, because they had not yet started school, though that would only last until Monday, when they would both take their places at Bold Street, although Gillian would only be there until Christmas. She had passed the scholarship for St Hilda's with flying colours, and would start there when the spring term commenced. As Joy had expected, she herself had not managed to make the grade, so for the first time in their school lives the twins would be parted.

Now, Alex cleared his throat. 'I'll start by telling you what you already know: that you've done very well indeed,' he said, and gave Joy and Gillian his most charming smile. 'Of course I realise that things won't be quite so easy for you when you're back in school but you've proved you can cope, and cope well, what's more. Our meals have been on the table at the right time, you have dealt admirably with the complications of ration books and so on, and though there were one or two occasions when I heard raised voices as I entered the house, by and large you've worked well together.' He pointed at Gillian. 'You're the eldest, and I imagine once you start at St Hilda's in January you will have the most homework. Do you feel you will be able to continue to do your share, or shall we consider employing someone to clean and cook or do our marketing?'

'Oh, no,' both girls said in chorus, Joy clapping her hand over her mouth when she realised she had not been addressed. Gillian, however, enlarged on their reply.

'I'm sure we can cope, Daddy. Fanny told Joy that they give you cookery lessons at Bold Street school and we did think we might ask Mrs Lubbock, next door, if we could watch the next time she's cooking. I know you've never complained, Daddy, but you've had boiled eggs like bullets, spuds raw in the middle and sprouts with enough insects in them to feed an army. If Mrs Lubbock wouldn't mind giving us a few tips . . .'

Alex smothered a grin and said he was sure Mrs Lubbock, a fat, easy-going pensioner who had offered to give a helping hand, would oblige. Joy waved her hand energetically, as she did in class. 'Daddy . . . why can't we ask Mrs Clarke? Mrs Lubbock's ever so nice, but . . .'

'I know,' Alex said, smiling. 'She's not the best cook in the world. But her scones are all right, aren't they? And she knows how to fry an egg and boil a spud.'

'I'd rather watch Mrs Clarke cooking, if she were to offer. But she does so much for everyone that she probably wouldn't have the time. As for the cleaning and that, Gillian and me manage all right, though I do most of it, wouldn't you say, Gillian?'

Gillian gave a guilty smile. 'I like to read a book while I'm ironing or doing the washing,' she admitted. 'But Joy will manage really well. She's much more practical than I am.'

'How true!' Joy said fervently. 'But actually, I rather

enjoy cleaning and I'd like to learn to cook. As Gillian says, I'm not brainy, but I am practical.'

'That's so, and after all it's not a big house,' Gillian said firmly. 'We hardly ever go into the parlour and you do your own bedroom, Daddy, which only leaves us the kitchen, the bathroom and our room.' She turned to her sister. 'We can manage easy-peasy, can't we, Joy?'

'Course. And when we're back in school we shan't be here to make a mess,' Joy observed. She had decided frankness was their best course. 'I'd hate to have some old woman tellin' me how to dust, or scrub floors, or clean the perishing bath.'

Alex laughed. 'Right you are. But remember, if you begin to let things slide . . .'

'We shan't, honest to God we shan't,' Gillian said quickly. 'But if we do you can take away our pocket money and get paid help. All right?'

Her father held out a large hand, first to Gillian and then to Joy. 'Shake on it,' he said. 'We're a good team; let's hope we can keep it up!'

It was a freezing cold day in December and the twins were helping their teacher to clear up, for the school holidays were almost upon them and the following day they would be engaged in a school production of the nativity play. However, this was not the only reason they had chosen to stay behind. They were avoiding Pat Seddon, a large and aggressive girl who had come top of the class until the advent of the Lawrence twins . . . and bitterly resented the ease with which Gillian in particular dealt with lessons.

Ever since they had started at the school, Pat had made

no secret of her dislike of the twins. Knowing that Gillian would be off to St Hilda's at the start of the spring term, she had done her best to make their lives a misery, though whilst in class she contented herself with muttering insults too low for a teacher to hear. She, and sometimes a little gang of her cronies, would follow them home jeering and taunting, and if they caught them up it would be to call names, to give one of them a spiteful shove or a clack, or even to try to push them into the road.

'Gillian, 'er gracious ladyship,' Pat would shout in a would-be posh accent. 'She thinks she's too good for the likes of us so she's goin' to St Hilda's, but they'll soon cut her down to size. And miserable Joy's as thick as two short planks, so she is! Oh aye, they gives theirselves airs and graces, but they ain't nothin' special, nothin' special at all.'

The twins did their best to ignore both Pat and her pals, but by and large it was easier to stay late at school – 'gettin' in wi' the teachers', Pat would call it – and walk home through the gathering dusk, provided they were back in time to get a meal together and start on their homework. Besides, the shops were bright with Christmas to come, and though the wartime shortages showed no hint of easing the windows at least looked colourful and jolly, and so the twins rather enjoyed the late walk home from school.

'What'll you do when I'm at St Hilda's, though? You'll be on your own then,' Gillian said as the two of them left the school premises, wrapped their scarves round their mouths, and set off for home. 'Suppose I stop off the tram at your school and we walk the rest of the way together?'

Joy snorted. 'I'm not scared of bleedin' Pat Seddon,' she said scornfully. 'I'll get a gang of me own and we'll have a grand battle. Anyway, she's leaving school at the end of the spring term because she'll be fourteen by then. I'll be right as rain, just you see!'

Chapter Three

Joy awoke on Christmas morning with that wonderful excited feeling which only Christmas can bring. She sat up cautiously and knew without even looking that Gillian, too, was awake and sitting up. But nevertheless she spoke in an excited whisper.

'Gillian? What time is it? Can we get up yet?'

'Shouldn't think so, it's very early,' Gillian hissed back. 'Which bed?'

'Yours,' Joy said. 'There are stockings, though Daddy said we were too old. Shall we . . . ?' As she spoke she seized her bulging stocking – actually one of Alex's fireman's socks – and leapt into her twin's bed, snuggling down and hugging the exciting object to her nightgowned breast.

Cuddled close, both girls examined their trophies, not needing their eyes to tell them what the stockings contained. 'Paperback book, a bag of humbugs, a tin whistle – don't you dare blow it, Joy, or you'll wake the whole perishin' street – and an orange,' Gillian said. 'Yours will be the same . . . oh, and there's something crumbly done up in a paper bag, in the heel . . . shortbread! I bet that's old Ma Clarke's contribution.'

'Don't call names, she's ever so nice,' Joy muttered sleepily through a mouthful of humbug. 'I wonder what the books are. But wasn't it sly of Daddy to say we were too old for stockings and then to give us one each anyway? I reckon he's the best daddy in the whole world.'

'He's grand,' Gillian agreed. 'Have you ever wondered, Joy, how he came to have such a horrible mother? If Daddy's the best then Grandma's the worst; and she'll come to dinner and tea like always and grumble about every single thing. Gravy's too thin, stuffings's too rich, chicken upsets her digestion . . .'

Both girls dwelled beatifically, for a few moments, on thoughts of the dinner to come. The previous day, while Gillian was cleaning the kitchen and Joy the bathroom before heading out to the market on Great Homer Street to search for Christmas Eve bargains, someone had knocked on the front door. Gillian had flown to answer it and returned with a cardboard box, well wrapped in string and sticky tape. 'It's a Christmas present from the Dodmans,' she had said breathlessly, dumping the parcel on the kitchen table. 'It's addressed to the Lawrence family, so I suppose we can open it, can't we?'

'I think we ought to,' Joy had said. 'Daddy won't mind if we jump the gun, because it's bound to be something to eat.'

It was. When the wrappings were laid aside, a chicken had been revealed, trussed and ready for the table. Both girls had given squeals of delight before carrying the precious bird into the cool pantry and placing it reverently in the meat safe. 'What a blessing it's arrived before we go bargain-hunting, though,' Gillian had said devoutly. 'Aren't the Dodmans the kindest people you could meet? We must write them a really long, newsy letter to thank them, and tell them all about our Christmas.' This being agreed upon, the twins had resumed their work.

51

Now, their attention returned to the failings of their grandmother. 'When I was little,' Joy said musingly, 'I used to wonder . . .'

'. . . if Daddy were a changeling,' Gillian finished, and both girls broke down in giggles. 'Only changelings are usually small and trim with pointy ears and a faraway look in their eyes,' she added. 'Oh well; at least Auntie Serena and Uncle Perce are okay . . . and Daddy's asked Mrs Clarke to dinner, because of course she offered to do the cooking, and she's made the pudding and actually found some brandy for the sauce . . .'

'She's ever so nice,' Joy said sleepily. 'Only she'll have to bring perishin' Dilly. They say chicken bones can kill dogs if they crunch them up . . . if I was to slip one or two under the table . . .'

'You wouldn't,' Gillian said confidently. 'I know she's snappy and smelly, but it would be murder and I know you wouldn't do that, nor me neither. Besides, I dare say Dilly's company for Mrs Clarke when we aren't around.'

'Mmm, hmm,' Joy droned. 'Goo'night, Gillian. Sleep dreams.'

Gillian chuckled. 'It'll be morning before you know it,' she said before she followed her sister's example, and slept.

'Dinner's on the table! Come along, Grandma, Uncle Perce!' Joy's shrill voice reached the two adults sitting in the parlour, placidly listening to the wireless and occasionally commenting on the good smells coming from the kitchen. 'Mrs Clarke's just putting the vegetables out and Daddy's carving the bird . . . oh, the bread sauce is still on the back of the stove, but come through anyway.'

Everyone obeyed with alacrity and very soon the chicken was carved, the vegetables, bread sauce and gravy were served, and Alex was holding up the wishbone. 'Who wants to see if they can win themselves a Christmas wish?' he demanded. 'Shall we say the two youngest may have a tug of war over this?' He turned to his daughters. 'Can you remember how to treat a wishbone?' he asked. 'You're only allowed to use one of your little fingers . . . hook it into the wishbone like this . . . and the one who gets the larger piece may have a Christmas wish.'

'We're too old for baby games . . .' Gillian was beginning, when Joy interrupted, giving her sister a meaning look. Nothing pleases Grandma more than to see us quarrelling or behaving badly, the look said. So come on, twin, play the game for Daddy's sake if nothing else.

'Why not? When we were at the Dodmans', it was whoever got the silver threepenny bit in the pudding who had the wish,' she said. 'Come on, Gilly, be a sport!'

'Well, if you ask me . . .' Gillian began, then saw her grandmother about to give tongue and changed her mind. 'All right; give me a hold of it,' she said. 'And then let's eat, 'cos it strikes me a Christmas dinner shouldn't be allowed to go cold!'

Grandma nodded grimly and picked up her knife and fork in a very businesslike manner whilst the girls tugged at the slender wishbone until it broke, Gillian crowing victoriously as she displayed the larger piece, quite forgetting that she had thought the ritual babyish a few minutes before. 'Go on, then, have your wish,' Joy said, smiling at her twin's triumph. She picked up her knife and fork and began to eat. 'And if I find the silver three-penny bit in my pudding . . .'

'. . . you'll choke on it,' Gillian said, laughing. 'Then when we've finished our dinner you and I will wash up and clear away and the oldies can have a snooze in front of the parlour fire. And then we'll open our presents!'

'I refuse to be counted as an oldie,' Mrs Clarke said, winking at Alex. 'So I'll give a hand with the washing-up whilst you two young 'uns put away. Then we'll lay the table for tea with the crackers your aunt and uncle brought and bring out the Christmas cake, and after that we'll talk about opening presents.'

There was a groan from her youngest listeners, but Alex said placidly that good things would always wait, and got to his feet. 'And this evening, after the twins have gone to bed, we'll have roast chestnuts and a little glass of something hot,' he said. 'Go on, girls, start clearing away. And don't let Dilly get a whiff of the chicken bones; I believe they're bad for dogs!'

'It was the best Christmas ever,' Gillian said sleepily as the twins climbed into their beds and snuggled down, for it was a bitterly cold night. 'Even Grandma was nicer than usual, and Auntie Serena is a darling. How she stands Grandma . . .'

'It's a good thing she does, though, or Grandma might have to come and live with us,' Joy said with a strong shudder. 'I once asked Auntie Serena how she put up with Grandma and she said she could do so easily so long as they lived next door to one another and did not share the same house. She said she can always walk away at the moment.'

'Well, good for her,' Gillian said. 'And now let's go to sleep or we'll not be able to enjoy the pantomime tomorrow. Incidentally, what did you wish for when you found the threepenny bit?'

'M.y.o.b.,' Joy said immediately. 'Come to that, what did *you* wish for when you got the wishbone?'

Gillian snorted. 'Shan't tell you,' she said. 'Nosy parker! Actually, if you really want to know, I wished you had a few more brains so you could come to St Hilda's with me. Wasn't that altru . . . altruis . . . nice of me, I mean? Oh, and I had a little extra wish whilst I was about it. I wished I was beautiful, with gleaming black hair and dark eyes and big bosoms. Now tell me what you wished!'

'I wished I might be a fireman when I grow up,' Joy said wistfully. 'A fireman like Daddy, of course. I know it isn't allowed now, but by the time I'm twenty or thirty . . .'

'Oh, you!' Gillian said, pretending to smother a chuckle in the bedclothes but making very sure, Joy realised, that her twin heard her amusement. 'You could be in Control, mind, like our mother was, but I suppose that isn't good enough for my thick twin; she's got to be on the hose, dragging it in and out of burning buildings, dodging falling masonry, climbing the ladder to rescue folk trapped on the first floor . . .'

'Shut up!' Joy growled. 'I know it's dangerous and very hard work but I wouldn't mind that. And wanting to be a fireman is a good deal better than wanting to be perishin' beautiful. Coal black hair and big bosoms indeed! Some chance, Gillian Lawrence!'

'Both will come to me in time,' Gillian said with dignity.

'You can dye hair, you know, and bosoms grow – sort of pop out – when you're older. And if you get out of bed and try to hit me I'll scream for Daddy or Mrs Clarke, so there!'

When Gillian awoke on the day after Boxing Day her first thought was of the pantomime they had seen the previous evening. The tickets had been Grandma's Christmas present to Alex and his daughters, though it had been Auntie Serena's idea, of course. Grandma's idea of a Christmas present was to hand over a box of hand-kerchiefs which someone had given her the previous year, or a pair of felt slippers, usually several sizes too large. But on this occasion, thanks to their aunt, Grandma's present of three tickets to the pantomime had been a splendid treat.

They had gone to the Empire Theatre to see *The Queen of Hearts* with Jimmy O'Dea. Because the Dodmans had never taken them to the theatre, Gillian and Joy had had only the haziest recollection of what a pantomime was all about and this, if anything, had increased their excited anticipation, which had been amply rewarded. Gillian, far more conscious of being thirteen and a half than her sister, had watched Joy enter enthusiastically into the spirit of the story, bouncing up and down in her seat yelling 'Look behind you!' and almost splitting her sides with laughter whenever the Dame appeared on the stage.

After the show they had gone home to have a supper of leftovers, or so Alex had warned, but when they had reached No. 77 it was to find Mrs Clarke in their kitchen, just withdrawing from the oven a large golden-topped pie. 'It's only what was left of the chicken and ham, and a good deal of potato,' she had said, smiling at Alex. 'But it's an icy night and so I thought it would be more welcome than cold meat.'

'You put me to shame, Mrs Clarke,' Alex had said apologetically, unwrapping his scarf and taking off his navy serge coat. 'If I'd thought, I'd have bought you a ticket for the pantomime and we could all have gone together.'

'Nonsense!' Mrs Clarke had said briskly. 'Why should you do any such thing? The tickets were a present from old Mrs Lawrence, so that you could have a family outing. I've been perfectly happy cooking the pie and I'll be even happier to share it with you.'

It had been a wonderful ending to a wonderful evening, Gillian thought now. Joy had insisted upon relating the plot of the pantomime and most of the jokes to Mrs Clarke, who had proved to be a most satisfactory audience, laughing and gasping in all the right places. 'I'm going to be an actress when I grow up,' Joy had assured them as they had begun to clear away the meal. 'If I'm not a fireman, that is.'

'You're daft, you are,' Gillian had said, with a mixture of amusement and scorn. 'Shall we walk you home, Mrs Clarke, or will Daddy do that?'

'Daddy will do it while you two wash up,' Alex had said. 'And as soon as you finish, off to bed with you, or you'll be too tired to get my breakfast tomorrow morning.'

'Are you on early shift tomorrow, Daddy?' Joy had asked anxiously. 'If so, you'll be pretty tired yourself. Do let us walk Mrs Clarke home . . .'

Alex had laughed but shaken his head. 'No, no, I'm

on the night shift,' he had said reassuringly. He had taken Mrs Clarke's coat and helped her into it, though she had protested that no one need walk her home.

'It's only a step,' she had reminded them. 'I can be home in five minutes or less.'

'I dare say you could, but it's after eleven at night and the pavements are icy. If you were to slip . . .'

'Oh, very well, if you insist,' Mrs Clarke had said, turning to the children, who were starting to wash up the supper things. 'Back to normal tomorrow, girls!'

Now, lying snugly in her bed, Gillian reviewed the day ahead. Because Alex would be on call all night, he would have a rest after lunch, so she and Joy would make themselves scarce for the afternoon. After that, she meant to get back into her study routine, since she was desperately keen to catch up with her future classmates at St Hilda's.

Sighing, she sat up on one elbow and looked at the face of the little alarm clock on the small table between the two beds. Even as she did so, Joy sat up too.

'Whazza time?' she asked sleepily. 'Oh, I've dreamed all night about the pantomime . . . I wish we could go every night.'

'It's time to get up,' Gillian said cruelly, for in fact they had no need to leave their beds for another half-hour. Joy immediately began to throw back her bedclothes and Gillian laughed and admitted she had been teasing. 'It's seven o'clock,' she said, 'and since school doesn't start for another week . . .'

'You beast!' Joy squeaked. She threw her pillow at her twin's head, then produced the paper hat which had come from her cracker on Christmas Day and plonked it on her head. 'What'll we do today? I know you'll want to study this morning, and as Daddy's on nights we'd best do any shopping this afternoon so the house will be nice and quiet and he'll be able to have a proper sleep. Oh, I might as well get up because I'm wide awake now.' As she spoke, Joy slid out of bed and padded across to the window, wincing as her feet touched the cold lino- leum. She twitched the curtain back. 'There's a hell of a nasty wind blowing and it's raining, or sleeting; thank heaven we haven't got to go out this morning,' she said, returning to her bed. She sat down upon it and reached for her slippers. 'Bags I the bathroom first.'

The day went much as the girls had planned. Gillian studied in the morning and after they had had their lunch and Alex had departed for a snooze, they went shopping. At their father's suggestion, they bought a recipe book for Mrs Clarke to thank her for cooking their Christmas dinner. 'Of course most of the things in the book are on ration now, or unobtainable,' Gillian remarked, leafing through it, 'but that won't always be the case; everyone says rationing will begin to ease off when the weather improves.'

'Which isn't yet by a long chalk,' Joy said gloomily. She had just spent her last sweet coupons – as had Gillian – to buy Grandma a quarter-pound box of Black Magic chocolates to thank her for the theatre trip. 'I wish we could just post the chocolates through her letter box and then come straight home. But Daddy would be livid if we did that.'

'No, we've got to go in, but we needn't stay long because the weather's so frightful,' Gillian pointed out.

'I just hope the old devil doesn't ask us to tea. Last time she did she gave us Marie biscuits whilst she gobbled a huge slice of Battenberg cake, saying rich food was bad for children.'

'She won't ask us to tea because the weather's so appalling,' Joy said hopefully. 'If you ask me it'll snow before morning.'

The two girls had done all their shopping and dropped it off at No. 77. Now they were queuing patiently for a tram which would take them right across the city to their grandmother's street. Despite upturned coat collars, thick scarves and gloves they were beginning to feel chilly as the sleet was blown into their faces and the gale tried to snatch the hats from their heads. Gillian was about to suggest that they should leave delivering Grandma's chocolates until the following day when a tram drew up beside them. A quick glance at the destination board told them that it was the one they wanted and they hurried aboard. 'Not long now and we can hand over the chocs and head for home,' Gillian said cheerfully, giving her sister's gloved hand a quick squeeze. 'Poor old Joy! I know how you hate the cold, but it's warmer in here than outside and soon enough we'll be back in our own kitchen putting the kettle on for a nice hot cup of tea.'

Chapter Four

As Joy had predicted, the weather showed no sign of improvement, and after only a few hours of fitful sleep that night she was woken by the sound of hail lashing against the windowpane, driven by a howling wind. For a few minutes she lay on her back in the small bed, listening to the storm outside and mulling over the events of the last few days, until she realised, in the way one does, that her sister, too, was awake.

She sat up on one elbow. 'Gillian?' she whispered. 'Haven't we had the best Christmas ever? Oh, we used to have fun wi' the Dodmans, and the Goodys' Christmas party was grand, but it wasn't the same. Why, even Grandma didn't manage to spoil it, though I thought she would. But she seemed pleased with everything, especially the chocolates and the embroidered hankies . . .'

'She thought we'd embroidered them ourselves,' Gillian hissed, giggling. 'I opened me mouth to tell her different but I caught Daddy's eye and saw him giving a little shake of the head, so I said nothing. They really were pretty, those hankies, even though they were second-hand – we must have washed them five times at least – so she were right to be pleased.'

'And Auntie Serena liked the sachets of lavender to put in her underwear drawer,' Joy hissed back, then spoke in her normal voice. 'Why ever are we whispering?

We can't disturb Daddy because he's on Watch, and though Mrs Lubbock says knock on the wall if we need her when Daddy's on nights, I reckon it would take a regiment of fellers playin' the trombone to wake her.'

'Oh, I expect she'd come thumping round to the back door if we screamed at the tops of our voices . . .' Gillian was beginning when both girls heard the sound of the fire bells reverberating through the storm. With one accord they leapt out of bed and made for the window, knowing that if they leaned out and looked to their right they would probably see the fire engines, fully manned, emerging from the station. Alex would be riding shotgun, as he called it, sitting next to the driver – Chalky or Fred Finnigan – and ringing the bell, a task the girls knew he greatly enjoyed, and though he would not approve of them leaning out of the window on such a wild night, Gillian thought – and knew Joy thought also – that to see the engines charging past, with all their Blue Watch friends aboard, was worth the telling-off they would probably get when their father returned home.

Joy reached the window first and pushed it open to its fullest extent. 'Beat you . . .' she began triumphantly as her twin tried to elbow her aside, but before she could get another word out the wind had seized the open pane and brought it crashing back straight into her face.

For a moment, Joy knew blinding pain and felt blood trickling down her brow, saw the scarlet of it and felt the chill of the icy wind. Then she fell into the black pit which had opened up before her and knew no more.

For one awful moment, Gillian had no idea what had happened. Her sister slid down from her position at the open window and landed in a tumbled heap on the floor, and Gillian began to scold her whilst leaning perilously out to grab the window latch. It was only as she began to pull it closed that she realised the big pane was there no longer. Casting a startled glance around the room by the light of the nearest street lamp, she saw glass starring the floor, the windowsill and her sister's inanimate form.

'Joy?' she whispered. 'Are you all right? Did the glass hit you?' As she spoke, her sister's head rolled a little, revealing a face covered with blood and spears of glass.

Then, Gillian screamed.

Despite Joy's earlier comments, Mrs Lubbock was up the stairs and into the bedroom within moments of Gillian's beginning to bash at the wall between the two houses. Wheezing and clutching her chest she turned on the light, screwing up her eyes against the sudden brightness. 'Wharrever is the matter?' she demanded. Gillian jumped to her feet and seized her fiercely, turning her round and beginning to propel her back towards the stairs.

'The window slammed in Joy's face; she's hurt real bad,' she said wildly. 'You go to the telephone and ring for an ambulance; I'll stay with her so she's not afraid when she wakes up.'

'Perhaps I oughter tek a look . . .' the old woman began uncertainly. 'The ambulance folk is bound to ask me . . .'

'She took the glass full in the face and she's unconscious,' Gillian said, aware that not only her voice but her whole body was shaking. 'Tell 'em there's blood an' glass everywhere, tell 'em our daddy's away to a fire somewhere with the rest of Blue Watch. Tell 'em . . . oh, tell 'em anything you like, so long as you get help.'

'Right,' Mrs Lubbock said. She descended the stairs ponderously and the last Gillian saw of her was her long nightgown disappearing through the front doorway.

Gillian returned to her sister and knelt down beside her once more, without even noticing that she was kneeling on shards of broken glass and adding her own blood to that of her twin. 'Joy?' she whispered. 'When I said I didn't like being a twin, and I didn't want to look exactly like you, I didn't mean it, honest to God I didn't. I wish to God I'd reached the window first, 'cos I've got more sense than to let go of the latch, which is what you must have done . . .' She looked at the window and felt the icy wind blowing through the jagged gap, and realised that her sister would not have had the strength to prevent the gale from first taking the window from her grasp and then flinging it back in her face. Despite her much-vaunted brainpower, she herself would probably have done no better.

Gillian sat back on her heels; what should she do, what should she do? She supposed she ought to clear up the glass and noticed, for the first time, that her knees and the palms of her hands were covered in blood.

She and Joy had attended First Aid classes at the village school, but now that she could have done with their advice she could recall nothing about injuries caused by glass. All she could remember was that in some circumstances it was dangerous to move an injured person. She stood up and, after another look at her sister, dragged the patchwork quilt from the nearest bed, which happened to be Joy's, and tucked it round the inanimate form. She remembered something about hot drinks for shock and gently smoothed a hand across her sister's cheek, hoping

64

to bring her round, but Joy neither moved nor spoke, and looked so ghastly that Gillian's fear redoubled. She must get help, she *must*! The old lady would undoubtedly do her best, but she had not come right into the room, could not possibly realise the extent of Joy's injuries.

The neighbours on the other side of No. 77 were old and would be little help in an emergency, Gillian thought, but further down the road there was sensible Mrs Clarke, and further still Mrs Finnigan, whose eldest daughter was training to be a nurse; she might know what to do. Yet suppose Joy comes round and finds herself alone and tries to come downstairs, or simply gets into bed, pressing the glass even further into the cuts, Gillian asked herself. Oh, I must do something, I can't just sit here while Joy bleeds to death! I remember reading in a novel once that pressure stops bleeding, but I dare not press on any of Joy's cuts because of the glass.

Irresolute, she hovered in the doorway and was just turning to descend the stairs, deciding that she would simply go into the street and knock at any house which had a light showing, when she heard the sound of an ambulance approaching, its bell ringing loudly.

Gillian could not have said how she got down the stairs. She simply found herself outside the front door, with the sleet lashing her face and the wind seizing her tangled curls and whipping her white winceyette nightgown up above her knees. Two uniformed men came towards her and she saw Mrs Lubbock's fat, nightgowned figure approaching at a run from the direction of the telephone box. The foremost man caught hold of her arm and lowered his head until his mouth was on a level with her ear. 'What happened?' he asked, pushing her into No. 77 ahead of him. 'Something about window glass . . . it's to be hoped, young woman, that you've not called us out because your window's broke.'

Gillian jerked her thumb in the direction of the stairs and the men began to mount them, Gillian close on their heels. 'Our dad's a fireman; he's answering a shout,' she said briefly. 'Me sister heard the bells go down and opened the window to wave to the fellers, only the wind caught it . . .'

They reached the landing and in the dim light from the small electric bulb, which was all Alex considered necessary in the bedrooms, the two ambulance men took in the scene at a glance. The foremost sucked in his breath, then turned to Gillian. 'Fetch a brush and dustpan,' he ordered. 'Bring them to the door here, then get yourself some warm clothing – got any slippers? Good. Put them on and stay out of our way whilst we take a closer look' – he gestured to Joy's motionless form – 'at your sister.'

Infinitely relieved by their mere presence, Gillian nodded meekly, took her dressing gown from the back of the door and scuffed her feet into her slippers. Then she went downstairs but did not immediately fetch the brush and dustpan the ambulance man had demanded. First, she went into the kitchen and opened the front of the stove, riddling it briskly until the fire, which had been little more than a smouldering lump of coals, burst into flame. Then she put the kettle over the heat and went out of the kitchen, up the hallway and out on to the pavement. As she had guessed, Mrs Lubbock was standing there shivering, white with fright and with tears

66

running down her face. Gillian gulped, then fell into the old woman's arms.

'Oh, Gillian, I done what you said, and then I went round to the Finnigans' and tried to rouse young Daphne, only she's doin' nights at the Northern Hospital,' Mrs Lubbock quavered. 'The ambulance were awful quick, especially when I told them she were only thirteen and hurt real bad.' She sniffed and rubbed her eyes with the heels of her hands. 'Oh, I pray to God she ain't as bad as she looked! Course I couldn't see much, but there were all that broken glass . . . Shall I fetch your pa? Oh, no – you said he'd been called out. Wharrabout me brother Toby? He'll nail plywood over the broken window.'

Gillian thought of Mrs Finnigan, a tall, lively Irish woman, whose language when roused was said to be the envy of an Irish navvy, and of Toby Lubbock, who had kissed the Blarney Stone, according to Daddy, and had, it was said, half a dozen wives in every port. He was ashore right now, but would either of these persons do more than she herself could, which was nothing, except to wait for Daddy? The ambulance men clearly thought that any further action on her part could wait until her sister was safe in a hospital ward.

She turned back into the house, telling Mrs Lubbock rather sharply that the best thing she could do was brew a pot of tea whilst she herself spoke to the ambulance crew. Then she headed for the stairs, reaching them just as the two uniformed men, with Joy slung in a blanket between them, came carefully down the flight. Immediately, all her worries came surging back. The older of the two must have read the fear in her face for he slowed for a moment as he reached the foot of the stairs and smiled reassuringly at her.

'Ma and Pa out on the razzle-dazzle, it bein' Christmas? Oh, no – you said your dad's a fireman . . .'

'Her ma's dead,' Mrs Lubbock interrupted in a small voice. 'That's why I said I'd come over when Mr Lawrence is on nights, if the twins gorrinto any sort o' trouble. Little did I think . . .'

'Sorry, queen,' the man said. He glanced at Mrs Lubbock, hovering in the kitchen doorway, and addressed her kindly. 'Why don't you make yourself and your young friend here a cup o' tea and stop worrying. The young' un will be all right once we get her into hospital.'

Mrs Lubbock nodded eagerly, but Gillian shook her head. 'I'll go with my sister,' she said obstinately. 'If Joy wakes up to find herself alone in a strange bed she might make herself really ill, from fright and that.'

The ambulance man shrugged philosophically. 'You may be right,' he admitted as they left the house and lifted Joy carefully into the ambulance. 'Hop aboard, then . . . only what'll your pa think if he comes home to find the house deserted? He'll likely believe you've been kidnapped, and before we know it every scuffer in the city will be out searching for you.'

Gillian had already climbed into the ambulance, but the old lady, who had followed them outside, spoke up. 'I'll stay here and tell Mr Lawrence what's happened,' she volunteered. 'Better meself than the youngster here.'

The older man, in the act of closing the ambulance doors, turned to give her an approving nod. 'That's the ticket,' he said breezily. 'Be sure to tell Mr Lawrence to come straight to the hospital, though.'

'I will,' Mrs Lubbock said. Gillian leaned forward.

'Ta ever so, Mrs L, you're a real brick,' she shouted. 'And ask me dad to bring me some proper clothes, will you? I dare say a dressing gown will pass muster on the wards, but when Joy and me come home it will probably be full daylight, and folk will think I'm a queer kid to go walking the streets in me nightwear!'

Alex arrived in the large reception hall desperately anxious, for Mrs Lubbock had not been able to tell him much, save the name of the hospital to which his daughter had been taken. By the time he had got home it had been nine o'clock in the morning and, mindful of Gillian's shouted instructions, his neighbour had already gathered a supply of clothing for him to take to his daughters, so it was only a quarter of an hour later that he went through the swing doors and hailed a nurse carrying a large pile of different-coloured files. 'Excuse me, miss,' he called urgently, though he kept his voice low. 'Can you tell me where my daughters are? One of them has had an accident, and the other came with her . . . I've got their clothes here; if you can tell me where to find them . . .'

The nurse stopped and smiled at him. 'Are you Mr Lawrence? Joy was taken straight to theatre, but I imagine she'll back on the children's ward by now. If you'll hang on a moment, I'll take you up there.' She eyed the clothes he was carrying and cleared her throat uneasily before speaking again. 'I don't think Joy will be able to leave the hospital today – she's had an anaesthetic – but the other little girl – Gillian, is it? – will be grateful for something warmer than her dressing gown.'

'I'll wait,' Alex said eagerly. He had no idea where the

children's ward was and dreaded having to tour the hospital searching for his daughters. 'Was she hurt badly, my little Joy? Is that why Gillian's still here?'

The nurse, already pushing open with her hip a door marked *Medical Records*, immediately looked wary. She flapped a hand at him and called over her shoulder: 'I can't tell you because I don't know, but you'll find out more when you can speak to the ward sister.' She disappeared, letting the door shut behind her, but was back only moments later smiling a bright, professional smile which sat oddly on her pale, tired face.

The children's ward was called *Emily Jane*. Alex stood in the doorway, scanning the lines of beds stretching before him, and was still standing there when a small figure detached itself from its position at a bedside halfway down the long room and hurled itself into his arms. 'Oh, Daddy, Daddy, Daddy,' Gillian sobbed. 'It's all my fault! She's hurt ever so bad. They've done one operation, but I heard them talking. The tall man with the ginger moustache said they would wait until she was stronger, and then operate again. Oh, Daddy, I'm so frightened!'

Alex gave his daughter a hug and turned her towards the bed she had been sitting by. 'I'll just take a quick look at poor little Joy and then find the ward sister and see what she has to say,' he said. 'Oh, I've brought your clothes. Do you want to dress while I see Joy?'

Gillian was beginning to say that this was a good idea when the ward door swung open and a tall, angular woman in a navy uniform and starched white cap and apron entered like a tornado. She started to berate Alex for daring to enter her ward without first seeking her permission, then stopped short, peering at him before seizing his arm and turning him towards the doors through which she had just entered. 'I'm sorry, Mr Lawrence, but rules are rules, as I'm sure you would be the first to appreciate. You may see my patient for just five minutes, and then Gillian will show you the way to my office.'

Alex stared, a slow smile spreading across his face. 'Hetty!' he exclaimed. 'Well, if it isn't Hetty Bowdler. I didn't recognise you at first, what with the uniform and all, but you've not changed. You always were bossy, even when we were in school. I didn't know you were a nurse, though.'

'I'm Sister Ashley, actually,' she said, giving him a little push in the direction of Joy's bed. 'I'm afraid you'll find your daughter a bit of a mess, but children heal quickly. Now don't forget, come to my office in five minutes.'

Alex would have liked to say that he did not mean to go home until his daughter could accompany him, but realised, perhaps fortunately, that this was foolish. He had no idea of the extent of Joy's injuries, nor of how long she would need to remain on the ward. Instead, he allowed Gillian to take his hand and tow him to Joy's bedside.

What he saw there frightened him; her whole head was swathed in bandages so that little of her face was visible, and tucked tightly into the high hospital bed her body seemed so small that it scarcely lifted the covers. Alex bent over her and saw that the bit of cheek and chin he could see was criss-crossed with stitches. He whispered her name but Gillian, still holding his hand, squeezed his fingers to get his attention, and spoke softly. 'She's con . . . oh, I think the word was concussed, Daddy. The man with the ginger moustache said that that was not a bad thing in the circumstances, whatever that means.' She shuddered convulsively. 'Did Mrs Lubbock tell you that we heard the bells go down? Joy shot across the room to the window – well, we both did – and opened it so we could wave as the fire engines went by, only the wind was so strong that it snatched the window out of her hand and smashed it into her face. Oh, Daddy, it were the awfullest thing you could imagine. There was blood and glass everywhere . . . and it were all my fault.'

'How could it possibly be your fault?' Alex asked. 'I expect you mean that if you were racing to see who could get the window open first, it might easily have been you lying in this hospital bed. But please don't make things even more difficult by blaming yourself.'

Gillian turned dark, haunted eyes up to his. 'All my life, just about, I've complained that I didn't want to be an identical twin. You can't deny it, Daddy, you know it's true. And now . . . and now . . . we'll never be identical again,' she ended, and Alex saw tears well up and spill down his daughter's pale cheeks.

He opened his mouth to repeat that she must not take any blame on herself, then changed his mind. The poor kid had had a terrible experience; best not make it worse. 'Didn't you hear what the sister said?' he asked instead. 'Children heal quickly, that's what she said. All right, for a couple of weeks, maybe a couple of months, Joy's pretty looks will be spoilt by the stitches and then by the scars. But they'll fade soon enough and folk will start driving you mad again by saying "Like as two peas in a pod" whenever they see the pair of you side by side.' He gave her a little shake. 'So don't let me hear you blaming yourself for what's happened to poor little Joy. Just be proud that your quick thinking got her into hospital within minutes of the accident's happening, from what I can gather. And now take me to Sister's office.'

'All right,' Gillian said, though Alex could hear the reluctance in her tone. 'I'll show you the way there, but I'm not leaving Joy until she's ever so much better, Daddy. Don't let them try to make me!'

Joy came to herself after what might have been minutes or hours. She was in total darkness and could see nothing, could hear very little. All she knew was pain; she had an agonising headache, movement was impossible, speech even more so. Sometimes she thought she heard a voice she recognised, a voice she loved, but it never said a word she could understand, and if she tried to concentrate the voice whirled into the darkness, leaving her alone with the pain.

Time passed, though she had no idea whether it was minutes, days or even weeks. She did not know who she was or why she seemed to be lying, trussed up like a chicken, on what felt like a hard board. The board made the pains in her limbs even worse and for one awful moment she remembered something about Christmas and a chicken . . . was she the chicken? But before she could begin to get seriously anxious, the scene in her mind changed. She saw Father O'Reilly from the Holy Martyr School, who was reputed to beat his pupils on a daily basis, and wondered if he had been wielding his cane upon her. But then the father's face, which had been pale with spite, went scarlet and began to waver, as though under water, and Joy was once more alone in deep darkness, without even the voice to give her a hold on reality.

'But Daddy, it's been three whole weeks, and she's still here! When are you going to talk to the man with the ginger moustache again? He's the boss, isn't he? Last time he came to see Joy, Sister told me to scarper, so I waited until she left and slipped under the bed. He came with a load of students and he talked and talked, but though I tried ever so hard I couldn't really understand what he was saying. Perhaps if you speak to him . . .'

Gillian and her father were sitting in Sister Ashley's office, where they had taken refuge whilst the doctor's ward round was in progress. Now, Alex smiled at Gillian, trying to sound more positive than he felt. 'I've spoken to the doctor and he was most understanding, but the truth is that until Joy regains consciousness he won't know the extent of her injuries or what other treatment she may need.' Glancing at his daughter's worried expression, Alex decided to change the subject. 'What worries me, darling, is that you've not returned to school, though the spring term started weeks ago. The teachers at Bold Street know that because of what's happened you won't be taking up your scholarship at St Hilda's until after the Easter break, but naturally, when we made the arrangement, Miss Batchelor assumed that she would have you until then. She understands that it may be many weeks before Joy can attend school again but I do think, my love, that you should return to Bold Street for the rest of this term. Otherwise you'll fall behind and when you start at St Hilda's you'll be struggling to catch up with the rest of your class.'

Gillian snorted. 'The work Joy and I were doing before Christmas was kids' stuff,' she said dismissively. 'But in a way you're right, Daddy, and I should be working, particularly at French and Latin, because we didn't do those in the village, and don't at Bold Street of course, and I'll need Latin if I'm to matriculate.'

'I'll speak to Miss McCullough and see if we can arrange some private tuition,' Alex said. 'But you must promise me that you'll return to Bold Street school for the rest of the term. When Joy comes round, you can be with her after lessons, but already some of the staff have made it plain that you should not spend so much time on the ward. They know you and Joy are twins, of course, but rules are rules, and . . .'

'I know, and I'll do as you say and start school again tomorrow,' Gillian said. 'I'll hate not being here, but I'll pop in whenever I can. I can bring my homework and do it sitting by her bed, quiet as a mouse.'

Alex laughed. 'I dare say the staff would allow you to come in straight from school instead of at visiting time,' he said. A sound in the corridor outside made him get to his feet just as Sister put her head round the door.

'Ward round's over,' she said breezily. 'You can go back to the ward for ten minutes, but then you'll want to go home and get yourselves something to eat. We'll see you at visiting.'

Half an hour later father and daughter were ensconced in their kitchen, where Alex brewed the tea whilst Gillian made a plateful of cheese sandwiches. When their make-shift meal was finished, Alex told Gillian to get out her schoolbooks and try to do some work whilst he went up to St Hilda's and asked Miss McCullough to recommend a language teacher. 'And don't try to go back to the hospital until I'm home and can go with you,' he instructed her. 'It's no good trying to hurry things, you know; that was something else Mr Burton said.'

'All right, Daddy. I'll do my school work for a bit and then take a look in the pantry and see whether there's something we can have for supper,' Gillian said submissively. 'And I'll try not to hurry things.'

'Well, queen, your sister's illness is teaching you one thing: patience,' Alex said. 'And waiting is something you've always found difficult. You've always wanted everything yesterday.'

This made Gillian laugh, and the two parted. By the time Alex returned, he had arranged for French and Latin lessons with a retired teacher, and Gillian had written an essay, cleaned the house and peeled a pan of potatoes. Alex gave her a hug. 'You're a good little lass,' he said approvingly. 'I know Sister said come back at visiting time, but I think we'll go to the hospital now, instead of later. I've arranged for Vera to sleep in Joy's bed again, so you've got some company, because I'm on shift. You like Vera, don't you? She's a good kid.'

'Daddy, she's fifteen, not a kid at all,' Gillian said disapprovingly. 'But you're right, she's nice and I like her. Of course she's no substitute for you – or Joy for that matter – but although I know it's silly, I still don't fancy being alone in the house at night.'

She took her coat down from its hook and the pair left the house and hurried towards the hospital. As they reached it, Gillian turned to her father. 'Isn't it odd,

Daddy? I feel really excited, as though something nice were about to happen. Do you think . . . ?'

They pushed through the swing doors to find Sister Ashley hurrying towards them. She had a big smile on her face. 'She's come round!' she said in a high, excited voice. 'Matron said to send someone to fetch you, only here you are!'

Joy had felt for some time now that she was once more approaching the normal world, though not by any means in a normal fashion. She felt as though she were at the bottom of a well, surrounded by water, though she could breathe easily. She was rising up through that water towards flashes of light and the sound of voices and she knew that if she tried hard enough, her head would break the surface and she would be able to look around her, see where she was and why.

For a long time, however, the effort involved in getting to the surface was too great; she simply did not have the energy. But then something inside her head seemed to whisper that if she did not try her strength soon she might find that there was no strength there; that she was no longer capable of escaping from this horrible half-world in which she floated.

The idea frightened her so much that she took her courage in both hands and headed upwards . . . not towards light, exactly, because the flashes were all around her, but towards . . . oh, towards sounds, smells, people!

Her head broke the surface and she moved it a tiny bit and realised that it rested on a pillow; moved a hand and felt sheets, some sort of warm coverlet . . . it was night-time, the darkness was absolute, but at least she was not the only person in the world awake. She heard a voice, high and excited, though she could not make out the words. Then there was the sound of running feet, someone breathing very hard as though they were the owner of those feet, and then someone caught her hand and lifted it, held it against something soft. A cheek? Yes, it must be a cheek, and the owner of that cheek was crying; the wetness of tears ran down between her fingers even as a voice spoke close to her ear.

'Joy? Can you hear me?' The voice spoke breathily, jerkily, but – oh bliss! – Joy could hear and understand every word. I'm back, she thought exultantly. If someone would just turn the light on I could see where I am . . . but I *think* it's a hospital, or at any rate a bed, though it's not my bed . . .

'Oh, Joy, can you hear me?' the voice said again and this time Joy was able to put a name to it, knew it was Gillian speaking. 'Oh, Joy, we've been so worried, it's been so long . . .'

Someone else took her other hand, shaking it gently back and forth, and Joy knew that it was her father, and that he was in some distress. She took a deep breath and turned her head towards him. She had thought she could not speak, but to reassure Daddy, and her twin of course, she would make the effort. 'I'm back,' she said, and scarcely recognised her own threadlike voice. 'It's dark . . . is there a light?'

Three weeks after Joy had regained consciousness the surgeon, Mr Burton, took Alex to his office and broke the appalling news that he doubted whether Joy would ever regain her sight. He had operated again, and the following day meant to remove the bandages, so he was warning Alex of the worst possible outcome. He wanted him – and his daughter – to be present at ten o'clock the next day.

'When the bandages come off she may need reassurance,' he told Alex. 'Oh, of course we are all hoping that she will have some sight in the right eye; it was the left which was worst affected. But just in case . . .'

'Are you telling me that my girl may be blind?' Alex whispered. 'Oh, my God, my God!'

'I'm telling you no such thing,' the doctor said sharply. 'Never give up hope, Mr Lawrence. Just be on the ward by ten o'clock tomorrow morning, if you please, and then we'll see what we shall see.'

Alex would have kept the surgeon's words from Gillian, but she had guessed that Mr Burton would not have taken her father off to his room to impart good news, and in the end Alex told her almost word for word what the man had said. Like Alex, she was shocked and horrified, but she was still so grateful that the surgeon and his team had saved Joy's life that she was able to take an optimistic view. 'I'm sure Mr Burton was just telling you the worst thing that *might* happen, not what *would* happen,' she pointed out. 'It'll be grand to see her give us a smile, laugh at something we say . . .'

'Yes, it will,' Alex said, trying to sound hearty and convincing and not succeeding very well.

Gillian looked up at him, suddenly serious. 'I shan't sleep tonight,' she said quietly. 'I'll be on my knees, praying that our Joy's eyes will be working again when they take the bandages off.'

Alex squeezed her hand. 'You won't be the only one,'

he admitted. 'Even if we get a shout I'll be thinking of my little girl. Oh, Gillian, I hope to God you're right and Joy's eyes will be working when those bandages come off.'

Whilst Joy was in hospital Alex had arranged for Vera Hutchins from across the road to come and sleep at No. 77 whenever he was on nights. That evening, Gillian did not mention the fact that the surgeon would be taking Joy's bandages and dressings off next day. Instead the two girls made themselves a meal, cleared everything away and then sat over the fire with their knitting and chatted of this and that.

'Wonder how you'll like that there St Hilda's, when you start,' Vera said idly, holding the piece of knitting she was working on up against herself. She peered inquisitively at the work Gillian held. 'What's that, then? Mine's a lacy top for when I go dancin' in the summer.'

'Squares to make into blankets for African babies,' Gillian said. 'Didn't you knit them when you were at Bold Street?'

'Oh aye, that's right,' Vera said. Her needles, Gillian saw, fairly zipped through her work compared with her own slow progress. 'So as I were sayin', how d'you think you'll gerron at St Hilda's, without your twin to back you up?'

Gillian gave Vera a pitying look. 'We're thirteen, not three,' she said reproachfully. 'As for twins backing each other up, well, often we disagree just like other people do; sometimes we're worse *because* we're twins, if you understand me. But I might not take up the scholarship, though I haven't told Dad yet. He's keen for me to go, but whilst Joy is still struggling to get over the accident . . . oh, I don't know, it seems mean to go off to St Hilda's when Joy's so poorly. Still, time will tell.'

Vera nodded sympathetically. 'Aye, you're afraid young Joy may miss you, even miss the arguing,' she said. 'But she's a nice kid, your Joy. She'll soon make pals at Bold Street and be as happy as Larry. And she won't have to work like stink, which you will, young Gillian, because everyone from round here who's gorra scholarship says it's awful hard work keepin' up.'

Soon after this the two girls went up to bed, Vera to snore all night and Gillian to lie awake, staring at the ceiling and worrying over her twin, until the church clock chimed two and she fell into an exhausted and nightmare-ridden sleep.

Joy awoke after a sleep so deep and delicious that she felt, had it not been for the bandage round her eyes, she could have jumped out of bed, run along to the canteen or the kitchens or wherever it was they prepared food and helped herself to the biggest plate of porridge in the world. But then she remembered she had had an operation on her eyes and felt a thrill of excitement. Mr Burton had told her that he and his team would be doing a ward round at ten o'clock that morning, when he meant to remove the bandages and dressings, so that they – and Joy herself, of course – might see how successful the operation had been.

Joy sighed. She had been told that her eyes had been badly damaged by the jagged glass which had speared her when the windowpane had crashed back into her face. Mr Burton had operated twice at the time and then again last week, and he was hopeful that he would not need to do so again. Joy certainly hoped so, because when she had come round after the final operation she had felt very poorly for several days. Today, however, was different; she felt well and was looking forward to her breakfast, though that must be some time away for the ward was totally quiet . . . no, not totally quiet. She could hear the snuffling of little Amanda in the next bed, who had had her tonsils out, the rustle as a child turned over in its sleep and, far off, the click of a nurse's shoes as she hurried along a distant corridor.

Joy sighed again; she had noticed how much better her hearing had become since the accident and guessed that this was because she had been deprived of sight whilst her eyes healed. Idly, she wondered whether her hearing would become duller once more when the bandages came off.

They were such good bandages, too! They had not allowed so much as a chink of light to penetrate their folds. And all of a sudden it occurred to her that, since today was 'bandages off day', she could give herself a little preview. Why not? She could hear, now, the distant clatter of crockery and guessed that the staff were laying up the early morning tea trolleys, for hospitals came to life at six o'clock. The trolleys had not yet begun their journey from kitchens to wards, so if she just poked a finger up under the bandages she could smooth everything down again before the orderly reached her.

Joy wriggled up the bed a bit, then began to fiddle with the irritating bandages which obscured her vision. It was odd that she could see nothing but blackness; she would have thought some light at least would have filtered through the cotton. She poked at it and managed to slide a finger up the side of her nose, which should have let in at least some light. There was something on her face, below her eye, something sticky. She tried to look down, and then, with an impatient jerk, she pulled the bandage clear of her eyes.

Then she screamed.

Gillian and Joy came out of the hospital hand in hand, while Alex carried Joy's little suitcase, circling round them like a sheepdog who finds itself in charge of two very foolish sheep, Gillian thought. She whispered as much to her twin, but Joy was concentrating on her feet and did not comment.

'The taxi's here, my loves; I'll just open the door and help Joy in whilst the driver gets the luggage aboard.' Alex had flung open the door of the cab and now he pressed gently on Joy's head. 'Don't go banging your noggin on the taxi roof,' he said cheerfully, though with a shake in his voice. 'This is the happiest day I've had for a long time, because once you're back home we'll be a proper family again; I don't intend to spoil it by taking you back to Casualty with a bump on the head!'

Gillian, following Joy into the taxi, laughed dutifully, but Joy's face did not change, nor did she speak. Gillian filled the gap by chattering to her father as he climbed into the cab's front passenger seat, but though Alex tried to respond Gillian could see it was a real effort, so she sank back in her seat and let her mind go over the past few weeks.

Once Joy's bandages had been removed, Alex had told Gillian that Mr Burton had said, with real regret, that he had done everything possible but had to admit failure; unless there was a miracle, Joy would never see again.

Gillian thought that the next few weeks were not going to be easy. Of course, it would be hardest and worst for Joy, who had been in hospital for more than three months and would have found it hard to re-join the outside world even had she not lost her sight. But both herself and her father would suffer almost as much, he from his inability to do more to help, and she from the feeling that she would be deserting her sister when she went off to her new school after Easter.

The taxi drew up before No. 77 and Alex got out, but whilst Gillian was still struggling to emerge from the vehicle and before her father had got the key out of his pocket, the door shot open and Grandma Lawrence came out to stand at the top of the three small whitened steps, still in her outdoor clothing and with her face set in its habitual expression of discontent.

Gillian, halfway out of the cab, stopped short, staring. Grandma seldom left her small house save for a monthly visit to her chiropodist, occasional forays into Fuller's café, and funerals of friends and acquaintances. Grandma never missed a funeral, always arriving in a cab and attending first the church service and then the wake in order to see how many members of her generation were still at the obsequies and not, so to speak, taking the central role. Gillian touched her sister's arm. 'Grandma's at our house; heaven knows how she got in, but she's standing in the doorway, scowling,' she whispered. As Alex straightened up and saw his mother, Gillian grabbed his jacket. 'What's *she* doing here?' she demanded. 'She never visits, except at Christmas.'

Alex turned and grinned at his daughter. 'I don't know, and I don't know how she got in, either,' he hissed back. 'Heaven defend me . . . is that a suitcase that I see behind her? Oh dear God, she can't mean to come and stay . . .'

Joy, who had clearly overheard the exchange, began to say that things were bad enough without adding a disagreeable old woman to the mix, but Gillian hushed her and then helped her twin out on to the pavement. 'Dad will deal with her,' she whispered. 'Poor old thing, she's probably only trying to help.' As the girls approached the front door Gillian kept up a running commentary, hoping to see her sister smile, even if she could not raise a laugh. 'Grandma's in her Sunday best,' she murmured. 'You know, her black coat with the fur collar which you once said was made out of dead cats, and her black cloche hat with the artificial violets pinned to the crown. Gracious, she's wearing those boots that lace and button from ankle to knee; I wonder how the devil she got them on without you or me to do the laces up for her.'

'Auntie Serena probably went round,' Joy said. 'In fact it'll be she who ordered the taxi and gave the driver our address and everything, same as she does at Christmas. Oh dear heaven, don't say Auntie Serena's hidin' in the parlour! I just hope Daddy kicks them out at once, otherwise I mean to be very, very rude indeed.'

'You mustn't; she's Daddy's mother, don't forget, and we both like Auntie Serena,' Gillian murmured, guiding Joy across the pavement. 'I expect she's just popped in to say welcome home, poor old thing.'

'Huh!' Joy snorted, and shook off her sister's helping hand. 'Do stop treating me like a new-born baby. I can get into the house without you shoving me. There are two steps . . . oh, oh, oh!'

'Three,' Gillian said wryly as her twin sprawled on the hall floor. She glared at her grandmother, who had stepped hurriedly back to avoid being mown down, and heaved Joy to her feet, not surprised to see her sister's mouth wobbling dangerously. What a homecoming! Grandma had never bothered with them much before, so why should she do so now? But Daddy had finished paying the cab driver and now he came over and slipped a strong arm round Joy's waist.

'Don't try to run before you can walk,' he said dryly. 'Isn't that what Mr Burton said? I expect Grandma has just popped in to make us all a cup of tea.'

'I were comin' to stay to give a hand like,' Grandma said in a hurt tone which Gillian had never heard her use before. 'Oh, Joy, me love, if I could tek your place . . .'

'Well you can't,' Joy snapped as her father led her down the hallway and into the kitchen. 'The doctor at the hospital said I should be allowed to learn where everything is, and that means everybody, too. You'll just clutter up the place, Grandma. Go home!'

'Well, if that's how you feel . . .' the old lady began indignantly, but her son interrupted.

'It's early days, Mother,' he said gently. 'Come into the kitchen and have that cup of tea – Gillian will make it, won't you, darling? And then I'll get another taxi and take you home.'

His mother sniffed. 'Tryin' to help . . . tryin' to do me best,' she muttered. 'And that's all the thanks I get. I were going to get Serena to bring round the old camp bed which you used to use when you were a lad . . .'

By now they were all in the kitchen and Gillian had filled the kettle and put it over the flame. She was getting cups down from the sideboard when her father spoke again. 'Oh, Mother, it's really good of you, but it's not necessary, honest to God it's not. Why, you're used to sleeping in a double bed; you'd probably roll off that little camp bed the first time you tried to turn over.'

Grandma sniffed again. Upon entering the kitchen she had sat down on the only comfortable chair and now she took off her hat and patted her crimped grey curls before replying. 'The camp bed weren't for me, it were for you,' she said indignantly. 'I were goin' to sleep in your bed, and why not, pray? You spend a good deal of your time, nights, waitin' for a call-out, so you're used to sleepin' in a bunk. I don't suppose the camp bed would be much different.'

Gillian, pouring water from the kettle into the teapot, kept her head averted to hide her amusement, and saw her father put a hand up to his mouth to disguise a grin. He had begun to say that he did not fancy the camp bed since it had not been made for a grown man but for a boy when Joy interrupted. 'Daddy is *not* going to sleep anywhere but in his own bed, or in his bunk at the fire station,' she announced firmly. 'And how did you get into the house anyway, Grandma? I'm sure you weren't invited.'

'I told 'em at the station that I'd got a cake for you, and needed to gerrin to mek a cuppa to go with it,' Grandma muttered. 'One of 'em – a young feller – said he'd get in through a back window what had been left open.'

'Breaking and entering,' her son said, smiling. 'I

imagine it was Chalky; he's like a perishin' mountain goat for climbing. Well, Mother, where's this cake?'

The old lady heaved herself to her feet and went, groaning and with a hand to the small of her back, over to the pantry, returning with a very small jam sponge, the sort Gillian recognised as being the cheapest confectionery sold by the baker down the road. But it's the thought that counts, she told herself, and ignored Joy's whispered demand to be told if it were a rich fruit loaf or a Battenberg, her particular favourites.

Alex, however, said firmly that it was a jam sponge, and very nice too, though Joy gave a contemptuous sniff. 'I like fruit cake,' she said. 'I may not be able to see what Grandma's brought, but I know what I like.'

Grandma glared at Joy's small, pale face. 'You've not got false teeth,' she snapped. 'Them fruit cakes have nuts in; I can't abide nuts.'

'But you aren't the one who's just come out of hospital.' Joy's face was flushing with indignation, and Gillian judged it time to interrupt.

'I'll get you a fruit cake when I go marketing tomorrow, if I can,' she told her sister. 'I know the war's over but everything worth having is still on ration, and what isn't on ration isn't usually available, unless you buy black market.' She poured four cups of tea to the accompaniment of grumbles from her grandmother and some mutterings from Joy, then went and stood beside Joy's chair so that she could guide her twin's hand to the cup.

Once Joy, with both elbows on the table and her cup held between her hands, was sipping, Gillian fetched a knife from the dresser drawer and divided the cake into four equal pieces. She handed a slice each to her grand-mother and her father, waited until Joy, with considerable caution, put her cup down, and then walked round the table, speaking cheerfully as she did so. 'Here's your share of the cake, Joy.' She tried to put the cake within Joy's reach, but her sister snatched her hand away, shaking her head vehemently.

'I don't want it,' she said bluntly. 'Take it for next door's chickens.'

Gillian began to expostulate, thinking her grand-mother's feelings must be lacerated by such a response, but Grandma got to her feet more swiftly than Gillian would have believed possible and picked up the rejected slice. 'I'll take it home for me supper,' she announced. Then she gave Joy's hand a quick little pat. 'I'll find you some fruit cake next time I go shoppin',' she promised. 'If I tell 'em in the baker's it's for a poor little blind girl . . .'

Gillian was watching her sister's face and saw the pain, but also the fury, and felt she could scarcely blame her twin when Joy began to tell her grandmother, shrilly, that if she did any such thing she, Joy, would go down to the baker's . . .

Gillian took a deep breath, wondering how to stem her sister's words, which were becoming increasingly aggressive, but her father got in first. 'That's enough, Joy,' he said firmly. 'Grandma spoke without thinking; she didn't mean to insult you.' He turned to his mother. 'We've all had a long and tiring day; it's time I fetched that taxi. You and I must have a serious talk on the way home.' He looked from his mother to Gillian, then put a gentle hand on Joy's shoulder. 'If I leave the three of you here, will I come back to find that a battle has been fought in my nice clean kitchen, or will you call a truce for ten minutes or so?'

Gillian gave a reluctant chuckle. 'Of course we will, Daddy,' she said and pinched her sister's hand as it lay on the table. 'We'll both remember that Grandma doesn't mean half she says, and anyway I'm sure you won't be long.'

Alex nodded. 'I'll be as quick as I can,' he promised. 'Mother, if I give you a pan of potatoes to peel, do you think you could do that for me whilst I'm gone? And there's a letter from Ireland for the twins from their other grandmother. It only arrived this morning, so it might be nice if Gillian read it to Joy. And no squabbling; is that agreed?'

Gillian murmured that of course they would do as their father wished, but Joy simply tightened her lips and said nothing. Grandma, on the other hand, creaked across to the sink and peered at the colander full of potatoes awaiting attention. 'Me char peels spuds for me,' she announced. 'Me hands is too rheumaticky to handle a knife.'

'Use the potato peeler,' her son said, struggling into his overcoat and opening the back door, which promptly let in a draught of air that made Grandma give a protesting squawk.

'Shut the perishin' door, boy,' she demanded. 'Do you want us all to die of pewmonia?'

Gillian chuckled and squeezed Joy's hand once more, reflecting that if Grandma had managed to prevail upon her son to let her stay with them, hand-pinching would have become a second language. Then she went over to the sink and took the potato peeler from her grand-mother's shaky old hand, knuckles swollen with rheu-matism and veins standing out like knotted ropes. 'Why don't *you* read the letter from Granny O'Keefe, Grandma?' she asked gently. 'I'll peel the spuds – it won't take two minutes. Or tell you what, why don't you pour us all another cup of tea? By the time you've done that, I'll have finished the spuds and can get going on the letter, because Granny O'Keefe's writing is terrible difficult if you aren't used to it.'

Grandma sniffed but surrendered the potato peeler with alacrity and trundled back to the table. She picked up the teapot, groaning at the weight of it, and poured three cups. 'No point in pourin' one for the boy,' she announced. She looked anxiously at Joy, then turned to Gillian. 'Can she hold the cup if I put it into her hands?' she enquired. Of course it was the wrong thing to say.

Joy jumped to her feet, knocking her chair over and making a wild, sweeping gesture which, had her grand-mother already placed the tea before her, would have sent it flying to the four winds. 'I'm going up to my room!' she shrieked. 'Does the silly old fool think I'm deaf as well as blind? I'll tell her where she can put that cup of tea . . .'

'That's enough!' Gillian ordered. 'Just you stand still, Joy Lawrence; you've knocked your chair over and you haven't had a chance to get to know where the table and chairs and things are yet, let alone how many stairs lead to our room. Look, I'm standing your chair up; will you please sit down on it and stop making an exhibition of yourself.' She waited until her sister, sobbing dryly beneath her breath, had sat down again, then turned to their grandmother. 'Grandma, I want you to promise me that you won't open your mouth again until Daddy gets back. I know you don't mean to upset Joy, but I'm afraid you keep doing so.' She looked around her wildly, then seized a newspaper from where it lay on the dresser and thrust it into her grandmother's hands. 'It's today's *Echo*; have a read of it whilst I deal with the spuds.'

Chapter Five

When her father returned from taking his mother home, Gillian half expected him to give them both a telling-off, but Joy was so utterly weary that when he came over and lifted her off the kitchen chair to give her a cuddle, she simply buried her face in the breast of his jacket and wailed. 'Oh, Daddy, Daddy, I'm so sorry,' she cried between sobs. 'But Grandma said all the things I've been afraid of hearing, all the things they never said in hospital, even if they thought them. Why, even the lady in the unit never called me the blind girl, not even when I was un-ungrateful, and t-told her what to d-do with her white stick.'

Alex chuckled and Joy heaved a deep sigh and curled her arms up round his neck. 'You're the best father in the whole world,' she said contentedly. 'I know what you said about making haste slowly is true . . .'

'It wasn't me who said that, it was Night Sister,' Alex pointed out. 'But she was right, of course. And now that there are just the three of us, we can begin to plan how we are going to live our lives. You do know, darling, that you will have to attend school. Oh, not immediately; the summer term doesn't start for a couple of weeks, so you've all the Easter holidays to grow accustomed.'

Later, in their bedroom, Joy admitted to Gillian that

she was dreading the return to school. 'I wouldn't say so in front of Daddy because he's got enough worries without me adding to them, but even though the teachers will probably do their best I'm sure the other kids will find me a bleedin' nuisance,' she said despondently.

The girls were sitting on their beds, Joy undressing slowly and carefully, and before replying Gillian moved from the foot of her bed to its head since Joy had turned to face that direction. 'Of course it will be strange at first, but everyone will want to help you and of course the teachers will be there to talk you through everything. You'll be fine, honest to God you will.'

Joy patted her bed until she reached the pillow, then delved beneath it for her warm winceyette nightgown. She slid it over her head and stood up to shake it down to her ankles, giving a little satisfied nod as she found the three buttons at the neck and did them up. Then she turned slowly round, pulled back the covers and climbed carefully between the sheets. 'I suppose it doesn't much matter when I start school again,' she said. 'But I'll dread it, whenever I start.'

Gillian, who had undressed with great rapidity and donned her own nightgown, climbed into bed too, then looked across at her twin, who was still sitting up. 'Lie down, darling Joy,' she said gently. 'Remember, I offered to give up my scholarship, but you wouldn't have it. If you want to change your mind . . .'

'I don't,' Joy said quickly.

'That's all right then,' Gillian said. 'Is there anything you want, a drink of water beside your bed? If you need the jerry in the night you'd better wake me up.'

'I don't want anything,' Joy said abruptly. She lay down and pulled the covers up. 'As for using the jerry, I almost never do. Just because I'm blind it doesn't mean I'll start bedwetting, you know.'

'Oh, don't be so daft,' Gillian said crossly. 'If you're going to snap and snarl at everyone who tries to help you, you'll soon not have a friend in the world.'

'Sorry, sorry,' Joy mumbled. 'You don't know what it's like, nobody does. I keep telling myself to be cheerful and look on the bright side, but when all you can see is black . . .' Her voice wobbled into silence.

Gillian jumped out of bed and dropped on her knees beside her sister. She flung her arms round Joy's neck and pressed her cheek against hers. She said nothing and presently felt Joy's arms go round her, felt also a trickle of tears run from her sister's sightless eyes and down her cheek. 'I'm sorry too; sorrier than you'll ever know,' she muttered. 'Will you think I'm copying Grandma if I say I wish I could take your place? I'm not even sure if it's true; I just wish I could help you, take some of the burden.'

'Well you can't,' Joy said gruffly. She gave a small – a very small – giggle. 'Now if you were to say you wished we could have an eye each, just the one . . .'

Gillian giggled too, though there were tears in her eyes. 'An eye in the middle of our foreheads, you mean? Like the feller in Greek mythology – Cyclops, he was called.'

'I wouldn't care where the eye was, so long as it worked,' Joy said in a small voice, rubbing her wet cheek against her twin's. She sighed. 'Oh, I do love you, Gillian!'

*   *   *

Joy lay for some time in the darkness, which was deeper and more dreadful than any darkness she had ever known before. It had been bad in the hospital, but for some weird reason, which she could neither understand nor attempt to explain, she had believed in her secret heart that when she got home she would be able to see, if not everything, at least the difference between day and night. When Gillian left her side to return to her own bed, she knew a desolation so complete that she was unable to prevent a sob from rising to her throat. She did not let it escape, however. She had not cried once in the hospital, but it seemed that the moment she got home she became a whirlpool of emotions and a positive crybaby.

Fairly or not, she blamed this on her grandmother. She had so looked forward to leaving the hospital and getting home, back to the dear, familiar house to which she and Gillian were only just becoming accustomed again. Arriving to find Grandma in possession had been a shock, and then the old woman had said unforgivable things . . .

Hastily, Joy burrowed down the bed. Don't think of Grandma, or of being blind, or anything else nasty, she commanded herself. Think of nice things, like Daddy taking us round the fire station tomorrow to reintroduce me to his crew, and all the school pals who weren't able to visit me in hospital coming round to say hello. But it was no use; the tears continued to flow. I'll be brave once I get used to things, Joy told herself in her cage of hateful blackness. Tomorrow I'll be nice to everyone and – and make the best . . .

She felt the sob begin to fight its way up her throat

once more and buried her head in the pillow. Please God, let Gillian be asleep so she can't hear that I'm crying, she prayed. Please God, make me brave, like Daddy was when Mummy was killed. Please God, let me learn to cope with the dreadful dark!

After her first couple of days trying to learn the route she would take to school when the summer term started and Gillian took up her scholarship, Joy admitted to her twin that she did not think she would ever be able to go to and from Bold Street alone. Whilst they were walking she clutched Gillian's arm as a man who is drowning seizes a life belt and Gillian, the impatient, never uttered a word of complaint, though she did tell Joy, laughingly, that her arms would soon be black and blue from shoulder to wrist. 'We should try to go a few paces along the pavement with me walking alongside you but not touching,' Gillian suggested, but Joy only managed half a dozen stumbling steps before clutching Gillian's arm again and announcing that she felt giddy.

Gillian, sighing, told her father that they would simply have to have some help. 'Joy is getting more dependent with every day that passes, instead of less. She dreads the thought of going to a special school, but I'm beginning to think it might have to come to that.' Her father, however, was reluctant to take such a drastic step after such a short time.

But then they had a piece of luck. One of the elderly firemen, who had been beginning to find the work more than he could manage, had given in his notice and taken a job at a large commercial bakery. The young man who had been appointed in his place, Jerome Braddock, happened to mention that he had a brother who had attended the London school for blind children as a child of eight, and was now working part time whilst attending the St Saviour's school in Liverpool, which was where those without their full sight were taught a trade of some description so that they could learn to be self-supporting.

Alex promptly buttonholed his new crew member, who listened with real interest when Alex told him about Joy and said that if it would help, he would send his brother round to No. 77 to meet Alex's daughter. The young man was a few years older than the twins, but like Joy he had been blinded in an accident, and lacking a twin to guide him he had gone to the London school for help and training.

After speaking to Jerome, Alex discussed the situation with Gillian, and they decided that they were not helping Joy by letting her rely on her twin so completely. 'Perhaps this young feller will persuade her to stop using you as a prop, which can only be an improvement on the way things are at present,' Alex said. 'I hate to see my dear little girl afraid of moving without holding either your hand or mine.'

He realised, however, that it would take both tact and persuasion to get Joy to meet the young man, and employed both, finally being forced to give her an ultimatum. 'Either you meet this young fellow tomorrow or I take you down to London for an interview at the special school there,' he said, though it wrung his heart to see the fear on his daughter's small face.

'All right, I'll meet him if you insist, but why should you think he knows better than I do what's best?' Joy asked. 'Oh, Daddy, if you're bringing him here so that he can persuade me to go to that special school, *please* don't try to make me. If you do, I'll run away, honest to God I will.'

Alex laughed. 'Some chance you'd have of running away when you won't even let go of Gillian's arm to see how you get on without her,' he said. 'Now, your visitor's name is Colin Braddock and he's sixteen or seventeen years old; not a boy really, but a young man. I've never met him myself but his brother, Jerome, is a grand bloke, lively and hard-working; if Colin's anything like him, you'll get along, so let me have no more argument. I shall be on Watch, but Mrs Clarke has baked scones and ginger snaps and Gillian will make the tea, so all you will have to do is chat to Colin and listen to what he tells you about both the special school and St Saviour's, though of course you're too young to attend the latter yet. I know you won't be rude' – Alex crossed his fingers behind his back – 'but try to show him you mean to follow his advice, even if it goes against the grain.'

'All right,' Joy said crossly. 'But I really won't go to the special school. And I'll be fourteen in May, old enough to work – I suppose I could go to St Saviour's in Liverpool if I had to.'

'Let's tackle school first,' Alex said tactfully. He did not wish to remind Joy of how she had wasted her time at the Devonshire village school, nor how hard he had had to plead with the headmistress of Bold Street to put the twins in the same class when they came home. In fact, if he were honest, he knew that Joy would have had to remain at school for an extra year, just to catch up with other children her age. But it would not do to say so; poor Joy had troubles enough. 'One day at a time, darling. Meet young Braddock for a start and see what he advises . . .'

'See?' Joy said scornfully, and immediately repented. 'Oh, Daddy, I'm sorry. What a horrid thing to say! I know you're right, and I'll listen to what this fellow has to say, honest to God I will.'

The twins had been practising the walk to and from Bold Street and now, as they neared their home, Joy squeezed her sister's arm and pulled her to a halt. 'Hang on a minute. When that chap arrives, don't you dare go off and leave me. Oh, why did that wretched Jerome have to perishin' well interfere? Now will you promise me you'll not leave the room even after we've had our tea? It tires me out talking to someone I can't see; you should try it some time.'

Their father had arranged for Colin Braddock to come round at about four o'clock, when the girls would have been back from their walk for a sufficient length of time to put fresh fuel on the fire, brew a pot of tea and lay out Mrs Clarke's scones and ginger nuts upon the kitchen table.

Despite her initial unwillingness to meet the fireman's younger brother, Joy admitted to her sister that she was feeling curious as she and Gillian resumed their progress along the pavement, arm in arm. When they reached No. 77 Gillian produced her key and pressed it into Joy's hand. 'Go on, do your party trick,' she exclaimed. 'Let us in so I can get going on the tea, and for once, young lady, you can perishin' well give a hand.'

In normal circumstances, the girls would have gone in through the back door which led straight into the kitchen, but today, because they were having a visitor, Gillian had decreed that they should use the front entrance. 'Three steps, remember, up to the door. Then the hallway – don't walk into the umbrella stand – and then the kitchen, first door on your left,' she said. 'If you weren't so obstinate about carrying a white stick, I bet you could fly up the steps and go straight as an arrow into the kitchen.'

'I couldn't; I'm far too afraid of falling,' Joy retorted. 'Still, I bet I can unlock the front door, although it may take me a few tries.'

Gillian watched as her sister fumbled the key into the lock, tried to turn it, realised it was in on the slant and corrected it. When the door swung open, Joy turned and gave a triumphant grin in Gillian's general direction and Gillian realised, with a little shock of surprise, that it was the first time since before the accident that she had seen Joy's mouth curve into that delicious smile. She remembered how Joy used to clown in class, making the other pupils helpless with laughter, and found herself wishing fervently that Joy would smile more often, but one had to be happy to smile.

She opened her mouth to congratulate Joy on unlocking the door, then changed her mind. Joy would think she was being patronising, and in a way she would be right. After a whole week at home, unlocking the front door was a very tiny accomplishment and one which in other circumstances would not have warranted any comment at all. So she watched Joy push the door open and walk into the house, merely following her and saying as she did so: 'And now to get the tea for this feller. Isn't it odd, entertaining someone we've never met and who has never met us.' She giggled, encouraged by the memory of that smile. 'Who introduces who to who . . . or should that be whom?' she added, and tried not to feel cast down when her sister neither smiled again nor spoke but merely shrugged before fumbling her way into the kitchen and sitting down in her usual chair.

'I don't care; the feller can call me Fido if he wants,' she said indifferently. 'What do you want me to do? Only don't say slice bread or peel spuds because you know Daddy won't let me handle anything sharp.'

For a moment the old Gillian pushed the new meek one into the background. 'You can do nothing, as usual,' she said crossly. 'Just sit there while I do all the work, and maybe when the chap leaves you can wash up for once.'

Joy was so surprised that for a moment her mouth hung open. Then she closed it with a snap. 'How can I wash up when I'm not allowed to touch knives and forks?' she asked querulously. 'You're unkind, Gillian Lawrence! You don't know what it's like . . .'

Gillian felt a wave of irritation sweep over her, but conscientiously pushed it back. 'You're right, I don't know what it's like; how could I?' she asked reasonably. 'But I'm doing my best, and I'm not at all sure that you are. If I split the scones . . .'

'I can't butter them; I'd make an awful mess of it, and besides, you know Daddy said . . .'

'. . . Daddy said you weren't to use sharp implements,' Gillian repeated wearily. 'All right, you can chat to me whilst I get the tea ready, and then when Mr Braddock has gone home I'll wash up as usual.'

'All right, and I'm sorry I was cross,' Joy mumbled. 'Before, I was the one who did most of the housework, wasn't I? And you were the clever one who whizzed through your homework in no time and thought me an awful dunce. You're still the clever one, of course, but I'm not much use in the house any more.' She cocked her head on one side. 'What's that noise?'

Gillian had heard nothing, but now she listened and thought she could make out a tapping. Quickly she ran to the back door and tugged it open. It was a sunny day, and the young man making his way across their yard with the aid of a white stick wore no coat and was clad only in a light jacket and grey trousers. His fair head was bare and he must have heard the back door opening for he paused and spoke. 'Is this number seventy-seven? I've an invitation to tea from the two young ladies who live at number seventy-seven and I've come the back way because Mr Lawrence told my brother that there are no steps to the back door.'

Gillian glanced behind her into the kitchen; Joy had actually got up and was coming, very slowly and carefully, towards the sound of the young man's voice. 'Wait a moment whilst our guest comes in,' Gillian said to her, then turned and addressed the visitor. 'Yes, this is number seventy-seven; I'm Gillian Lawrence and my sister Joy is beside me. Stay there and I'll come and take your arm.'

The young man grinned. 'Don't you worry yourself, I can find my way; you go and put the kettle on,' he said breezily. 'I'm an old hand at tackling new places, though it's not always easy. Folk are such fools; they know I can't see but they still put a low stool directly in my path and apologise madly when I measure my length.'

Both girls laughed, though Gillian thought her sister did so grudgingly; then she watched as the young man used his stick almost as though it could see. When he was within a foot of the doorway, he tapped both sides of the architrave lightly, and walked into the room as confidently as though he had visited them many times. Once in the kitchen he held out a hand, which Gillian hastily took. 'Are you Gillian? How d'you do?' he said, then turned his head. 'Where's t'other one? If you say something, Joy, I'll use the sound of your voice to direct me to your side . . . unless there are any chairs or tables in the way, of course. But my stick should warn me of obstacles if I use it correctly.'

Joy, standing between their visitor and a table, took a deep breath. 'I don't know where you are, so I don't know whether there are any chairs in the way,' she said grumpily. 'If you let Gillian guide you . . .'

She stopped as a hand reached out and took her own. 'How do you do, Joy? Oh, and I forgot to say I'm Colin Braddock, though of course you must have guessed that.' Having shaken Joy's hand, he patted her shoulder, saying proudly: 'Bet you can't do that. It's one of the things the LSB taught me, how to gauge a person's height from their voice. It took me a while to judge, but I got it right first go, didn't I?'

'You did,' Joy said. She fumbled in the air for a moment, then laughed, actually laughed aloud, and addressed the newcomer almost pleasantly. 'Oh, give me your hand, Colin, and I'll take you to a chair. I know this kitchen pretty well and my father and Gillian make sure that things stay where they're put and don't get moved around. I can't visualise new places, I don't know why, but I can see this kitchen inside my head. I know where the fire is, and the pantry, and the sideboard – oh, everything, just about . . . and then there's Gillian to see me right, so I don't really have to make much effort.'

Gillian saw that Colin had held out his hand on her sister's words, and after a couple of fumbling attempts Joy had grasped it and was leading him to the chair at the head of the table. She sat down next to him and turned towards Gillian, who was pouring tea from the old brown pot into three enamel mugs. Before Joy's accident, they had used a beautiful old china tea service whenever they had afternoon tea, but after Joy had broken two cups, a saucer and two plates, Alex had decided that the ones they used at the fire station would be both sensible and practical. Joy must have noticed and guessed the reason for the change, but she had said nothing.

'Gillian's pouring the tea . . .' she began, and was interrupted.

'How do you know?' Colin said. 'Don't say you're just guessing, because I shan't believe you. I think you're already learning that there are other senses besides sight. Hearing is a tremendously important one for the blind. Go on, tell me how you know your sister's pouring the tea.'

'I *was* guessing . . . well, I thought I was,' Joy said. Then Gillian saw her sister's mouth begin to curve at the corners. 'Gosh, I know what you mean! If I listen hard I can hear the splash of the tea into the mug . . . I can even tell roughly where Gillian is standing.'

'Well done,' Colin said approvingly. He turned towards Gillian as she placed the tin mug on the table before him, deliberately putting it down with a clatter. 'Thank you, Gillian.' He inhaled gustily, lifting his chin and reminding Gillian strongly of the Bisto kids in the advertisement. 'I can smell that someone's been baking!' He sniffed again. 'Scones, and I believe I can catch a whiff of ginger; don't say you've provided ginger nuts!'

Joy was gazing towards the sound of his voice, her mouth rounding into an O of astonishment. 'You hardly *need* your eyes!' she exclaimed. 'Is that what they taught you at the London school? I *won't* go there – it's hundreds of miles away – but perhaps when I'm older I might go somewhere local, like St Saviour's. That's where you go now, isn't it? What are they teaching you?'

'I'm learning Braille and typewriting; they teach both at the London school, but I was only there six months, until I could re-join my normal school, and I was too young for those classes – they were for the older pupils. Now I'm at St Saviour's part time; the rest of the week I make handbags in a big factory down by the docks. Incidentally, the London School for the Blind – the LSB – is known as "Blinkers" to the pupils; a nickname, like.'

Gillian laughed appreciatively, but Joy merely tightened her lips. 'I suppose it's funny, in a way,' she said grudgingly. 'But I don't want to talk about it since I won't go to a boarding school far from home.'

'I know; your father explained that because you were twins you needed to be together. Perhaps if I'd had a twin, I'd have opted for staying at home and teaching myself, as you say you will. Only, if I'm honest, Blinkers is – oh, absolutely first-rate. They teach you things which you couldn't possibly learn anywhere else: self-defence, for instance. I dare say you think that you'll never need to fight off an attack, but you never know. Blind girls and boys can make enemies just like sighted ones.'

'I don't want to know, thanks very much,' Joy cut in, hunching her shoulders. 'Perhaps when I'm older I'll go to the local place – St Saviour's – but for now home's good enough for me. And as for self-defence, why, no one can possibly be taught such a thing.'

Gillian came back to the table at this point and put two plates down before Joy and Colin, each containing a thickly buttered scone and a couple of ginger biscuits. 'Our neighbour down the road did the baking,' she explained. 'Before the accident, Joy was the housewifely one; I'm ashamed to say I hated cooking and cleaning and did all I could to get out of doing my share. So now you could say I'm getting my just deserts because I have to do it all myself.'

Colin swallowed a mouthful of scone and tutted. 'Well, we can't have that, can we, Joy? Despite your blindness, you've got to learn to cook and clean. A pretty girl like you will have a house and a husband of her own one day, and you can't expect your sister, even if she is your twin, to keep your place decent as well as her own.'

Joy's lip trembled. 'It just shows that you don't know everything,' she muttered. 'I might have been pretty once – quite pretty anyway – but that was before the accident. Now I've got train tracks all over my face and my eyes feel truly horrible, sunken and closed all the time, so I don't see why I should bother to learn to cook. I'll have to share Gillian's house when we're grown up whether she likes it or not.'

Gillian reached across the table to take hold of her sister's hand, just as Colin did the same. Gillian tried to withdraw, but he would not let her, so they ended up as if they were playing hands on top and Joy was laughing, though with a catch in her breath. Nevertheless, Gillian knew that her sister's feelings were still somewhat delicate on the subject of her appearance. 'Look, Joy, it's time you stopped putting yourself down, particularly as you're only guessing,' she said severely. 'You do have scars still, of course you do, but they'll disappear with time, and since you're still my identical twin I'd rather you didn't talk about us as if we were monsters of ugliness.'

Joy gave a watery little giggle. 'Yes, but my eyes . . .' she began, only to be swiftly interrupted.

'Oh, shut up!' Gillian said sharply. 'Just be thankful that you won't be scarred for life or anything like that. And let me tell you that someone who didn't know about the accident couldn't possibly tell from looking at you that you can't see; not if you wore your dark spectacles, that is.'

The spectacles were another sore point. Joy hated them, could not see the point of wearing them when they could not make her sightless eyes see, and now she said as much.

Gillian turned to Colin. 'You aren't wearing glasses at the moment, but do you do so sometimes? I know you use your white stick, and now that you've shown us how useful it can be perhaps Joy will start using hers. Spectacles are different, though. *Do* you wear them?'

'No,' Colin admitted after the briefest of pauses. 'But if you don't want people to look at your eyes, specs are the answer.' He put his hand on Joy's arm, then slid his fingers down until he could grasp her wrist. 'Why do you fight everything, even things that will help you?' he asked gently. 'Perhaps I was luckier than I realised when my parents sent me to the LSB. I didn't know a soul there, not one single soul, and I wasn't quite eight years old. I couldn't afford to refuse any help that was offered, any friendship even. I grasped at everything, and now that I look back I can see that the other children taught me as much as or more than the teachers. All the little tricks that I use as a matter of course I learned from Freddy, Sam and Phil – they were my particular friends – but of course when you're all in the same boat, everyone helps everyone else.'

Joy heaved a sigh. 'It sounds a lot too perfect to me,' she announced. 'Just because you were all blind, surely that was no reason to be pals?'

Colin chuckled. 'You're right, of course. Once I got settled in, I made enemies as well as friends; well, not exactly enemies, but there were a couple of boys who would deliberately move a chair in the classroom, or make me an apple pie bed, or tell the teacher that it was I who had pushed a smaller boy aside in the dinner queue. But it was no worse than being a new boy in an ordinary school and we soon settled down. Indeed, the boys who began by teasing me quickly discovered that two could play at that game. I would hear the scrape of a chair being moved into my path and avoid it, then get my own back some other way. I became one of the best listeners in the school, though we were all pretty good.'

'Well, it doesn't sound as bad as I thought it would be,' Joy said grudgingly. 'It's rather like Angela Brazil – *The Naughtiest Girl in the School* – you know, boarding school japes and all that. But japes or not, I won't leave my home and my twin.' She sighed. 'Talking of Angela Brazil makes me remember that I miss reading more than anything.'

Colin had finished his scone as she spoke and picked up one of the ginger biscuits, holding it beneath his nose and sniffing before taking a bite. 'Yummy! If it tastes as good as it smells, I'm in luck.' He turned his attention from the food to Joy once more. 'What a little goose you are! Have you never heard of the Talking Books Service? You have to have a note from your doctor, but once you are a member the books – which are records really, of course – come free through the post and can be enjoyed by the whole family.'

'Oh,' Gillian said, entranced at the thought of having a book read to her whilst she worked and hoping that Colin had not noticed her sister's lack of response. 'I listen to the wireless now when I'm ironing, or washing up, but we don't have a gramophone.'

'They lend you one; you can keep it for as long as you need it,' Colin said cheerfully. He bit into the biscuit. 'Yes, it *is* ginger – my favourite.'

This made Gillian remember something which had puzzled her before. 'Colin, earlier you said you could smell scones and ginger biscuits. I've been sniffing ever since and I can only smell them when I hold them under my nose. Is there something wrong with *my* sense of smell?'

She sounded so worried that Colin laughed. 'Oh dear, you've found me out! Your father asked my brother whether I liked scones and ginger biscuits, because he had asked a neighbour to do some cooking for him. I thought the neighbour would probably do a bake in your kitchen and I wanted to impress you.' He pretended to hit his forehead with the back of his hand. 'Exposed as a liar and a cheat,' he said mournfully. 'Will you ever forgive me, girls? But I meant it for the best. Normally I would have realised at once that there was no smell of baking, but I was so keen to get on good terms with the pair of you that I spoke without thinking.'

'Without sniffing, you mean,' Gillian said, giggling. 'Well, we'll forgive you for pretending to smell baking since you've told us how to get hold of these talking books. Have you any more tips which would help Joy to become more independent?'

Joy made a hasty movement and took a breath as though about to speak, but then closed her mouth without uttering a word. Gillian looked thoughtfully at her twin and knew, with a stab of real disappointment, just what was going through her mind. Joy did not want to become independent. Not unnaturally, she was afraid of the big dark world which now surrounded her and had come to rely on having, so to speak, her own personal interpreter, who told her everything that was going on. She would pretend to take on board all that Colin was offering, but would obstinately refuse to act on his advice. She would continue to cling to her twin, making excuses which Gillian and Alex would find hard, if not impossible, to refute. Gillian looked across at Colin; had he guessed what Joy had been about to say? If so, he chose to ignore it.

'I think I've said enough to give you both food for thought,' he said. He turned towards where he knew Joy was sitting. 'At first I thought you were lucky to have your twin to help, but I'm not sure if that's really so. Perhaps being alone sharpens one's senses, makes one both warier and, in the end, more self-confident.' He picked up his mug and drained it, then stood up, pushing back his chair and setting his mug down on the table. It was so near the edge that Gillian reached across to pull it to safety, but Colin was clearly aware of the danger. He slid his hand along the table, pushed the mug towards the centre and turned to the back door. When he reached it, which he did in a couple of strides, he picked up his stick, which he had leaned against the wall, and turned back to the girls. 'Thank you for a delicious tea; I hope I've been of some use,' he said, with his hand on the latch. 'If you would like me to pop in now and then to see whether you've come across any problem which I might be able to solve, just send me a message. I'm going round to the fire station now to meet Jerome so we can walk home together. Is there anything you would like me to say to your father?'

'Tell him I'm getting fish and chips for supper,' Gillian said hastily. 'And if you could spare the time to pop in now and then, I'm sure we would both appreciate it, wouldn't we, Joy?'

Joy muttered something beneath her breath which both Gillian and Colin chose to ignore. Colin had begun to open the door and winced as the draught cut through the gap. 'Thanks again, girls!' he said. 'And don't forget, if you want to get in touch with me, get your dad to speak to Jerome; he'll pass the message on.'

'Thank *you*,' Gillian said gratefully, and was ashamed when Joy said nothing. As soon as the door closed behind their visitor, she turned a reproachful gaze on her sister, knowing she could not see it but also knowing that her disapproval would be reaching her twin in positive waves. 'Joy, how could you be so bleedin' rude and ungrateful?' she said angrily. 'That poor feller came round to do what he could to help, and . . .'

'You thanked him,' Joy said sulkily. 'And I don't want him to come round here interfering. I didn't like it when he said I'd do better on me own. He doesn't understand how lost I should be without you.'

'That's the whole trouble; he *does* understand, and you don't like it,' Gillian said, though when she saw the expression on her twin's small, pale face it was all she could do not to fling her arms round her and promise to stay with her for ever. 'Daddy and I have been worried that you were beginning to rely on either me or him for everything, and from what Colin said we were right to be anxious. Darling Joy, we only want to do what's best for you. So why not accept the help Colin was offering with a good grace?'

Joy sighed. 'I'm already learning the way to school, but it will probably take me months and months,' she said, her voice quavering pathetically. 'But I suppose I'll have to use that bloody stick and wear those damned spectacles, though I don't see— Hey, be careful, you nearly knocked me over!'

'Sorry,' Gillian apologised, for her violent hug had

indeed caused her sister to sway perilously. 'It's just so good to hear you saying you'll use the stick and wear your specs! Both these things are a step forward, because once folk know you can't see they'll be really eager to help. Wait until I tell Daddy you've agreed to use your stick!'

'Well, how did it go?' Alex asked hopefully, when Jerome had performed the introductions and left Colin in the small office where Alex was doing his paperwork. He was not sorry to be interrupted; he was responsible not only for writing reports on the fires Blue Watch had attended but also for planning duty rotas for the coming week, a task hated by all sub-officers. 'I bet Joy was pleased to be able to talk to someone who shared her problems, wasn't she?'

Colin looked uncomfortable. 'I don't want to tell tales out of school . . .' He hesitated, and Alex sighed.

'Oh, no. Gillian said Joy would resent anything which parted the pair of them, and I suppose she was right. Go on, what happened?'

Colin gave a brief résumé of his visit, assuring Alex that he had been warmly received by Gillian but not hiding the fact that he believed Joy had resented what she no doubt considered to be his interference. 'She's frightened, that's the truth, and no one can blame her for that,' he said. 'But tell me, Mr Lawrence, what were they like before the accident, your daughters? I bet Gillian led, but did Joy just meekly follow? Although you say they are identical to look at, they seem to have very different personalities.'

'You're right. They looked identical, but inside their

heads they are – were – quite different. And I think they are still, though Joy doesn't laugh like she did before, or joke, or tell funny stories. I think she's still too shocked and hurt to be her natural, loving self. But surely she'll grow accustomed and become the old Joy once more, don't you think?'

'Time will tell,' Colin said guardedly. 'It's a hard thing to lose one's sight, but I've come to terms with it. We must hope that Joy will do the same.'

Alex looked hopefully at his visitor, reflecting that there was no clue in the bright, intelligent face that the blue eyes were sightless. He had to keep reminding himself that this chap could see no more than Joy could. He said as much, but Colin shook his head. 'No, that's not quite true. I can tell day from night, though only just. Nothing more than that, but it's a great deal better than total sightlessness. I said nothing about it to Joy – she was resentful enough as it was – but I'm aware I'm one of the lucky ones.'

Alex tried to imagine a world in which the only differ-ence was darkness or light, and failed dismally. He looked with deep respect at his companion, then remem-bered that to Colin a facial expression meant nothing. 'I shouldn't have thought you lucky, exactly,' he said mildly. 'You don't seem much better off than my little Joy . . .'

He was interrupted. 'How can you possibly think that?' the young man said incredulously. 'You have to use some imagination, Mr Lawrence; close your eyes and see black-ness, nothing but blackness. Then, very slowly, let the blackness become less dense, turn to charcoal grey, with a – oh, a sort of fluttering at the edges. Not light, as such, but a lighter darkness. And you know the night's over and the day's begun.'

Alex was silent for a long moment whilst his mind grappled with the effort of making himself see what his companion had described, then he shook his head and gave up. 'I accept what you say; you are lucky compared with someone who is totally without sight. But I couldn't imagine what it's like, hard though I tried.' He paused, and then said bluntly, 'Tell me, how did you get on with Joy?'

Colin sighed. 'Not well. She doesn't want to be helped if it means separation from her twin, but if you ask me, Mr Lawrence, it's a good thing that Gillian means to take up that scholarship to St Hilda's. For one thing, it's only fair; she's clearly a very intelligent girl and deserves a chance. And for another, leaning on her sister the way she does will quickly ruin Joy's chance of becoming an independent person. Why, she whines like a baby if she sees she isn't going to get her own way, and though the humour is still there, lurking, she pushes it down pretty quickly if it looks as though her prop – that is, her twin – is going to move back a pace or two. For her sake even more than Gillian's, therefore, the two should be separated. Mind, I'm no expert; it's only my opinion.'

'I think you're probably right, but just to be on the safe side I'll have a word with her teachers, and perhaps with the doctors who looked after her in hospital,' Alex said, feeling rather guilty. He had asked for Colin's opinion, and announcing that he was going to put the same question to others seemed the height of ingratitude, but to his relief Colin did not seem to see it that way.

'Good; then neither Gillian nor Joy will blame me if you go ahead and separate them, at least during school hours,' the young man said, getting to his feet. 'I hear Jerome coming to pick me up.' He held out a hand, which Alex shook, just as the door to the small office opened and Jerome entered the room. 'I've offered to pop in from time to time, to see if I can help Joy with any problems that might arise,' Colin said. 'But I shan't do so; not unless they send me a message by yourself or Jerome.' He laughed and turned to where his brother stood in the doorway. 'Gillian's getting fish and chips for supper; shall you and I do likewise, Jer?'

Towards the end of the Easter holidays, when the weather had greatly improved and the bulbs in the local gardens were in bright bloom, Alex managed to get Gillian alone, not always an easy task. On this occasion, however, Joy was at home listening to the wireless whilst Gillian was trying to buy soft fruit to stew, so when Alex, who was on day shift in the yard supervising Blue Watch's drill, saw her outside the greengrocer's shop, he came across to join her. He told her that everyone he had consulted, from the hospital doctors down to the teaching staff at Bold Street, had said that Joy would never learn independence whilst she had her twin at her beck and call. 'Gillian's like a little slave,' old Mrs Lubbock next door had said rather disapprovingly, and even gentle Mrs Clarke had said she thought both girls would benefit from attending different schools and meeting different people. When Alex had asked Sister Ashley what she thought, her reply was unequivocal.

'Her sister has become her eyes, which isn't fair on

either of them,' she had exclaimed and Alex, who valued her opinion, found himself in agreement.

Gillian told Alex that she was prepared to return to the secondary school after the Easter holidays if it would make life easier for her twin, but her father shook his head. 'It won't make life easier for her in the long run,' he assured her. 'Remember, she's accepted that you'll be taking up your scholarship to St Hilda's as soon as the holidays are over, so she knows she had better start thinking for herself instead of letting you do it for her, because that's what she's been doing, queen. Perhaps you think I'm being cruel, but those who know best don't agree. Look at Colin, for instance. Eager to help, saying he'd pop in whenever Joy wanted, and we've not seen hide nor hair of him since that one visit because she simply won't ask him to call. Instead, she clings to you like a perishin' limpet to a rock and it's not right nor fair for either of you.'

Gillian eyed her parent curiously. 'You say Joy has accepted that we'll be going to different schools in a few days, but what do you mean to do about getting her to school and back? It's all very well to say she knows the way – she does – but she simply can't walk to school by herself. Why, groups of schoolchildren could push her off the pavement, not meaning any harm. What's more, she'll need someone to tell her what the traffic is doing, where the kerbs are and so on, otherwise she'll end up under a bus. You can't take her, I can't either, so what's the answer to that, eh?'

Alex sighed at the mere thought of the trouble Joy might get into if she tried walking to school by herself, but he shook his head chidingly at Gillian. 'Of course

I've thought of that, silly! Do you remember Mr Williams, who is one of my Watch? He's got a son, Edward, who goes to the Bold; he's in his last year. I've asked Mr Williams if the boy can take Joy to and from school, and they're both willing. Does that satisfy your scruples, young woman? Edward's fifteen, and in the special class for boys and girls who are particularly bright, so he should be able to look after our Joy, no problem.'

'Have you told Joy that a boy will be taking her to and from school?' Gillian asked suspiciously. She chuckled. 'Oh dear, she's not going to like it, Daddy. Couldn't you find a responsible girl who could give an eye to her?'

'No,' Alex said firmly. 'I wanted someone I could trust, and the fact that Edward's father is a member of Blue Watch means he's family, as we say. So if Joy doesn't like it I'm afraid she'll have to lump it.'

'When are you going to break it to her?' Gillian asked, hefting her basket on one arm. 'If it's now, I'll make myself scarce. She'll be as cross as crabs, Daddy, and you can't really blame her. Alone in the dark . . .' She shuddered. 'It must be dreadful. But, you know, I thought that Colin chap gave her really good advice. He told her to use any aid she could get hold of, but she never has, even though she promised to use her stick and wear her glasses so that folks would realise she was blind. Well, when I go to St Hilda's she'll perishin' well have to use the stick, if not the spectacles.'

'And she'll have the rest of the Easter holidays to go over the route to school with you,' Alex said, but he could hear the uneasiness in his own voice. 'Surely with Edward's help she'll be able to get to and from school safely enough? It's a great pity she didn't make any friends before Christmas, when you and she were both at Bold Street.'

'It's being a twin,' Gillian explained. 'We tend to do everything together so other children leave us alone. But I dare say Joy will remember some of the other kids in her class once she starts at the school again.'

'And I've spoken to Miss Batchelor,' Alex said. 'She's going to get one of the more responsible kids to stick by Joy until she's managed to learn the layout of the school. Folk are really good; I believe they like helping when asked to do so. Look at the young Williams boy, for instance. I don't believe he's ever met either of you, but his father said he would be happy to accompany Joy to school.'

'Edward Williams,' Gillian said thoughtfully. 'Is he that boy who's a bit of a swot? If it's the one I'm thinking of, he's gingery and wears specs.' She giggled. 'We used to call him Silly Willy because he's such a dream, but he is clever, I know.'

Alex pulled a face. 'Don't be so sharp, young lady. And don't you call him anything but Edward, because he's got a kind heart and your sister mustn't be put off walking with him; not until she's more independent, anyway.'

'Right,' Gillian said as she moved towards the doorway of the greengrocer's shop. 'See you later, Daddy; and good luck!'

Joy was in bed lying in her own particular dark, listening to the tiny sounds which those who had sight would not even notice. The wind rustling the leaves of the tree which grew only a few yards further up the street, an errand boy breathing noisily as he passed along the pavement below their window, someone starting up a car and cursing mildly when the engine did not fire at the first attempt.

It was the first day of the summer term, the first time she would walk to school with only a strange boy for company, for in order for Gillian to get to St Hilda's on time she would have to leave very much earlier than Joy would, as St Hilda's was on the opposite side of the city. She would have to catch a tram to the Old Haymarket, then change to one which would take her all the way to her new school. Joy, on the other hand, would simply leave the house by the front door when the boy Edward called for her, follow the pavement along until her stick told her that she had reached the kerb, and wait there, listening for the sound of turning traffic, listening even more carefully for someone about to cross. She had been forced to agree that Edward might call for her, but told herself stoutly that she had no real need of him. She had practised the walk to school over and over with Gillian, and was sure she could now do it without a companion to warn her of approaching hazards or see her across the three side roads which lay between her home and the school. The fourth road she would turn into, walking along it for forty paces – she and Gillian had paced out all the distances which would affect her – and only then would she wave her despised white stick in an imperious fashion, cross the road and go straight through the wrought-iron gates into the school playground. The boy Edward would be with her, since Daddy had arranged it, but she was pretty sure that by the end of the week she would be able to dispense with his services.

Joy sighed and turned her head restlessly on her pillow. Nights were always the worst, long black hours which she dreaded, but this night had been longer than all the rest. She would have liked to get out of bed and climb in with her sister because to cuddle close to someone eased her dread of the dark. She knew it would not be fair, however; Gillian needed her sleep because today was her first day back at St Hilda's, as it would be her own first day at Bold Street. There would be thirty other girls in Gillian's class, and her sister did not know a single one of them. Unlike Joy at Bold Street, Gillian would have a different teacher for every subject and would not stay in her own classroom for the duration of each day but, with the other girls, would make her way to one teacher's classroom for maths, another's for geography, the library for English and so on, and so on. At least once Joy reached the haven of her own classroom she would remain there for every lesson, only leaving for break at eleven and school dinner at one. And when afternoon school finished, she would hang about until Edward called for her, whereupon they would walk back home together.

The girls had a small alarm clock, its tick comforting Joy because it proved that time was passing, but Gillian had refused to set the alarm the previous evening, saying that it would not be fair to wake Joy hours before she needed to get up. Gillian had to leave the house by twenty to eight at the latest, whereas Joy, even walking slowly, could reach her school in good time if she left the house an hour later. When she had told Gillian to 'set the bleedin' alarm 'cos I'd rather get up early than be responsible if you didn't wake in time', Gillian had assured her there was no fear of that, since it got light so early now that she'd probably wake up ages before she needed to get out of bed.

Now, Joy heard a creak as Gillian turned over, and then other little sounds which meant her sister was not only awake but getting out of bed. She sat up on her elbow. 'What's the time, Gillian?' she whispered. 'I know you're getting up so I'm getting up as well. Are you excited? I know you laid out your uniform last night and my navy skirt and blouse and things are on my chair. You wash first.'

'Oh, Joy, and I was trying so hard not to wake you,' Gillian said remorsefully. 'I meant to wash and dress ever so quietly, go down and prepare breakfast and then come back and give you a hand. I expect we'll make a mess of things today because it's all new to us, but we'll grow accustomed. We're going to have to get extremely organised though, otherwise you'll be hanging around the house waiting to go and I'll be scampering up the road and probably jumping aboard the wrong tram. Now be sensible; back into bed until I'm ready to help you.'

'Shan't!' Joy said baldly. 'You get washed while I brush out my hair, then I'll wash while you do yours. Then we can go downstairs together and have our breakfast. I'll listen to the wireless when you're gone; they give plenty of time checks, so don't worry that I'll be late. Is it proper daylight already?'

'Yes, it's actually sunny. I wish I didn't have to leave so early, but that boy, what's-his-name, Edward, told

123

Daddy he'd give our door a knock around half past eight. I know you think you'll be able to manage without him, but if a van or lorry turned off the main road right into your path . . .'

'Oh, don't be such an old hen,' Joy said crossly. 'As you say, we've practised and practised and I haven't been squashed flat yet. But if it makes you happier, I'll let him walk beside me, for the first week at any rate.'

She got her reward as she was pulled into Gillian's embrace and given a hard hug. 'Oh, Joy, you're a princess,' Gillian said fervently. 'You've no idea how I've worried about you crossing those wretched side streets. I *know* you're sensible and will wave your white stick, I know you listen to the difference in the engine's note when a driver changes gear to take the corner, and I know you try to cross when others are doing so. But I'll stop worrying altogether if I know you're going to let Edward walk alongside you. Just for a bit, you know,' she added hastily, sensing her sister's disapproval. She splashed water on to her face and then rubbed it briskly dry. 'Your turn now, twin!'

'Are you sure you'll be all right?' Gillian asked for the hundredth time, her voice anxious, yet already a little preoccupied. Joy smiled; I'm quite useful for taking people's minds off their own troubles, she told herself. Gillian hasn't given a thought to her new school until this moment, when she's all set to go, and realises that she will be leaving me here alone. She could picture her sister, in her green blazer and striped green and white cotton dress, with her straw hat on the back of her head and her big brown satchel slung over one shoulder, standing in the open doorway and gazing anxiously at Joy herself, who was sitting at the table eating bread and jam and listening to the wireless. 'Joy? Are you sure you'll be all right? You won't try to make toast, or – or wash up? Daddy wanted Mrs What's-her-name to come in early so that she'd be here by the time he left for work, only you got so cross . . .'

'I'll get cross again if you don't shut up and go,' Joy said sharply. 'Don't treat me as if I was a perishin' baby! We've gone over it again and again, I've agreed to take me white stick even if this here boy turns up as arranged . . .' She heard her sister's gasp as the possibility of Edward's not turning up occurred to her, and knew a fresh bogey had arisen in poor Gillian's mind. For a moment she thought vengefully that it served her sister right, then she relented. 'He'll come, and if he doesn't, I'll be sensible, honest to God I will.'

'How sensible?' Gillian asked suspiciously. 'Go on, if he doesn't turn up what'll you do?'

'I suppose I'll have to go round to the fire station and ask Mr Williams what's happened to him,' Joy said rather gloomily. She had no wish to frighten her father into believing this Edward to be untrustworthy.

But apparently her answer satisfied Gillian, for Joy heard a swift rush of feet, then felt her sister's breath on her cheek and the panama hat digging into her ear as her sister gave her a hurried kiss. 'You're a good girl,' Gillian said. 'I love you as much as I love our daddy and I wish . . . oh, I wish . . .'

'You wish you were thick, like me, so we could go to the same school together. What a liar you are, Gillian Lawrence,' Joy said. 'For God's sake, bugger off before you have us both in tears. Have a wonderful day; you can tell me all about it over tea.'

'All right. Tea shouldn't be a problem because Daddy's got Mrs Clarke to bake a cake, so when you come in you won't have to wait for me before you start to eat . . .'

'I know, I know, I *know*!' Joy almost screamed. 'Everything will go according to plan, except that you'll ruin it all by missing your tram. See you tonight, twin. Be good.'

Chapter Six

Edward Williams brushed his lank, sandy hair, polished his spectacles, straightened his tie and shrugged himself into his worn grey jacket. He had agreed to accompany Joy Lawrence to and from school with very mixed feelings. So far as he was concerned girls were a blot on the landscape, and he considered his school life to be quite hard enough – fat boys suffer all sorts of abuse – without inviting the taunt that only a blind girl would consent to walk to school with him.

However, he had agreed to take Joy to and from school because his father was a member of Alex Lawrence's Watch and it would have been difficult for him to refuse. Like everyone else in the area he had heard about Joy's accident, but the true awfulness of it had not come home to him until he had seen her stumbling along clinging to her sister's arm. Before the accident, the twins used to dart in and out of other pedestrians on the pavement, calling to each other and laughing, but now Gillian walked slowly and carefully whilst Joy clutched her arm as a drowning man clings to a spar.

Edward was in the year above the twins at school and knew them by sight so now the difference between the two girls, who had been identical, was immediately obvious. He had watched the pair of them surreptitiously during the Easter holidays as they practised the walk to school, and had felt truly sorry for Joy, for he had never realised before what a big part expression plays in one's looks. Gillian's face showed complete confidence and command, whereas now Joy always wore a worried frown. He knew of course that this was because she was concentrating fiercely upon following her sister's instructions; once or twice he had been close enough to the pair of them to hear Gillian's voice as she warned her sister of some upcoming obstacle, but now he thought it a dreadful thing that Joy had lost not only her sight but her pretty looks as well. However, perhaps as time went on she would regain some of her old carefree attitude, along with her delightful smile.

So when his father had told him that Alex Lawrence wanted someone responsible to accompany Joy to and from school he had agreed to do it, though with some secret reservations. But Edward liked Alex – everyone did – and besides, the sub-officer's recommendation would stand him in good stead if he applied for a job with the fire service; he trusted that by the time he was an adult he would no longer need his spectacles, for bad eyesight could spell disaster to any chance of becoming a fireman.

At this point in his musing, Edward reached the front door of No. 77. For a moment he hesitated, suddenly reluctant. What should he say when Joy came to the door? Before the accident the twins had never even noticed him; the fat boy who was bad at games, couldn't swim, excelled at nothing save schoolwork, which only interested the teachers. He had always been a loner, though not necessarily from choice, whereas the twins, compared to him, appeared popular with most of their fellow pupils. However, he was not going to stand here looking an idiot, with his hand raised to knock . . .

He knocked too softly, then too loudly, and was just wondering whether she had given him up or gone with someone else when the door shot open and Joy appeared in the doorway. 'Yes?' she said sharply. 'Who is it?'

It was weird, because although she was wearing darkened spectacles she appeared to be looking straight at him, yet he knew this could not be so. He felt his face grow hot. Oh, dammit, this was worse than his worst imaginings! He cleared his throat and his voice, when he spoke, did not sound as it should. 'It's me, Edward Williams, what's come to walk to school wi' you.' In his agitation his accent had thickened. 'Didn't no one tell you I were comin'?'

'Course they did; I've been waiting for your knock,' Joy said briefly and he saw she was already wearing her coat and carrying her white stick. 'But I thought you'd come to the back door because of the steps.' Edward began to apologise, but she interrupted. 'It don't matter; I know these perishin' steps by heart,' she told him. 'You'd best come to the front door every day – every school day, I mean.'

She locked the door as she spoke, and posted the key, on its length of stout twine, back through the letter box. Then she descended the steps, tapping the edge of each one with the stick, and hesitated at the bottom. 'If you don't speak, I don't know where the devil you are,' she said rather gruffly. 'I always know with Gillian, of course, 'cos it's different for twins, but you'll have to tell me when a kerb's coming up, or when there's an obstacle on the pavement.'

'You could hold my arm,' Edward offered.

'No I couldn't; the whole point of your calling for me is so that I can get more independent. Anyway, what a fool I'd look, hanging on to the arm of some feller I don't know from Adam. There'll be no need for you to touch me, thank you very much! Just you walk alongside me and throw out the odd word now and then, and we'll manage . . . or I hope we will, at any rate.'

'If that's what you want,' Edward said, rather huffily. 'But what I want to know is, if you don't want to hang on to my arm because I'm a feller, why didn't your dad ask a girl to call for you? Oh, and slow down, there's a side street coming up.'

Joy obediently slowed and, turning to her unseen companion, gave him a cheeky grin. It was the first time her expression had changed from one of mixed anxiety and annoyance since she had greeted him in the doorway of her house, and he grinned back, remembering too late that she would not have known had he put out his tongue and crossed his eyes. He spoke hastily. 'Well? Why didn't Mr Lawrence pick a girl?'

'There isn't a girl living near enough who Dad would trust to be able to pick me up if I fell, or stop me whacking someone with my white stick,' she explained. 'Besides, your dad's a member of the fire brigade; my dad always says the firemen are like a family and he wouldn't want to ask a favour of someone he didn't know well. So that's why you got the job. I s'pose he is paying you?'

Edward grabbed her arm, too annoyed to remember that she had forbidden him to touch her. 'No, of *course* no one's paying me,' he said angrily. 'It ain't as though I have to go out of my way, because I pass your house

130

every day, and we're heading for the same school. And stop wrigglin' and tryin' to throw me off, because this here kerb is the high one and I've watched you and your sister taking it real slow and careful, so I reckon we've got to do likewise.'

He had indeed watched the Lawrence twins negotiating this particular kerb and had seen how carefully Gillian guided her sister and how they worked as a team, for there was a grid to be avoided as well as the steep kerb itself. 'Oh, we're there, are we? I didn't realise we'd reached it because you kept gabbling on,' Joy said disagreeably. 'Where's that bleedin' grid? I don't want to get my stick stuck down it, 'cos if you've watched me and Gillian, you'll know it's stick first, then I come down sort of sideways . . . and I have to trust you to tell me that there's no traffic coming before I start me darin' descent.' She had spoken quite pleasantly, and Edward was so surprised by her Scouse accent and the sudden change of tone that he turned to stare at her and was annoyed with himself when her frown descended once more. 'I may not be able to see you but I can tell you're gawpin' at me as though I were some sort of freak,' she said crossly. She raised her voice to something perilously akin to a shout. 'Where's that bleedin' grid, you – you *boy*, you!'

Edward began to giggle, and then to laugh, and to his astonishment his companion began to laugh as well. For a moment, they stood on the edge of the kerb, almost doubled up with mirth, and then a passer-by stopped to offer help and Edward, mopping his streaming eyes, thanked the woman but said they could manage, and then turned to Joy. 'The grid's right in front of you,' he said. 'And I weren't gawping, honest to God I weren't. There's nothing coming, so turn sideways and pat with your stick like I've seen you do, then lower yourself on to the road and we'll be across in two ticks.'

Joy obeyed, and having negotiated the worst part of their walk they became, if not friendly, at least more at ease with one another. When they reached the school Edward accompanied her through the big wrought-iron gates and across the yard to the doorway marked *Girls*, where he had to leave her. All around them, other children took no notice of either Joy or Edward, but continued to laugh and play games. Edward knew they were waiting for the bell to ring, whereupon they would line up in classes and enter the building in a sedate fashion when given permission to do so.

It appeared that Joy, however, was an exception to this rule. When they reached the doorway, she stopped for a moment and turned to her escort. 'Daddy's arranged for me to be allowed to go in as soon as I arrive, because there's always a scrum in the cloakroom and he's afraid I might get knocked about,' she informed him. 'When school's over, I'll meet you by the gate five minutes after the bell. But if you're kept in for rowdy behaviour, you'll have to get someone to pass a message to me.'

Once again, Edward heard the jibe in her tone, but no longer resented it. 'You think because your father trusted me to take you to and from school I can't even know the meaning of the word rowdy,' he said. 'Well, you're right; I want to be a fireman one day, so I have to keep on the good side of the teachers and that means I have to study hard; I can't afford to play the fool. So I'll be at the school gate almost as soon as I hear the bell for going home time.'

'Right,' Joy said briskly, and, turning, disappeared into the building. Edward waited for a moment, listening for the tap of her stick, but the only sound was that of her receding footsteps as she made her way, he presumed unerringly, into the girls' cloakroom. Of course, she must have learned that much before her accident, he reminded himself. He kept forgetting that the twins had come back from Devonshire last October, and had attended Bold Street school for several weeks. So though Joy had not visited it since her accident she must, he assumed, have some idea of the layout of the place, and indeed some recollection of her classmates, which would be a help.

Turning away and going back across the playground towards the boys' entrance, Edward reflected that it had not been nearly as bad as he had feared. To be sure, Joy had had a couple of goes at him, and it would have been nice had she said thank you, or even goodbye, before marching off into the school, but he could understand why she had been a little stiff. He imagined himself having to ask a fellow pupil to accompany him to school and knew that he, too, would have resented being so dependent upon another person. There had been a couple of occasions when he had thought he could see the old, happy-go-lucky Joy struggling to get out from the hard shell which blindness had erected around her. He was sure that as time went on she would become more at ease with him, and less critical.

When the bell sounded and his line was formed, he entered the school without a single comment from anyone on his new job. They don't notice me at all, or care who

I walk to school with, he told himself rather sadly. He wished he was popular, like some of the other boys. There was Jenkins, for instance . . .

The teacher's voice telling his pupils to get out their exercise books brought Edward abruptly back to reality. He fished in his desk, produced both his history exercise book and his copy of *Life under the Tudors*, and wrenched his mind from the present to the carryings-on of Henry VIII and his six unfortunate wives. The teacher was writing a list of a dozen questions on the blackboard, telling the boys to put away their textbooks and write their answers, in pencil, in their exercise books. 'Then you will hand your books in, get out your textbooks and read Chapter Seven whilst I correct your answers,' he said, beginning to walk up and down the aisles between the desks as he did so. When he reached Edward, he stopped for a moment and looked over his shoulder at the page Edward had already produced. 'Well done, Edward. I can always rely on you to hand in neatly written work. Now tell me, did I see you this morning with that little blind girl from Class 3B? A friend of yours?'

Edward did not know whether to feel gratified or offended, since he felt that a normal boy of fifteen would scarcely befriend a girl nearly two years younger. But no one sniggered or even looked towards him and the teacher's question had been fair enough. 'Her dad's in the fire brigade, same as mine, so Mr Lawrence asked if I'd walk to and from school with her until she gets used to it,' he explained. 'But I wouldn't call her a friend exactly, though she's a nice enough kid.'

Mr Johnson guffawed. 'Never let it be said that a lad

in my class looked twice at any girl,' he said, and gave Edward's shoulder a playful punch. 'You'll be singing a different tune in a year or two, young man. But perhaps you fancy the other sister; they're identical twins, aren't they? If so, you'll make a good pair, because you're pretty bright, like . . . Gillian, isn't it? She won a scholarship to St Hilda's, anyway, which is no mean feat.'

'Yes, sir,' Edward mumbled. Mr Johnson had always been a bit of a joker, but it didn't do to cross him. 'During the Easter holidays, Gillian – she's the older twin – went everywhere with Joy, the one I'm taking to and from school. It's because Gillian's starting at St Hilda's today that her pa needs me to help out.' He waited for a snigger from the boys at the desks surrounding his own, but for once they were concentrating on their work.

'Well, I'm glad one member of my class at least has a social conscience; the rest of them don't even know the meaning of the phrase,' Mr Johnson said. 'Starting today, is she, eh? She'll have a lot to talk about when she and her sister meet up this evening.'

Gillian got off the tram at the end of her road and waved to the girls who were still aboard. She had been a little anxious lest her new schoolfellows snub her or ignore her, but instead they had vied to take care of her as the class moved from room to room. In fact she had had a fantastic day and was still glowing with pleasure.

Furthermore, until today she had not realised how the burden of her twin's dependency had weighed her down. When she was with Joy she could not relax for one moment. Her eyes were not only on the pavement ahead, but also keeping a lookout for possible dangers:

a dog on one side of the road and a cat on the other could spell disaster for someone who could see neither, so Gillian would warn her sister to slow down, to hang on to her arm and not to worry if she heard the screech of brakes and the shouts of passers-by. It would only be the dog darting into the traffic or the cat streaking up a side street.

When they met someone they knew, Gillian would tell Joy who it was in a whisper, and they had made this into a sort of game – *Mrs Tudor Williams on our port bow* – so that when the woman greeted them they could chorus: 'Hello, Mrs Williams. Nice day, isn't it?' Mrs Williams must know that Joy could not see her, but she would answer the greeting placidly. If she felt astonishment, she would not show it. This, Gillian soon discovered, went for anyone they met and greeted. So she not only had to warn Joy of possible hazards, but of approaching acquaintances as well.

It had worked beautifully and Gillian had not realised, until now, what a strain she had been under. Going into a new class in a new school with a great many other girls, none of whom she had met before, she felt the freedom of being without her twin as a real blessing. She might have felt guilty, knowing Joy was alone in her dark world, but instead she suspected that Joy, too, would benefit from their separation. With the intuition which she imagined all identical twins must share, she had a mental picture of Joy talking to other members of her class, maybe even laughing and joking with them, showing off a little to that boy – what was his name? Oh yes, Edward Williams – on the walk to and from school. All the little tricks which Colin had mentioned on his one visit and which Joy had scornfully refused to use should come into play now that she did not have Gillian to be her guide and her eyes, and Edward would surely be impressed.

When they had practised the walk during the Easter holidays, Joy had not really used the white stick, nor listened with all her might to discover what was happening around her. Instead she had wagged the stick in a desultory fashion, tapping the kerb all right and checking now and then on the shops they passed, but relying on her sister to warn her of possible dangers. Now she would have to use the stick in earnest, and Gillian just hoped she wouldn't make a rude comment – she was quite capable of it – if Edward was slow to warn her of approaching hazards. It wouldn't help to antagonise the lad.

Now, Gillian danced along the pavement, but slowed to a sedate walk as she neared her home. Joy should have been in for a good half-hour, but given her past perform-ance she had probably done nothing towards getting their tea. Oh well, Gillian told herself, bypassing the front door of No. 77 and diving down the jigger, Mrs Clarke has made us a cake, so we can have a slice of that, and it won't take two minutes for the kettle to boil. Supper will be later, when Daddy comes in. She crossed the yard and reached the back door on the thought, beating a brief tattoo on it before reaching for the latch, so that Joy would know it was she entering the room. She pushed open the door carefully though, in case Joy was standing near it, but when she entered she saw that her sister was sitting at the table eating whilst behind her steam was beginning to issue from the kettle on the stove.

Gillian gasped, a hand flying to her mouth. 'Joy, you know you're not supposed to light the gas and I've heard you saying times without number that you shouldn't handle knives. How did you cut that slice of cake without using a knife? Or has Mrs Clarke been round to give you a hand?'

'I did have a little bit of help, but only with lighting the gas,' Joy said with a small self-satisfied smirk. 'I filled the kettle myself and put it on the cooker. That Edward insisted on coming in and lighting the gas for me . . . well, no, that's not fair. He stood by and watched while I used the gas lighter – it's easy, isn't it? – and then he buzzed off. He asked me if I would like him to cut the cake; he was probably angling for me to give him a bit, only I wouldn't.' She waved the slice of cake she was eating. 'Cut it myself, no trouble! I would've started on the spuds for tonight's supper only Dad must've done 'em before he went to work. At any rate, there's a pan full of peeled ones on the draining board and there's what feels like chops in the meat safe.' She grinned at her sister, her pleasure in her achievements so great that she was pink-cheeked. 'Here, let me cut you some cake whilst you make the tea; I don't reckon I'm up to pouring boiling water into the teapot, though I dare say it'll come to me in time.'

'I'll cut the cake as well if you like,' Gillian said eagerly, but her sister shook her head and turned in the direction of Gillian's voice, for the older twin had moved across the kitchen and was taking the kettle off the gas as they spoke.

'No need, thank you very much. It's easy to cut a cake made in a loaf tin; a round one would present more of a problem.' As she spoke she had risen to her feet, pulled the cake towards her and picked up the knife. She grinned at her sister and Gillian could tell that Joy knew exactly where she was by the sounds she herself was scarcely conscious of making: the lifting of the milk jug, the adding of the tea, probably even the stirring in of a spoonful of sugar to each mug. But Joy was turning to her, her fingers resting lightly on top of the cake. 'One inch or two?' she asked playfully. 'I had quite a large piece and advise you to do the same; it's absolutely delicious. When the summer holidays come, perhaps I'll get Mrs Clarke to teach me simple cookery. Nothing too dangerous, and you may have to put stuff into the oven for me and get it out when it's cooked, but it would be fun, and helpful, don't you think?'

'Gosh!' Gillian said. 'It would certainly be nice if we could cook. I'll have a large slice, please . . . and when we're settled, I'll tell you about my day and you can tell me about yours.'

Presently the sisters were seated opposite one another, both munching cake and sipping tea. 'It's just like the old days,' Gillian said. 'I'll tell first, shall I?'

'Yes, sure; only don't forget that when Daddy comes home we shall have to tell the whole thing again,' Joy said. 'He'll want to know what I thought of Edward and whether I think I'll be able to cope without you . . .' She heard the impatient little movement her sister made, and spluttered into her tea. 'Sorry, sorry! Carry on, Jeeves!'

Nothing loth, Gillian began her tale, starting with what she thought most important. 'Well, I didn't know a soul in my class and I was dead nervous, honest to God I was. But as soon as—'

'You? Nervous? That I should see the day!' Joy cut in derisively. 'You don't know the meaning of the word nerves, girl . . . Oh, sorry again. I didn't mean to interrupt. Go on; my lips are sealed.'

'Your lips are sealed?' Gillian squeaked. 'That'll be the day! Dad always says your tongue runs on wheels and I've no reason to think you've suddenly changed. But I'll take your word for it that you won't interrupt again; nod once for yes and twice for no.'

Joy snorted and blew cake crumbs, but nodded once and Gillian started to speak again. 'Well, the girls were friendly as friendly. No one looked down on me; in fact, quite the opposite. They damned nearly fought over who was to sit next to me and at dinner time everyone wanted to give me one of their sandwiches, or a few crisps, or even an apple. It seems that we have to take a packed lunch once a week, but we can buy a hot school dinner on the other four days. They aren't expensive and the girls say they're good value, but most of the pupils in my class take sandwiches every day because their mams do a hot meal each evening. There's one girl I particularly liked, and I think she liked me. Her name's Helen and she's got lovely curly fair hair and eyes that laugh, even when her mouth doesn't, if you see what I mean. She lives quite near the school – very handy – and she's got a lovely soft voice, you'd like it. And she's easily the cleverest in the Lower Fourth.'

'I bet she won't be the cleverest, not now you're in her form,' Joy said proudly. 'I know it was only the first day, but did you have tests and that?'

Gillian nodded and took another bite of cake, speaking rather thickly through it. 'Yes, we did, and I must admit

I came out of it pretty well. French was a surprise; they've been learning the language for ages and of course it isn't part of the curriculum at ordinary schools, but Mademoiselle Cousteau's French lessons must have been really good because I'm way ahead of the class in the spoken word and only a trifle behind in written work.'

'So you truly enjoyed your first day?' Joy asked. 'Although you never said so, I know you worried that the other girls might despise you because you were a scholarship girl, but I take it that no one thought worse of you because of it.'

'As I said, everyone wanted to sit next to me, or take me from one classroom to another,' Gillian assured her sister. 'I was really popular.' She was intelligent enough to realise that this popularity might not be of long duration, but whilst it lasted it was very sweet. She said as much to Joy, who shook her head.

'You're pretty and clever and now that you've not got me tied round your neck like the albatross in the poem you'll make heaps of friends,' she said decidedly. Gillian began to protest, but Joy hushed her imperiously. 'Hang on a moment. You aren't the only one who has news to impart. Are you ready to hear the story of *my* day?' She put down her empty mug and smiled in the general direction of her sister. 'You'll have to cast your mind back to those two months at the Bold Street school before Christmas, when I was able to see. The truth is, I don't have to imagine what the boys and girls look like from their voices; I just have to use my memory. Oh, at first it's bound to be difficult, because I never took much notice of people's voices when I could see, but now I can't I have to get to know which face goes with what

141

voice, if you understand me. Well, today, I hung about the cloakroom until the bell went. Then I waited until it was quiet and went very slowly and carefully into our old classroom. I don't mind admitting that at first it was . . . oh, awful! I heard all the chattering die away and the most dreadful feeling of desolation swept over me. I imagined stepping forward and finding a desk in my way, crashing to the ground, trying to scramble to my feet . . .'

'Oh, Joy darling,' Gillian said, her voice choked with tears. 'I'll give up St Hilda's – it's not that great anyway – and come back to Bold Street, so we can be together and I can tell you—'

'No!' Joy shouted. 'That would be the worst possible thing; it would ruin everything. The point is that as soon as they saw I was alone – and they must have guessed how frightened I felt – someone came over and took my hand. "Remember me?" she said. "I'm Susie. You and I sometimes shared a desk before Christmas, when your twin was doing special lessons with the top class. Are you going to wait for Gillian or shall you and me share a two-seater? It'll have to be in the front of the class because I don't hear too good. Where is Gillian, by the way?"

'I reminded her you'd started at St Hilda's and she gave my fingers a little squeeze and then led me to the desk we were to share. "*Do* you remember me?" she asked. "I've got sandy hair in two plaits and rather a lot of freckles. I'm quite good at English, but useless at maths and—"

'Someone else broke in, giggling. "She's gorra squint and no front teeth," a girl's voice said jeeringly. "Now

142

me, I'm Prue Edge and you won't remember me 'cos I were new at the beginnin' of last term, but if you want to know wharr I look like, just visualise Marlene Dietrich; folks say they can't tell us apart."

'Everyone laughed, including me, though I couldn't help thinking what a shame it was that I'd never see another cowboy film – or any film, for that matter – but I'm getting off the point. I did remember Susie all right, but there were other voices then, other hands patting me or giving my hair a tweak, people introducing themselves. For a moment it was frightening and how I cursed my stupidity in not learning as much about our fellow pupils as I could have done. But I wasn't to know . . . oh, never mind. Anyway, they were grand, Gillian, honest to God they were. By the time the teacher came in and rapped on her desk for order, I'd remembered most of the class and was beginning to put names to voices.

'The teacher was grand too; she was our class teacher. I remembered her from the time we spent in school before Christmas. I hadn't liked her much then; she was awful strict and wouldn't stand no nonsense.' Joy grinned at Gillian. 'Do you remember how ratty she got because we were squabbling about whose pencil case was which?'

'Course I remember; I thought she was beastly, but from what you've said perhaps she was right and we were wrong. Carry on then.'

'Right,' Joy said, reflecting that in an odd sort of way her day and Gillian's had really been very similar. 'Well, the teacher – Miss Roberts – said that since we'd started getting to know one another all over again she would introduce us properly. She came over to my desk, told me to stand up and then took my hand . . .'

143

'I hope you didn't flinch away,' Gillian said anxiously, remembering her twin's dislike of being touched, but Joy shook her head.

'No, of course I didn't,' she said indignantly. 'She was trying to help me. Oh, I know that before I've resented being helped by anyone but you and Daddy, but today I realised how stupid that is. Now I mean to accept any help offered, until I don't need it, that is. Blind people do become independent, don't they, Gillian? Look at that Colin. I know he went to the special school and learned all sorts of tricks there, but he was only eight. I'm nearly fourteen and I can work out for myself various ways of becoming independent. Not that I need to, because Colin said he'd come round to give a hand whenever I wanted; all I have to do is send a message by his brother Jerome, and he'll be here like a shot.' She giggled. 'He liked Mrs Clarke's scones and ginger nuts, didn't he? We'll have to get her to bake some more.'

'Just what do you think Colin can teach you?' Gillian asked curiously. She leaned across and pulled the cake towards herself, then picked up the cake knife. 'Do you want another piece? It *is* good, isn't it?'

Joy frowned and began to feel her way across the table, plainly searching for something, and when she addressed her sister her voice was reproachful. 'Now you've been and gone and done it, Gillian; I knew exactly where the cake was in relation to my plate and mug. I know you pulled it away because I heard the cake plate slithering across the table top, but I haven't a clue where it ended up.' She scowled in the general direction from which Gillian's voice had come. 'We've both got a lot to learn, you know, and you can start by not moving things

144

without telling me what you're doing. Go on, tell me where the cake is now.'

'It's right in front of you, where it was before,' Gillian said, hastily pushing it back across the table. 'The knife is lying on the plate beside it. Oh, Joy, you're quite right, we've both got an awful lot to learn. Now tell me what happened when Miss Roberts took hold of your hand.'

'You've spoilt my flow,' Joy grumbled. 'Well, Miss Roberts took me up to the front of the class and stood me beside her desk. Then she called the class out, one by one, and each pupil was told to give their name and any other information which might help me to recognise them. For instance, Susie said about her freckles and sandy plaits again, and Ella said she was short and plump, whilst Jane said she had shared my book at the carol service and didn't I remember how we'd sung the descant together. Of course when she said that I remembered her perfectly and took hold of her hand, moving my own up until I could touch her hair. It's weird, Gillian, because when I could see her I often longed to touch her hair. It's long and silky and I was just telling her that of course I remembered her perfectly when my hand reached her shoulder and stopped short . . . Gillian, I was so surprised that I gave a little yelp. "You've cut your perishin' hair off!" I said. "Oh, how could you, Jane? Your long hair was so beautiful . . ."

'"Yes, but it was getting too long; Mam said it was straggly and untidy and the hairdresser said it would grow stronger if I had it cut. I didn't reckon she would shorten it quite so much, though," Jane said. Everyone laughed, and Jane pointed out that I had long hair and asked if I'd ever thought about cutting it.

145

'After that, it were a whole lot easier because I started to use my memory in real earnest and by the time the bell went for break I'd got a pretty good idea of what most of the class looked like and which face went with which voice. And Miss Roberts said that I should go out when the bell rang for break when everyone else did, and she would choose the best-behaved pupil each morning to take care of me in the playground and see that I came to no harm. I was glad of that, because playtime's a bit of a scrum, isn't it?'

'You're right there,' Gillian agreed. 'So you went out with all the others; what were they doing? Playing Relievio?'

'What, in the playground? Very funny. No, first of all we had our milk and I ate the biscuit Dad gave me for my elevenses. Prue was milk monitor, which meant she had to collect the little bottles, rinse them out and take them down to the kitchens . . .'

'I know all about milk and milk monitors, goofy,' Gillian said. 'I was at Bold Street as well, you know. How would you manage if they made you milk monitor?'

'I'd be all right,' Joy said loftily, though her heart sank a little. 'Someone would have to take me to the kitchens and carry the milk crate through for me, but I could manage to rinse the bottles. But that's not the point; I'm talking about playtime, if you don't mind!'

Gillian smiled, then leaned across the table and rubbed her sister's cheek affectionately. 'Of course I don't mind. Carry on!'

'Right. Jane, Susie and I linked arms and went outside. The playground's pretty flat so they didn't have to warn me of any hazards that came up and we just talked about what we're going to do when we leave school. Of course it'll be a while before anyone has to make up their minds, but Jane's elder sister is at college doing an arts course and Susie means to be a hairdresser, like her mam. They don't get much money whilst they're training, but once they pass out or whatever you call it they can open their own salons and charge the earth.' She sighed wistfully. 'Wish I could be a hairdresser . . .'

'Oh yeah?' Gillian said mockingly. 'I can just see you brandishing an ear in your scissors and saying to the customer: "Does Modom like the new style? Or would she like it a little shorter?"'

Both girls collapsed and then Joy, listening carefully to her sister's hiccuping mirth, leaned across the table and seized some part of the other girl, patted what she assumed must be a shoulder and then grabbed a handful of her sister's long hair. 'I'd make a better hairdresser than you would, brain-box,' she said jeeringly. 'You'll probably end up teaching – dull work – or writing numbers in a big ledger, whilst I earn a huge salary as – as someone's secretary. Colin said they taught typing at St Saviour's, didn't he?'

'Ye-es,' Gillian said. 'But what a cheek; *you'll* be working in Woolie's, or sweeping the concourse at Lime Street station, or packing bags of sugar at Tate's . . .'

'Shan't!' Joy squeaked, and in a moment the two of them were locked in a fighting embrace and giggling like five-year-olds.

Alex, entering the kitchen quietly, stopped short, astonished at the scene before him. The twins were rolling around the floor, exchanging the wildest of wild punches

147

and laughing hysterically. Alex's presence had not been noticed and he reflected that his daughters were far too involved to see that a third party had entered the room. Indeed he doubted whether they would have looked up had he been accompanied by three brass bands, all playing different tunes. He grinned; this was like old times, but of course it would not do to say so. Instead he announced his arrival by seizing an arm of each daughter and pulling them to their feet.

'Why are you fighting? When I went to work this morning, I left two young ladies getting their breakfast. Now I come home to two hooligans rolling around on the floor, trying to gouge each other's eyes out. You'd better sit down at the table and tell me what it's all about.'

Still giggling, the girls went and sat down. 'It was only play fighting,' Gillian said apologetically. 'We were discussing our future . . . Joy said she wanted to be a hairdresser, which made me laugh, and then we started insulting each other, you know how it is. When we were living with the Dodmans we often had a good old fight, but not when they were around. They would have been shocked.'

'I'm shocked too,' Alex said, though with a twitching lip at the thought of Joy being allowed to wield scissors near some unfortunate woman's head. 'Well, if that's the way you behave when you're alone at home, perhaps I ought to get someone in when I'm not here myself . . .'

There were cries of protest from both twins. 'It's all right, Daddy, honestly it is,' Joy said fervently. If you're afraid that I might get hurt because I can't see, you're dead wrong. I only had to shout pax and Gillian would have given up at once. Twins never go too far, you know. Can't you remember how we used to fight when we were quite little kids?'

Alex cast his mind back. He could remember the twins from their birth right up to the moment when they had been evacuated; two pretty lively little girls, one with green ribbons on the ends of her plaits, the other with red ones. He grinned reminiscently. Now Joy had reminded him he could remember the fights, which had always been good-humoured; remembered how Bridget had said that Joy, the peacemaker, was also the first to dissolve into laughter. 'And laughter is a great healer,' Bridget had said. 'Gillian is clever, though rather impatient, but people love Joy because she makes them laugh.'

However, it was different now. He said as much, adding: 'Suppose the pair of you had rolled up against the table legs? Joy, my love, you might have whacked your head on something you couldn't see. I don't want to stop you playing, but I do think you're getting too old to fight. So unless you want me to pay someone to come in when I'm working, you'll have to learn to argue without coming to blows. Do you think that's possible?'

Clearly horrified, the girls chorused that they would be careful in future and would not fight again even in fun, though as Gillian put it they could scarcely promise never to disagree. 'Because although we're twins, we don't always like the same things or the same people,' she pointed out. 'For instance, Joy quite likes Irene Finnigan, so whenever we meet her in the street I have to stop to let the two of them have a chat. But she's not

149

my type, not really.' She snorted. 'All she thinks about is clothes and gossip!'

'She's all right; she's quite fun really,' Joy said defensively. 'Remember, Miss Clever Clogs, that she used to be at Bold Street, so she knows all the teachers and quite a lot of the pupils, which gives us something in common. Why did you pick on Irene, anyway?'

Gillian gave a little choke of laughter. 'Oh, Irene's not so bad really.' She turned to her father, who knew he must be looking baffled. 'Oh, Daddy, I was trying to show you that Joy and I often disagree, even if we are identical twins.'

'I see what you're trying to say,' Alex said mildly, 'but I don't understand why you don't like poor little Irene.' He turned to Joy, who was sitting next to him, and took her hand, letting her know that it was she he was now addressing. 'Don't listen to your sister, she's just jealous because she thinks Irene has a soft spot for me.' He puffed out his chest, Tarzan-like. 'And who can blame her for fancying a handsome chap like myself?'

Joy laughed. 'Oh, Daddy, everyone has a soft spot for you! Why, when we went to see Miss Batchelor that day to arrange for me to be allowed into school before the bell, she kept patting her hair and speaking in a fluttery sort of voice, and she's old as the hills; even older than you!'

'What a cheek; I'm not in my dotage yet, you know,' Alex said with mock indignation. 'And how do you know Miss Batchelor kept patting her hair?' His voice sharpened with hope. 'Can you see, just a little, sometimes? No, of course you can't, silly question. Only I don't understand how you knew.'

Joy sighed. 'I wish I could see a tiny bit; even if I could tell day from night it would be something, but it hasn't happened yet, though I'm sure it will some day. Sometimes I see flashes of brilliant white or violet light . . . but then they go away and it's nothing but dark once more.' She turned hopefully to where her father sat beside her. 'Wouldn't you say that's a sign that there is some sight in my eyes, somewhere? So you see, I do have hope.'

'And so you should,' Alex said heartily, though he had discussed this phenomenon with Mr Burton and knew that it meant nothing. However, he did not mean to tell his daughter that. 'So if you couldn't see your Miss Batchelor – who is a very nice lady and not as old as the hills at all, incidentally – then how did you know she patted her hair?'

Joy laughed. 'Guesswork,' she admitted. 'Was I right, Daddy? Did she pat her hair? Only I know it's one of her little habits because before Christmas we all noticed she did it whenever Mr Cadogan, who teaches PT, was around.'

Alex laughed too. 'You're a cunning little weasel and I love you,' he said, giving her a squeeze. 'So you've both had a good day at school, have you?' The twins imme-diately started to speak at once but Alex hushed them and stood up. 'Quiet. You can each tell me all about your day over supper, but right now we'd better start preparing things or it will be midnight before we get a meal.'

It was halfway through the summer term and Alex was sitting in the kitchen after the girls had gone to bed, waiting for a quiet knock on the back door. He was expecting a visitor, having given the regime of school, housework and marketing a fair trial before deciding whether he should employ anybody else to do one or other of those jobs.

Now that Joy had her confidence back – or at least some of it – she was rapidly beginning to pull her weight. She washed and wiped up, laid the table, made the beds and mopped and cleaned the floors. Of course she had accidents from time to time – their crockery was in constant danger – but otherwise she managed, with a certain amount of help from Gillian and Alex himself, to do her fair share of almost everything.

The exception was cooking. Gillian, bless her, Alex thought now, had taken over the preparation of their meals, but her pastry was like cement, her cakes would not rise and even quite simple things like scrambling eggs had caused at least two good saucepans to lose their bottoms. If it had not been for the shortages and the increasing severity of rationing, Alex thought they might have soldiered on, but, as he told his daughters, they simply could not go on wasting good food.

Apart from the cooking and serving of their meals, however, things were continuously improving. He had been delighted when the girls had both settled well at their respective schools, even more delighted by the realisation that Joy was coming to terms with her sight-lessness. She asked for help when she needed it but was proud of her own ability to solve the problems which arose, no longer railing bitterly against the fate which had made her fly to the bedroom window. Of course, being only human, she was occasionally a victim of black depression, when nothing seemed to go right and the future – a future in which she could not see – was something she could not bear to contemplate, but these fits were rarer than they had been at first, and there were times, Alex thought contentedly now, when Joy was her old optimistic, happy-go-lucky self.

So in one sense at least, things were going pretty well. Joy had confided in him that she did not think her blindness would last for ever, and though Mr Burton had told both Gillian and himself that only a miracle could restore Joy's sight, he had also said that no one should let Joy know as much. So when Gillian talked about her place in the rounders team, her hopes of representing the middle school at tennis, and like subjects, Joy simply said that when her sight returned, as she felt sure it would some day, she must have extra coaching so that she could compete with her twin once more.

But right now, at the end of May, a problem had arisen which neither Alex nor his daughters had allowed for. Clubs. St Hilda's ran a number of after-school clubs, for both sporting and academic activities. Gillian had said wistfully that she realised she could not join any, but Alex thought it a great shame that Gillian, who worked very hard both in class and at home, should be denied the more social side of school life. Accordingly, he had made his plans, and these included sitting alone in the kitchen, a good while after the twins had gone to bed, waiting for—

There was a knock at the door; a cautious knock. Alex, who had chosen a late-night interview in order that the twins should not be aware of it, smiled to himself and got to his feet. He walked over to the door and opened it quietly . . . then stepped back, eyebrows rising, mouth dropping open. Standing smiling hopefully up at him, and looking very young and pretty in a blue linen coat and high-heeled shoes, was Irene Finnigan!

Alex opened his mouth to ask her what on earth she was doing on his doorstep at this time of night, but he was so surprised that he actually took a step back, which Irene seemed to interpret as an invitation, since she immediately stepped past him into the kitchen, giving him a bright smile as she did so.

'Evenin', Mr Lawrence,' she said brightly, but Alex caught the strain in her tone and immediately all his chivalrous instincts came to the fore. The poor kid was nervous. She must realise as clearly as he did himself that it was an odd hour for a social call, so he assumed she needed help.

'Evening, Irene. What can I do for you?' he said at once, smiling to put her at her ease. 'It's rather late for visiting, but of course it's always nice to see a neighbour. Were you looking for Gillian? Or Joy? I'm afraid they've been in bed for an hour, and unless it's very urgent I'd not dream of disturbing either of them.'

Irene gave a giggle. It was a nervous giggle, and it made Alex feel extremely uneasy. What the devil was happening? This girl – well, young woman – was very little older than his daughters, so why was she looking at him under her lashes, whilst a tide of pink rose from her neck to the top of her forehead? And why was she wearing her best bib and tucker, he asked himself with considerable unease. Why was she calling at an hour when she must have known very well that the twins would be tucked up in bed? She had come round on other occasions and offered help for which she had been politely thanked, though they had never taken her up on any of her suggestions.

Alex cleared his throat. 'I'd ask you to sit down . . .' he began, and was forestalled.

'Thank you,' Irene said politely, and sat down in one of the kitchen chairs, twisting it to face him. 'I'm sorry it's so late, but someone said . . .'

She hesitated, and Alex jumped in at once. 'Just what did someone say?' he asked baldly. 'I'm sure no one said I encouraged young ladies to visit me after ten o'clock in the evening! So why are you here?'

Irene's face grew even pinker and Alex thought for a moment that there was a sly look in her big, pale blue eyes, but then it vanished and she was just a very young girl feeling the most awful fool, and he was not helping a bit. Dared not help, in point of fact. He liked all the Finnigan family and had no wish to alienate even this particular sprig by telling her bluntly to go home. 'Why are you here?' he repeated, and then, aware of the brusqueness of the remark, softened his tone. 'I'm sorry, Irene, but I'm puzzled . . .'

'Why, I'm applyin' for the job. Surely you realised?' Irene said quickly. 'They said you wanted folk to come when the ki— the children, I mean, were in bed, so I come round after ten, like you said.'

'Like I said?' echoed Alex blankly. 'But I didn't . . . I haven't . . . I don't know what you're talking about.'

Irene sighed, but the betraying flush in her cheeks deepened. 'Some of the women were chatterin'. They said as how you wanted a – a companion, a friend like, to be wi' young Joy from around four until t'other one, or yourself of course, come home. They said that now, while the evenings is light until quite late and the weather's clement, your Gillian will be attendin' after-school classes . . . I think that's what they said. And they said as how you wanted someone to keep Joy company whenever you or Gillian ain't here.' She peered at him anxiously. 'Ain't that right? Have I gorrit wrong? Only that *was* what they were sayin', the women in Platt's grocery t'other evenin'. And I'm real fond o' young Joy. I'd be happy to come in when needed and wouldn't ask no payment, honest to God, Mr Lawrence, sir.'

Alex took a deep breath; this was not going to be easy! 'I'm afraid you've got hold of the wrong end of the stick,' he said politely. 'I couldn't possibly ask you – or anyone else – to give up their free time without paying them. And of course during the school holidays we won't need any help at all. It's true that Gillian is coming home a good deal later than Joy, but . . .'

Another knock sounded on the back door and Alex's heart descended to his boots. Now things might be awkward indeed, if this was the person he was expecting. But he smiled at Irene and said in a low voice: 'Off with you, young lady. The visitor I was waiting for has just arrived.'

As Irene got reluctantly to her feet he went across and opened the kitchen door, gesturing for Mrs Clarke to enter. He smiled at her, then turned to Irene. 'Goodnight, Irene. Thank you for your offer of help, but . . .'

He opened the door wider and Irene slipped out, keeping her eyes down and her head averted as she and Mrs Clarke passed one another. Alex was about to close the back door, saying pleasantly: 'I'm sorry about the muddle . . .' when Irene suddenly turned back.

'What say we share the job – me and Mrs Clarke?' she said eagerly. 'I remember old Mrs Platt saying that there were some trouble over cookin' . . . if you was wantin' help in that quarter . . . ?'

Alex was starting to feel that he shared Gillian's opinion of this young visitor; the girl was downright pushy. After all, she was an uninvited guest, whereas he had asked Mrs Clarke to pop round. He was beginning to bid Irene a rather cool goodnight when Mrs Clarke interrupted. 'If this young lady is one of Joy's friends, then maybe the child might prefer her company to that of a woman old enough to be' – she smiled a trifle ruefully – 'her mother . . . though not her grandmother,' she finished rather roguishly. 'What do you think, Mr Lawrence? I'm very fond of your daughters and will enjoy giving them cookery lessons, but of course we must not forget that Joy will always need help, so the girls must learn to cook as a team. I take it that that was why you asked me to come round this evening?'

Poor Alex stood by the open back door, not liking to shut it in Irene's face, yet none too keen to have her listen to his discussion with Mrs Clarke, for he had every intention of offering that lady a small hourly sum for time spent in his home.

Irene took matters into her own hands by coming back into the kitchen, closing the door behind her and addressing the older woman. 'I'm no hand at cooking and me mam's no great shakes, so I'd be glad of a lesson or two meself,' she said eagerly. 'And as I were tellin' Mr Lawrence here, me and Joy's good pals so I wouldn't expect no rumer . . . rumer . . . no money for keepin' the kid company when there's no one else around.' She turned her head and looked pleadingly at Alex. 'Honest to God, Mr Lawrence, I reckon it's the ideal solution.'

Alex decided it was time he took control of the situation. He went over and opened the back door again, but this time kept a firm hold on the handle. 'I know you mean well, Irene, but Mrs Clarke and myself have to talk,' he said, ushering his unwanted guest firmly out into the back yard.

Irene was still looking over her shoulder and talking of her willingness to come in whenever she was needed when she gave a shriek and cried that there was something in the yard; it had just bumped against her legs . . .

Alex began to say irritably that it must be a neighbour's cat, but Mrs Clarke pushed past him, bent down and seized something, then straightened, revealing that one hand was hooked into the collar of her pug. 'I'm that sorry, Mr Lawrence,' she said breathlessly. 'I brought Dilly out for an airing but of course I wouldn't bring her into your kitchen . . . if I'd known you had a visitor, I'd never have let her loose in your yard.' She turned anxiously to Irene. 'Did she bite you, love? I expect you startled her, walkin' out all of a sudden the way you did.'

'I don't know; my leg hurts! If that little bleeder has laddered my nylons . . .' Irene began in anything but a forgiving voice. 'I'd best go back in the kitchen, check what the little beast's done.'

But Alex had had enough. 'No you don't, young lady,' he said grimly, barring the way. 'You said something had bumped into you, which might mean a ladder in your nylons, but scarcely a rent in your person.' Suddenly, the humour of the situation struck him and he had hard work not to start laughing. He controlled his mirth, however, and turned to Mrs Clarke. 'Take Dilly into the kitchen, Mrs C. She can have one of the biscuits you baked last week; there are a few left in the biscuit barrel.' He turned back to the younger woman, who was balefully examining her nylon-clad legs in the light from the kitchen door. 'Off with you, Irene. Thanks for the offer; if at any time I decide to take you up on it, I'll let you know.'

Back in the kitchen, he and Mrs Clarke exchanged rueful grins whilst Dilly slobbered over a ginger biscuit, lying in front of the fire as though she owned the whole house. 'I'm awful sorry,' Mrs Clarke said apologetically. 'I'll leave Dilly at home another time; you won't want her messing up your nice clean kitchen. But I always give her a walk last thing and I've been too busy all day to give her much attention, so I thought I'd trot her round here, leave her in the yard whilst you and I had our little chat, and then walk her up as far as the bomb site. I usually let her off the lead there so she can have a good sniff around.'

Alex grinned. 'And bite the bums of any lovers unwise enough to pursue their frolics in what they assume to be a secluded spot,' he observed. 'I hope I needn't tell you, Mrs Clarke, that young Irene was an uninvited guest? Apparently she'd been in Platt's the other day when some of the customers were discussing our problems and decided to take a hand . . . well, there was no harm done, as it happens. Actually, I asked you to pop in so I could see if you'd consider a sort of part-time job. At present Gillian comes home from school about half an hour after Joy, but she would like to stay on for various after-school clubs, which would mean she wouldn't get home until seven or eight at night, sometimes later. St Hilda's girls can use the tennis courts, the cricket nets and the sports field until nine o'clock at night, but Gillian has been unable to take part in any of those extras because she's had to get home to be with Joy. Oh, not always, but as you know, I don't have regular hours.'

'Yes, I understand, and if Joy would agree we could work out a timetable which would suit us both,' Mrs Clarke said, nodding. 'I could bring my knitting round, or do some cooking for you, or Joy and I could go out together, perhaps to the park, or just for a stroll.'

'That would be wonderful, and of course I'd pay you an hourly rate . . .' Alex began, only to be peremptorily hushed.

'No, no; why should you pay me when I'd be using your gas cooker? To say nothing of ingredients, because I'd be bound to borrow a little salt or the odd spoonful of jam from time to time. I'll charge you for any ingredients I buy, as I always have, but not for my time!' She clicked her tongue. 'Why should I expect payment for enjoying myself?'

On this point, however, Alex was determined to be firm, and in the end they agreed on a small sum to be paid weekly. They also agreed, to Alex's secret surprise, that Mrs Clarke would ask Irene Finnigan to take her place when either she herself was busy, or Joy wished to attend some event which Mrs Clarke knew the girl would enjoy more in the company of someone her own age.

Alex had demurred at this, not wanting Irene to get her foot in the door for fear she would take advantage in some way. He said as much to Mrs Clarke, who shook a reproving finger. 'She means well, and she'll be able to do a number of things which are beyond me,' she said frankly. 'Don't you worry, Mr Lawrence, I know what you're thinking, but be sure I'll keep her in check. She's not a bad girl, but she's at an awkward age, neither one thing nor t'other.' She smiled understandingly at her companion. 'You'll find out all about the difficulties of rearing young girls in a couple of years when Joy and Gillian become . . . what is it the Americans call them? I know, bobby-soxers.' She chuckled, and got to her feet. 'Break it to Joy before she goes off to school tomorrow, and let me know if she approves. Goodnight, Mr Lawrence. Dilly? Come along, old lady, stir your stumps.'

Alex hurried to open the back door, thanked his visitor sincerely and watched as Mrs Clarke and the fat little dog crossed the yard, went through the gate and turned right along the jigger. Only when they were out of sight did he close and lock the kitchen door and with a deep sigh, for it was well past eleven o'clock, begin to lay the table for breakfast before making his weary way up the stairs to bed.

Irene had gone home thoroughly disgruntled with her evening, but the next day Mrs Clarke called round at the Finnigans' and asked for a word with her, then explained how things stood and said that if Irene were agreeable they would share the task of being with Joy when she needed them.

Irene had been thinking gloomily that she might as

well forget her cunning plan to infiltrate the Lawrence household, but now it seemed as though fate, far from being set against her, was actually on her side. Of course it was a pity that for the most part her entering No. 77 would be the signal for Alex to leave it, but that was a problem which could be overcome once her foot was in the door. And me knees are under the table, she thought.

Oh, how I love Alex Lawrence, she told herself gleefully, and how exciting was a secret love for an older man, which she must keep locked within her own breast. For Irene was quite bright enough to realise that if Alex or his daughters guessed what her true feelings were she would be immediately dismissed – oh, not for the real reason, of course, but for any trumpery excuse they could dream up. Gillian, she already knew, did not like her much and would not hesitate to see her off with a flea in her ear if she made an obvious play for Alex. But softly, softly, catchee monkee, she told herself. Once they're used to me, I'll work something out, make an excuse to stay for an extra five minutes when he comes in from work, meet him in the street and say I want to chat about Joy . . . oh yes, I can be a match for young Gillian if I put my mind to it.

Chapter Seven

It was late June and Gillian, who was good at all sports but excelled at tennis, ran across the court and whacked the ball as hard as she could into the tramlines on her opponents' side of the net. 'Game, set and match,' Gillian's partner announced happily. She mopped her brow. 'Well done, Gillian. Phew, isn't it hot? I could do with a drink.'

The two approached the net to shake hands with their opponents and Gillian glanced sideways at the green-painted bench which stood alongside the grass court. As she expected, it was still occupied. David Rogers, Keith Bain and Paul Everett were applauding languidly whilst little Twiggy Woods was hastily closing his book and shoving it into his satchel so that he, too, could applaud.

'Well done, you two,' the large, heavily built girl on the other side of the net said, seizing Gillian's hand and pumping it energetically up and down. 'You're really good, easily first team material.' She grinned across at Gillian's partner. 'You aren't bad either; if your backhand wasn't so weak . . .'

'It's all right, Eleanor, I know Gillian carries me,' Shirley Smithson said regretfully. 'I really like tennis but I'm not nearly good enough to play for my year, let alone the school. But as Miss Rutledge says, it isn't winning that counts . . .' she grinned as the other girls chorused: 'but how you play the game.'

The girls turned away from the net, Eleanor's partner going across to lower it whilst Eleanor herself looped it off the grass, for they knew they were the last people to use the courts that evening. Then they walked over to the boys, who immediately stood up. 'Well done, all of you,' Keith said. He picked up Gillian's sports bag from where it lay against the legs of the bench and slung it over his shoulder, the action making it clear, without words, whom he meant to accompany back to the school building.

The other young people dropped behind and Keith looked Gillian up and down. She was in tennis whites because the girls were not allowed on the courts in school uniform, but they had to change back into it before they left the grounds. Gillian was conscious that her whites were a pretty poor affair when compared with those of the other three girls, but though at first this had embarrassed her, it no longer did so. With a good deal of help from Mrs Clarke, she had made herself a short pleated skirt and had bought from Paddy's market a white Aertex shirt and a pair of white ankle socks. Plimsolls had been difficult since the ones on sale in the market were mostly black, but Irene, who had accompanied Gillian and Joy on the shopping expedition to buy her sportswear, had pounced on a pair of sand-coloured pumps. 'These are your size,' she had said triumphantly. 'Me mam always says you can get anything in Paddy's market, and ain't she just right?'

'Yes, they'd fit, but they're no good,' Gillian had said rather scornfully. 'I *told* you, they've got to be white.' But

Irene had sighed theatrically and picked up a small bottle full of some milky-looking liquid.

'You paint 'em wi' this,' she had said briefly. 'It's really to cover dirty marks on proper white pumps, but I reckon if you buy two bottles – it's quite cheap – then it'll cover the brown all right.'

And so it had proved, Gillian thought. The brown pumps were now white plimsolls, and no one had so much as noticed that her footwear was scrupulously repainted after each game. She headed for the changing rooms, which were not really changing rooms exactly but a couple of small sheds left open for girls using the sports facilities and wanting to change back into their ordinary clothing. Gillian reclaimed her bag from Keith and joined her fellow pupils in the first shed. They changed with much chattering and laughter, pulling aside the lace curtain and peeping through the small window at the backs of the boys, all pupils of the Grosvenor Public School for Boys, which was no more than half a mile away from St Hilda's. It was not only the Grosvenor boys who were interested in Gillian either, as she well knew. Several boys from the secondary school made a habit of hanging around the tram stop and then joining her for the walk home. It was nice to be popular, though sometimes Gillian was uneasily aware that being liked by the boys could mean being disliked by other girls. However, this did not worry her unduly; why should it? She was only fourteen and enjoyed having friends of both sexes. There could be no harm in a little gentle flirtation.

In her school uniform once more, Gillian brushed her hair vigorously and then turned to her partner. 'Are you ready, Shirley? St Hilda's is shut now, so we can't get a drink from the cloakroom, but there's a drinking fountain in that little garden where the council school kids go. Do you want to pop in there?'

Shirley shook her head. 'No, thanks. I'm going to buy me an ice cream from that van which is always parked outside the gates.'

Gillian finished off her toilet, said cheerio to their opponents, who were still changing and chatting, and linked her arm in Shirley's, leading her out of the changing shed before turning to her and speaking in hushed tones. 'Oh, Shirley, you can't. You know very well we're not supposed to eat in the street. And ice cream is the very worst sort of eating; Miss McCullough would have a blue fit!'

'She won't know; she'll have gone home hours ago,' Shirley said gaily. She was a small blonde girl, snub-nosed and pretty, popular with staff and pupils alike. Even Miss Rutledge had a soft spot for Shirley, although she did not excel at any games and Miss Rutledge, as gym mistress, tended to favour sporting types.

Gillian was still protesting that Shirley was taking her life in her hands by eating an ice cream in the street when they re-joined the boys. Keith immediately took Gillian's bag and slung it over his shoulder once more. 'It's heavier with your kit inside than it was with your school uniform,' he observed. 'What's this about an ice cream?' He brushed a hand across his glistening forehead. 'I wouldn't mind a cornet, or even an ice lolly.' He grinned at Gillian. 'Tell you what, we'll dare each other; then if we get caught we can plead—'

'Insanity,' Gillian said wrathfully. She turned to Eleanor

166

as their opponents, now clad in their summer frocks and blazers, with their panamas on the backs of their heads, joined them. 'What do you think, Ellie? You're a year ahead of us, so you can advise us. Keith wants to buy an ice cream – so does Shirley, for that matter – but I'm sure if we do we'll get caught and probably expelled or something awful.'

'Six of the best,' little Twiggy murmured provocatively. 'Only girls don't get the cane, do they? Oh, to hell with it, fellers! I say we go into the ice cream parlour on Smiffy and eat the ices in there. Anyone short of a few coppers?'

Everyone had a few pennies, though Gillian's had been destined to become her tram fare. She said as much, but Keith waved this aside. 'I'll walk you home,' he said at once. 'Got any homework? If it's maths, and you need a bit of help, we can do it as we go. You can read the questions out to me and I'll jot down the answers on a bit of rough paper. Then, when we reach your house, you can jolly well take me in and introduce me to your twin sister. I'm dying to meet her and you've met Bain minor and minimus, so it's only fair.'

Gillian giggled. She knew it was the custom at public schools to refer to three brothers as major, minor and minimus, since for some absurd reason Christian names were not used, and it was quite true that she had met Keith's brothers, two little boys with the faces of angels and the dispositions of fiends. Bain minor had asked her when she and Bain major meant to name the day, causing poor Gillian to go red all over, and Bain minimus had advised her strongly to steer clear of his big brother. 'He nicks all the chocolates out of the Quality Street tin and then blames us,' he had said in an aggrieved tone. 'Don't

167

you have nuffin' to do with our big brother, Miss Lawrence.'

'Well, young lady? Will you introduce me to your sister if I walk you home?'

'If she's in,' Gillian said cautiously. She reflected that since it was a nice bright evening Irene and Joy might have had an early supper and then gone off to Prince's Park, or some other pleasant spot. Joy was especially fond of the Garden for the Blind, about a mile away from their home, because the neat paths had been made with geometrical straightness and were lined with sweet-smelling blooms, not only roses but other perfumed plants such as mignonette and lavender.

'Righty-ho,' Keith said. 'Off to the ice cream parlour, ladies and fellers, and damn the consequences.'

When Alex returned from work, he found three girls chattering animatedly, and Mrs Clarke withdrawing a tray of Cornish pasties from the oven. Alex's mouth watered; these delicacies were one of many delicious things Mrs Clarke made regularly and was teaching both Irene and Joy to make as well. They had by now worked out a good routine for cooking. Joy had what Mrs Clarke described as light hands, so she was the one who rubbed the fat into the flour, then added water, or even egg yolk, judiciously, and formed the dough into a ball. She would then flour the table, working entirely by touch, and roll her pastry out, brushing a hand across it every few minutes to ensure that it was neither too thick nor too thin. Once all her pasties were ready, Mrs Clarke or Irene would pop them into the oven and withdraw them when they were cooked. Only someone who had watched Joy's

168

struggles over the past weeks could appreciate her pride in those pasties, Alex thought, smiling round the room.

'Evening, Mrs Clarke, evening, girls; something smells good,' he said easily. 'Well, Mrs Clarke, how are your pupils coming along? Don't tell me my little Joy is responsible for those beautiful golden brown pasties?'

Joy looked towards Alex's voice, smiling seraphically. 'Yes, Daddy, it was me. Gillian brought some boy round to meet me, but Irene and I had gone for a walk down by the Mersey and by the time we got back he'd gone. It doesn't make much difference to me, of course, because I wouldn't have been able to see him, and I'm quite glad he didn't see me . . . I mean, I'm not like Gillian to look at any more and people expect identical twins to *be* identical.'

Gillian looked up. She had spread her homework out on the table and was busily writing, but now she wagged a reproving finger. 'You're daft, you are,' she said affectionately, flicking back the long hair which hung to her shoulders. 'We are still alike, only as we've got older we've changed, as folk do; experience changes everyone, I think. But I'm going to have my hair cut as soon as I've time, so if you want to be identical again you should jolly well have a haircut too.'

Alex expected Joy to exclaim that hair or no hair she knew very well she was now nothing like her pretty twin, because hard though they had all tried to convince Joy that the scars had faded to near invisibility and she was now as pretty as ever, they had had no success. 'You would say that, of course, because you're kind and you love me,' Joy had said the last time Alex had tried to convince her. 'But don't think I care, Daddy; looks aren't everything.'

169

But now, sitting round the kitchen table and discussing hairstyles, Alex was able to watch the girls closely without their being aware of his scrutiny. Joy of course could not possibly see him, but she was rapidly developing a sort of sixth sense and often knew when someone was staring at her. Gawping, she called it. 'It's not fair,' she had explained to Alex when he had gently reprimanded her for speaking sharply to her grandmother, but though Joy had apologised to the old lady she had told Alex that before her accident she had known better than to gawp at someone who could not gawp back. 'Besides, when I was a really little girl, three or four, Mummy told us staring was rude,' she had reminded him. 'Still, I won't tick Grandma off again if it upsets you.'

Now, Alex considered the three bright young girls before him with very real pleasure. No one would guess from looking at her that Joy was blind; they would just think her a very pretty girl with bright brown hair, a straight little nose and a mouth that smiled often. Her eyes were usually half closed, but this was not immediately apparent because her expression was so lively. He thought that few people, meeting her for the first time, would realise that she could not see.

Irene, he decided, made an excellent foil for the twins. She was a brown-eyed blonde, with a pert little nose and a neat figure. Taller than either of the twins and a couple of years older, she had achieved her ambition of becoming almost a part of the family and Alex treated her as though she were indeed his daughter, making sure that she took home little treats for her younger brothers and sisters; two of the Cornish pasties, for instance, would go home in Irene's basket, to be enjoyed as a late supper by any member of the Finnigan family around.

The conversation at the table was growing heated. 'I don't care what you say, Gillian; you can cut your perishin' hair or leave it long, or dye it sky-blue pink if you want,' Joy was exclaiming. 'It's different for me. You spend hours in front of the mirror every morning, prettifying yourself, but even if I could see I couldn't be bothered.' She gave a disdainful snort. 'You always cared about your appearance much more than I did, and for me, hair is just a nuisance. When it starts tickling my collar then I know it's too long, and it's tickling my collar now. Besides, Daddy cuts mine; he'd do yours if you ask.'

'I know what you mean, but it needs proper cutting, which costs a mint,' Gillian said ruefully, tugging at her long locks. Her hair was a good deal longer than her twin's, but Joy, of course, could not know that. 'Look, have you heard of the hairdressing school at the technical college? The girls learning to be hairdressers need people to practise on, so they'll do your hair for nothing. They work late on a Thursday evening . . . what say we book ourselves in for next week or the week after? Only I'm told most hairdressing establishments charge extra for long hair because it's more difficult to cut – don't ask me why.' She turned to Irene. 'Have you ever had your hair done at the tech? Yours could do with reshaping.'

'Ooh, listen to who's talking! Old gorse bush herself,' Joy said, grinning. She turned to face Irene. 'Come over here and let me run my magic hands over your lice-ridden bonce, so I can tell if my sister's right.'

'You cheeky young . . .' Irene began, then glanced

self-consciously at Alex, who guessed that she had been about to use a word of which he would not approve. He thought, not for the first time, that though Irene fitted well into the Lawrence household she was still a tiny bit in awe of him. But the conversation had moved on and now it was Gillian speaking.

'Right then; are you on, Joy?'

'If you two are, I suppose I might as well come along,' Joy said with what her father saw was feigned indifference.

'Right,' Gillian said briskly. 'Then I'll go down to the tech on Saturday and make three appointments for a wash, trim and set.'

Irene objected, saying that she only wanted hers shaped, but Joy overruled her. 'Susie, one of my friends at school, is going to be a hairdresser when she's old enough. She says the girls are taught to cut your hair when it's wet, though I'm not sure why,' she informed the other two. 'What does it matter, anyway? Since they don't charge, we might as well have whatever's on offer.'

The girls agreed and Mrs Clarke, who had put another tray of baking into the oven as soon as the pasties were out, opened the oven door and produced a batch of jam tarts. 'Does the tech do older folks' hair as well?' she asked hopefully. 'I could do with a nice trim and a set, or even a permanent wave. You might add me to your little group.'

'I'm pretty sure they charge for perms, but we could ask,' Gillian said, but Mrs Clarke laughed and shook her head. 'No, no, I was teasing you. I cut my own hair, because my curls are what I was born with, so I don't need a perm.' She glanced at the clock over the mantelpiece. 'It's time we were off, young Irene,' she said briskly. 'It's still not dark out so I won't offer to walk you home.' She crossed the kitchen, took her coat off the peg and put it on. Irene stood up too, though reluctantly, and Alex was grateful when Mrs Clarke held open the back door and ushered Irene out. He hated having to send the girls up to bed so that Irene would leave, and realised Mrs Clarke understood his dilemma when she turned in the doorway and winked.

'Thanks, Mrs C,' Alex said, knowing that this remark could be taken two ways. 'See you on Wednesday.'

Gillian was as good as her word and booked herself, her twin and Irene into the hairdressing department at the tech. They were all to be seen between half past five and seven in the evening and had decided amongst themselves that Joy should be first, Gillian next and Irene last. Joy demurred at being first because she would be waiting for quite a long time. 'But you'll be sitting in a comfy chair in the foyer,' Gillian pointed out. 'Don't make difficulties, kid!'

The tech was on the opposite side of the city, only a stone's throw from the Grosvenor School and even closer to a private school called St Mary's. According to Gillian, pupils who failed the entrance exam to St Hilda's would always be taken on by St Mary's, so there was considerable ill feeling between the pupils of the two schools. As the three of them, arms linked, made their way past St Mary's tall, wrought-iron gates, Gillian gave her opinion of the pupils in no uncertain terms. 'Good thing they're so near the tech, because when they fail to get their School Certificates they pop into the tech and sign on to be hairdressers, or cooks, or uncertified teachers,' she said gaily. 'See if I'm not right.'

'Hey, steady on,' Joy said mildly. 'Irene and myself aren't at St Hilda's, nor we aren't borin' brain-boxes like you are, but that doesn't mean we're inferior in any way.'

'I'm inferior because I work in a shop, but I don't give a tinker's cuss; the money's okay and the work's all right,' Irene said with assumed placidity, but Joy felt the other girl's grip on her arm tighten for a moment and was truly annoyed with her twin, knowing that Gillian had hurt Irene's feelings and knowing also that Gillian wouldn't care. She got on all right with the older girl but had made it pretty clear that theirs was a working relationship and not a friendly one. Joy, on the other hand, really liked Irene, appreciating her sense of humour and her helpfulness, and enjoyed her stories of shop life.

However, right now was no time to tell Gillian off; if she had done so, she would only have embarrassed Irene, so she changed the subject. 'I know we've just passed St Mary's, but whereabouts is the Grosvenor? That feller you say you like, your pal Keith what walks you home sometimes, is at school there, isn't he?'

Gillian gave a little squeak, bounced on her toes and then patted her sister's cheek with her free hand. 'Well done, oh you of the mighty intellect,' she said mockingly. 'Yes, Keith's at the Grosvenor and it's not only him who likes to walk me home and dance attendance; half the boys in the Upper Fifth want me to go out with them, only Keith's the best looking and has the most money, so I graciously allow him to buy me meals and take me to the flicks.'

'Gillian Lawrence, you're the most conceited little pig who ever breathed,' Joy said indignantly. 'And it's all lies anyway. You've never had a meal out with any Grosvenor boy, regardless of whether he's as rich as Croesus or poor as a church mouse. If our daddy could hear you . . .'

'Oh, shut up, the pair of you,' Irene said, and Joy felt her two companions slow down and then turn into what she took to be a doorway. 'If I'd known you was going to squabble like a couple of four-year-olds, I never would've agreed to come along.' She turned to face Joy and the younger girl felt Irene's breath on her cheek as she sank her voice to a whisper. 'There's a big glass door ahead of us with a desk facing it, and heaps of people just sort of milling around in the foyer. I expect they've all come to make appointments or to attend classes, so we'll go straight to the desk and tell them we're here. There are no obstacles so far as I can see. In we go!'

Joy sat herself down in the swivel chair to which Gillian guided her and felt her sister turn the chair, Joy presumed, so that it faced the mirror. 'My sister's here for a haircut—' she began, but was immediately interrupted.

'It's all right, the lass can tell me if I'm going wrong,' a voice well above Joy's head remarked. A hand reached out and took her own. 'Hello, Miss Lawrence; I'm doing your hair this evening. I'm Francesca, a final year student, which means I'm on what you might call the home stretch. In a few weeks I'll be working in a salon, having served my time.' She released Joy's hand and patted her shoulder. 'So you see you're in good hands. Your friend

175

is with Sharon; she's in my year too. Now if you'll just bend over the basin, I'll start by giving your mop a good wash.'

Joy reached out and gripped the edge of the basin. Her hearing was acute and she was rather gratified to realise that Gillian had not thought it worthwhile to warn the hairdresser that her client could not see. As the water began to spray on to her head and Francesca's fingers to work shampoo into her scalp, she set her imagination to work. Francesca must be tall – her voice had come from well above Joy's head – and judging by the feel of her fingers she was thin. And I think she's a brunette, though I don't know why, Joy mused to herself as the older girl rinsed, squeezed and wrapped Joy's head into a towel. Yes, a brunette with brown eyes and probably very short hair, or possibly a bun, or even a ponytail. She's older than me, of course, and she's not got a local accent. Joy giggled to herself, remembering her sister's words earlier. Perhaps she really is from St Mary's, which is why she's got a nice posh voice.

Her musings were interrupted as the hairdresser began vigorously rubbing her head, keeping up a flow of gentle chat as she did so. She asked Joy which school she attended and immediately Joy knew she was smiling because her voice lightened. 'Well if that ain't a lucky coincidence,' she said. 'I went to Bold Street too, right up until I got my School Certificate. Do they still have a special top class for the bright ones, so's you can get qualifications?' She did not wait for Joy to answer, but prattled merrily on. 'I were – was, I mean – really happy at Bold Street. Mr Lang taught the top class and my mam still swears that if it wasn't for him I'd never have got where I am today.'

176

Joy had expected to feel a degree of apprehension when she felt the scissors against her neck but in fact, because of the hairdresser's constant chatter, she soon realised that all she had to do was to put her trust in Francesca, and presently the older girl moved away for a moment and then came back.

'That's you done; like the back? Is it short enough? If not I can always trim more off, though personally I think it's just right and suits you.'

Joy thanked her politely, said it was just fine, rose from the chair and put a shilling piece into the girl's hand, as Gillian had instructed.

She realised she had no idea which way to turn and was wondering whether she would have to tell the hairdresser that she could not see after all when she was saved by Gillian, who must have been hovering nearby and now came across to take her hand. 'I say, you look really good,' she said in a low tone as the two wended their way across the foyer. 'I've not been done yet, and nor has Irene, but I'll sit you down in the foyer and one or other of us will come out to you as soon as we can.'

'All right; I'll wait for you here,' Joy said as Gillian guided her to a low chair. She felt it carefully and then sat down. 'Are there magazines?' she asked, suddenly visited by inspiration; if there were magazines and Gillian could hand her a couple, she would pretend to be absorbed and carefully turn the pages, ignoring what was going on around her. She knew there were still people in the foyer, but only three or four, and she assumed they were waiting for their appointments and would not take any notice of her.

'Magazines?' Gillian chuckled. 'Yes, there's a low table

a few feet away from you; you're sitting about a foot to the right of the glass entrance doors.' Her voice changed and Joy knew that Gillian was now examining the magazines. 'There's *House Beautiful*, *Ideal Home*, a couple of those hairdressing ones showing different styles and a couple of weeklies. You'd better have *Ideal Home* because that's a monthly and therefore pretty bulky, and *Woman's Weekly*. It's as old as the hills so no one's likely to ask if they can have it after you.'

Joy felt the magazines land in her lap and knew her sister had turned away, then turned back. 'Irene was waiting to go under the dryer when I suddenly remembered you'd want someone to take you to a chair.' She chuckled, a trifle ruefully. 'I'm glad I'm having your hairdresser and not Sharon; she's covered Irene's head with bristly-looking curlers. Since it was my idea to come here, I'll get the blame if Irene emerges with frizzy hair.'

Joy laughed, but shook her head. 'What makes you think they'll do anything but cut and wash your hair?' she asked. 'That's all Francesca did to mine. Does it really look nice?'

'Yes, she's cut it into a bouncy, silky bob. But I'd better love you and leave you now,' Gillian said. 'Are you sure you'll be all right by yourself? You won't move, will you? Only you didn't bring your white stick or anything.'

'Oh, really, Gillian, I'm quite capable of sitting in a chair and pretending to read a magazine until you and Irene come out,' Joy said crossly. 'Do go away.' She bent her head over the page before her, pretending an interest she could not possibly feel. 'Don't hurry back on my account; remember the ear in the hairdresser's scissors?'

Both girls laughed and Joy waited until her sister's foot-steps had gone. Then she turned another page, wondering what delights might be before her had she but eyes to see.

It must have been ten minutes later when somebody tapped her on the shoulder and spoke in her ear. 'Excuse me, miss, I wonder if I could trouble you to give up your chair? Old Mrs Bennett here has come early for her appointment and you're in the only chair available.' The speaker sighed gustily. 'There's usually others – chairs, I mean – but as you can see, we're having a refit. There will be new chairs next week, but right now . . . if you wouldn't mind . . .'

Joy rose to her feet and another voice spoke, an elderly voice, wheezy and breathless: 'Thank you, m'dear. I'm ever so grateful.'

Joy smiled politely and heard the leather creak as the old woman sat down. For a moment she stood very still, wondering what she should do. She could not stand about for perhaps half an hour like a cigar store Indian, getting in people's way. She hooked her spectacles out of her jacket pocket and perched them on her nose, then realised she was still holding the magazines and laid them in the old lady's lap. She moved a couple of feet away but she knew there was a low table, laden with magazines, somewhere in her vicinity and did not want to make a fool of herself by tripping over it and sending the table and its contents flying.

She was still wondering what to do when the old lady spoke again. 'I'm that sorry to have axed you to move, missie,' she wheezed. 'But if you goes out through them glass doors, you'll see a wooden bench . . . It's a nice sunny evening, and you could sit there while you wait for your pals.'

'That's a really good idea,' Joy said appreciatively. 'But I promised my sister and her friend that I wouldn't wander off. Can you see the bench from here?'

She heard the old lady turn in the chair and then say, in a rather surprised tone: 'Well bless me, I see it as clear as daylight.' She must have pointed. 'See, by that low stone wall, summat green; that's the bench. Can't you see it?'

Joy sighed; truth will out, she told herself. 'I'm extremely short-sighted,' she said, reflecting that she was not exactly lying, though neither was she telling the complete truth. 'If I go through the doors and keep going straight, will I reach the seat without tripping over any obstacles?'

'My, your sight must be poor,' the old lady said. Joy heard the creak as she turned in the chair again. 'No, if you go straight through the doors and continue in the same direction, you'll find yourself at the wooden bench after half a dozen steps. When your sister comes for you she'll see you through the doors, or she'll see me sitting in your chair, if I've not been called through, and ask where you've gone. So if you fancy a bit of a walk, just pop back and tell me and I'll pass the message on.'

Joy thanked her and stood for a moment, getting her bearings. How she wished she had brought her white stick! But even as the thought crossed her mind, she felt a breeze on her cheek and started forward. Someone had come in and was holding the door for her. Hastily, Joy went through it, nodding her thanks to the person she could not see and heading for the bench, which was nearer than she had imagined; she found it by cracking her knee painfully upon its wooden slats.

Muttering a curse beneath her breath, she was about to sit down when someone took her arm and a girl's voice spoke in her ear. 'Miss Lawrence? I've a message from your friend. She wants you to go into the tech by the side door – it's more direct – and sit with her whilst she's being attended to. Me and my friend will show you where to go.' As she spoke she took Joy's left arm and someone, her friend presumably, took hold of the right. 'All set? Off we go, then.'

'It's very kind of you, but don't walk too quickly,' Joy said a little breathlessly, for the second girl, who had not yet spoken, was walking rather fast, forcing Joy to do likewise. 'I take it you meant my friend Irene, or did you mean my sister?'

'I dunno,' the girl who had already spoken said. She turned to the one on Joy's right. 'Did she say she was Miss Lawrence's sister?'

The other girl shook her head; Joy heard her hair rustle softly as she did so. 'No, she just said, "Would you fetch my friend."'

'It must have been Irene then, I suppose,' Joy said as they turned a corner and she felt the cold shadow of the college building sweep across her, cutting her off from the warm sunshine and the sounds of people entering and leaving. 'Where is this side door then?'

'It's not far now,' the girl on her right volunteered. She had a harsh voice and for the first time Joy felt a prickle of unease. It occurred to her that it was not like either Gillian or Irene to ask total strangers to assist her. 'We'll cut through the shrubbery,' the harsh voice continued.

'Don't suppose you've ever been round the back here, but don't fret, we're nearly there.'

Joy felt herself being hustled between bushes; she smelled lavender and roses, whilst the cool leaves of laurel and azaleas brushed against her. But now the girls who held on to her so tightly did not feel like people anxious to assist, but rather like captors. She began to protest, trying to pull herself free from the grip on her arms, but one of the girls must have stuck her foot out just as the other one gave her an almighty shove, and Joy found herself sprawling on gravel. Someone twisted her on to her back, sat on her chest and began to rub earth and tiny stones into her beautiful new hairdo. She tried to free herself, wriggling and kicking and demanding angrily just what the girls thought they were doing, whereupon a large hand was placed suffocatingly over her mouth.

'Cut that out!' one of the girls snapped; the one with the squeaky voice who had held Joy's left arm. She snatched the spectacles off Joy's face, ignoring her protestations, and Joy heard, with dismay, a crunching crack as one of her captors deliberately trod on them, giving a hoarse laugh as she did so. 'Oh, we're so grand, we have to have sunglasses to protect us from the glare,' the girl said in a mock posh accent. 'You came here for a cheap haircut, didn't you? Well, you're going to get a good deal more than that if you ever so much as glance at the grammar school lads again, you nasty little flirt.' She turned to the other girl; Joy knew she had done so by the change in her voice. 'We're going to teach you a lesson you won't forget in a hurry, aren't we, Ev— I mean, aren't we?'

'That's right,' the hoarse-voiced one said gloatingly.

'You won't have that pretty face when we let you go, that's for sure. And don't try to yell out because no one will hear you and we'll make you suffer worse. That's a promise.'

One of her attackers dealt Joy a sharp slap across the face and she was just trying to tell them they had the wrong pig by the ear when, faintly, she heard footsteps and someone whistling a catchy tune. Her tormentors were too busy threatening and hitting her to notice, so Joy bit the hand gagging her with all her might and, as the owner of the hand snatched it away with a very unladylike curse, took a deep breath and put all her strength into a mighty shriek. Shriller than any train whistle, it split the air, and before her attackers could muffle her again she yelled: 'Help, help, HELP! Thieves, robbers, murderers!'

Abruptly, the weight was lifted from her chest as the footsteps grew closer and a voice called out: 'Where are you? Hello?'

Shakily, Joy sat up, hearing her attackers begin to panic. One of them started to say it had just been a bit of fun, but the other told her to shut up and run and to Joy's immense relief she heard their footsteps recede, even as other, firmer footsteps approached.

'Hello?' The man's voice was nearer. 'Hello? Who's yelling murder? Where are you?'

'I think I'm in the shrubbery at the back of the tech,' Joy called back.

The man turned into it; she could hear him pushing his way between the low-growing bushes, his footsteps urgent, until they stopped in front of her.

'Did you see two girls?' she said. 'They attacked me.'

She felt strong hands take her own and pull her gently to her feet. 'Which girls? You poor kid; are you much hurt?' the man asked. 'They certainly have roughed you up.'

'Oh, I ache in every limb and I'm bruised all over, but it could have been a lot worse,' Joy said. She shuddered at the recollection. 'If you hadn't come along . . . well, anything might have happened. You didn't see them, I take it?'

'No, I was trying to reach you and didn't so much as glance around me, though I did get the impression of someone running away from the path I took to reach you,' her rescuer said. His voice changed. 'You must have known them, otherwise why would they attack you? You've got to go to the police. An attack with that ferocity could have had tragic, if not fatal, consequences.'

'I didn't know them; they mistook me for someone else.'

'Ah, I see,' the man said. He released her for a second, during which time he must have picked up her glasses, for he pressed them into her hand. 'I take it these are your specs? I'm afraid they'll never be any use to you again and I guess you're blind as a bat without them.'

'Very true,' Joy said, rubbing her head vigorously and feeling, with distaste, the dirt and little stones in her hair. 'If you don't mind, I'd be grateful if you'd take me back to the college foyer. My sister and her friend will be wondering what on earth has become of me.'

'Of course I will; and whilst we walk, you can tell me exactly what happened,' the man said. His voice changed. 'But why are you smiling? You said yourself that your attackers bruised you all over.'

'Was I smiling?' Joy said, surprised. She knew the reason all right but had no intention of admitting it to her new friend. She was smiling because with the realisation that she had been mistaken for her twin had come the certainty that she must still be pretty; even without her spectacles she must be unscarred. Others had assured her of this many times but she had thought they lied – oh, out of kindness, but mainly to comfort her. Her attackers, however, had no reason to lie. They had accepted without question that she was Gillian – pretty, clever Gillian whom all the boys admired – so her fears that she was ugly must be groundless. But her rescuer was repeating his question so Joy answered hastily, if not truthfully.

'Well, I suppose it's because you've rescued me and I feel safe now. My sister and I came to the technical college to have our hair cut and styled . . .'

Joy chatted brightly until he drew her to a halt outside the big glass doors and pushed them open, ushering her inside. 'Can you see the reception desk? It's straight across from here,' he said. He had been holding her arm, guiding her carefully, but now he released it, giving her a gentle push towards the reception desk as he did so. 'You must get someone to take you along to the First Aid room. You can get cleaned up there and have your hurts seen to. I expect you're well aware that you've grazed the palms of your hands and your knees, and there's a big black bruise on your forehead . . . but you said your sister would be worried, so no doubt she'll take over. I'm sorry, I can't hang around. It was just luck that I heard your screams because I was simply killing time before making my way to the station . . .'

Joy scarcely heeded his words as she heard Gillian gasp out her name and then two sets of running footsteps as her twin and Irene rushed across the foyer, both asking questions at the tops of their voices, though her sister's tones prevailed. 'Joy, my darling, whatever has happened to you? And where have you been? You're filthy dirty and there's blood running down your legs – oh, you're getting a black eye – did you fall? We've been so worried, Irene and me . . .'

'I've been in trouble, but I was rescued by this gentleman,' Joy said, gesturing to her left where her new friend had stood. 'I know you'll want to thank him . . .'

Joy stopped speaking. There was no one by her side; her rescuer had gone.

Chapter Eight

When the girls came into the kitchen after the attack, Joy with her knees bandaged, sticking plaster on the palms of her hands and an enormous bruise on her forehead, Alex and Mrs Clarke exclaimed with horror, even though it soon became obvious not only from Joy's wide smile but from her whole demeanour that she was not seriously hurt. She explained quickly what had happened and also aired her theory that she had been mistaken for Gillian, and Mrs Clarke, clucking like a hen with one chick and pouring cups of tea for everyone, said that in her opinion mistaken identity was no excuse.

Alex, who had listened with some alarm to Joy's story, thought ruefully that though he would say nothing right now he believed he understood why the attack had come about. His darling Gillian was pretty, lively and very intelligent, but she had a sharp tongue and did not hesitate to use it. He guessed that she made enemies without even realising it, and besides, flirting with another girl's boyfriend was always a dangerous thing to do. Knowing Gillian as he did, he guessed that she had been guilty of that if nothing else and that this had rebounded, not on Gillian, but her twin.

However, Mrs Clarke, getting scones out of the pantry and handing them round, was still fuming. 'I don't care who they thought they were beating up,' she said roundly. 'They ought to be flogged!'

Alex, once he had realised with great relief that Joy's wounds were largely surface ones, grinned at his daughters and asked what was wrong with boiling oil. Everyone laughed, easing the tension, but Gillian said rather stiffly that she was the one who should have been flogged or boiled in oil. 'I left Joy in the foyer whilst I had my hair done,' she began, very pink about the gills, and by the time Mrs Clarke was offering a second cup of tea they all knew how it had come about that the bullies had been able to pick on Joy.

Alex saw that both his elder daughter and Irene were truly distressed, for as soon as Gillian stopped speaking Irene broke in. 'If anyone's to blame – apart from them horrible girls, that is – then it's me,' she said sadly. 'I'm the oldest by two years; I should never have agreed to leave Joy waiting in the foyer by herself. And oh, Mr Lawrence, my hair were finished ten minutes after Joy's was.' Alex saw with some dismay that tears had formed in Irene's big blue eyes. 'I were real pleased with it and wanted to book another appointment, so I weren't thinking about Joy . . .'

'Oh, shut up, the pair of you,' Joy said crossly, but Alex saw that her smile still lingered. 'If anyone's truly to blame, it's me. If I'd explained to the old lady that I was blind, I'm sure she'd have fetched help of some sort. But I suppose I was too – too proud, and I reckon I owe those girls a debt in a way.' Her hearers looked astonished, as well they might, Alex thought, and listened closely as his daughter continued. 'They mistook me for Gillian! Don't you realise what that means? It means I'm

188

not hideously scarred, or totally changed, the way I thought I was. It means Gillian and myself are still identical twins.' She turned towards where she knew her sister was sitting. 'So yah boo sucks to you,' she said gaily. 'I'm afraid you're landed with me, Gillian Lawrence.'

'But we *told* you . . .' Alex began, then stopped short as Mrs Clarke shook a reproving finger at him.

'Of course we told her; all her friends and relations, all of Blue Watch, probably half the school as well told her,' she said. 'And silly Joy just thought that because we loved her, we were being kind. Those evil girls didn't love her and there was no reason for them to pretend. They must know Gillian pretty well and yet they didn't hesitate to grab Joy when they saw her alone. Clearly, it never crossed their minds that she wasn't Gillian.'

'Gosh!' Gillian said, her voice awed. 'Well, I'm going to have to be careful because I'm nowhere near as brave as Joy and I don't fancy having my face smashed in, which is the only way, it seems, that we can stop being identical twins. Oh, Joy love, I'm so very sorry.'

After Mrs Clarke had left and before he went off to the fire station, Alex decided that a word or two of reproof and advice might not come amiss. Irene was putting on her coat whilst the twins were washing up the tea things, so he cleared his throat and caught Irene's arm. 'Wait a minute, queen. There's something I have to say and I think you should hear it,' he said seriously. 'What happened this evening must be a lesson to all of us. The mistakes that were made might easily have ended in tragedy. I saw the three of you go off and reminded Joy to take her white stick, but she said that when you're all together she never takes it because she hangs on to an arm of each of you and it would only get in the way. That was mistake number one; I should have insisted that where Joy went, the stick should go also. Mistake number two happened when the three of you reached the tech and you all went your separate ways, forgetting how vulnerable a blind person can be in a seeing world.' He turned to the older twin, giving her a rueful grin. 'I didn't want to say anything in front of Mrs Clarke, Gillian dear, but mistake number three is that flirting is a game you enjoy playing, but others – the girls with whose boyfriends you flirt – clearly don't find amusing. In fact, in this case at least, I believe it bred hatred and a desire for revenge.'

'Oh, Daddy . . .' Gillian began, her hands flying to her hot cheeks, but before she could even begin to defend herself her sister interrupted.

'Does she flirt?' Joy asked with genuine interest. 'I thought she did, you know, but it's one of the many things which are difficult to judge when you can't see. Irene?'

'Yes, I'm still here, standing by the back door waiting to go home,' Irene said rather resentfully. 'Your pa grabbed me before I could escape and of course he's right, because I'm sure all of us will be a lot more careful in future. But I don't flirt, not really, despite being older than both of you.'

Joy giggled. 'Of course you're older than both of us, because we're twins,' she reminded her friend. 'But I don't understand . . . what has flirting to do with age? I'm the same age as Gillian and I'm sure I wouldn't even want to flirt, even if I knew how to do it!'

'Irene Finnigan, what a liar you are!' Gillian said in a

shocked tone. 'You *do* flirt! You flirt with Daddy and Chalky White, and the fellow in the greengrocer's shop; why do you think he gave us an orange last week? It was because you made sheep's eyes at him and when he asked you to go to the flicks next time there was a Laurel and Hardy on you said you might go along if you had nothing better to do.'

Alex broke in hurriedly, horribly aware of the hot colour flooding Irene's cheeks and knowing that Ronnie White, also known as Chalky, a member of Blue Watch, rather liked Fred Finnigan's lass. 'That isn't flirting, that's just being friendly,' he said. 'And now I think we've had enough discussion for one night. Remember, though; sometimes an innocent act like walking home with someone else's boyfriend can lead to real trouble.' He let go of Irene's arm and patted her hot cheek. 'Off with you, young Irene, and don't you worry about what our Gillian says. She doesn't always think before she speaks, and that can be hurtful, but don't take any notice. You're a really good, helpful girl and I think of you as my third daughter. Daughters don't flirt with their fathers, so Gillian was clearly barking up the wrong tree. Goodnight, queen.'

Irene slipped out of the back door, closing it carefully behind her, crossed the yard and headed for her own home, glad of the cool night breeze on her hot cheeks. She was a prey to conflicting emotions; it was nice that Alex admitted she was both good and helpful and had more or less accused Gillian of fibbing when she had called Irene a flirt. On the other hand, though, she had no desire for Alex to think of her as a daughter, for she had loved him – yes, it was real love, not infatuation, as folk would say – for absolutely ages, years probably.

She turned into the main road, still bustling and busy despite the lateness of the hour, and lingered for a moment, wishing that Alex had suggested accompanying her as far as the Gadwall fire station, as he sometimes did. But she supposed that had he done so, Gillian would have jeered, and that would have been very hard to take.

Irene sauntered along the pavement, gazing into shop windows. She was paid weekly by the grocer and spasmodically by Mrs Clarke, and usually had a small fund put aside for such things as dancing shoes or a seat at the theatre. She was saving up for a black taffeta skirt, these garments being all the rage amongst those who frequented the Grafton ballroom, and stopped before a window display which included a number of pretty blouses in pink, blue and primrose yellow. She sighed. Blue suited her and would go well with a black taffeta skirt, but fashion decreed that the blouse must be white. She moved on, and suddenly remembered that since Alex was working the night shift, her father would be doing the same. She glanced at her wristwatch and realised that by the time she reached home the younger members of her family would be in bed, leaving her sister Daphne and her mother to gossip over a hot drink in the Finnigan kitchen, and she, Irene, had news to impart, as well as a wonderful new hairstyle to display.

Irene thought of the dramatic events of the evening and of Alex's words of praise. She began to hurry.

In the Lawrence kitchen, Gillian was hanging the cups on the dresser – Joy could hear the tinkle as the cup handles slid over the brass hooks – and Joy herself was carrying the uneaten scones back into the pantry. They usually had a cup of cocoa and a scone or a couple of biscuits before going to bed, but had agreed not to do so tonight since it was getting late.

Alex was beginning to say that the girls should go up to bed at once after such an eventful day when Joy cleared her throat meaningfully. 'Hang on, Daddy; don't walk out on us just yet,' she pleaded. 'I've got something rather important to say.'

'Right, sweetheart, but make it snappy,' her father said. 'I take it it's something you didn't want Irene to hear?'

'No, no, I don't mind who hears,' Joy said at once. 'But I don't want you, or anyone else, to get the wrong impression. You know I've asked Colin Braddock to come round once or twice – well, of course you do, Daddy, because you've taken messages to Jerome for me – well, when those girls were attacking me, I realised that if only I'd done as Colin had suggested and gone to the LSB, I should have been taught self-defence. As it was, it never occurred to me that someone might mean me harm. I should have sensed danger, but I didn't. I let them grab my arms whilst we were still only yards from the main doors into the college, whereas if I'd been trained the way Colin said, I should have pulled free then. Even if I'd only refused to go with them, someone would have come to my aid. So, in a way, the fact that I was beaten up was my own fault. But it's a mistake I shall never make again – not just being so gullible, but turning down a marvellous offer like a place at the LSB. So, if you'll agree, Dad, I want to start there at the beginning of next term.'

Alex said nothing for a moment, but when he did speak he sounded bewildered. 'But Joy, love, you've always said you'd not move away from home. If you're frightened that the girls may come after you again . . .'

'No, it's not that,' Joy said quickly. 'I think perhaps what those two girls did to me was a – a sort of catalyst, if that's the right word. It occurred to me then how little I've done to grow used to being blind, to tackle it if you like. To be honest, for one awful moment I thought I – I might be going to die . . . oh, I don't know, but in that moment it seemed to me that I was a pretty feeble sort of person not to try to improve my lot in life.'

Gillian, who had been clattering dishes in the sink, came over to the table and put a hand on Joy's shoulder, giving it an affectionate squeeze. 'I would be so glad if good did come out of such a terrible incident,' she said. 'But won't you be lonely if you go to the LSB? And I can't forget that if I'd stayed with you . . .'

Both Joy and her father cried out at this, Alex saying that one should not dwell on past events which couldn't be changed, and Joy protesting that she should have been perfectly capable of looking after herself. 'And if I go to the LSB, it isn't just self-defence I'll be learning, but a great many other things as well. As things are at present, what sort of work could I do? I shan't pass my School Certificate, but even if I did it wouldn't increase my chances of getting a job because I'm blind. Oh, I'm sure I'll be able to see again one day, but that day may not arrive for ages, so in the meantime I want to go to that school and learn Braille, and touch-typing, and . . . oh, all sorts.' She turned to where she knew her father was sitting. 'And anyway, next term Edward will be

194

moving on to take the Higher School Certificate at that grammar school on the far side of Prince's Park. He's said he'll talk to his pals and choose someone really responsible to take his place, but he won't have to do so if I'm in London. So what d'you think?'

There was a long silence, during which Joy could imagine Alex and Gillian staring at her, open-mouthed. They must remember how adamant she had been against any suggestion that she attend the school. But surely the explanation which she had just offered them must be sufficient to allay their fears that she would be dreadfully lonely so far from her family and all their friends. She realised she was crossing her fingers and burst into speech again.

'Daddy? Gillian? What do you think?' she repeated. 'Even before the attack I was beginning to see I'd been an idiot to turn down the chance of going to the LSB. But I was still dithering until one day last week, when Colin came calling; you were at work, Daddy, and Gillian was playing tennis. He said he could stay with me for half an hour, so I decided to ask him more about the school. I know I snubbed him when he tried to talk about it before, but I've realised lately that it's downright stupid to criticise something you know nothing about. And honestly, once Colin began to talk, I suddenly saw what a fool I'd been. Daddy, it sounds a fantastic place; they've got a gymnasium, games courts . . . all sorts of things, and all geared to people who've lost their sight. Did you know they take you to a theatre where there are listening devices especially for the blind? You plug them in and put earphones on and a voice tells you what's happening on the stage; not when the cast are actually speaking, of course, but in the quiet bits, which would baffle anyone who couldn't see. And of course they teach you all the things you'll need when you are at work, like Braille and touch-typing. Colin made me see how daft I'd been, and when I said I was thinking of taking his advice and asked about money, he told me about that, too. He said the Institute would pay my fees, but of course I would need an allowance for food, clothing, bus fares . . . that sort of stuff.' She turned her head towards her father who was sitting in his usual place at the head of the table. 'Daddy? Would it stretch our budget too much? If so . . .'

'We'd have to feed and clothe you if you only sat at home all day,' Alex said. Joy could hear from his voice that he was surprised, but realised that he was also delighted. 'Only, are you sure it's truly what you want, queen? You've always been dead set against leaving home, being parted from Gillian . . .'

'I'm certain sure,' Joy said firmly. 'I've wasted three months whining and pottering about the house, and now I'm going to take my future into my own hands.' Once more she sensed her father's surprise, and laughed. 'That's what Colin said when I told him I was thinking about applying. Will you help me with the papers and things, Daddy? Only I can't fill in forms or write letters, which is why touch-typing will be such a boon. Oh, Daddy, do say you understand!'

'I understand, and I'm sure Gillian does as well,' Alex said slowly. 'We'll both help you in any way we can. Oh, queen, how I've longed to hear you say something so positive! I've talked to Colin several times when he's come to the station in order to walk home with Jerome, and he's said over and over how important it is for someone who is blind to take every bit of help and advice they can get. As you know he only attended the LSB for a short while, but wishes he had been able to stay for the whole of the three-year course. If you can stick it, my darling, you'll very soon realise how many doors such a course can open for you. I've never talked about it to anyone apart from Colin, because I thought your mind was dead set against it, but now, if you're truly sure . . .'

'Oh, I've grown up a lot in the past three months,' Joy said. 'And when someone grinds dirt into your hair and hits you and swears at you, it's time to do something about it. Believe me, I've thought it all out and it's what I want. Gillian? What do you think?'

'I think you're doing the right thing, and besides, you can always change your mind,' Gillian said. 'If you hate it, a telephone call to the fire station will bring us running.' She leaned over and rumpled Joy's hair. 'I wish I had your courage, old girl, but I'll back you all the way whatever you decide to do. If there was a school here in Liverpool . . .'

'But there isn't,' Joy cut in at once. She smiled broadly. 'Think of it! London and all the theatres and museums and galleries, all the parks and squares and gardens . . . and all the people at the school who are in the same boat as myself! Oh, Gillian, I can hardly wait – and I'll be home for the school holidays, of course.'

'If you're as sure as you sound, I'm all for it, though we'll miss you most dreadfully,' Gillian said. 'And you'll miss us; that goes without saying. But you'll start at this school in September, I suppose, so we've got all the summer holidays to get used to the idea. And remember we've got our trip to Devon to look forward to first!'

The long-awaited visit to the Dodmans had been a delight from start to finish, despite the inevitable tears when the twins, whooping with joy, had run into the arms of their kind foster-parents, Gillian leading Joy by the hand and practically casting her on to Mrs Dodman's welcoming bosom. Far from being embarrassed by his wife's show of emotion, Mr Dodman had had to clear his own throat once or twice when Joy had run her hands over once-familiar objects and announced that she had not truly appreciated them before, but would never forget them now. A happy week had been spent by all, and on the long journey home Gillian had declared that the Dodmans must be the best second-best parents in the world.

Now, sitting between her father and Gillian in the taxi which was taking her on the first stage of her journey to a new life, Joy reflected that the change she faced was no less momentous than the one which had confronted herself and Gillian on evacuation day so many years before. Alex was going to accompany her right to the school, and would carry her large suitcase, whilst she held her white stick and had a haversack slung across her shoulders.

Gillian was coming along to see her off and would then catch a bus or a tram out to St Hilda's, for though she had begged to be allowed to go to London as well both Alex and Joy had vetoed the idea. 'You're in the Lower Fifth now and a responsible young lady; it won't do your reputation any good if you aren't in class for the first day of the autumn term,' her father told her. Joy, more frankly, had said that she would need all her father's attention on this, her first journey of any length since the accident. 'I know you, twin,' she had said severely when Gillian had pleaded to accompany them. 'You'll keep butting in to point out something of interest, or you'll swing round and knock against my haversack when trying to get someone's attention. Or you'll start chattering when I need to be able to listen.'

They had been sitting in the kitchen whilst Alex, brow furrowed, drew little maps in a small notebook, telling the twins that he was trying to discover the best route from Euston station to the school. Gillian had pouted. 'How can you be so mean, Joy Lawrence? I don't chatter . . . well, not much anyway, and I could help Daddy to understand his street maps. In fact, I'm pretty sure that your best route isn't by foot at all, nor by taxi. You should go by underground; you'd be there in two ticks. If I were with you . . .'

Alex and Joy had both cried out at this suggestion and Joy had smiled to herself; already, quite without meaning to do so, Gillian had been proving how her irresistible urge to take over any expedition would make itself felt, and Joy knew, without quite knowing how, that Gillian had acknowledged the justice of the reproof and had been smiling guiltily to herself.

But that had been a couple of days ago, and as the taxi drew up outside Lime Street station Joy could visualise the scene, the bustling concourse and the milling crowds of people. From within the station she could hear the screech of brakes and hiss of steam as a train drew in to one of the platforms.

'Out with you, darling!' That was Alex's dear voice

and Joy could see, in her mind's eye, the anxiety on his face, for her father was a stickler for timekeeping and would be afraid of not being able to find their reserved seats, or mislaying their tickets, or simply missing the train altogether. She scrambled out of her seat in the taxi, ducking to avoid bumping her head or catching her haversack on something, and landed safely on the pavement, white stick extended, hand slipping easily into the crook of Alex's arm.

She felt Gillian arrive next to her and the three of them set off, Gillian giving the running commentary which had been so helpful when Joy first left hospital. Lately, however, being more experienced, Joy occasionally found it an intrusion, though she would never have dreamed of saying so.

They were early, but Alex refused to go to the buffet for a cup of coffee and perhaps he was right, for the train arrived early too. Joy and her sister exchanged a quick kiss and a few joking remarks as to their future conduct. 'No more flirting with the fellers; just you stick to the one you said you liked best . . . Keith, wasn't it?' Joy quipped. 'And keep your thieving paws off my Edward!'

'*Your* Edward? You're just a babe, far too young to have an Edward of your own,' Gillian said, giggling. 'Or do you mean Teddy? I know you've got a teddy, I saw you popping him into your case when you finished packing last night.'

'I did nothing of the sort, but if you mean I'm too young to flirt . . .' Joy began, then had to snatch at her hat to prevent Gillian from grabbing it.

'Do stop fooling about, you two,' Alex said wrathfully.

'I think our seats are reserved in carriage G. Come along, Gillian, make yourself useful; find carriage G and our seats, then you can buzz off.'

Gillian obeyed, and presently the twins sobered up and gave each other a quick hug. 'Good luck, young Joy,' Gillian said and Joy could hear that the other girl was fighting back tears. 'Take care of yourself and keep in touch, and if you're unhappy, just you phone Control; they'll get a message to us and we'll be with you in no time.'

'I can't write, but very soon I'll be able to type and then I'll be in touch – ha, ha – at least once a week. But you've got no excuse, so I expect letters from you weekly, if not daily. Someone will read them to me, I'm sure.'

Joy heard the carriage door swinging wide and someone leaned out and took her suitcase, even as her father thanked the unknown and lifted her on to the train before climbing aboard himself. He guided her to her seat, which was a corner one, and as they began to move instructed her to wave, since Gillian was doing so on her side of the glass. Joy obeyed, waving vigorously, and then, as the train picked up speed, she settled back in her seat. 'I do hope she wasn't crying,' she said, lowering her voice as she remembered that there would be other people in the compartment. 'Poor Gillian! But she loves St Hilda's, and although Irene won't be needed when I'm not there I'm sure she'll still pop round from time to time.' She lowered her voice still further. 'I like Irene, don't you, Daddy?'

'Very much; as I said, I think of her as my third daughter,' Alex said. 'And now tell me, queen, how did you know Gillian was trying to grab your hat? Your hand went up to your head to protect it two or three seconds before Gillian reached out.'

There was a puzzled pause whilst Joy thought this one over. How *had* she known? But having had it pointed out to her, she realised that she often knew what Gillian was doing, or might presently do. Sometimes she knew, perhaps from experience, just how Gillian would react in certain situations. But there were other times – the hat-snatching episode just now, for instance – when she supposed, doubtfully, that she must have guessed.

But she knew Alex would be staring at her and waiting for an answer, so she frowned to show him she was considering his question, then answered as truthfully as she could. 'I'm not sure, Daddy, but I think it's a twin thing. Before the accident we often knew what the other one was thinking; sometimes we both spoke an identical sentence at identical moments, but I don't know how it works.' She sighed deeply. 'Oh dear, I can't really explain, though I'm doing my best.'

Alex grinned. Joy could not see the grin, but she could feel it in her bones; and now explain that to anyone, she told herself. But her father was speaking. 'Yes, I remember you both coming out with the same remarks at the same time; you do it still. I wonder whether it will work when you're miles apart, though? It'll be interesting to see whether you get moments of knowing what Gillian's doing, or saying, or thinking. And now I've a suggestion to make. I think you should stop calling me Daddy and shorten it to Dad. How do you feel about that, then?'

Joy gave a gurgle of amusement. 'I never knew you could read minds, Dad,' she said. 'I've been going to suggest it for at least a week, but somehow I've never had the opportunity. I expect Gillian will jump at it; unless she'd prefer to call you Father, of course.'

They both laughed and then Joy heard her father stand up and fumble around in his coat, which he had put up on the rack as soon as they had entered the compartment. Presently she felt a rather sticky paper bag being thrust into her hand. 'Have a humbug,' Alex invited.

Joy took one, though not without difficulty, for she guessed that the sweets had been purchased a couple of days before and were now very sticky indeed. 'Thank you, Dad, they're my favourites; you *must* be a mind reader!' she said. The two Lawrences sat back in their seats and prepared to enjoy the journey, Alex describing the scenery through which they rushed until his voice slowed and Joy realised he was falling asleep. Smiling to herself, she leaned against his shoulder and presently dozed off herself.

The journey went well and Alex hailed a cab outside Euston station, having decided, despite Gillian's advice, that he would not tackle the underground railway system when burdened with a heavy suitcase and accompanied by a daughter waving her stick to the peril of passers-by. Joy chattered at first, then fell silent, and by the time the taxi arrived at their destination she was clinging to Alex's hand, all her bright optimism and self-confidence gone.

Alex paid off the taxi and hefted the suitcase, then gripped his daughter's hand firmly in his free one. Together, they approached the enormous building. 'No steps, just very large glass doors and a wide hall; no rugs or little tables or any such obstacles, but right opposite the doors a big desk with two young women seated facing us,' he said as he guided Joy inside. 'Here we go! Smile, sweetheart, because the ladies are smiling at us!'

Smiling obediently, though with a fluttering heart, Joy clung to her father's hand and as they stopped before the desk, she turned towards him. 'Don't leave me until I know where I am,' she hissed. 'Oh, Daddy, I feel like a rabbit when it sees a weasel.'

Alex gave a choke of laughter, then squeezed Joy's hand. 'I won't,' he promised, then leaned towards the desk. 'Excuse me, ladies, this is my daughter, Joy Lawrence; she's come to join the school. I trust we've come to the right place?'

Two hours later, Joy was already beginning to feel a good deal less frightened. She had been allotted a helper, a girl of her own age called Amy Freud. They would share a small bedroom and go everywhere together until Joy had learned the layout of the big building.

She and Amy, with Alex tagging rather self-consciously along, had visited the cloakrooms, the dining room, the recreation room and gymnasium, and various classrooms. And then Joy had heard her father's breathing become agitated, recognised the rustle as he pulled up the sleeve of his jacket to examine his watch and guessed that he was afraid of missing his train.

She and Amy were hand in hand, but now she pulled her new friend to a halt and turned to face her father. 'I'm all right now, Dad,' she said, trying to infuse her voice with more self-confidence than she actually felt. 'Amy and me want to do things which you'd simply find boring: counting how many paces there are between our room and the stairs, for instance. And I want to have a really good explore in the gymnasium.' She grabbed her father's hand and gave it a squeeze. 'Oh, Dad, I know what you're thinking; you're afraid you'll miss your perishin' train! And you really mustn't do that because Blue Watch is on call tonight and I've heard all about Murphy's law, so if you were to miss the train Blue Watch would have a shout, sure as eggs is eggs.'

'Blue Watch can manage perfectly well without me and they know there's a chance that I won't be back in time. But I don't fancy hanging about Euston station for three or four hours, so if you're sure you don't mind . . .'

Joy began to say in rather a wobbly voice that of course she did not mind, but Amy cut in. 'There's a private study room on the ground floor what we use for interviews with parents or relatives. I'll take you along there and when you've said your goodbyes and that you just open the door, Joy, and holler my name. I shan't be far away and I'll come running.'

Joy smiled; the other girl's accent intrigued her. It was so different, not only from the Scouse accents by which she had been surrounded for the last eleven months, but from the soft Devonshire burr to which she and Gillian had become accustomed whilst living with the Dodmans. She imagined that it must be what they called a Cockney accent since she had heard echoes of it both at the station and from the cab driver. But now was no time to discuss such things. Amy opened a door and ushered Alex and Joy through it, closing it firmly behind them.

'This is very cosy,' Alex said approvingly. A chair scraped across the floor and he settled Joy in it, then took another himself. 'Darling Joy, I've saved a little surprise for you which I hope will make parting easier. We are having a telephone installed at home . . .'

Joy gave a muffled shriek and abandoned her chair, casting herself rapturously into her father's arms. 'Oh, Daddy – Dad – you're the most wonderful man on earth,' she exclaimed. 'But won't it cost an awful lot? I promise that when I telephone home I'll just say a few words and then slam the receiver down. Oh, Dad, I'm so lucky to have you!'

Alex laughed and Joy could visualise how his slow smile would spread across his face and how he would smooth down his thick hair with both hands as he replied. 'I'm glad I've done the right thing for once, because you will be able to phone us direct, instead of having to go through Control. And we, of course, will be able to telephone the LSB from the comfort of our own parlour, which is where the telephone people are going to install the instrument. There's a long queue of folk wanting telephones, but we're being treated as a special case because of your being only fourteen and attending the LSB. You see, I know you won't be able to write to us until your touch-typing is pretty good, and I know Gillian didn't like the idea of having her letters to you read by a stranger, so a telephone was the obvious answer.'

'I hope you've warned her not to chatter on and on, the way she usually does,' Joy said severely. 'But I've just thought, Dad. If I ring you on the school telephone, then it will be they who pay, won't it? And I do believe I shall have an awful lot to tell you once I've been here a week or two.'

'You will have to use the public box down the road,' Alex said. Gently, he disengaged himself from his daughter's tight embrace. 'I must go, queen, or I'll miss the through train which will get me to Liverpool a good deal faster than the other one. I've arranged with Miss Hibbert, who is in charge of your year, that I'll telephone our number through as soon as we're connected. Now, let me see you open the door and give a good yell. And when Amy arrives, I really must be on my way.'

Joy sighed but nodded, walked carefully across the room, opened the door and called her new friend, but her voice came out far more softly than she had intended. She felt her father's hand in hers, heard him inhale and guessed that he was about to shout for Amy himself. Then he expelled his breath in a long hiss, gave her hand a squeeze and then released it. 'Good girl; here comes your friend. Do you want me to describe her to you? She's about your height and thin, with very dark brown hair . . .'

Joy had meant to leave her white stick in the bedroom, for she never carried it indoors in her own home, but Amy had laughed and reminded her that the LSB – Blinkers – was large and totally strange to her. So now Joy tucked her stick under one arm and reached up to give her father a hug and a kiss on the cheek. 'Go and catch your train, and if you hear footsteps pattering after you you'll have to give me a good ticking-off,' she said rather tearfully. 'Oh, Dad, I know I'm going to enjoy myself and learn lots, but right now I just wish I could hop into your pocket and go home with you.'

'Well, you can't, because you'd regret it for the rest of your life; besides, the term is only twelve weeks long and when you come home it'll be almost Christmas,' Alex said bracingly. 'Goodbye, sweetheart. Be good.'

Amy had joined them, and now took Joy's hand in a firm grip as she stood facing the glass doors through which her father had disappeared. She was striving to keep a happy smile on her face, but all of a sudden she felt abandoned and bereft. If only she hadn't poked her head out of the window in the gale that black and terrible night! Oh, if only Gillian were here, close beside her, holding her hand and describing everything before her! She longed to break away from Amy and run after her father; run all the way to Liverpool if necessary. Standing stock still and listening intently, she heard her father's footsteps fading and was almost startled when a voice spoke in her ear. 'I know how you feel, Joy; we've all had that horrible feeling when we knows our mums and dads are leavin' us in a strange place and goin' back home without us. You must feel especially bad 'cos he's real nice, your dad, real understandin'. Wish mine were like that; still, there you are, can't have everything. My old ma's a proper treasure; what's yours like?'

Joy fished a hanky out of her pocket and blew her nose. 'My mum died when I was nine,' she said huskily. 'She was a real treasure, too, just like yours. I suppose that's why Daddy never married again – because Mummy was such a darling. But it was a long time ago. And once I know my way about I'll be all right, I expect.'

'Oh! Well, it's sad that you lost your mother when you were so young,' Amy said briskly. 'But these things happen.' She cleared her throat. 'If you don't mind me pokin' me nose into your business, I'd advise you not to call your parents Mummy and Daddy; the other kids will think you're toffee-nosed if you do. Mum and Dad is fine.'

'Right; my dad and I had agreed that Daddy sounded babyish anyway,' Joy said submissively. 'Thanks for warning me, Amy.'

'That's all right,' Amy said. She sighed gustily. 'I guess your dad's halfway back to the railway station by now, so what do you want to do till supper time?' Joy felt the other girl squeeze her hand and was obscurely comforted. It was good to have a friend, especially one as bright and willing to help as Amy appeared to be. 'Best to keep occupied,' the other girl continued. 'Tomorrer there'll be lessons, talks from the teachers, rules to be explained, so right now we'll do whatever you fancy.'

Joy felt the only thing she wanted to do was to be alone, to go up to the little room she and Amy would share and simply bury her head in the pillow and howl like a wolf, but she knew she could do no such thing.

'I'd like to explore the gymnasium, if it wouldn't bore you,' she said, keeping her voice steady with an effort. 'I bet when I tell my sister about it she'll think I'm making it up. I mean, you just don't associate people who can't see with ropes and wall bars and beams and so on. I wish I could see them, but feeling them would be pretty good, so if we could go along there . . .'

'Good idea; the gym's a grand place and you'll be surprised how quickly you'll be able to use the apparatus,' Amy said. 'Off we go, then. Hang on to me and I'll talk you along the corridors and into the gym.'

Alex had vowed to himself that he would not look back, and strode purposefully away from the school, but at the corner he could not resist a quick peep and immediately wished that he had resisted. Joy stood close to the glass doors, still holding the other girl's hand but with an expression on her face which was enough to break his heart. Even at this distance he could see – or fancied he could see – her yearning and, turning away and continuing his walk to Euston station, he felt every sort of heel. What would Bridget have said if she could have seen him abandoning their child to that great, square building? But Bridget would have understood that this new life his daughter was embarking on was at her own wish and would, in the end, be greatly to her advantage. Sighing, Alex straightened his shoulders and increased his pace.

Chapter Nine

Gillian was hurrying home from the tram stop, anxious to get indoors, for it was bitterly cold and today was the last day of term for both St Hilda's and the LSB. She knew that Mrs Clarke and Irene would be busily dressing the tree, hanging paper chains and, in the case of Mrs Clarke at least, putting the finishing touches to a welcome home cake, beautifully iced and with Joy's name picked out in little silver balls on the top.

Gillian smiled to herself and slowed down to look into the shop windows as she passed. Despite the fact that the war had been over for more than a year, rationing was still in force and unrationed food was scarce, though the spivs and wide boys who ran the black market seemed able to get you most things if you had sufficient money. The Lawrences, however, could not possibly have afforded black market goods, even though Alex still worked at the market on his days off, Gillian reminded herself. And anyway, she, Irene and Mrs Clarke had managed to get hold of most things they needed both for Christmas Day itself and for Joy's homecoming.

Gillian slowed in front of a particularly enticing window. She had envied Irene the frilly pink blouse which the girl had splashed out on a few weeks before. 'It's going to be my gift to myself,' she had said, grinning at Gillian. 'Actually, my mam paid half. I've been invited to a party on Christmas Eve and I wanted to wear it then, but Mam put her foot down, so it'll get its first airing on Christmas Day. What's Alex buying you?'

'Dunno,' Gillian had replied truthfully. She had hesitated, glancing under her lashes at the older girl. How much did Irene know? Despite the fact that their father didn't have to pay for his daghters' education, she knew he was frequently worried about money; he still paid Mrs Clarke to do a bake for him once or twice a week but otherwise he and Gillian ate as cheaply as they could. Even so, there were always expenses cropping up which their budget had not taken into account, but when she had said she really ought to leave school and get a full-time job he had pulled a face and forbidden her to do any such thing.

'Being hard up is part of life,' he had told her. 'Everyone's in the same boat; even the country itself. I find it hard to accept that we're having to pay back huge amounts to America from that lend-lease thing which was in force during the war, whereas the Yanks are rebuilding Germany for free. But don't you understand? More than anything else, I want you to go to university; you'll be the first member of our family to do so.'

So Gillian had taken a temporary Saturday job as a counter assistant at Bunneys, 'just for the Christmas rush', she had told her friends. The money she earned had helped; she knew that. Alex had grinned at her and said her twin would be envious, but they both knew that this was just a joke. Joy had told them that she saved most of the allowance Alex paid her and would not need any extra for Christmas presents.

'I've only bought little, useful things,' she had said, the last time she and Gillian had talked on the telephone. 'And there's nothing I want, honest to God there isn't.'

Gillian knew, however, that Alex had already bought her twin thick woollen gloves and a matching scarf, and suspected that she would find an identical set parcelled up beneath the tree with her name on it when they opened their presents on Christmas Day.

Turning regretfully away from her contemplation of the beautiful clothes in the window of the small drapery shop, she jumped when a hand descended on her shoulder and a voice spoke in her ear. 'Well I never did; when did *you* get home? I went into the fire station last week to have a word with your dad. He wasn't there, but one of the fellers in Red Watch said you wouldn't be back till tomorrow.'

Gillian swung round and stared up into the face of the young man whose hand still gripped her shoulder. He was tall and not conventionally good-looking, with a Roman nose and a determined chin. He was wearing a long striped scarf but no hat, and his eyes were very bright. But he was looking down at her, his expression suddenly wary. 'Joy? Don't you recognise my voice?' He let go of Gillian's shoulder abruptly, and she saw a flush stain his cheekbones. 'My God, I'm so sorry; what a fool I am! You must be Joy's twin; Gillian, isn't it? Of course I should have realised it might be you, but I was so surprised to see Joy – or someone I thought was Joy – home a whole day early that her having a twin went right out of my head.' He smiled suddenly and Gillian

213

saw that though she had not thought him handsome, he became rather attractive when he smiled. 'Will you ever forgive me?'

Gillian had been too surprised to comment, but now she said accusingly: 'How can I forgive you? I don't have the faintest idea who you are or how you know my twin. I suppose everyone knows that Dad's a fireman, but . . .'

The young man smote his forehead. 'Of course, we've never actually met, though we were at Bold Street school at the same time last year. I'm Edward Williams. My father is a member of Blue Watch, Billy Williams.'

Gillian gasped. 'Now I know who you are; you're the lad who used to take my sister to and from school. I *do* remember you from Bold Street . . .' She hesitated, and Edward laughed.

'And you thought I was a bit of a weed, a swot who seldom played games and certainly never excelled at anything but schoolwork,' the young man finished for her. He grinned reminiscently. 'And so I was. I was afraid the other fellers in my class would rag me for walking to and from school with a girl, but I soon stopped caring what anyone thought; your sister's real brave and good fun as well. I couldn't see her over the summer holidays because I got a job on a farm near Denbigh, but to tell you the truth it was Joy, talking about what fun she'd had when you and she were evacuated to Devonshire, who decided me to take the job. The farm is owned by my uncle Meirion; he was knocked over by a charging heifer and broke his leg, and whilst he was in plaster he wanted someone to help out. He insisted on paying me, but you don't want to know about that. The outcome of it all was that I was away from Liverpool for seven weeks, and when I got back I heard that your sister was already at the London School for the Blind. You could have knocked me down with a feather, because she had been so set against leaving home. To tell you the truth I was quite peeved that she'd not consulted me; I was jealous of Colin, I do believe. I thought about writing to her, but I was afraid she might not like it, since she would have to get someone else to read my letters to her . . . but I meant to call on her the moment she arrived back so that we could catch up on each other's lives.'

'Oh yes, I remember Joy saying that you'd got a place at the new grammar school. What's it like? Is the work terribly hard? But I seem to remember Joy saying that you'd matriculated a year early, so you must be pretty bright.'

Edward grimaced. 'I don't believe I'm particularly clever, but I work very hard,' he said. 'I wanted to join the fire service before I went to the new school, but I changed my mind when a pal began to extol the advantages of a university education.'

'I'm the same,' Gillian said. 'Not that I wanted to be a fireman, though Joy always swore she did. She used to say that by the time she was in her twenties, the rules would have changed and female firefighters would be perfectly acceptable. But of course the accident changed everything. As for me, hearing the senior girls talking about the marvellous life led by undergraduates convinced me that I'd love it, so that's what I'm aiming for.'

'Then we're both in for a great deal of work in the next few years,' Edward said, falling into step beside her as Gillian moved away from the draper's window. 'But what am I thinking of, discussing my own future – and past – when it was Joy I wanted to know about! How is she getting on at this special school? Is she happy? How long will she be there? And what are your plans for the rest of the school holidays? Will it be all right if I come round the day after tomorrow? That will give you a whole day to exchange news; would it be an intrusion if I popped in at about two o'clock?'

'I'm sure it would be all right, but if you want to be certain, you could ring up at about twelve,' Gillian suggested, blinking at the rush of questions. 'I dare say Joy will have some last-minute shopping and I can't accompany her because I'll be working at Bunneys – I'm a Saturday girl – so you could be useful . . .' she laughed, 'as well as decorative.'

Edward laughed too. 'Oh, you've got a telephone, have you? How did your dad wangle that? They're as rare as hens' teeth amongst the common herd. But give me your number and I'll ring before I call. Gosh, it'll be grand to see young Joy again and hear all her news.'

Joy awoke early, as she had done for almost all of the past twelve weeks, roused not by the school bell which was rung vigorously by a member of staff at seven thirty each morning, but by the clock of an ancient church about half a mile from the LSB. Lying there, she wondered for a moment why she could feel faint stirrings of excitement, and then remembered that today was the last day of term and there was to be a Christmas treat for all pupils aged between fourteen and eighteen. They were to go in a coach to an ice rink – imagine that, Joy thought, awed

– where sighted volunteers would take them out on the ice. Joy hugged herself; she would be assigned to a partner who would teach her – or try to do so – how to swoop gracefully across the ice, enjoying the experience without actually coming a cropper.

Amy had never been to the ice rink, since she had only joined the school the previous January, but she had heard ecstatic reports from others and passed these on to Joy. 'They say it's the *atmosphere* which is so lovely,' she had enthused. 'Even if you're no good on the ice, it's the greatest fun. Of course most of us can't see anything at all, but they say the rink is lit by coloured fairy lights, and there are special treats for the kids from Blinkers. Lovely hot drinks which you can suck through a straw; savouries, like cheese puffs and sausage rolls, and dear little iced cakes with glacé cherries on top. They let us stay on the ice for a good hour, then we take off our skates and go to a special room where the food and drink is set out, and after that we return to the rink – that's when they let members of the public in – and take our seats for what they call community singing. It's mostly carols and Christmas songs, and instead of gramophone records there's a real band. When that's over, we line up for the coach and come home.'

Joy, who was beginning to know Amy well, had guessed that she would be clasping her hands with delight and beaming from ear to ear. 'Gosh!' she had said, beginning to smile at the prospect of such a treat. 'Who pays for it, though? There are an awful lot of us in Derby House alone . . .'

'It's only for us Derbyites,' Amy had assured her friend. 'The kids in Franklyn are much too young and the boys

217

have an outing of their own. And as to who pays, Bella Mills says it was started by some rich old feller whose daughter was born blind, but now I think they've set up some sort of fund.' She had sighed impatiently and dug Joy in the ribs. 'What does it matter who pays? Oh, Joy, I'm that excited!'

Naturally enough, Joy had clamoured for more information; what clothes she should wear, who provided the skates, and how long would they remain at the rink? But Bella Mills, who had gone on the Christmas treat twice, had told Joy that Miss Hawkins would keep them back after their last class and explain everything far better than she could herself.

This had proved to be the case and by the time the girls were helped up the three rather steep steps into the coach, they knew just what awaited them. Joy had imagined that the skates would be fastened somehow to her sensible brogues, but Miss Hawkins had told them that the skates were part of a special boot which laced up to the knee. When they arrived the girls would be lined up on benches and a member of staff would come along, check their shoe size and help them to change into the skating boots. 'Then your partner will come along and help you on to the ice. And from that moment you will be in his charge.'

Amy cleared her throat. 'Are all the volunteers men?' she had asked rather nervously. 'Why aren't they ladies?'

Somebody laughed and Joy could hear a smile in the teacher's voice as she replied. 'Because it needs a fair amount of strength to take a beginner round the rink when she can see nothing, and may find the simplest movement difficult,' she had said. 'But don't worry about it; the volunteers are all extremely experienced and if, like me, you've got wobbly ankles and no sense of balance, they'll just take you back to one of the rinkside seats and give you a running commentary on what's happening on the ice, so please, girls, don't *worry*. I and three other members of staff will be present, so if you're not happy, ask your helper to find one of us.'

Now, clambering down from the coach, the girls formed into a crocodile and were led by Miss Hawkins into the rink. The teachers helped them to find the long wooden changing bench and told them to take off their shoes and put them in the sacking bags which had their names in relief upon them. There was a good deal of noise: people shouting, laughing and instructing. It sounded as though half the world was present, but Joy knew that the rink was temporarily closed to everyone but the pupils and staff of the LSB and guessed that the noises she could hear were echoes caused by the ice and the great domed ceiling she had been told was above. She was relieved of her drawstring bag and helped into her skating boots by a cheerful young woman who sounded not very much older than Joy herself. Apparently she had several different sizes of boot but was sufficiently experienced to guess Joy's size correctly at the first attempt. Once the boots were laced, she took Joy's hands and pulled her to her feet. 'I bet you feel really odd, don't you?' the woman said, laughing. 'You're on rubber matting, not ice yet, so don't try to slide your feet. Ah, here's Ralph. He's your partner for the evening, so I'll leave you in his capable hands . . . I take it you are Amy Freud?'

Joy would have corrected her but the woman had already gone back to the few pupils still sitting on the bench; she heard her cheery voice saying: 'Jennifer Bates? You look like a size six to me, so we'll try that first.'

Then Joy felt her hand taken in a much larger one and a deep and pleasant voice said: 'Amy Freud? I'm Ralph, your partner for this evening.' He was still holding her hand and now he shook it, saying laughingly: 'Now we've been introduced, we might as well get on to the ice and see whether you're comfortable there. Don't forget, the moment you feel uneasy or suspect that you're about to fall, you must let me know.'

'Right,' Joy said rather breathlessly as she felt her skates leave the rubber matting. 'Ooh, how very strange it feels! And just for the record, Ralph, I'm not Amy Freud, though she's my best friend. I'm Joy Lawrence. I wonder what made the young lady who gave me my boots think I was Amy? Oh, I know! We put our shoe bags down in the coach – we were sharing a seat – and I expect we picked up the wrong ones.'

'That sounds likely,' her new friend agreed. 'Now I'm going to put my arm round your waist and you must follow suit. We won't go very fast, or very far, until you've got the feel of the ice. But what I want you to remember is to slide your feet and keep your toes pointed outward . . . no, no, not at right angles to your body, child, just slightly outward. The quickest way to engineer a fall is to try to skate pigeon-toed; in fact that is how you stop. Are you ready? Then off we go!'

An hour later Joy put her hands to her flushed cheeks as her partner guided her to a rinkside seat. She was smiling and turned immediately to the man beside her. 'Oh, Ralph, I can't thank you enough. It's the most exciting thing I've ever done in my whole life! No, that isn't true, but it's the most exciting thing I've done since I lost my sight. Moving at speed, feeling the wind rush in my face and learning how to avoid other couples when you warned me they were in our path . . . well, I can't explain how wonderfully free I felt.' She laughed. 'No white stick, no dark spectacles, no steps up and down to be negotiated. No wonder the school brings pupils every year for the Christmas treat! But it must be awfully hard on you, having to slow your pace to suit mine and supporting my weight when I got muddled and tried to go right instead of left.'

Her companion took her hand and wagged it gently up and down. 'My dear young lady, you're a natural skater, a natural athlete in fact. You have an enviable grasp of balance, even on ice and without being able to see your surroundings. If it wasn't for your disability . . . So please don't feel sorry for me. Having a pupil like yourself is ample reward for missing a few hours of solitary skating. And I shall definitely advise you to take part in the dancing . . . Did they tell you that the best skaters, and their partners, do a sort of Paul Jones on the ice? We hold hands and whirl round three times, then change partners. It's quite tricky, but don't worry, we all make sure each new fellow has a good firm hold of you before we let go.'

Joy bounced in her seat. At that moment, she told herself, she was sure she could have circled the rink alone and done all sorts of fancy steps, for such praise had never before come her way. In fact, she reflected, she had never had the opportunity to enjoy organised sports. The playground at Bold Street school was all right for hopscotch and skipping ropes, but nowhere near large enough for hockey or lacrosse. Once every two or three weeks, the children were marched in a crocodile to a recreation ground on the outskirts of the city, where they played cricket in summer and rounders in winter. However, because of the long walk in both directions, the time available for a game was short and no one had ever taken much notice of Joy's abilities on the sports field. But Ralph was talking, so Joy dragged her mind back to the present.

'I've been meaning to ask you whether you'd ever skated before you lost your sight?' he said in his deep, pleasant voice. And upon Joy's shaking her head, he suggested that she might have gone roller skating in the past, or played some other game which demanded natural balance.

Joy, however, shook her head again. 'Not that I can remember,' she assured him. 'But if there's an ice rink in Liverpool, I'll get there somehow, honest to God I will. I believe it's the only sport that a blind person can play . . . if you can call it playing, that is.'

'Ah, you're from Liverpool, are you? I think there is an ice rink there; I know the city quite well as I work for a large firm and in the course of my business I've travelled pretty extensively. However, good though you are, you might find yourself in serious trouble on a rink which was open to the public. Young lads act the fool, young girls show off, and you'd not have a sighted partner to keep you out of trouble.' He patted her hand again. 'Or would you? It's odd, isn't it? We're total strangers thrown together by the luck of the draw, so to speak, yet already we're friends. And all I know about you is that you're at the LSB and have a natural sense of balance.' He laughed and pinched her cheek. 'And what do you know about me, young lady? I know you can't see me but I've been a volunteer at this shindig for a number of years and know that when someone loses one of their five senses the other four grow stronger and do their best to compensate.'

He paused, plainly waiting for a reply. Joy thought hard; taller than her by at least three inches and sturdy too, for her arm had not encircled his waist. She was pretty sure he was quite a lot older than her, at least ten years, which would make him twenty-four or thereabouts, and since he'd been a volunteer at the rink for years and had said he travelled for his firm, he was probably nearer thirty. She had noticed the faint scent of Brylcreem, but, though she thought hard, could discover no other clues. 'Well, you're taller than I am, with longer legs . . .' she began, and when she finished he cried: 'Bravo!' and filled in what she had not been able to guess.

'I've dark hair, a little long for fashion, brown eyes and a broken nose, the result of a collision on the ice, so be warned. But I see they are lining up for the Paul Jones; unless you want to be left out we'd better get across there right away.'

Joy had never been to a dance but she had heard Irene talking about the Grafton ballroom and knew that when a Paul Jones was announced, any dancer could tap another on the shoulder and they would at once change partners. She realised of course that that could not happen in this instance, but she got the general idea and hurried fearlessly on to the ice. She was determined to wring every last drop of enjoyment from this wonderful visit because it would probably be her only chance to come to the ice rink; she thought that a second year at the LSB would put an unfair burden on the family finances. After all, a girl of her age could earn money and she would not want Gillian to miss out on her college education just so that she, Joy, could stay on at the LSB. On the other hand, pupils usually remained at the school for the full three-year course and she knew her father would strain every nerve to keep her there.

Five minutes later a voice came over the tannoy, indicating that the free skating period would be rounded off by a dance session in which the more experienced of their guests could join. Joy waited expectantly as the music swirled then died, and the tannoy explained that the dance would be done without music since the dancers needed to be able to talk to one another.

'Off you go; first pair, second pair . . .' the voice instructed, and Joy soon found herself enjoying yet another new experience. Ralph counted the swirls clearly, and as they completed the third he let go of her hands. Before she had a chance to feel nervous other hands seized hers and another voice counted the swirls, then thanked her laughingly for the pleasure and handed her on to her next partner.

Joy revelled in every moment. She became so accustomed to the swirls that she counted in unison with her various partners, and actually began to recognise hands. Some were elderly, others very young. Some had short nails, others longer ones. Some she supposed must be manual workers since their hands were calloused, whilst others probably worked in shops or offices, since their skin was soft and well tended.

She had circled the rink twice before she became conscious that she was listening not just for the voices of her various partners, but for another sound as well; what was it? Oh! Someone was whistling the very same tune that her rescuer had whistled that evening in the shrubbery at the tech!

Listening hard, she lost concentration and for the first time slipped and fell, causing considerable consternation amongst her fellow skaters and bringing down several others. The whistling stopped abruptly and somebody, she could not tell who, bent down and lifted her to her feet. Before she could do more than catch her breath he said airily: 'All in a day's work; hang on to the rail and you'll be all right.' Joy began to stammer her thanks, but the whistler – she was sure it was the whistler – had gone.

By the time she had dusted herself down and assured all and sundry that she was unhurt, the session was over, the dancers were leaving the ice and Ralph was taking her to the changing bench, where she swapped her boots for her old shoes before heading towards the supper room.

Once settled on a comfortable chair with a plateful of goodies before her, she asked Ralph if he could identify the man who had been whistling when she fell. 'I didn't know anyone had been,' Ralph said. 'I was concentrating on the task in hand, which was more than you were doing, you bad girl! Fancy crashing into the couple next to you and causing mayhem, and you easily the best beginner I've ever encountered! Have you tried the cheese puffs? Mrs Lincoln makes them and won't give anyone the recipe; they're really good.'

'No, I've not had one yet,' Joy told him, curbing her impatience. 'Look, this is really important to me, more important than cheese puffs. Way back last June I was rescued from a very nasty situation by a man I didn't know, and have never met again to my knowledge. Because I'm blind I never saw his face, and since he left without giving me his name I'd no means of tracing him. Only before he came in answer to my shouts, I heard someone whistling the very tune that someone was whistling just now.'

Ralph shrugged; she could hear the movement and guessed that he thought her quest for the whistler both foolish and fruitless. 'Coincidence,' he said briefly. 'If you're desperate to find out, however, I could ask over the tannoy, only we aren't supposed to whistle or hum or do anything which might make a skater lose concentration, so he might not own up. If you'd been badly hurt, we would all have been in trouble.'

'Oh, it doesn't really matter,' Joy said regretfully. 'If only I knew the name of the tune he was whistling! But I suppose it wouldn't make much difference. Oh, and there was a very slight smell of lavender, but I think that was because he'd brushed against a lavender bush when he came running through the shrubbery.'

'Probably,' Ralph agreed. He put something into her hand. 'This, my dear girl, is a cheese puff. When you've eaten it, we'll go and take our seats for the carol singing.'

Joy meekly agreed to do as he said and presently, after

all the special guests from the LSB had taken their places alongside their skating partners, the big doors at the back of the hall were flung open and those members of the public who had bought tickets for the carol singing joined them. Ralph told Joy that whilst they were eating, the staff had erected a platform on the ice for the orchestra. 'They're taking their places now,' he said, and described the scene as the members of the orchestra crossed the ice with some trepidation and took their places on the platform. The conductor, he told her, was thin and aristocratic-looking, with white hair that waved down to his shoulders and flashing blue eyes; he was wearing a dinner jacket with a white frilled shirt and pointed patent leather shoes. 'He will announce the carols, and someone is coming round with song sheets, written in Braille for you and neatly typed for me,' Ralph said. 'Not that you will need it; I've noticed on previous occasions that you girls do a great deal of memorising and know the words of most popular carols and Christmas songs off by heart.'

'Yes, you're right. I remember carols, poems and all sorts which I learned before I had my accident,' Joy said in a low voice. She chuckled. 'It's a good thing I do, because Braille is awfully difficult; it will take me the entire year, or longer, to learn to read with my fingers.'

'I can imagine . . .' Ralph was beginning when the conductor began to speak.

'We will start with a really well-known carol,' he said in a light but pleasant baritone. 'It is number three on your song sheets.'

'It's "We three kings",' Ralph whispered. 'I'm sure you know it perfectly.'

The orchestra began to play, the voices around the rink swelled and soared and Joy began to sing. She had always been able to carry a tune, and was unselfconscious when the conductor said: 'And the next carol will be sung by the young ladies from Blinkers alone. Sing up, girls!'

She heard herself singing gaily, heard Ralph say with almost unflattering astonishment: 'By God, you can sing better than most of the so-called songsters one hears on the wireless,' and rejoiced in the fact that she had perhaps a tiny talent.

In addition, she had heard the whistler again, which might mean that they were under the same roof. She could not recognise him, but perhaps he might recognise her. The very thought sent a trickle of excitement through her; oh, if only he would spot her, come over, speak! She told herself that she did not care if he was old or young, fat or thin, handsome or ugly. He had saved her once from a very frightening situation and just now from an embarrassing one, and on neither occasion had she been able to express her thanks properly. If only, oh, if only he would approach her! If he began to whistle once more when the carols were over, perhaps someone might point him out, and even though she would be unable to see him she could ask him if, way back last summer, he had been the person who had come to her aid.

She sang her way merrily through the rest of the concert, but only half her mind was engaged in singing. The other half, she felt, was willing her rescuer to come to ask her how she did and what she was doing here, for the last time they had met had been in Liverpool, a long way from an ice rink in London.

But when the music finished and the girls were lining up to return to their coach, hope died. No one had come near her, no one had whistled again, or spoken her name. As she thanked Ralph for all his help and climbed aboard the coach, she told herself severely that she was being quite ridiculous and must not let one solitary incident spoil her pleasure in that wonderful Christmas treat. It simply must have been a coincidence; what would her rescuer be doing in London if he lived in Liverpool? Come to that, what had he been doing in Liverpool if he lived in London? Unable to answer either question, she decided that when she got home the following day she would tell Gillian all about it, including the fact that someone in that vast auditorium had been whistling the very tune her summer rescuer had whistled before he had heard her shouts for help.

Back on the coach once more, she and Amy chatted away, laughing over the mix-up which had caused Joy to be mistaken for Amy and Amy for Joy. 'I did tell my partner that he was calling me by the wrong name, but he just laughed and squeezed my hand and told me not to keep letting my feet slide together and not to bend half forward as though in anticipation of a fall. He was quite strict really, though very nice, so I told him that he shouldn't blame me for my faults when he would keep whistling under his breath. I'm telling you, that can be very off-putting when you're straining your ears to catch his instructions, and—'

Joy had been leaning back in her seat, dreamily remembering the feel of the ice beneath her skates and Ralph's firm grip on her waist, but she sat up straight so suddenly that Amy gave a squeak of surprise. 'What's the matter? Don't say you've forgotten something . . . but they checked us all ever so carefully. They checked our shoes at least twice, if not three times, because of the muddle.'

But Joy was not listening. 'What was he whistling?' she almost shouted. 'Do stop gabbling on and tell me what *tune* he was whistling.'

There was a short pause before Amy spoke, her voice a touch sulky. 'What tune *who* was whistling? Honestly, Joy, I'm not a mind reader, you know. Incidentally, can you and your twin read each other's minds? I've often wondered.'

'Oh, Amy, please, please do stop talking and *think*,' Joy said urgently. 'I've never told you, but when I was at home in Liverpool something rather horrid happened. Two girls attacked me and I was rescued by a feller I heard whistling as he came up the path – which was why I yelled for help. I never had a chance to thank him properly, but if your whistler was the same as mine I'd really love to meet up with him.'

'Ye-es, I can see that,' Amy said, having thought it over. 'But I think my partner was whistling snatches of music rather than one tune. And honestly, Joy, it's almost unbelievable that the man who came to your aid in Liverpool was the same feller who partnered me this evening. It sounds awfully romantic but it would be too much of a coincidence if it were the same man, don't you agree?'

Joy sank back in her seat with a sigh. 'I suppose you're right,' she said regretfully. 'Oh well, never mind. But if I ever meet the chap who saved me from being beaten up I'd like to be able to thank him properly, because he was meeting someone and hurried off before I had a chance to tell him how grateful I was.'

'And you were going to reward him with a loving kiss, I suppose?' Amy said sarcastically. 'He's probably fat and forty, with a shiny bald head and those teeny little glasses . . . pince-nez, aren't they?' She laughed, and after a moment Joy laughed too.

'But even if he's one of the seven dwarfs, I would still love to meet him again,' she assured her friend. 'It's odd, isn't it, that whenever I'm in trouble I'm saved by someone who's whistling . . .'

'Oh, nonsense, you daft girl,' Amy said bracingly. 'The feller on the ice rink was probably the one who knocked you over – he certainly didn't save you from a horrible fate, anyway.' Joy heard a rustling and felt a paper bag pressed into her hand. 'Have a sherbet lemon!'

Joy sat in the corner seat in which one of the older pupils had settled her, and propped her white stick carefully by her side. She was ostensibly in the charge of the guard who would come along the train whenever they were nearing a station to make sure she was all right and would assist her to alight when they reached Liverpool Lime Street. She knew that her haversack was on the rack above her head, and in the pocket of her coat nestled a florin and a packet of jam sandwiches wrapped in greaseproof paper. The money was to buy a drink and the girl who had brought her as far as the train had reminded her severely that she must not leave her seat, but must get a fellow passenger, or the guard, to purchase anything she might need.

'What if I need a pee?' Joy had said mischievously, but the older girl had only laughed, given Joy's shoulder a friendly pat and shouted: 'See you next term, littl'un,' before abandoning her to the pleasures and perils of the journey.

After the train had begun to chug out of the station, Joy had spent the first ten or fifteen minutes familiarising herself with the voices of her fellow passengers. They were a mixed lot: an elderly man with a broad Lancashire accent, a woman – presumably his wife – who kept interrupting when he spoke, a couple of young persons whom Joy guessed to be the grandchildren of the Lancashire couple, and two elderly ladies who chatted in low voices, whilst a constant clicking told Joy that both were knitting industriously.

At first Joy listened to the conversation of the adults, then switched her attention to the children. She judged them to be eight or ten and simply by listening soon knew their names – Tammy and Terry – and the fact that they were brother and sister. They had come to London to see an exhibition at the Natural History Museum and were eagerly rehearsing how they would describe their adventure to their friends.

Joy had visited the museum with a party from the LSB, and of course hadn't seen the exhibits with her own eyes, but the member of staff who had guided them from room to room had described everything so vividly that Joy could see it all in her mind's eye, and shared in the children's awe and delight over the vast fossilised dinosaur which dominated the main hall.

Presently, however, she began to wonder who would meet the train. It might be Gillian, eager to tell of the triumphs and disasters which had occurred at St Hilda's, or it might be her father. Not Irene, because she would be at work, and though Mrs Clarke, according to Gillian, spent almost as much time in their house as she did at home, she doubted that the older woman would come to the station. If no one turned up, there was an arrangement that a porter, forewarned, would take her and her suitcase out to the taxi rank. But she thought it very unlikely; this was a momentous occasion, her very first return to Liverpool after twelve whole weeks away. She could not imagine her father not making his way to the station, probably a good hour before her train was due. Joy hugged herself. To be met by Dad would be best! She had spoken to him on the telephone about once a week, but because of the cost these conversations had been short, and though he had replied to her increasingly competent letters, it was briefly; Alex was not a good correspondent.

Gillian, on the other hand, had written long letters, mainly keeping her twin up to date with her life at St Hilda's, which was fair enough, Joy thought, since she had done the same in reverse. Gillian had a friend called Keith, mention of whom had appeared at frequent intervals in her letters, and another, Paul, who had also been mentioned often. Joy assumed that Keith and Paul were boyfriends, but she was still not sure precisely what a boyfriend was. And I don't care either, she told herself defiantly now, digging out her packet of sandwiches when she heard the rustle as other travellers produced food. I remember Dad telling Gillian that flirting was dangerous, though, so perhaps there's safety in numbers. I'll find out when I get back; after

233

all, we've got the whole of the Christmas holidays to tell each other all the things we couldn't put in letters, or say over the telephone. Oh, I can't wait to get back to dear old Liverpool!

Chapter Ten

Summer 1949

Alex was sitting at the kitchen table, absently rubbing a yellow duster across his shoe whilst contemplating the list of shopping which he and Mrs Clarke had arranged to do between them. When Gillian burst into the room he greeted her vaguely, indicating a couple of rounds of toast with a jerk of his head. 'Good morning, queen; you're up early considering it's the first day of the holidays. Does this mean you're going to give me a hand with the shopping?'

Gillian slid into the chair opposite her father's, reached for the first slice of toast and began to butter it, shaking her head as she did so. 'No, I told you before I was planning to see Keith. Oh, don't worry, I'll be at the station in time to meet Joy's train, but Keith's off to his holiday job at noon and I promised him . . .'

'All right, all right,' Alex said peevishly. He reflected that Gillian was a good girl, but somewhat single-minded. She kept declaring that her friendship with Keith was just that, but behaving as though the two of them were joined at the hip and could not be parted for long. 'As for meeting Joy, there's no need for that because I mean to go to the station myself. It's just that we still need some little extras for our celebration high tea and what with rationing and shortages it could take ages to find the things we want.'

Gillian took a big bite of toast. 'What sort of little extras?' She smiled hopefully. 'I know the cake's done because Auntie Clarke told me she's keeping it at her house so I don't go peeping, and there's cold ham in the meat safe . . .'

'Never you mind; since you can't help with the shopping you'll have to wait until teatime to find out,' Alex said. 'And come to think of it, since it's a celebration for both you and Joy, it should be a surprise to both of you as well. So go off with your Keith, my love, but be back here by five. If you aren't, we'll start without you.'

'Celebrating my passing my end-of-year exams seems a bit excessive, doesn't it?' Gillian said. 'Is the tea still hot?' She tapped the side of the pot, then poured milk into a mug and added the tea. 'It's Joy who's been made Student of the Year.'

'For the second time,' Alex added proudly. 'Oh, I know they're only internal exams, but nevertheless . . .'

'We're both bleedin' brilliant,' Gillian said provocatively, knowing that her father hated to hear his daughters using bad language. 'Ho yes, we're kids a feller can be perishin' proud of.'

Alex laughed. 'You get it from me,' he observed. He stood up. 'I'm off; the shops are open and you never know, they say the early bird catches the worm.'

Gillian shuddered, but stood up as well. 'So you're going to feed us on worms, are you?' she said. 'In that case I'm off too, and you can clear away the brekker and wash up yourself!'

As she spoke she was putting on her jacket and tugging

open the back door. Alex still hoped to delay her so that she might at least help with the washing-up, but Gillian shot through the door and slammed it behind her. Alex began to clear the table, noting that they also needed mundane things such as bread, and the sticky buns the twins always enjoyed.

As soon as he finished the washing-up and clearing away, Alex checked the pantry and decided that if he could buy some nice fruit and get to the baker's before they ran out of bread, that would just about complete his marketing. Had Gillian obliged by helping with the shopping, he would have stayed at home to give Mrs Clarke a hand, but as it was he had best get the marketing bag and start his search at once.

Five minutes later, he was out on the sunny pavement, smiling and nodding to passers-by. Several people stopped him to congratulate him on the fact that he would soon have both his chicks back in the nest. Mrs Lubbock next door must have seen him through her parlour window, for she popped out and pressed a brown paper bag into his hand. 'A few sweeties for your lasses,' she wheezed. 'I remember how they used to spend their pocket money on humbugs, afore rationin'. Tell young Joy to pop round any time she feels like a chat.'

It was the same all the way to St John's market, where Alex joined a queue at one of the stalls. He had hoped to buy some strawberries, since they were not only in season but also the girls' favourite fruit, but there were none on view. However, he remained in the queue, thinking how strange it would be to have both the girls home at the same time, if not for good, at least for several weeks.

Last year, Gillian's school had arranged an exchange for her, since she was doing languages and her teacher thought she would benefit from a stay in France during the summer holidays. Gillian had jumped at the chance, and had left on the first leg of her journey within hours of her twin's arriving home. 'We're like that little Swiss cottage which tells the weather,' Gillian had said gaily at the time. 'When the old grandfather pops out, it's going to be fine, but when it's the old grandmother, look out for squalls!'

Joy had laughed, giving her twin an exuberant hug. 'It'll seem really strange to be back in Liverpool without you, but I dare say I'll grow accustomed. And Irene is going to take a week's holiday whilst I'm home, so I shan't be lonely.'

'And all your old pals will come calling and take you about,' Gillian had pointed out. 'Then there's Dad, and Mrs Clarke, and that girl who works at the corner shop and was in your class at Bold Street . . . you'll hardly miss me at all, but mind you write at least once a day!'

To make up for her sister's absence the previous summer, Alex had bought a very old Remington type-writer and given it to Joy as a belated birthday present, and this had enabled her to write to her twin, if not daily, at least weekly. Alex remembered, with a twisted grin, how Joy had hammered away on the keys, sending reams of paper winging its way across the Channel to the little village in France where Gillian had been staying. And of course he also remembered Gillian's rather rare replies, for it seemed she had been having an exciting time, thanks to being the only English girl for miles and therefore much sought after by students wishing to practise their language skills.

Alex reached the head of the queue and handed his list to the young assistant, giving her his most appealing smile. She was a pretty girl, and vaguely familiar. He was just wondering whether she was one of the girls' friends when she leaned towards him, giving him a conspiratorial smile. 'Mornin', Mr Lawrence,' she said cheerfully. 'D'you remember me? I used to go about wi' Irene when we was just out of school. I'm Lucy Biggins.' She giggled. 'Me and Reenie used to hang around the fire station, hoping you'd come out and have a word. She had a crush on you – I did meself – but a'course that were years ago. She nicked a bunch of chrysanthemums off her Dad's allotment for you the day your kids came home after the war; she were right grateful you didn't go gabbin' to Mr Finnigan because she would ha' got a rare wallopin' if he'd knowed it were her. And now if you'll pass me your marketin' bag, we'll see what I can find, 'cos I know your Joy's comin' back later today.' She leaned across the counter, beckoning Alex to do likewise. 'How many punnets o' strawberries would you like?' she hissed. 'We've still gorra few left, for our special customers, like. And we've some rare nice tangerines . . .'

Presently Alex paid, thanked Lucy sincerely and left the market, having reclaimed his bag. He peeped into it and saw that the girl had done him proud, for there were no fewer than four punnets of strawberries, ranged carefully along the top of the bag, and beneath them he could glimpse a variety of fruit and vegetables, enough to make the celebration tea a real success.

Baker next, Alex told himself now, remembering with

considerable relief that Mrs Clarke had offered to call on the butcher and buy anything needed for her baking, such as lard and sausage meat. Hefting the heavy bag, he wondered whether he should take the greengrocery home and then come out again, but decided against it. He meant to buy a couple of loaves of bread and some sticky buns from Sample's; better to get them now and save himself a double journey, though he would have to persuade the baker to give him a paper carrier bag, for putting anything heavy on top of the strawberries would be asking for trouble.

He was striding along the pavement, whistling a tune beneath his breath and enjoying the warmth of the sun on his bare head, when someone shouted his name and he saw Fred Finnigan approaching, a broad grin on his face. 'Mornin', Alex,' the other fireman said. 'I hear young Joy's comin' home today. Want a hand wi' that bag? You're bendin' over sideways wi' the weight of it!'

Alex grinned too, but shook his head. 'No, this one isn't too heavy, but if you've time to spare you might come with me to Sample's. I want a couple of loaves and some buns . . .'

'And you've no more room in that there marketin' bag,' Fred guessed. 'Yes, I'll come along and give you a lift wi' your loaves.' He peered into the bag. 'Looks like . . . cor, strawberries! Someone's gorra pal in high places!'

Alex raised a quizzical eyebrow. 'You think so? Come off it, Fred; if anyone knows all my business, it'll be you, so you must know I got the strawberries because of my well-known charm, not because me and the Prime Minister are hand in glove.' Fred guffawed, but said it wouldn't surprise him who his sub-officer knew.

Alex grinned. 'Young Irene's in and out of our kitchen like a perishin' Jack-in-the-box, so if I palled up with King George she'd tell you,' he said. 'Not that I'm grumbling, because your daughter's a jewel,' he added hastily. 'I'll give you this, Fred; you've brought her up right. She's always willing to help, no matter what the task in hand may happen to be . . . but of course now she works in Lewis's she has to be careful of her hands.' He chuckled. 'She's bought herself a pair of rubber gloves, keeps them in a cupboard under the sink and wears them when she scrubs the kitchen floor or washes the pots.'

The two men had fallen into step and were chatting as they walked, but at Alex's words Fred tilted his cap over his eyes and then pushed it to the back of his head, doing a double-take. 'Irene, scrubbing floors?' he said incredulously. 'Well, I admit she talks a lot about you Lawrences and Ada Clarke, and we knew she did a bake occasionally, but as my good lady will tell you, mention scrubbin' a floor or lightin' a fire and Madam's off, shoutin' over her shoulder that the mannykins at Lewis's has to have perfect hands and nails, and she ain't riskin' her job, so there!'

'Oh well, perhaps it isn't her who scrubs the floors and light the fires . . .' Alex began only to be swiftly interrupted.

'Oh aye? Then it'll be the little people, I suppose? I trust you leave a saucer of milk by the fire before you go to bed, 'cos they's mortal fond of warmed milk.' Fred chuckled hoarsely. 'Pull the other one, Sub-Officer Lawrence, it's got bells on!'

Alex gave a reluctant laugh. 'Well, she's been a great

help to me, and Lewis's must regard her highly since they allow her to show their gowns. She told me that the chief buyer examines their nails before she'll let them put on the dresses they're supposed to be modelling, and if anyone's aren't perfect they're told to go back to their counters.'

'Oh aye, she's said the same at home,' Fred said. 'She ain't clever, like your Gillian, but Mother and me's proud of the way she's got on. I reckon she'll end up head sales lady, or summat o' that nature.'

Alex nodded. 'In fact last summer, when Gillian was in France, your girl just about saved my bacon. Whenever I had to leave Joy, either Irene, or Mrs Clarke, or even old Mrs Lubbock next door, kept an eye on my girl. Even now, though Joy's seventeen years old, I shall worry about leaving her in the house alone. I know it's foolish; she's had three years at that fantastic school in London, but I'm still nervous. She tells me she's been taught how to avoid accidents and how to behave if one happens, but I'm a good deal happier when she's with Irene. Mrs Clarke does her best – she's wonderful too – but she's not a teenager and doesn't pretend to be, whereas Irene's only two years older than the twins.'

His companion grunted. 'Aye, I know what you mean,' he said. 'I reckon it's hard on your Joy, always walkin' in the dark. Being with someone her own age must make it easier.'

Joy sat in the train looking forward to the now familiar journey, knowing it was the last one. She had travelled to and from the LSB eighteen times, she calculated – no, sixteen times, because last year she had not returned to

Liverpool for the Easter break since the school was taking scholars who could afford it to Paris for a week. It had cost six pounds, not counting spending money, and Joy knew that the firemen had had a whip-round to enable her to have her first experience of foreign parts.

Now, however, that seasoned traveller, Joy Lawrence, made herself comfortable, for she had been allowed on to the train before the other passengers, and went through her checklist. Suitcase on the rack above her head, along with her navy blue duffel coat, her purse in the small handbag on her lap, her white stick leaning against the side of the compartment, for she had naturally taken a corner seat. Even though she was now seventeen years old she was in the nominal charge of the guard, but he had recognised her from other journeys and chatted quite like an old friend, assuring her that since this was a corridor train he would visit her between stations, just to make sure that she was all right and didn't need help.

'But I leave the train at Crewe, so from there to Lime Street the new guard will keep an eye,' he had promised her. 'Pa meetin' you, is he?' He had chuckled. 'First time I was told to keep an eye on you I thought I'd be in big trouble for neglectin' me duty when I saw what I thought were you on the platform at Lime Street before the train had stopped. Didn't know you was a twin, see?'

Joy had seen, and had understood his confusion. As she waited now to see how many other passengers would join her, she remembered that very first journey, the jam sandwiches which had oozed all over her best jumper, the friendly little boy who had got off the train to buy her a drink and had only just got on again before the train left. She also remembered how the drink had splashed all over her when the train jerked.

How different it was now! When the canteen staff at Blinkers had asked her what she would like in her sandwiches, she had specified Spam or paste and had suggested they provide her with a screw-topped bottle of pop or milk to slake her thirst; indeed, clearly a seasoned traveller!

Somebody slid back the door of the compartment and Joy, whose hearing was acute, listened to a whispered conversation with some amusement. 'What d'you reckon? But this train's usually crowded, and I promised Ethel I'd save her a place . . .'

'What's wrong wi' asking her? She may be blind, but I reckon she ain't deaf.'

Joy turned towards the speakers, giving them a broad smile. 'There's no one in the compartment but myself, so you're welcome to join me,' she said cheerfully. 'And the train is always crowded until it reaches Crewe, when half the world seems to get off.'

Joy heard the door of the compartment being pushed right back and several people entered, one of whom sat heavily down next to her and patted her hand. 'Thanks, miss. Truth to tell, the perishin' train's fillin' up fast. We's a party of ladies from Chester what's been to a convention up London, so we'll be leaving the train at Crewe too. Where's you from?'

'Oh, I'm from Liverpool,' Joy said at once. 'I'm going home; my school term finished yesterday and it was my last. So now I'm an ex-pupil of the London School for the Blind.'

'Oh aye?' her neighbour said. 'I've heard of that place;

it's reckoned to be the best.' She wheezed as she spoke and a large and comfortable thigh was pressed against Joy's side. Already Joy realised she was building up a picture of the woman beside her; fat and elderly, but also competent and good-natured. She must be both to have fallen into conversation with me, Joy thought; many people lack the courage to start to talk to a stranger who can't see who is addressing them.

Joy sensed that her neighbour was waiting for her to enlarge on her comment. 'Yes, the LSB really is the best,' she said. 'I'll miss it most awfully, but of course home is even better.'

At this point other members of the party began to chatter amongst themselves, including Joy's neighbour, and Joy was able to lean back and listen, or to read her book, for she had brought a copy of *Lorna Doone* in Braille to stave off boredom. Once her companions had got used to watching her fingers fly over the dots they began to discuss their London trip and presently there was a rustling as they produced their packed lunches, so Joy was able to do likewise without embarrassment.

The train reached Crewe on time and Joy wished her fellow travellers a good onward journey and wondered whether she should get her case and coat down from the rack so that she was ready when the train reached Lime Street. The new guard had not yet appeared, but previous experience told her that someone would be available if she needed assistance, so she settled back in her seat just as the compartment door, which the women had shut behind them, slid open once more. A man entered, speaking to someone behind him as he did so. 'I'll stay on this train now until it reaches Lime Street; you'd best get off or you'll miss your own connection. You'll be back tomorrow, I take it?'

'Yes, I should be in by teatime,' his companion agreed. 'See you then.'

'Right. Goodbye for now.'

Joy heard retreating footsteps, then heard the man who had first spoken dumping something heavy on the floor and also the soft slithering sound as he removed his coat. He slung it on the rack, did likewise with what she imagined to be a suitcase, and then he must have spotted her for the first time, obviously taking in the significance of the dark glasses perched on her nose and her white stick. 'Excuse me, miss,' he said. 'I trust these seats aren't taken?'

'Not as far as I know,' Joy said cautiously. She found herself hoping that the guard would come along, because she usually preferred to travel with other female passengers. However, the man's voice was low and pleasant enough, in no way threatening, and since it was a corridor train she could always collect her possessions and pretend she had reached her destination, whereas in reality she would simply walk along the corridor and go into the next compartment. But her new companion was settling himself in the corner seat opposite and getting out, from some sort of briefcase or bag she presumed, what she took to be reading matter of his own, possibly papers, for there was a good deal of rustling.

The train began to move and Joy slid her fingers across the open page of her book. She found her place and was about to start reading once more when the man opposite her spoke. 'Aha, I see you can read Braille. May I hazard a guess that you are a pupil at the London School for the Blind?' Joy agreed that this was so and the man continued, 'I thought I knew your face. I have given talks there from time to time.'

A large firm hand suddenly reached out and took Joy's, shaking it vigorously. Joy steeled herself not to squeak; had he no imagination? A hand reaching out of nowhere is not a pleasant experience for one who cannot see the owner. But he was talking again. 'I'm Dr Slocombe. How d'you do, Miss . . . er . . . but I am anticipating. If you've been at the LSB for two or three years, surely you must have heard my name?'

Joy bit back the words 'I don't know your name and don't want to, either', because that would sound rude, not the sort of thing one would say to a man in his forties, which she imagined he must be. She was not good at judging age, however, but guessed that as a medical man he was probably nearer forty than twenty. Then she remembered that not all doctors were medics; he could be a doctor of anything. However, she had disengaged her hand from his, and when he repeated his question she answered truthfully. 'No, Doctor, I don't think I've ever heard your name before,' she said, wishing that she could return to her book. 'But as one gets further up the school, one is allowed to pick and choose which lectures one attends; what is your subject?'

'Despite being a doctor of medicine, I am a great believer in the power of faith,' the man said quietly, and it seemed to Joy that his voice deepened. 'And I believe in the capacity of the human soul to rise above the mundane worries which beset those with disabilities.'

She knew he was leaning close to her, could actually feel his breath on her face. She drew back a little,

247

beginning to feel the first stirrings of real disquiet. If this man knew anything about blindness, he should know better than to invade her space. However, she answered with assumed nonchalance. 'Oh, religion,' she said. 'That's probably why I never attended your . . . er . . . lectures. My family—'

He cut across her and now his voice was soothing, almost hypnotic. 'No, no, not religion; faith, my dear young lady, comes in many guises. Do you have faith?'

'Faith in what?' Joy asked bluntly, and moved still further back in her seat. This was dreadful! She now felt thoroughly uncomfortable in this man's company, and longed to escape; yet good manners forced her to remain where she was since she could scarcely pretend to be leaving the train between stations.

She felt her companion's fingers brush her hand once more and some sixth sense made her snatch it away sharply, so that, instead of her fingers, he fumbled with her copy of *Lorna Doone*, which fell to the floor. Joy dived for it and so did he, and for a brief instant they banged heads, dislodging her glasses, which she hastily reinstated. The man began to apologise, handing back the book, but Joy had had enough. 'Look, Dr Slocombe, as you know, I can't see your face,' she said, 'which makes for difficulties when talking to someone I've never met. Since I assume we have both provided ourselves with reading matter, I hope you won't think me rude if I suggest we make use of it.'

Joy could hear her voice trembling and hoped that he would think it was with annoyance rather than fear. She opened the book again, her fingers clammy, and held it defensively before her face, not attempting to read.

'In a moment, my dear young lady,' the doctor said, his voice deepening to an even warmer and more intimate note. 'But first, this question of faith. Has it never struck you that miracle cures have been granted to those who have faith? Have you never heard of faith healers? I am one myself, and have seen many instances where faith alone has caused the blind to see, the lame to walk . . .'

'Ah, then you don't have to convert me, Dr Slocombe,' Joy said with all the firmness she could muster. 'I am perfectly certain that I shall regain my sight one day; it's just a matter of when, not if. And now if you don't mind, I'm going to read my book.'

'No, no, of course I don't mind; reading is a great comfort, and I'm delighted to have come across a convert to my way of thinking,' the doctor said. 'Would you like me to describe the passing scene? I can tell you have a vivid imagination; probably you are making pictures behind your lids all the time. Have you ever practised thought transference?'

Quite without her own volition, Joy found herself on her feet, staring in the man's direction. 'I said I wanted to read my book but you seem determined to prevent me,' she said, and her voice came out with scarcely a quiver. 'I think it will be best if I change compartments.'

Her companion laughed in a self-satisfied sort of way. 'There's no need to rush off just because you don't understand how faith can heal,' he began.

Joy was still on her feet, ready to reach up for her case and coat, her heart beating wildly. She could not – would not – stay in this horrible man's company, no matter how rude it might look to walk out on him. She reached for her coat, which fell to the floor, and Dr Slocombe laughed gently and stood up too. He put both hands on her shoulders, pressing her back into her seat. 'Now settle down, my dear. Don't be afraid of faith healing; if I have magic it is the white sort, not the black, and you and I really should talk. I honour your belief that one day you will see again – I'm sure you are perfectly right – but I think you may need my assistance. I have premises on Rodney Street in Liverpool . . .'

But Joy had heard enough. She tried to get to her feet once more, but the man's hands descended again, pinioning her shoulders just as the compartment door slid open and a voice she guessed was the guard's said: 'I'm just checkin' my passengers . . .' His voice sharpened. 'Is somethin' amiss? Oi, what d'you think you're doin'? Take your hands off of that young lady's shoulders!'

By now, Joy would have done almost anything to escape from the doctor, so she burst into hurried speech. 'I – I want to change my seat for one in another compartment, if I may. I want to read my book, and—'

'There's nothing amiss, my good man,' the doctor said loudly, almost drowning Joy's voice, though his tone was now more honeyed than ever. 'The young lady is confused; I've offered to see her safely off the train when it reaches her destination, and hand her over to the care of her family. I assure you—'

Desperate to get away from her unwelcome companion, Joy interrupted. 'Don't listen to him! He has nothing to do with me. I'd prefer to travel with lady passengers, please.'

The doctor began to reiterate that his only intention had been to befriend her, but the guard cut across him ruthlessly. 'Hasn't the young lady made it clear that she don't need your help? A grown man should know better than to intrude on a young girl like this 'un. Good day to you. Foller me, miss.'

Joy heard the guard pick up her coat and shake it – the carriage floor was probably dusty. He placed the garment round her shoulders, collected her stick, and then picked up her case and tucked her hand into the crook of his elbow. 'There's a compartment a bit further along the train wi' a couple of lady schoolteachers in it,' her rescuer said. He shut the compartment door firmly, ignoring the fact that the doctor was still speaking, and began to lead Joy towards the front of the train, patting her hand gently as he did so. 'Sorry, miss, not to 'uv come along afore, but I've had a bit of trouble with a dog; animals are supposed to be muzzled and restrained before enterin' the guard's van, and this one weren't, so I thought I'd best deal wi' it before checkin' on you. I'm rare distressed that you were havin' a bit of trouble and I'll be along to help you off the train when we reaches Lime Street.'

'Thank you so much; you are good,' Joy said gratefully. 'But don't worry about me when we reach the station because my family will be waiting. Oh, I forgot my stick and my book!' She turned to the guard as a compartment door – presumably the one containing the two school-teachers – slid open. 'Could you possibly go back and fetch them? Only I can't face that fellow again, honest to God I can't; I think he must be a little mad!'

'I've go your stick here, and I'll pick your book up on me way past,' the man assured her, settling her into a seat and putting the stick into her hand. He took the coat from her shoulders and laid it beside her, then heaved her suitcase on to the rack above her head, telling her as he did so that she was not to try to take it down, or to put on her coat. Then he addressed the schoolteachers. 'This young lady is in my care; I'm leavin' her wi' you but I'll be back in plenty of time to see her safely off the train with all her belongings.' He cleared his throat. 'One of our other passengers was tryin' to get a bit too friendly.'

The schoolteachers voiced their shock and distress and promised the guard to take good care of their new travelling companion. They offered to help her off the train and find her family for her, but the guard assured them this would not be necessary. 'No, no, she's best to remain officially in my charge,' he assured them. He turned to Joy. 'Whass the book called? I don't want to pick up the wrong one; that feller's so cross he'd doubt-less accuse me of stealin'.'

Joy laughed. 'It's *Lorna Doone*, but since it's in Braille you can't mistake it for anything else,' she said. She was already beginning to recover from her fright, but when she remembered the man grabbing her hand, his hold so tight that she could not at first break it, she felt quite sick. She had planned to run away from him, but would she have actually done so when it came to the point? She doubted it. He could see to foil any such attempt; she could not. And besides, innate good manners are not always a help in a difficult situation.

But the guard was telling the schoolteachers that he would be obliged if they would remain in the compart-ment until he returned, and they were assuring him that they would, so Joy sank back in her seat and smiled at her new companions. 'Thank you so much,' she murmured. 'Do you know, I've travelled home by train – oh, a heap of times – and never had trouble before. I'm so grateful to you for staying with me.'

Alex was thinking that the train would never come in, that something must have happened to delay it. Yet when it did steam alongside the platform, a glance at the clock told him that it was a mere five minutes later than scheduled.

He grinned ruefully; he had arrived at the station a whole hour before the train was due and had seethed with impatience for no good reason. Others who had been waiting to meet it pressed forward, but Alex knew better than to try to do so. Joy would have been told to remain in her seat, and no matter how anxious she might be to join her father he knew she was too experienced a traveller to ignore the instructions which must by now, he thought humorously, be engraved on her heart. He remembered the frightened little girl of three years ago, who had clung to his hand when they had first entered the LSB, and the almost equally frightened child who had sat glued to her corner seat when she had returned twelve weeks later to her home city. It had been her first journey alone and Alex had watched her through the window as the train had drawn to a halt, had seen her cringe back in her seat, clutching her white stick, her head swinging from side to side as though her ears might tell her what her eyes could not: that the train had arrived at her destination.

Alex had longed to push past the descending passengers, make his way to his daughter's side and give her a great big hug, but had known better than to do so. The instructions from the LSB had been plain: the guard would come along with a porter in close attendance. They would see Joy off the train; the porter would carry her luggage and would remain with her until she was claimed by a friend or relative.

It was safest and best to follow the rules, even though Alex knew that now he would be meeting a slender young lady of seventeen, with smooth golden-brown hair cut into a pageboy bob, for the years at the LSB had turned that frightened child into a delightful and self-confident young woman.

Walking along the length of the train and peering into the windows, he saw Joy and instinctively raised a hand to wave, then dropped it again, cursing himself for a fool. Apart from the white stick and the tinted glasses, she looked no different from any other seventeen-year-old. In fact, as he watched, she stood up, felt along the rack and began to ease her suitcase down on to the seat. She had been reading a very large book, which he guessed must be in Braille, and now she opened the suitcase, slid the book inside, then picked up her coat and glanced towards the compartment door.

After five minutes or so, most of the passengers had alighted and Alex was just beginning to wonder what had gone wrong when he saw the guard and a porter come along the corridor and slide back the door of Joy's compartment, talking and smiling. The porter seized Joy's suitcase whilst the guard helped her on with her coat, and then the two men came out into the corridor again and descended from the train. The next moment Alex was lifting Joy down and twirling her round, whilst she kissed him and reminded him that she was a grown-up and could have managed to descend the steps without help from anyone.

The guard, meanwhile, stood waiting and grinning and Alex hastily put his daughter down and turned to press a shilling into his hand and a sixpence into the porter's. 'Thank you very much . . .' he began, but was interrupted by a beaming Joy.

'Oh, Dad, I had a bit of trouble on the train. It was nothing to worry about, just a silly old man trying to make conversation, but the guard told the man off and moved me to another compartment. He was so kind.'

'It's all part of the job, miss,' the guard said formally. He smiled at Alex. 'Your daughter could probably have managed wi'out me; she's a very independent young lady, and I reckon she were just about to leave her seat anyway. It were just luck that I came along in time to carry her traps.'

'Well, we're both very grateful,' Alex began, but was once more interrupted. Joy turned and faced the direction from which the guard's voice had come. 'You were marvellous, but there's one more thing you can do for me,' she said. 'What did he look like, that fellow? Was he old or young? If I met him again I'd know his voice, of course, but I'd like to know a bit more about him, just in case.'

The guard made a doubtful noise. 'I don't know as I remember him much,' he said, then brightened. 'He were wearin' a sports jacket an' flannels, an' so far as I recall, he were dark-haired. Truth to tell, he looked respectable; should 'uv knowed better than to annoy a young lady.'

Alex watched a very sweet smile spread over his daughter's face as she thanked the guard again, and reflected that she was more like her sister than ever. She was holding out her hand to be shaken, and the guard took it gingerly, bade her farewell, and walked away in the direction of the station offices.

Alex took her hand and tucked it into the crook of his arm. 'We'll get a taxi since your suitcase looks pretty heavy and there are always queues for buses at this time of day,' he said, picking up the case and heading for Lime Street. 'Come along, darling! I'm sorry there wasn't a reception committee to meet you, but Irene's working, Mrs Clarke is cooking, bless her, and Gillian is—'

'Right here,' Joy said triumphantly. 'Where's she been, Dad? She must have bought a platform ticket or the ticket collector wouldn't have let her come this far, even.'

'No, love, she's not here,' Alex said. 'Her friend Keith has a holiday job down on the coast and he's off later today, so she said she'd see us back home in time for tea. What made you think—'

Joy frowned, opening her mouth to speak just as a familiar voice said: 'There you are! I tried to catch you up so that we could be a little reception committee, but I had to queue for a platform ticket with what seemed like a hundred schoolchildren ahead of me, and by the time I came through the barrier you'd disappeared.' Gillian clutched her twin in a warm embrace and Alex smiled to himself. He had hoped that Gillian might ignore his hasty words and come to the station anyway, which was precisely what she had done.

'I'm glad you managed to make it, queen,' he said happily. 'And now take Joy's other hand and we'll be home in two ticks.'

*　*　*

256

When they arrived at No. 77 Gillian helped Joy out of the taxi and on to the pavement whilst Alex paid the driver and hefted Joy's case. 'Mrs Clarke must have been watching for us,' Gillian whispered, 'because she's got the door open and is standing on the front step smiling like mad.' She chuckled. 'Dilly's standing beside her, grinning and dribbling, so mind how you go . . . oh, it's all right, Mrs Clarke couldn't have realised she'd followed her out of the kitchen; she's picked her up and is shutting her into the parlour.'

Joy laughed. 'If that horrible animal was grinning and dribbling it was probably in anticipation of a nice chunk of leg,' she said. She climbed the three steps, not bothering with her white stick, and gave Mrs Clarke a kiss, then sniffed. 'I smell something delicious,' she said happily. 'I had sandwiches on the train and a drink, but it seems hours since food last passed my lips. What time are we having tea?'

'As soon as you like,' Mrs Clarke said, leading the way into the kitchen. 'But I reckon you'll want to clean up first; trains are mucky things in my experience and though it ill becomes me to remark on it, you've a smut on your nose and a smear across your forehead, so you'll be all the better for a visit to the bathroom.'

'I know, I know, don't nag,' Joy said cheerfully. 'Gillian told me in the taxi that I look as though I've been mining coal. I'll go and have a good wash whilst you brew the tea.' She gestured to the room around her. 'Any changes? Chairs in different positions and so on? I've got my stick, of course – the kids at Blinkers call them our extra eyes – but if everything's in the right place I think I can probably reach the bathroom unaided.'

Joy was right and reached it without mishap. Rather to her surprise, Gillian came in with her and shut the door behind them, running the water for her, giving her the soap and guiding her hand to the towel rail, where a clean towel hung in readiness, before she spoke. 'Joy, how did you know I was at the station? I heard you tell Dad I was there before he saw me – he'd told me I needn't come so I know he wasn't expecting me. I suppose it's not important, but it just seemed strange.'

Joy said nothing for a moment. She soaped her face, neck and hands, rinsed herself off, and busied herself with the towel. Then she spoke. 'Look, Gillian, this is a huge secret; will you swear not to tell a soul if I . . . but you must swear first.'

'Of course I'll swear,' Gillian said at once. 'Go on, explain. I suppose you're psychic!'

'No, I don't think it's that,' Joy said slowly. 'It's – it's even better than that. I think I actually saw you. You were standing by the engine, looking at me.'

She heard Gillian's startled gasp, heard her sit down heavily on the edge of the bath with a thump before she replied. 'You *saw* me! My God, Joy, that's just wonderful! But why do you want it kept a secret?'

'Because it's never happened before and I'm scared that it may never happen again,' Joy said honestly. 'You know I sometimes get flashes of brilliant light, white or violet? Well, when I turned my head and saw you, it was the merest flash. In fact I was guessing when I said you were near the engine because I could hear the sounds of escaping steam and so on, and knew from which direction they came. At first I was terribly excited, but then I thought I might have imagined it because you and

I have that twin thing which means we often say the same thing or wear the same clothes without consciously choosing them.'

'Ye-es, I know what you mean,' Gillian said at last, and Joy guessed that her sister, too, was having difficulty in accepting what she had just said. 'But aren't you going to tell Dad? Even if you won't tell anyone else, surely you'll tell him.'

Joy shook her head. 'No, I'm not going to tell anyone until my sight comes back completely, which I'm sure it will. And now we'd best get down to the kitchen because Mrs Clarke will have tea on the table and from the lovely smell of baking, it's going to be a good one.'

'In a moment,' Gillian promised. 'But wouldn't it be wonderful if we walked into the kitchen and you were able to see the celebration spread which Dad and Mrs Clarke have made for you? There's a bright red jelly castle on mashed-up green jelly grass, and a beautiful cake with *Welcome Home Joy* written in pink icing on white, as well as Mrs Clarke's famous vegetable pie. And the firemen had a whip-round and bought a bottle of sherry – horrid stuff – which Mrs Clarke has made into a sherry trifle, though there is still enough left for us to have a drink of it, if we want.'

They were about to leave the bathroom when something else struck Joy. 'Two things,' she said slowly. 'The first is that Dad said your Keith was leaving Liverpool today and you were going to spend your time with him whilst he was still around. Why didn't you? The second thing is that some horrible old man got fresh with me on the train; I can't tell you about it now or we'll be late for this celebration tea. That'll have to wait till bedtime,

259

but there's nothing to stop you telling me why you came to the station after all.'

Gillian gave an exaggerated sigh. 'Keith was leaving from Central station and when I got there he was surrounded by his parents and all their friends and hardly noticed me. So I thought, damn you, Keith Bain, gave him a quick wave, and came over to Lime Street to welcome my darling sister.' She opened the bathroom door, ushered Joy through on to the landing and handed her her white stick. 'Was he attractive, the man who got fresh, I mean? Oh, I know you said he was horrible and old, but how do you *know*, Miss Clever Clogs? He might have looked just like Gary Cooper, or – or John Gregson.'

Joy chuckled, making her way down the stairs with her stick tucked under her arm and her hand gripping the banister rail. 'Anything's possible,' she admitted. 'But he was a doctor, which means he must be quite old, doesn't it? I asked the guard to describe him and all he told me was that he thought the fellow was wearing a sports jacket and flannels and had dark hair. Some help that was!' She slowed and turned to her sister, who was following her down the stairs. 'Did you see anyone on the platform who might have been staring at me and Dad?'

Gillian gave a scornful snort. 'On that platform? Well, I suppose you wouldn't know, but it was people soup, honest to God it was. Kids, adults, men in uniform . . . oh, all sorts. Even if your dirty old man looked like Leslie Howard and Clarke Gable rolled into one I wouldn't have noticed.'

Joy had reached the foot of the stairs and turned to her sister, a finger to her lips. 'No more now; I'll tell you the whole story later,' she whispered. 'I don't want to worry Dad, or spoil the celebration tea!'

It was not until the twins were in their room preparing for bed that the subject of Joy's experience on the train was raised once more. 'I don't understand why you're being so coy,' Gillian said rather indignantly. 'After all, according to what you've told me so far, you were rescued before the bloke could work his wicked wiles on you. So why don't you want to talk about him? If he didn't do anything awful – and I don't see how he could have done, on a public train – there's no reason not to tell me, your best friend and also your twin, just what went on.'

Joy laughed and hugged herself; it was lovely, she discovered, to be treated like a normal girl who might have to fight off unwanted attention, even if it was from what her twin had described as a dirty old man.

Furthermore, in the past it had always been Gillian who attracted the boys whilst Joy had been forced to play a listening role. She had had friends who were boys – Edward and Colin, for instance – but they had been just that: friends. Neither they nor she had looked for a warmer relationship. But now she was the one who had had an experience which Gillian wanted to share, and it was Gillian who was begging for details of Joy's acquaintance instead of vice versa. She realised she was longing to 'tell all', as the saying went.

'Now that we're alone, I'll tell you the whole story, right from the beginning,' she said. 'It was really weird. You see, the train emptied at Crewe, so I was alone in the compartment until a man joined me. In my mind's eye I see him with thick, white wavy hair down to his

261

shoulders, like Wild Bill Hickok, and a big white moustache. He told me his name was Dr Slocombe, and said that he sometimes lectured at Blinkers, so assumed I must know him. But I didn't.'

Joy told the story exactly as it had happened, and when she got to the bit where she had felt his breath on her face Gillian gave a gasp. 'How absolutely dreadful!' she exclaimed, and Joy was pleased that her twin's reaction was exactly the same as her own. 'Did you give him a slap across the face? I think I would have just jumped up and run away . . . but I suppose, not being able to see, you could scarcely do that.'

'I wanted to; I did jump up,' Joy admitted. When she got to the point in her story where the doctor had actually put his hands on her shoulders, trying to press her back into her seat, she heard Gillian gasp again. 'Then the compartment door slid open and the guard appeared, like St George rescuing the maiden from the dragon. I've never been so glad to see anybody in my whole life – well, I know I didn't see him, but I heard him asking what was amiss. Of course the doctor tried to explain but the guard grabbed my stick and my suitcase, slung my coat across my shoulders and hustled me out into the corridor. I think he was quite ashamed that he had not checked on me at Crewe, which of course he should have done. But there was this dog . . .'

At the end of her story Joy waited for her twin's reaction, but none came. 'Well? If he really is a medical man and has lectured at Blinkers, I suppose it's just possible he might know something that all the other doctors have missed. Only the truth is I'm sure he's a fake and I hated him; he scared me and I think he knew I was frightened.

So I intend to forget all about him and carry on with my normal life.'

'I think you're right,' Gillian said slowly. 'I read a story in the papers recently about a young man who provided himself with a white coat, a stethoscope and a clipboard and went into hospitals, telling the patients he was a houseman. He examined wounds and dressings and ordered the nurses about for more than a year without being detected. He even assisted at minor operations – in fact it was only when a particularly bright theatre nurse queried the advice he was giving that he was unmasked – ha ha, forgive the expression! He gained nothing from the impersonation, except I suppose he enjoyed the kudos of being thought to be a medical man and having power over a great many pretty nurses. Your Dr Slocombe may be what they call a confidence trickster, the same as the feller in the article. However, if his plate is really up in Rodney Street then I suppose he's what he says he is. The faith healing business is different, though I know faith healers exist and it's possible that some have had good results where ordinary medicine has failed. But I think they mainly cure things like headaches and . . . and rheumatism.'

Joy giggled. 'And I'm not suffering from either,' she said buoyantly. 'Well, Rodney Street or no Rodney Street, I didn't like or trust the so-called doctor. It wouldn't surprise me in the least to discover that he was a fake.' She reached out a hand, which Gillian promptly took. 'I've just had an awful idea, though. He talked about thought transference and things. Do you suppose that was the reason I thought my sight had returned, just for a moment? A bit like believing someone can cure your

263

headaches, only it's just – just kidology, if there is such a word?'

'Oh dear, I suppose it might have been,' Gillian said. 'If so, perhaps we really ought to check up on this Dr Slocombe. If he stirred up something in your mind . . . oh, I don't know, it's a real mystery. Tell you what, can you remember what I was wearing when you thought you saw me?'

'No, it went too quickly,' Joy admitted. 'Oh, how I hate mysteries. But I'm sure I did see you on the platform, Gillian.'

'It's really strange,' her sister said, 'but it's certainly given us food for thought.'

'Oh, I'm sick of the whole subject; let's talk about something different,' Joy said. 'Tell me about Keith. I know he's nice because you wouldn't go around with him if he wasn't; I know he's good-looking because you wouldn't want an ugly boyfriend and I know he's athletic, because you watch him playing rugger in the winter and cricket in the summer. And you both play tennis, even though you hate being beaten and he nearly always wins.'

Gillian laughed. 'Clever girl. You've hit the nail on the head; he's tall, around six foot, I suppose, with dark hair, dark brown eyes and a very determined chin. He spends so much time out of doors that he's always got a tan, and he's got nice white teeth which you can see when he gives his gorgeous smile. But you'll meet him soon enough and I know you'll fall for him; all the girls do . . .'

'Stop, stop, stop!' Joy said, laughing. 'You make him sound like a gypsy's horse – all those strong white teeth

– but I don't want to buy him. And now let's go to sleep or we'll never get up in time to make Dad's breakfast tomorrow.'

'But I want to talk about the mysterious doctor,' Gillian objected. 'Oh, Joy, you beast, you aren't to go to sleep until you've satisfied my curiosity on all fronts . . . Joy? Don't you dare go to sleep. I'm your older sister, and . . . Joy?'

A snore answered her, and though Joy knew that Gillian would recognise it for what it was – a fake – her twin must have been pretty tired herself, for she snuggled down, saying as she did so: 'Aren't I mean to treat my little sister so unkindly on her first day home! G'night, you pest.'

'G'night,' Joy murmured sleepily, and heard Gillian laugh before she plunged into slumber.

Chapter Eleven

When she awoke next morning, Joy was immediately aware of sunshine streaming in through the open window and falling warmly across her face, and also of the traffic noises which told her it was very probably time to get up. She had a little alarm clock with the numbers raised so that she could read the time by touch, but she had not yet unpacked it so lay on her back trying to work out what time it was.

She had barely begun to identify the sounds coming through her open window, however, when the church clock struck seven and she heard Gillian's snores stop abruptly. Then, as though she had realised that today was a holiday, her sister sighed deeply, mumbled something and began to snore once more.

Joy swung her legs out of bed and moved cautiously to where she knew her chair stood. Last night she had been so tired that she had not put her clothes in order as she took them off, but it didn't really matter. She would carry them across to the bathroom, lock herself in and sort her clothes out once she was washed. For a moment she dithered, remembering that she had worn an old school dress for the journey, knowing she was bound to get it dirty; today, it would be nice to wear something fresh in honour of the warm sunshine. But she could change later; for now she would dress and go downstairs so that it would be she who would make Alex's breakfast, unaided by her twin.

Having locked herself into the bathroom, she did her usual check, though she knew that nothing much changed in this particular room, lavatory, bath and hand basin being fixtures, though the cork-top stool could be moved – had been moved, in fact. She laid her clothes upon it and began to wash, and was struck by a sudden thought. She had been puzzled at the time when Dr Slocombe had said he imagined she was a pupil from Blinkers and thought he recognised her, and so had accepted without question his claim to have lectured at the school. Now, however, she chided herself for not remembering she had been wearing her summer uniform. Of course he had recognised it and, wanting to start up a conversation, had used the fact not only that she was reading Braille but also that she wore the uniform of the most renowned school for the blind in the whole of Great Britain.

One mystery solved, Joy told herself with satisfaction as she finished washing and dressing and left the bathroom. It just goes to show that if one uses one's brain the inexplicable becomes plain, and what was frightening turns out to be commonplace. All right; he told a lie in order to get my attention, and once he'd done that he thought I might become an extra patient for his practice; that's assuming he really is a doctor, of course.

She descended the stairs, concentrating so busily on Dr Slocombe that she forgot to count the steps and had to grab at the newel post to stop herself from falling when she reached the hall. She went into the kitchen, realising at once that the curtains were still drawn across and the room was empty, though she would have been hard put to it to explain how she knew. Perhaps it was a stuffiness in the atmosphere and the fact that had someone been in the room they would have greeted her, but at any rate she knew she was alone and rubbed her hands gleefully. She had stolen a march on both her father and Gillian, and now she would put the kettle on, lay the table and get out the hay-box in which Alex made the porridge. His daughters had told him how the Dodmans made porridge, putting the ingredients into a special closed-lid pan which was then placed in a hay-box to simmer until morning, and Alex had seized eagerly on the idea.

Now Joy set about her work, and was just wondering whether it was too soon to serve the porridge into bowls when she heard feet thumping down the stairs and turned to smile at Alex as he entered the kitchen. 'Morning, Dad,' she said cheerfully. 'Isn't it a lovely day? I don't know quite what Gillian intends to do, but I hope it includes a visit to one of the parks.'

'Morning, queen,' Alex said. 'What a fantastic girl you are to be up so early on the first day of the hols! As for what Gillian intends, I can tell you that. She means to do whatever you want and she's planned a surprise for later in the week, which I expect she'll tell you about. Where is she? No, don't tell me; the lazy little tyke is still in bed, probably dreaming about Keith.'

'Gillian tells me he's very good-looking and of course he's nice, that goes without saying,' Joy said, as she took the lid off the porridge pot and began to dole the steaming contents into two bowls. She tapped one of them with a finger. 'These are new; don't say someone other than myself has started breaking the crockery!'

Alex laughed. 'No, no, nothing so dramatic. Mrs Clarke saw four bowls in Paddy's market, with lids, which means we can dish out the porridge, or soup or stew for that matter, and then stand the bowls on the back of the stove to keep warm. Good idea, don't you think? As for Keith, he's a grand chap. You'll like him, I know.'

Joy nodded, and was about to suggest that she might fill Gillian's porridge bowl and put it on to the back of the stove when she cocked her head. Someone was coming quietly down the stairs and seconds later her twin came into the room, yawning widely. 'Morning, all,' she said. 'Isn't it a lovely day, though? Just perfect for a trip to Prince's Park.' Joy heard a scrape as her sister pulled a chair out and then a thump as she sat upon it. 'Who's the early bird then? I bet our Joy was too excited to have a lie-in on the first day of the holiday.'

Having dished up all the porridge, Joy sat in her own seat and accepted the mug of tea her father slid across the table towards her. She found the spoon and her twin pushed the sugar across to her; Joy scarcely fumbled at all as she began to spoon a small quantity on to her porridge. 'I'd love to go to one of the parks,' she said, picking up her mug and taking a mouthful of tea. 'Oh, Gillian, it's grand to be home so it is, but I wish I hadn't missed your Keith.'

Gillian gave a little crow of glee and her chair creaked as she bounced on it. 'But you haven't missed Keith,' she announced triumphantly. 'That's the big surprise which I've planned for you next Wednesday. I've bought two tickets for a coach trip to Llandudno, which is where Keith is working. He's waiting on at the Imperial Hotel and his day off is Wednesday. He's going to arrange for

us to have a meal in their dining room, which is tremendously posh. Isn't that good of him? So you see you are
going to meet my feller, if I can call him that.'

'That's lovely; two, no, three new experiences,' Joy
said. She ticked them off on her fingers. 'One, I've never
been to Llandudno, two, I've never visited a grand hotel
like the Imperial and three, I've never met your Keith,
though we've had one or two near misses.'

'Yes, I know, but his family owns a holiday cottage in
the Welsh mountains and they go off there as soon as
school breaks up. In the long vac – that's what they call
the summer holidays at Cambridge – Keith usually gets
a job, often down on the coast, which is why you two
have missed one another. You are pleased about
Llandudno, aren't you?' Gillian said rather anxiously, as
the two girls began to clear the table. 'Are you worried
by the fact that you'll be eating in a crowded dining
room, though? Because if so, you needn't be; Keith has
arranged for a really good sandwich lunch to be served
to us. And Dad's given me money to buy fish and chips
later on, which we can eat out of newspaper, sitting on
the pier and chucking bits to the seagulls.' Balancing a
large pile of dirty crocks in one hand, she squeezed her
twin's fingers with the other. 'We'll have a marvellous
day, I promise you.'

'You really like Keith, don't you?' Joy was saying as a
tram drew up alongside the queue in which they waited.
'Is this one ours? Where are we going, anyway? If we
get on, will someone give me a seat? Only I can never
find the strap hangers until one hits me in the face.'

'Yes, this one will take us to Smithdown; we can walk

from there to the park,' Gillian assured her. 'And I like Keith very much indeed. Oh, Joy, it's so great to have you home; you can't think how I've missed you! I know you told Dad you were going to get a job, but I don't see why you need to do so straight away.'

'I must start searching for one soon,' Joy said as they settled themselves on the hard slatted seats. 'Anyway, you'll be studying tremendously hard and will have no time for me. I'm not grumbling, but the sooner I find a good job and can earn a fair wage, the better. So don't try to put me off.'

Gillian sighed and raised her voice above the clatter and rumble of the tram. 'All right, all right, I suppose I've got to accept that you want to be independent,' she said. 'I know Dad said that he'd be happy for you to stay at home and become his housekeeper, but that's a one-way ticket, isn't it? He'd be happy, but you'd be bored to tears. So I suppose this holiday will be the last time we shall be truly together and able to please ourselves. Once you're working and I'm back at school, life will be pretty hectic, though I sincerely hope we'll have some sort of social life.'

Joy chuckled. 'I can't imagine you kicking your social life into touch,' she observed. 'I'm sure we'll manage to amuse ourselves one way or another. And remember, dear sister, all little birds have to leave the nest, and we're no exception. Besides, for the last three years, apart from school holidays of course, I've been in London and you've been in Liverpool, yet we've still managed to keep in touch.'

'Yes, that's true; you wrote endless letters, pages long, and I answered with short notes,' Gillian said.

'When you're studying all day it's downright boring to come home and find you are expected to write letters. Still, all that's over now because we'll both be living at home.'

Joy might not have been able to read her sister's face but she could certainly read her voice, and now she heard the dissatisfaction in it. For a moment she felt hurt, then chided herself. It was natural that Gillian, who had lived her own life throughout term time for the past three years, should feel a little resentful at the thought of sharing everything with her twin once again. It was not just that she would be sharing a bedroom – and Joy could remember very clearly how Gillian had resented such sharing before the accident – but now there was Joy's blindness to take into account. I'll try my very best to be independent, she promised herself. And I've other friends who will help to spread the burden, but I'm afraid it will be a long time before I can dispense with Gillian's help altogether.

But Gillian was still speaking. 'I admit I shall be studying harder than I've ever done in my life before, because I mean to get into Girton or Newnham if it's the last thing I do, and of course you'll be slogging away in some office, nine to half past five . . .'

She stopped speaking to guide her sister out of the tram and across the busy main road and Joy sniffed ecstatically as they entered the park. 'Lovely to smell grass,' she murmured. 'Oh, there are times when I still miss the country and the Dodmans dreadfully, don't you?'

'I do in a way, but whenever we have a free day and don't need to study Keith and I catch a bus into the country and go for a long walk, or we get the ferry across to Woodside or New Brighton. We're both great walkers and I'm hoping you'll take to it as well.'

'I haven't done a lot of walking in London, though I used to enjoy it when we lived in Devon,' Joy acknowledged. 'Keith's a medical student, isn't he? I remember you writing that he had deferred his National Service, just as Edward has done, in order to take his degree. But look, Gillian, I don't want to play gooseberry when Keith gets back from Llandudno. Right now, though, in this lovely park, I feel I could walk miles and miles, but that's only because I know you won't let me bump into trees or trip over stones.' She tugged on her twin's arm, pulling her to a halt. 'What's that I can smell? Are we near a rose bed?'

'That's right; there's a bed of beautiful velvety red roses and a seat . . . here, I'll take you to it and you can sit down and bury your nose in a rose.' Gillian giggled, sitting Joy down and joining her on the bench. 'I'm a poet and I didn't know it,' she said gaily. 'No, don't reach for the roses, because of the thorns. There's one quite near which you can sniff to your heart's content whilst I hold the stem.'

'There's a garden specially made for the blind near Blinkers,' Joy said dreamily. 'I expect there's one in Liverpool too. Oh, and Gillian, I've been meaning to ask you if you have ever visited the ice rink. Silver Blades, I think it's called. You never said anything when I told you about the Blinkers Christmas treat, so I didn't like to suggest that you and I might have a go together.'

'Keith and I went once after you'd said what fun it was and I can well understand your enjoyment, but

273

you've got to remember, old love, that the sort of private session which Blinkers arranged just wouldn't be possible for ordinary folk like us. The rink was tremendously crowded and I was put off the whole idea when I was knocked over by a group of boys within ten minutes of taking to the ice. They were very apologetic, but I grazed my knees and the palms of my hands and didn't fancy having another try, so Keith took me home. After he had cleaned my wounds and applied TCP, we more or less decided that skating was not our thing.'

'Didn't Keith like it either?' Joy asked. 'You said in your letters that one reason you and he got on so well was because you both excelled at sports. Doesn't ice skating count as a sport?'

'I suppose it must, but Keith really wasn't keen. However, if he would come with us, we might try to take you on the ice at a beginners' session, but personally I think it would be jolly dangerous.'

Joy inhaled the glorious scent of the rose which her sister was holding under her nose, then got to her feet. 'All right, I'll abandon that idea, because in my heart I always knew it would be impossible,' she said regretfully. 'And whilst Keith is in Llandudno, I'd love to go on country walks with you. But when he comes home you can jolly well go off without me, because two's company and three ain't. Does Irene have a regular boyfriend?'

Gillian chuckled. 'Irene. Well, yes and no,' she said. 'Dad may not know it but she's still crazy about him. Oh, she tries not to show it, but she's never got over her schoolgirl crush, if you can call it that. Dad hasn't got a clue, of course; poor old Irene tells him there's a good film on at the Odeon or a special dance at the Grafton and he tells her to go along and enjoy herself. Then Irene says she doesn't like going to the cinema alone in case folk think she's hanging out for a feller – same at the Grafton, of course – and Dad fixes her up with one of Blue Watch, or with a girl like Vera Hutchins, who doesn't have a boyfriend either.'

'Poor Irene. But surely she must realise Dad's much too old for her?' Joy said, tucking her hand into her sister's arm as they abandoned the bench and began to walk once more. 'And most of Blue Watch are old as well, apart from Chalky White and Jerome. What does she do? Thank Dad politely and go off to the cinema or the ballroom with whoever he has suggested, making the best of a bad job?'

'That's right. But she keeps trying, hoping that one day Dad will realise that she's the woman for him.' Gillian laughed. 'Some hope! But you never know; when you and I leave home, Dad'll hate it. He's always taken care of people and perhaps he would regard marriage with Irene as just that.'

'I doubt it,' Joy said after some thought. 'I'm very fond of Irene, but . . .' She stopped speaking; there was gravel underfoot now instead of grass and when she drew in a breath she could smell coffee and reflected that she just fancied a drink and one of the sultana scones for which the park café was famous.

She said as much to Gillian, who gave her arm a squeeze. 'How do you know we're heading for the café?' she asked. 'After so long away I thought you would have forgotten.'

'I smelt coffee,' Joy explained. 'And since it's such a

275

nice day they'll surely have some tables outside; is one free?'

Gillian assured her that they could sit outside and settled her sister at one of the green-painted tables, then went into the café, emerging presently to place a tray on the table before Joy. She sat down, told Joy that her coffee was already sweetened and her scone buttered, then returned to an earlier subject. 'Joy, you know you said you wouldn't want to make a third with Keith and me on our country walks? Well, by the time he comes back from Llandudno, I hope you'll have a boyfriend of your own, or if not a boyfriend, a fellow whose company you enjoy. That's why I brought you to the park, because this afternoon there'll be a couple of cricket matches, and where there are cricket matches there are boys.'

'Oh, Gillian, it's too soon . . . and you know how I hate meeting strangers,' Joy said, dismayed. 'Look, I'll go off with Irene when Keith reappears . . . or someone else I know. Vera Wotsit if you like, or Chalky, if he's feeling generous and doesn't mind bear-leading a blind girl.'

'That's not a very nice thing to say. Chalky's a good bloke and he's known you since you were knee high to a grasshopper, so I'm sure he'd be delighted to squire a lovely young lady on a country walk, even if she does happen to be blind,' Gillian said sharply. 'Honestly, Joy, you mustn't have a chip on your shoulder about young men.'

'Young? Chalky's thirty if he's a day, and really, Gillian, you've got to give me time to make my own friends. Your Keith won't come home until September and he'll be back at university in October, so I have a whole month to find someone – either a boy or a girl, I'm not fussy – to go around with.' Joy took a large bite of her scone and then several mouthfuls of coffee before she spoke again. 'And now, if you'll kindly stop your matchmaking plans, why don't you ask me what I would like to do this afternoon?'

'But surely you'd like to watch the cricket match . . . no, no, I don't mean that, but surely you'd like to meet some of the fellers I know who'll be playing?' Joy heard a certain desperation enter her twin's voice. 'I don't like to think of you all on your ownio when Keith comes back. '

'Don't be so daft; as if I could be alone when there's Dad, and Irene, and dear Auntie Clarke, as well as count-less neighbours and friends,' Joy said at once. 'Besides, I may land a job next week for all you know. So now will you listen whilst I tell you what I'd like to do after we've had some lunch?'

'Carry on then,' Gillian said resignedly through a mouthful of scone. 'Will we have time to take a boat out on the lake before lunch, do you suppose? I thought you'd like that, but maybe I was wrong.'

Joy reached across the table to pat her twin's arm but missed and patted the table instead. 'I'd love to take a boat out, especially if you'd let me have a go at rowing,' she said. 'But this afternoon I thought we might go and see Susie. Do you remember her? She was in our class in Bold Street that first term, but we didn't get really friendly until after the accident when you'd gone on to St Hilda's. She lives quite near the cathedral, on Rathbone Street.'

'Oh, her,' Gillian said rather dismissively, then brightened. Joy could almost hear the thought arriving in her twin's mind that a friend like Susie might be very useful when she herself had no wish to accompany Joy on some expedition or other. 'Yes, I remember Susie; nice kid. And if she's not home we can walk up to the new cathedral and see how they're getting on with it. Then we can catch a tram into the centre and visit the shops.'

Joy finished her scone, drank the last of her coffee and stood up, waiting for Gillian to take her hand and guide her away from the maze of little metal tables which she remembered from previous visits. 'That sounds like fun,' she said appreciatively. She knew her twin loved the big shops and enjoyed shopping, whereas Joy herself, even before her blindness, looked upon shopping as a chore. However, she did not say so, merely remarking that if they were going to hire a boat they had best go straight to the lake, which she could guess was quite near, for the splash of water against the wooden hulls and the excited shouts of children would have led her in the right direction even if she had been alone.

The girls hired a rowing boat with hilarious results, for Joy had never rowed before and despite her sister's careful instructions caught many a crab, drove the nose of the boat into the bank and showered the pair of them with lake water. When they returned to the shore Joy asked her twin whether many people had been staring at them, but Gillian assured her that this was not so. 'Remember, it's the beginning of the school holidays so there are a good few dads trying to teach their kids to row,' she said. 'You think you're the only person missing the water altogether and landing on their back in the bottom of the boat, but it was happening all around. I bet not one other person on this lake, or watching from the bank, realised that you're blind. Honest Injun, Joy, you've done awfully well. I think we ought to come up here whenever we've got time and money to spare, so that you can add rowing a boat to your other accomplishments. Would you like that?'

Joy assured her that she would like it very much indeed and hurried happily out of the park, along the pavement and into the café of their choice, holding far more lightly to Gillian's arm than she had done at the start of their expedition.

Lunch was cheap and cheerful – minced beef and onion pie and mashed potatoes followed by stewed fruit and custard – and when they set out to catch a tram towards Rathbone Street Joy was still thinking how nice it would be if she could become at home on the water and impress her father with her new skill. When they got aboard the tram, Gillian remarked that considering the soaking they had endured on the boating lake they now looked very respectable, for their clothes had dried whilst they enjoyed their lunch and they had taken the opportunity to nip into the ladies' cloakroom, where Gillian had tidied first herself and then her sister.

They got off the tram at Mount Pleasant and stood for a moment whilst Joy guessed Gillian was trying to decide which way to turn; she was soon proved right.

'Dammit, it's years since I came up here and I can't remember the quickest way to the cathedral,' Gillian said crossly. Her voice brightened. 'But I reckon we can't go far wrong if we read the street signs . . .' She broke off and caught hold of Joy's hand, giving her fingers a gentle squeeze. 'Oh, Joy, you'll never guess where we are. We're at the top of Rodney Street!'

Joy gave a squeak. 'Well, of all the strange things! I say, Gillian, now we can see for ourselves whether the old fellow on the train is really a doctor . . .'

'Or whether he's a young man,' Gillian put in. 'You told me the guard said he was dark-haired, so he might not be all that old.' Her tone was teasing and Joy reflected that the very word 'doctor' had brought to her twin's mind, as well as her own, the picture of an elderly man. 'We'll be like Hercule Poirot and Captain Hastings, searching for clues.'

'But we've already got the biggest clue of all, which is his name,' Joy objected. 'How can we find out whether he really is a doctor?'

'Oh, Joy, what a fool you are,' Gillian said, but her tone was teasing and she squeezed her sister's hand again as she spoke. 'We shall have to examine every brass plate as we pass each front door. Slocombe's an unusual name, so if we come across it we'll know it's your travelling companion.'

'Not that we shall come across it,' Joy said at once. 'I just cannot believe that the fellow was a doctor; doctors don't behave like that, trying to force themselves on total strangers.'

Three-quarters of the way down the street, Gillian was beginning to say that it looked as though Joy had been right, for they had come across many names – some of the brass plates detailing more than one medical occupant – but not a single Slocombe, when she clutched her sister's arm so tightly that Joy exclaimed.

'I was wrong,' Gillian hissed in a thrilling undertone. 'He *does* exist! His name is R. P. Slocombe and he has a list of letters after his name longer than any other doctor we've seen so far.'

'We haven't seen any doctors,' Joy objected with a chuckle. If Gillian would persist in acting the Great Detective then she should get her facts right. But her sister, though she laughed, gave Joy's hand a little pinch.

'You know what I mean. Well, what's our next move? How about booking an appointment with his receptionist?'

Joy shuddered. 'You can if you like, but I shan't. I tell you I didn't care for him at all, so I've no intention of waltzing straight into the lion's den.'

There was a pause whilst Gillian, presumably, thought things over, then she spoke with all her usual decisiveness. 'All right, I take your point. I could go in alone and try to make an appointment . . . no, that won't do.' She cursed under her breath. 'What a bloody nuisance it is to be identical twins! He might not know me, but he'd recognise me as you, and he'd think . . . Oh, stop giggling, Joy. You know very well what I mean.'

'Yes, but now we know he's genuine why can't we just go round to Susie's house, see if she's home?' Joy said plaintively. 'I've been close to Dr Slocombe once and I don't want to repeat the experience. Oh, Gillian, let's keep walking. I'm sure people are staring at us.'

'They aren't, and I'd still like to take a look at the man himself,' Gillian said obstinately. 'We can't possibly hang around here until he comes out, though, particularly as he'll almost certainly live on the premises; they're huge houses. There would be heaps of room for Dr Slocombe, a wife, half a dozen children and even a servant of some description . . .' She broke off abruptly and her voice, which had been pitched at a normal level, sank to a whisper once more. 'There's someone in the front window! He's quite young, with fair hair and horn-rimmed spectacles . . . oh, but he'll be a patient, of course; I remember someone telling me once that all the waiting rooms are in the front and the consulting rooms at the back of these houses, so that passers-by can't see what's going on.' She let go of Joy's arm for a moment. 'If we were to make our way round to the back of the house, we might be able to look into old Slocombe's consulting room and see if he's old or young, or handsome or ugly. Then at least we should know what manner of man was trying to seduce my little sister.'

'Well, I'm not interested,' Joy began, only to feel her arm firmly seized as Gillian began to hurry her along the pavement.

'Shut up and be guided by me, in every sense of the word,' Gillian ordered brusquely. 'Every household has to have dustbins and dustbins have to be emptied.'

'But what's the point?' Joy asked breathlessly as she was hurried along. 'What have his dustbins got to say in the matter?'

'The dustbins will be in a back yard, and the yard will abut on the next road parallel to this one,' Gillian said. 'There'll be a wall, of course, but if we go through the gate we'll be able to see the window of the consulting room and with luck we'll get a really good view of the doctor. So if we turn right and right again, and count the back doors, or gates, or whatever they are, we'll find ourselves at the back of old Slocombe's house. What do you think?'

'I want no part of it,' Joy said at once. 'Oh, I know you, Gillian Lawrence! You make a habit of rushing in where angels fear to tread, but I'm the cautious twin, remember?'

Gillian laughed. 'I know it's not much of an idea, but you never know. Tell you what, I'll knock on the window and pull faces, and when he comes roaring out you'll hear his voice.'

'What do I want to hear his voice for? We know he's genuine and therefore he's the man on the train,' Joy said. 'I wish I'd never started this. All I want to do now is go to Susie's; I certainly don't intend to go prancing around his premises. Remember, he knows me even if I don't know him. He gave me the creeps. Oh, Gillian, do let's go.'

Gillian heaved a sigh. 'You needn't come with me, but I intend to go round the back and see if I can get a look at him.'

Joy was about to object again when Gillian abruptly turned right up a side street, pulling Joy with her, and after a very short distance turned right again. 'This is the road that runs along the backs of the houses on Rodney Street,' she told her sister. 'There are walls, quite tall ones, but they wouldn't be impossible to climb if you're reasonably agile, and once on top I shall have an excellent view of your doctor's premises.' After a few minutes, during which Joy heard her counting under her breath, she stopped again. 'Ah, this will be the one. Even if I only see his back view, at least I'll know if he's middle-aged and respectable . . . Oh, look at that!'

'Look at what?' Joy asked. 'Oh, don't do anything foolish, please Gillian!'

'There's a door in the wall,' Gillian said, still holding Joy firmly by one arm. She swung her round until Joy could feel she was in a corner where two walls joined. 'Stay there and don't move, no matter what,' she instructed. 'I shan't be a tick; don't you worry, dear Joy. No one will even think of a spy approaching via the dustbins!'

'Oh, Gillian, don't be an idiot. It's far too dangerous,' Joy said. 'What does it matter if the doctor was speaking the truth or lying like a flat fish? And anyway, we know he's genuine because of the brass plate . . .'

She stopped speaking. She knew that her sister had gone, leaving her most uncomfortably situated, pressed into a corner and presumably at least partially hidden by a tree whose branches drooped over one of the walls. She had no idea what was happening and felt both frightened and alone. Fortunately, however, she had her white stick, and if Gillian didn't return for her she could tap her way back to Rodney Street and ask any passer-by for directions. But right now she was far too worried that Gillian might get into trouble to think more than fleetingly of her own predicament. Trespassing on someone else's property was wrong and could put the trespasser in court, she believed. Gillian, so bold and unafraid, would be bound to get into trouble.

And she was right. She heard a door creak as her sister entered the yard, heard the softest of sounds as she began to move across it. Then there was a scuffling noise and someone said: 'I'll just put the sack out ready for the dustmen tomorrow . . . My God!' The voice became an angry shout. 'What the devil are you up to, young lady? How dare you . . .'

Even in her panic Joy did not think she recognised the voice and anyway she dared not move, pressing herself even further into her hiding place.

But Gillian must have lost her nerve, for the man's voice suddenly sharpened and there was a tremendous crash before the door creaked again and someone – it was Gillian, she knew – dashed past. Before Joy could react, a man's heavier tread ran past, and then there was silence.

Joy's heart was beating so hard that she was sure it could be heard a mile away, but the pursuit had passed her by, apparently without the chaser having so much as noticed her. Gillian, of course, had clearly not wanted to draw attention to her by speaking and the man, intent upon catching Gillian, had not even seen her, she supposed. Indeed, if he really was the doctor and not an assistant or even a patient, she was very glad he had not spotted her, because if he had he would have realised at once that she was his acquaintance from the train. Blind girls are not exactly ten a penny, she told herself ruefully as the running footsteps died away.

She stood very still, trying to blend in with her surroundings, and waiting. The time seemed to stretch endlessly, but she forced herself to remain just where she was whilst a distant clock chimed, first the hour and then the quarter. Only when half an hour had passed did she move her head from side to side, listening intently, for sometimes she could sense someone approaching by this method even if there was no actual sound. Having done her best to make sure that she was alone, she set off in the direction of Rodney Street, walking extremely slowly and using her stick to ensure that she stayed on the pavement and did not stray on to the road.

The wall ended and she turned left, then left again, and was pretty sure she had regained Rodney Street. She paused on the corner, as though to check her whereabouts, and heard footsteps coming towards her. She listened. Not Gillian's; she knew her sister's tread. A man? Almost certainly. Joy cleared her throat. She pretended to be interested in the building she was passing, feeling her heart begin to hammer then slow to a normal beat as the sound of the man's footsteps grew fainter and disappeared; she assumed he had entered one of the houses. She began to walk slowly along once more. More footsteps; a woman with several small children gathered them about her and then moved to one side and Joy smiled her thanks. Other people came and went but no one took the slightest notice of her. And then she heard lighter, almost dancing footsteps coming towards her along the pavement. Gillian!

Seconds later she felt her hand seized in her twin's warm, familiar clasp and a voice, with laughter bubbling beneath the words, spoke in her ear. 'Oh, Joy, I'm so sorry – what must you have thought! I went back to where I left you . . . but we can't talk now.'

'But what happened? Did the feller catch up with you, or is he still searching?'

Gillian gave a breathless little laugh. 'You could say he's given up; he's gone back to his house, anyway. But

I can't tell you any more than that until we're safely home.'

'Aren't we safe now, then?' Joy asked apprehensively. 'I thought you said . . .'

'We're safe all right; I just don't want to tell you what happened until we're alone. Oh, what an adventure . . . I dare say you've had one of your own as well, but we'll both have to wait. Tell you what, shall we run? Just for fun, not because we're being chased. The pavement's pretty smooth . . . ready, steady, go!'

It could be a frightening thing to be running with all one's might in complete darkness, in a strange place, with no knowledge of why one runs or where, but Joy trusted Gillian completely and the edge of laughter in the other girl's voice was very comforting. The twins often ran, arms tight round each other's waists, and Joy loved the feeling it gave her of being ordinary, like other girls. Besides, Gillian had made it clear that they were not running from any danger. She still kept giving tiny, purring laughs, and Joy felt obliged to remind her, somewhat breathlessly, to warn her of possible hazards. A tilted paving stone here, a wall sticking out too far there, a woman with a pram and toddlers at heel approaching, a side road to cross . . . Gillian mentioned them all as they ran until, at long last, she pulled Joy to a halt and they both stood still, panting, but somehow exhilarated, having reached Mount Pleasant at last, Joy assumed. 'Right, here's the tram stop,' Gillian informed her twin in a triumphant voice. 'Goodness! I should think you and I could represent our country in the three-legged race in the Olympics!'

Joy smiled. The danger, if there had ever been any,

had clearly passed, but even so she knew she would feel a good deal happier once they had left Rodney Street far behind. The traffic noise was considerable, but her keen ear picked out the roar of an approaching tram and she pinched her sister's arm. 'Is the tram I can hear coming ours?' she asked hopefully. 'Are we at the end of a long queue or will we be able to get aboard?'

'Wave your white stick and they'll push us to the front,' Gillian said, giggling, knowing full well that her sister would scorn such tactics. 'I wish I could tell you, but it's too weird . . . too personal.' She lowered her voice. 'What's more, I can't explain with half Liverpool listening. Oh, Joy, I just wish you could have seen me . . . only I can't tell you yet.'

Joy had had enough. 'Shut up!' she said. 'If you want to keep your secret, keep it. Just get me on this tram or I'll – I'll simply walk away from you, so there!'

Gillian giggled. 'All right, all right, don't get in a bate,' she said quickly as the tram drew up alongside them. 'Yes, this one will do very well. Hop aboard.'

Joy hoped Gillian would tell her story as soon as they reached home, but when they entered the kitchen they realised that this would be impossible, for the room contained not only their father, Irene and Mrs Clarke, but also someone else: a young man. Irene began to say that Joy would be delighted to meet an old friend, but Gillian stepped forward and must have put a hand over Irene's mouth for her words were cut off abruptly. 'Shut up, Irene Finnigan,' Gillian said reprovingly. 'You'll never guess who it is, Joy, not in a thousand years.'

Joy thought hard and then addressed the stranger. 'Say

something, just to give me a clue,' she said. 'You could try saying "Hello, Joy", or a whole sentence if you'd rather.'

The stranger laughed and might have begun to speak had not Joy given a crow of triumph and held out both hands. 'Edward!' she squeaked. 'I'd know your laugh anywhere. But you're at university! In your last letter you said you were doing end-of-year exams and thought you might have to go to a crammer in the summer vac. So why are you here now?'

'Because I passed everything so don't need a crammer,' he said. He had taken her hands, but he let them go in order to sweep her into a hug, planting a resounding kiss on her cheek. 'I've not seen you for months, which means I get to kiss you.' Then he took her hand again and guided it to his shoulder. 'Say "Haven't you grown, Edward, and aren't your shoulders broad!"' he said. 'I'm incredibly handsome – well, I'm still spotty of course, and my squint hasn't gone, and nor have my freckles. Then there's my wooden leg . . .'

There was a howl of derision from Irene and Gillian and the sound of a slap. 'Twerp!' Gillian shouted. 'You talk too much. And you were so pleased that you'd had an offer of a place at Cambridge, yet you're at Liverpool after all. Why was that?'

'Wanted to live at home,' Edward said after an infinitesimal pause. 'Mam and Dad aren't getting any younger . . . Well, young Joy, notice any changes?'

'You are an awful lot taller. Gillian and I don't seem to grow much,' Joy said ruefully. 'We haven't changed at all, I don't think.'

'Well, you're twins,' Alex said comfortably. 'And I must

say, darling Joy, that in every respect you and Gillian are . . .'

'. . . as like as peas in a pod,' the twins chorused, and Joy, still holding tightly to Edward's hand, led him towards the kitchen table.

'You sit next to me, Edward, and tell me all about university,' she commanded. 'Is your friend Tolly home as well? What about Smithy, and old Bluenose? I'd love to meet them, because you made them sound so funny.'

'Funny they definitely are, but I don't intend to let you meet them because you might fall for one of them and abandon me to bachelorhood,' Edward said, and Joy could tell he was grinning. 'I see the table's laid for one of Mrs Clarke's wonderful teas; can I pass you a couple of Welsh cakes or some shortbread?'

'No you cannot, young man,' Mrs Clarke said before Joy could reply. 'The idea! Bread and butter with just a little jam comes first, otherwise these gannets would fill up on cakes and pies and just leave bread and jam for their elders.'

'Of course, I forgot,' Edward said apologetically. He put a plate down in front of Joy. 'Bread and jam, ma'am?'

Joy thanked him and began to ask him what his plans were for the summer vac. Edward said that he meant to get a job, since he needed to earn something, and his uncle who farmed in North Wales needed help over the summer and was prepared to take him on. 'It's live-in, which means I shan't have to shell out for grub, and the pay's not bad,' he said.

'And North Wales isn't far,' Joy said, beaming. 'Oh, Edward, you'll be able to come home when you aren't too busy. I promise I won't be a drag on you, but the more people who are willing to take me about the better. Mind you, I'm having a fortnight off and then I mean to start looking for work myself, so hopefully I shan't have all that much spare time. When do you start at your uncle's place?'

'I'm having the next two weeks off as well,' Edward said quickly, 'so you and I, Joy my love, will be able to catch up on each other's news!'

It was at this point that Gillian leaned across the table and interrupted Edward's polite offering round of Mrs Clarke's fruitcake. 'I say, Edward, did I hear you say you're taking a couple of weeks off?' she demanded. 'If so, might you be free next Wednesday? Only Joy and myself are going down to Llandudno for the day, to meet a pal of mine who's working down there. It would be really grand if you could come along to keep our Joy company.'

'Oh, I'm sure Edward has better things to do,' Joy said awkwardly. 'Wednesday's only a few days off, and I don't think he knows Keith . . . It might be awkward, too, since Keith's only expecting the two of us and you said he was giving us lunch at the Imperial.'

'It's all right, I can pay my way,' Edward said easily, and it occurred to Joy that her old friend was not only taller and broader, but more self-confident too. In fact she would enjoy spending the day with him, getting to know him all over again, but would he share her feelings? They had been good pals, but she was uneasily aware that she was still rather young for her age, and might seem boring company to a sophisticated young man of nineteen.

Plucking up her courage, she said as much, only to

be told she was 'talking daft'. 'We'll have a good laugh, just like we used to on our way to and from school,' Edward assured her. 'You don't want to put yourself down, young Joy. When did I ever get bored with you, answer me that! And you say this Keith feller is feeding us at the Imperial? I'd go along just for an excuse to get into that gorgeous place, and I'll pay for my dinner, because I'd have to eat somewhere, wouldn't I?' He took Joy's hand and squeezed her fingers. 'Let me come to the seaside, pretty lady,' he said, imitating a gypsy's whine, then changed to the shrill tones of a three-year-old. 'I'll be ever so good, Mammy, I'll be the bestest boy in the whole world if you'll take me wi' you to Llandudno!'

All through tea, Gillian hoped that she was concealing her wild desire to grab her twin by the hand and take her off to where they could be alone, because the events of the afternoon burned like fire in her mind and she was simply longing to tell Joy every detail of what had happened. Indeed at one point, when everyone was clearing away and washing up, she had grabbed Joy's shoulder and suggested, in a hissing whisper, that they might make some excuse to go up to their bedroom and have some time together. But Joy had given a wicked grin and shaken her head. 'No way, Gillian Lawrence,' she had whispered back. 'You were so keen not to tell me a thing earlier, you can jolly well keep your secret now, if it's worth keeping, that is.'

'Oh, but . . .' Gillian had begun, but Joy had wriggled out of her grasp and gone over to the sink, where Edward had given her his tea cloth and a handful of cutlery and started talking about a certain night when he and his pals, having imbibed rather too much beer, had gone to one of the parks and plunged naked into the lake. In the shouts of disbelief and amusement that followed Gillian had been forced to curb her impatience; her own story could not be told in this company.

When the clearing up was finished, Alex departed for his shift at the fire station, Mrs Clarke announced that she meant to take Dilly up to the park, since the dog had been cooped up in the parlour for several hours, and Irene suggested that the four of them might accompany the older woman, unless Edward had other plans, of course.

'Fancy that horrible little brute still going strong,' Edward commented as soon as Mrs Clarke had left the kitchen. 'I've still got the scars on my calf from where it tried to take a lump out of me before I went to university.'

Joy had been sitting down whilst the others put away crockery and cutlery, but now she stood up and made her way to where her jacket hung on a peg. 'We might as well all go with Auntie Clarke,' she said. 'Then we can discuss our plans for Wednesday.' She lifted her twin's jacket off its peg and held it out. 'It's all very well for you to invite Edward to accompany us, but who can say there'll be room on the coach for him? I think we ought to go down to the bus station right now, so Edward can buy a ticket. You've not even told him what time we're leaving.'

'Well we can't do both – walk Dilly and buy a ticket – because they're in opposite directions,' Gillian said crossly. This evening seemed interminable; if they had to accompany the wretched pug to the park and then turn round and make for the bus station, it would be midnight before she got to tell Joy what had happened in Rodney Street.

But Mrs Clarke did not want to take Dilly such a distance and said at once that they had better split up. She turned to Joy, who had donned her jacket and was waiting by the door. 'Irene, Gillian and I will go to the park whilst you and Edward go to the bus station,' she said, ignoring Irene's mumble that she'd had a long day at work and wasn't that keen on walking anyway. 'Edward came round to see you, Joy, and you've scarce had time to exchange half a dozen words.' So saying, Mrs Clarke bent to attach Dilly's lead, taking care to keep out of the reach of the dog's jaws, and led the way out to the jigger.

As soon as they were out of hearing of the others, Joy asked Edward if he was sure he wanted to go to Llandudno. 'I'd be perfectly all right with just Gillian and Keith, because although he's her boyfriend they won't get all lovey-dovey and embarrass me,' she assured him. 'Anyway, there might be somebody else I know on the coach who would take me about for an hour or so, or they could simply sit me on the sands and leave me to enjoy the sunshine.'

'Oh, *do* shut up,' Edward said imploringly. 'Provided there's a seat on the coach I shall come with you, and if there isn't a seat on the coach I'll catch an ordinary service bus, or come by train.' He gave the hand on his arm a little pat. 'And if there's no room on the trains or the buses, I shall walk; does that satisfy you?'

Joy laughed and capitulated, trying to match her stride to his. 'All right, all right, I give in; you're coming to Llandudno come hell or high water, and don't blame me if you're bored to tears.'

Chapter Twelve

It was late when the two girls climbed the stairs to their bedroom, but Gillian was still longing to tell her story. Yet where to start? She sat Joy down on her bed and settled beside her, going back in her mind to the moment when she had left her sister, safely tucked away, with the branches of some tree or other – Gillian was no naturalist – hiding most of her from view.

As she began to speak, she was transported back in time, living again the extraordinary experience which she had so longed for her sister to share. In her head she could see it like a cinema show, slowly unwinding before her inner eyes, exactly as it had happened. Haltingly at first, she began to tell her story . . .

Gillian glanced back at Joy and saw that she was as well hidden as possible, then walked quietly along the pavement until she reached the green-painted door in the wall. She had counted the doors and gates as she went along, and was pretty sure that this was the one attached to the house with Dr Slocombe's brass plate upon it. For a moment she paused, then decided that since she had no desire to steal from or otherwise desecrate the doctor's premises, there was really nothing to stop her just opening the door . . .

She put her hand on the latch, reflecting that she might

well find it would not give to her touch. But it opened easily, though it gave the sort of creak that might have drawn attention. This caused Gillian to pause once more and put her head round the door to view the property intently. There were two large ground-floor windows, both covered with crisp white net curtains, and a back door, neatly painted and bearing a small brass knocker. This seemed strange until Gillian remembered hearing that many of the upper floors in Rodney Street were let as flats, sometimes to the person who acted as caretaker; that would be why the back door to the house was so well maintained.

She waited a moment in case the creaking of the door which she had cautiously pulled to behind her had been heard by one of the house's occupants. Then she stole across the yard, hoping to be able to see at least something as she neared the infuriating nets. She was halfway to the house when, to her horror, she saw the back door open, and a man emerged with what appeared to be a bag of rubbish in his arms. He was speaking over his shoulder to someone she could not see, but his words came to her clearly. 'I'll just put the sack out ready for the dustmen tomorrow . . . My God!'

It was at this point that the man turned his head and stopped short, his mouth dropping open. Realising he had seen her, she gave a wavering smile, trying desperately to think of a good reason both for being on someone else's property and for lurking amongst the dustbins. She cleared her throat and began to say, of all things: 'Oh, I believe I'm in the wrong . . .'

But the man interrupted her, a scowl marring his

features. 'What the devil are you up to, young lady?' he said harshly. 'How dare you . . .'

Gillian began to mumble yet another unlikely explanation as the man dumped the bag he was carrying and reached out as though to grab her. 'No you don't!' he shouted. 'When I get my hands on you . . .'

Gillian took one scared look at the fury writ large upon his face and pushed the nearest dustbin towards him with all her might. It caught him across the knees; there was a yell of pain, a tremendous crash as the bin clattered to the cobbles, and then Gillian was away, jerking open the door into the back street and running with all her might towards where she had left her twin.

Her plan, if she had one, had been to grab Joy and make for Rodney Street, where there were people who might get in the pursuer's way . . . they would be able to dodge amongst them, being both smaller and slighter than their enemy. But the man, despite being bowled over by the dustbin, was already close on her heels and Gillian, panicking, made no sign as she passed her sister, pounding round the corner at full speed and setting off along the pavement in the direction of the part-built Anglican cathedral. There were side streets to dodge down, jiggers and alleyways which positively invited her to nip into them, but she continued to make for the cathedral. There would be hiding places there where she could tuck herself out of sight, but surely her pursuer would begin to grow tired before then? What, after all, could he do to her? She had stolen nothing, broken or spoiled nothing – the tipping over of the bin had been an accident, she told herself righteously, if untruthfully. In fact, now that they had left Dr Slocombe's premises behind, there was nothing of which he could accuse her, save of mistaking one courtyard for another.

She reached the cathedral and went to ground behind a large pile of stone blocks. She was breathing hard, her heart hammering, but she thought that she must have outwitted her pursuer. She was peeping hopefully out from behind the sheltering stones when someone grabbed her shoulders and pushed her back into the tiny space into which she had bolted, blocking any hope of escape with his body.

'Gerrout! Gerroff!' Gillian squeaked breathlessly. She tried to hit him, to push past him, but though his chest was heaving and his face flushed he held her prisoner apparently effortlessly.

'I'll let you go when you tell me what you were doing in our yard,' he said. 'Come on; the truth now! If you weren't up to some mischief then why throw the dustbin at me and run for your life? Only the guilty behave like that; believe me, I should know. I did my National Service in the Royal Air Force as a snowcap – that's a member of the military police, to you – and the only people who ran away from us were guilty as hell, and knew it.'

Gillian let her shoulders droop, hoping that he would move back a bit, but he stayed just where he was, staring at her with a grim expression. 'Haven't I seen you some-where before?'

'That's the oldest line in the book,' she muttered. She remembered he had spent time in the train with Joy, but her twin had been wearing dark glasses and she doubted whether he could have picked up on the likeness after such a short acquaintance.

He must have dismissed it, for he returned to his original point without waiting for her to say more. 'What were you doing in our yard?'

'I'm sorry, I didn't realise it was *your* yard, but when you started to bawl at me I was scared and like a fool I ran,' she said defiantly. 'For heaven's sake, what is there to steal in your dustbins, answer me that!

Her captor shrugged. 'God knows,' he said. 'But what's rubbish to one man may be precious to another. And anyway, I'm asking the questions, young lady! Just what were you after? The truth, please!'

Gillian sighed; this hateful man would have to know the truth. 'I have a sister who is blind and met a man on a train who told her he was Dr Slocombe,' she said slowly, choosing her words with great care. 'He said he had a practice in Rodney Street but I'm afraid she didn't believe him because he then went on to say that he was a faith healer. So you see—'

The man interrupted. 'So you came up to take a look. I can well understand that,' he said, and his tone was less belligerent; he even took a step back and for the first time his frown disappeared and he gave her a reluctant grin. 'Well, I can assure you that Dr Slocombe is genuine all right. He is also deeply religious and believes in the power of faith. In fact, he's my father – I'm a doctor too. But why were you so keen to check up on him?'

'I suppose natural curiosity,' Gillian said. 'But what does it matter? You've told me that Dr Slocombe really is a doctor and not some sort of confidence trickster, and I've told you why I was in your back yard, so if you don't mind I'll make my way back to the main road and catch a tram, or I'll be late for my tea.'

Her captor stepped back and Gillian moved to pass him, but as she did so he caught hold of her upper arms and pulled her towards him. Puzzled, she looked up into the dark face above her own. 'What on earth . . . ?' she began, only to be interrupted.

'I still don't know exactly what your game is, because I find it difficult to believe your sister could have met my father and not realised he was genuine,' he said. 'Still, I accept your word that it was so, and now it's paying the price time.' And to Gillian's astonishment he dragged her against his chest, kissed her hard and long, and then pushed her away from him.

Startled and appalled, Gillian put a hand up to wipe her lips, then turned to flee, scarcely heeding the words he called after her. 'That's what you get for trespassing,' he shouted. 'And if you trespass a second time, you'll get more of the same.'

Gillian, scrambling back on to the road, cast a quick glance behind her. He was not following her, but standing where she had left him, rolling a cigarette with finicky care and not so much as looking up from the task in hand. Even as she turned away she saw a mocking smile cross his face; a knowing smile. But Gillian did not intend to linger, and set off once more in the direction of her twin.

'He *kissed* you!' Joy's voice rose. 'He actually kissed you? What a nasty old man. I hope you smacked his face good and hard.'

Gillian giggled rather self-consciously. 'No, no, you've got quite the wrong idea; this was Dr Slocombe's *son*, remember. He's a doctor too, so I agree he's not young,

301

probably late twenties or early thirties. As for slapping his face, that was the last thing on my mind. I just wanted to get away because I'd abandoned you in that back street and was worried that you might get into some sort of trouble.'

'What did he look like?' Joy asked curiously, beginning to undress. 'It's hard for me to imagine a young man, because somehow just the title "Doctor" conjures up a picture of someone elderly; that's all I keep seeing whenever I think of that train journey.'

'Yes, but I told you, I never did see Dr Slocombe, only his son, and I imagine it was the father you met on the train,' Gillian pointed out. 'I'm awful sorry, but I never even got a glimpse of him. The son, however, is dark, with a thin face, very black brows which meet across his nose, and dark eyes.' She giggled again. 'To tell you the truth, Joy, most of the time he was so furious with me that I hardly liked to look into his face, but I think most girls would consider him good-looking.'

Joy pulled her dress over her head and went across to the alcove where the girls kept their clothes to hang it up, speaking over her shoulder. 'Well, queen, you certainly did have an adventure! But why on earth did he kiss you? I think it was a great cheek. If you'd screamed . . .'

Gillian laughed. 'No one was working on the cathedral, and so far as I can remember there wasn't a soul on St James Road, so what would have been the use of screaming? There would have been no knight on a white charger to come to my aid. Not that I needed one; he didn't try to chase me, and when I looked back he was just standing there, laughing.' She tossed her head. 'However, should we chance to meet again, I'll give him a good slap round the chops and tell him it comes from my sister.'

Gillian was already in her nightdress, having visited the bathroom before telling her story, and now she climbed into bed and watched as her sister followed suit. 'I notice you told young Slocombe I was your sister, not your twin,' Joy said as she got between the sheets. 'I'm glad, because he might describe you to his father and I'd rather Dr Slocombe never knew it was me checking up on him through you, so to speak.' She snuggled down the bed. 'How frightening to think he might have caught me!' She chuckled. 'I bet if he had done, I should have been the one getting a slap round the chops!'

Gillian giggled. 'Didn't I hear Edward telling you not to keep putting yourself down?' she demanded. 'Young Slocombe seems rather fond of kissing pretty girls, so he would have kissed you just as he kissed me.'

Joy snorted. 'Don't want to be kissed by anyone, except you and Dad,' she said sleepily. 'I wonder if Dr Slocombe really could help me to regain my sight, though? Perhaps I'll go and see him one day; or perhaps I won't.'

'I wonder what sort of doctor the son is?' Gillian said idly. 'Perhaps he's a specialist of some sort, because his father is, judging by the miles of letters after his name.' She gave an enormous yawn. 'Ah well, I dare say we'll never know because we're unlikely to meet again.'

But though she made the remark confidently enough, in her heart Gillian felt that Dr Slocombe's son would make it his business to find her before much more time had passed.

* * *

Alex got down from the fire engine and rubbed a dirty hand across a dirtier forehead. It was two a.m., and Blue Watch was on the night shift, which meant they were on duty from six p.m. to nine a.m. the following day. They had been fighting a warehouse fire since ten the previous evening, and now that it was out at last the crews had been able to leave the scene.

'Awright, boss?' Chalky fell into step beside him as Alex headed for the washroom. 'Got any plans? We're off for the next three days so I thought, the weather being so fine, I'd nip off to my uncle's farm on the Wirral where I've worked before, in me time off.' He stretched luxuriously. 'He's always glad of a hand at harvest time.'

Alex grinned at the younger man. 'The girls are off to the seaside for the day and I've got a date with a young lady,' he said, and watched his companion's eyebrows climb towards his hair. 'No, no, it's nothing serious – it's just that Irene, Fred Finnigan's girl, has got a day off. She can't go with the twins because the coach is full, so I said I'd take her on a steamer to the Isle of Man; she's never been there and it would make up for missing Llandudno.'

'And what does your other girlfriend say to that?' Chalky asked. 'Or should I say girlfriends, because Mrs Clarke's still got that 'orrible pug, hasn't she?'

'She has, but I wouldn't describe her as a girlfriend exactly; I'm nearly forty and she must be six or seven years older than me,' Alex said. 'Mind, you couldn't have a better pal than Ada Clarke. As you know, she works for us from time to time, but she also does a lot extra and won't take a penny for it.'

304

'Why don't you ask her to go with you as well as Irene?' Chalky suggested. He guffawed. 'Wharrit is to be popular with the ladies, eh? Only you don't want young Irene gettin' ideas. What say I come along as well to make up a foursome like? I've never been to the Isle of Man and I can purroff visitin' me uncle for another day.'

Alex frowned. Poor Irene had been trying to get him to herself for months and months; if she heard their twosome was to become a foursome, would it wreck the day for her? On the other hand, if he stuck to his original plan and only he and Irene went aboard the steamer, then she might read into it more than he intended. Alex sighed; what on earth to do for the best?

He began to soap his face and hands vigorously. He had seen the look Gillian had given her twin when Irene had told the twins triumphantly of the planned excursion, had seen Joy banishing a wicked little smile. He knew neither girl wanted him to get involved with Irene, knew too that they had never even considered an involvement with Mrs Clarke. Why, after all the years they had known one another, he still called her 'Mrs Clarke' or 'Auntie Clarke', had never used her first name, though he knew it well enough.

Alex reached for a towel, then glanced at the clock on the wall; if he went up to his bunk now, and provided there were no more shouts, he could have a good sleep and still get home when his shift was over in time to catch the twins before they set off for the coach station. Then he could tell them his change of plan regarding the trip to the Isle of Man. Yes, it might be wisest to do that. The twins and Irene were thick as thieves these days, and Alex knew they loved their Auntie Clarke almost as much as they would have loved their mother, had she lived. But they disapproved of Irene's obvious designs on their father and would probably applaud Chalky's suggestion of a foursome.

Hastily, Alex clapped the younger man on the shoulder. 'Are you sure you want to, old feller? Only we've been up all night so we'll only get a few hours' sleep before we have to be down at the quay.'

'I'll be fine; I'll get me head down straight away and be fresh as a perishin' daisy by the time she sails,' Chalky assured him. 'It's years since I had an outin' like this. How much will it cost, though? I'm not too flush right now.' Alex told him, and Chalky said he thought he could manage to pay his way since he had long wanted to see the Isle of Man. 'But what about Mrs Clarke? She ain't exactly rolling in riches,' he said.

'Oh, if Mrs Clarke is free, I'll pay for her willingly,' Alex said, 'but I won't be able to find out how she's fixed till I'm free at nine o'clock. And I'll tell the twins that the first ones home buy fish and chips for – let me see – fish and chips for seven.'

Chalky rubbed his hands. 'I like young Irene.' He looked at his officer from under thick fair lashes. 'And if she didn't have a crush on some feller old enough to be her dad . . .'

'That's enough, young Chalky,' Alex said severely but with a twitching lip as the two men left the washroom and clattered up the stairs. 'You don't know how to court a girl, that's your trouble. Boxes of Black Magic and bunches of flowers are unknown to you. Four penn'orth of chips and a seat in the back row of the flicks is no substitute for chocolates and roses.'

'Chocs is on ration, don't forget,' Chalky grumbled. 'As for roses . . . why, I dare say they'd charge me two bob for the scrawniest bouquet. Remember, I'm just a perishin' fire bobby, norra sub-officer rollin' in dosh.'

'Oh, ha, ha,' Alex said smartly. 'I suppose you wouldn't like to pop round to the Finnigans' as soon as we're off duty, and tell Irene that you and Mrs Clarke are going to come along?'

'Is that an order?' Chalky said suspiciously. 'Because if so, it ain't bleedin' well fair! She'll want me guts for garters when she hears I'm hornin' in on her day out.'

'Oh nonsense, she'll be delighted to have some young company,' Alex said briskly, crossing his fingers behind his back. 'And she's rare fond of Mrs Clarke – shall we suggest that Dilly comes along as well? I know how you love that little dog.'

Chalky made a rude noise but said that though unwilling, he would do the dirty work and tell poor Irene the bad news, provided Alex promised that the pug should be left behind. 'And if Irene screams and sticks a carvin' knife into me vitals then it'll be your blame, Mr Lawrence, sir,' he said gloomily. 'Come on, let's hear you swear on the Bible that Dilly won't be one o' the party.'

The twins were awoken by their father thumping hard on their bedroom door, then shooting it open. 'Wakey, wakey, rise and shine,' he shouted. 'You don't want to miss the coach and I don't mean to miss the steamer, so get yourselves out of those beds and down into the kitchen to make my breakfast.'

Joy scrambled out of bed and collided with Gillian

doing the same, just as their father crashed the door shut. 'Clumsy idiot,' both girls said in chorus, collapsing back on to their own beds and giggling helplessly. 'You're the clumsy one though, because you must have seen me,' Joy pointed out, standing up and heading for the door. 'Why didn't you dodge?'

'I had my eyes closed,' Gillian confessed. 'I was so excited last night when we came to bed that I couldn't sleep. I heard the church clock chime midnight . . .'

'. . . *We have heard the chimes at midnight, Master Shallow,*' Joy quoted dreamily, opening the bathroom door and beginning to pull her nightdress over her head. 'They say there's a Shakespearean quote for every occasion, but I suppose we're a bit young for that one.' She began to run water into the hand basin. 'Gosh, I thought today would never come, but now it has and I do believe it's a nice one; am I right?'

'Yup,' Gillian said briefly. She nudged her twin with a sharp elbow. 'Shove up, then we can both wash at the same time.'

Presently, Gillian dressed in a blue gingham frock and Joy in one of sunshine yellow, they descended the stairs to the kitchen. Alex was already there, sleeves rolled up, stirring the porridge whilst sipping a mug of tea. He grinned at Gillian, patted Joy's arm, then told them the change of plan and received their congratulations with a smirk. 'I guessed you'd be pleased that Auntie Clarke was sharing in the treat,' he said. 'And Chalky, of course.'

The three of them ate their porridge and drank their tea, then Joy began to wash up whilst Gillian checked the bag containing their swimming costumes and towels. When there was a knock on the door, which opened to reveal Mrs Clarke's rosy face, both twins greeted her with affection, but did not linger.

'We'll miss the perishin' coach if we don't get a move on,' Gillian said, snatching her jacket and her twin's from the hooks by the back door. 'Have a good day, Auntie Clarke, and Dad! See you this evening!'

'And don't forget; whoever gets in first buys the fish and chips,' Alex shouted as the girls, arms linked, went out into the back yard. 'Gillian, keep an eye on your sister if she insists on going in the sea. Remember she can't swim, but I know very well that won't stop her from having a go.' He laughed. 'If she kept on going, I might have to take ship for Ireland to catch up with her!'

As soon as the coach arrived in Llandudno Gillian began to look for Keith, but it was Edward who saw him first. 'There's a fellow standing over there who looks vaguely familiar. Yes, he's spotted you, Gillian; he's smiling and coming over.'

Joy immediately let go of Gillian's arm, and Edward caught her hand and led her forward, saying as he did so: 'Yes, I was right; the chap in the blazer and flannels is Gillian's friend. I've seen him before – our schools were in the same area of the city – but we've never actually met. Introduce us, Gillian.'

Gillian had been chattering away to Keith, but at Edward's words she swung round, flushing. 'Oh, how dreadful I am! Poor Keith hasn't even met my twin, let alone you, Edward.' She performed the introductions, explaining that Edward was the boy who used to take Joy to and from school when she, Gillian, had taken up her place at St Hilda's. 'It isn't everyone that I trust to take care of my twin,' she said, 'but both Joy and I trust Edward completely. Now, where shall we go first?'

Keith opened his mouth to reply, but Edward cut across him. 'Gillian should have explained that I mean to pay my way since I'm an uninvited guest,' he said gruffly. 'If the Imperial will allow me to share your lunch and to pay for it, then I'll be quite happy, but if not, I can get myself a sandwich and a cup of tea somewhere else and then meet up with you later.'

Keith laughed. 'It's all right, there'll be plenty of food for four,' he said. 'Because it's such a gloriously warm and sunny day, the housekeeper has packed me a hamper, so we can have a picnic either on the beach or up the Great Orme, whichever you would prefer.' He looked at Joy as though expecting her to speak, then looked quickly away, and Edward realised, with a slight sinking of the heart, that Keith was embarrassed by Joy's blindness and would avoid even addressing her directly if he could do so without appearing rude. Still, Edward comforted himself, by the end of the day Keith would grow accustomed, might even forget Joy's disability as her delightful personality made itself felt.

But Gillian was speaking. 'Oh, a picnic!' she said excitedly. 'That will be lovely. But where is this hamper? I see no sign of it.'

'It's back at the hotel; the housekeeper guessed you wouldn't want to lug it around all morning, so we're to pick it up from her room at half past twelve. As for what we should do first, it's entirely up to you. There's the pier, the beach, the Great Orme and of course the promenade, as well as some of the most impressive shops and big stores in the whole of North Wales. Take your pick.'

Edward saw Gillian open her mouth to reply and was pretty sure she would go for the shops, but a small, firm voice cut across Gillian's opening sentence. 'I'm going on the beach,' Joy said. 'There are plenty of shops in Liverpool, and though everyone raves about the views from the summit of the Great Orme, views don't mean much to me. But I've longed and longed for the beach and the sea, so if you will take me down there and leave me, I'll be happy as – as a sandboy.'

'I agree; I'd prefer to go on the beach and paddle – or even bathe – rather than trail round shops or play the machines on the pier,' Edward said quickly. 'If you two want to go off by yourselves . . .'

Keith began to say that they could meet up outside the Imperial Hotel at quarter past twelve, but Gillian interrupted. 'You're right, queen, it's a brilliant day and you aren't the only one who's longing for the beach,' she said, and Edward beamed at her; it might not be true – he still thought that left to herself Gillian would have opted for the shops – but she was a loving sister and clearly wanted her twin to enjoy this special day.

Keith had flushed up to the roots of his hair and was now muttering that of course he should have guessed that the sands and the sea were what people came to Llandudno for, and that his friends were no exception. So Gillian seized Keith's arm, Edward took Joy's hand, and the four of them set off for the beach.

The beach! Joy settled herself on the sand and felt the salt breeze on her face, lifting her hair and caressing her bare legs and arms, and knew an enormous rush of happiness. She had dreamed about this moment all week and now it had arrived and she was at the seaside! She knew that young ladies of seventeen did not normally dig holes, create sandcastles, or turn over rocks in the hope of surprising a crab or some other sea creature, but today she was just Joy, and meant to get the most out of this rare treat. Indeed, when she had a job and a salary she meant to save up until she had enough money to take herself, her father and Gillian to the seaside for a whole week's holiday, but that day was still far distant. For now, she would tuck her dress into her knickers and play!

Accordingly, she announced that she was going to make a sandcastle, and very soon Edward, Gillian and even Keith joined in, bringing her stones and seaweed to decorate what they assured her was becoming a vast and impressive edifice. Joy was aware that Keith was embarrassed by her blindness, but if he was as nice as Gillian said he was, then he would soon conquer what she realised was really a fear of the unknown. She wanted to get to know him better, however, and knew this would not be possible whilst he was ill at ease.

So she began to put herself out, catching his wet and sandy hand – having first ascertained that it was indeed his and not Edward's – and saying teasingly that he didn't want to dirty his nails by digging too deeply into the sand. 'You're afraid you'll be pinched by a crab or pulled down into Davy Jones's locker by an anemone, that's why you say you won't bathe,' she accused him. 'Can you swim? I can't, but Edward is going to teach me.'

'I can swim like a fish,' Keith boasted. 'I'll teach Gillian if Edward's going to teach you. Only we'll have to leave going in the sea for at least an hour after our picnic, otherwise we'll sink like stones and nobody will ever hear of us again.'

Joy crowed with delight at the mental picture of the four of them so swollen with food that they could no longer float, but refused to agree to put off at least a paddle. 'Just you roll up your trousers, you fellers, and give me a hand each and take me down to the sea!' she commanded. 'I don't mean to leave this beach until I've been in the sea as far as my knees. We can come back later, after our picnic and a trip up the Great Orme, and swim then.'

'And don't forget the pier and the prom, and all the other amusements,' Keith reminded her. 'If we do all the things you and your sister want to do, it'll be midnight before you get your swim. I know it sounds very romantic to bathe by moonlight, but I don't think it's wise.'

Joy chuckled appreciatively. 'I could bathe at midnight and never know it,' she said cheerfully. 'For me, you could say it was always midnight.' She wagged a finger to where she knew Keith was sitting. 'Don't feel bad about it; I always love it when someone forgets I'm blind and treats me like a human being. You'd be surprised how ordinary I am, apart from my lack of sight.'

For a moment there was a shocked silence, and Joy feared she might have gone too far, but then Keith laughed and a hand came out of the darkness and gripped her own. 'On your feet, my lovely lass,' Keith's voice said. 'I rolled up my trousers while you were speaking and I see Edward has done the same. So now we'll go a-paddling, and if you bunch up your skirt and tuck it into your belt we'll take you in as far as your knees, and chase off any intrepid crabs who try to take a nip at your toes.'

One hand gripped by each boy, Joy set off fearlessly towards where she assumed the sea must be, for she could hear the waves advancing and retreating, the crash as a wave came inshore and the crunching drag as it retreated, carrying a good deal of shingle with it. They entered the water slowly, and Joy was about to shout to her twin to join them when Gillian's voice spoke in her ear. 'What's all this then? I don't grudge you Edward, but did you have to steal Keith as well? I thought a four-some meant each girl had a boy, but now I see it means one girl has two boys and the other girl has to make do with her own company!'

Joy released Edward's hand for a second and stooped to scoop up a handful of seawater and splash it to where she imagined Gillian stood. She acted so quickly that Gillian had no chance to take evasive action and Joy realised she had scored a direct hit when she heard her sister splutter and spit. 'Serve you right!' she shouted, as excited and happy as any five-year-old would have been.

She grabbed Edward's hand again, just as her bunched-up skirt slid out of her belt and a moment later was clinging, wet and clammy, to her bare legs. She would have scolded Edward, but realised the two men were talking to each other. 'Have you got her?' That was Keith, his voice anxious. 'If so, I'll give Gillian a hand; I just hope she isn't going to blame me for ruining that pretty dress.'

'Of course I've got her,' Edward said, sounding

indignant. 'But why . . .' Joy felt him twist to look over his shoulder, then felt a silent laugh travel down the length of his arm and into her left hand. It was a most peculiar sensation and needed an explanation.

'Why are you laughing?' she demanded, as Keith released her right hand and splashed shorewards. 'What's happened? Oh, how I wish I could *see*!'

But the laughter was bubbling up now, impossible to suppress. 'Gillian tried to dodge when you chucked the water, fell backwards, and is now cursing and laughing and being hauled to her feet by her fellow, soaked to the waist,' Edward informed her, between chuckles. 'Oh my, someone's in for a scolding!'

Joy was sitting on a convenient ledge of rock, the sun warm on her bare shoulders, for she was still in her bathing costume, having thoroughly enjoyed herself in the gentle waves. In the time at their disposal, her bathe had had to be a short one and she could not pretend that Edward had taught her to swim, but he had held her chin whilst she flailed around and had then suggested that instead of the breaststroke she might start off with what he called a doggy paddle. 'Animals swim by nature, simply moving their legs as though they were running on land,' he had explained. 'Don't worry, I shan't let you go, but if you pretend you're Dilly I dare say it will help you to get the feel of the water.'

Joy had had great fun and, as Edward soon discovered, she was completely fearless. He had commented upon the fact, making Joy giggle. 'Why should I be afraid?' she had countered. 'I remember you saying that the sea was shallow for a long way out, and every now and then, when I drop my feet by accident, I can feel the sand. Do you think if I fell off a boat far out to sea I'd simply drown?'

'Yes, well, I don't think we'll put it to the test,' Edward had said firmly. 'Are you tired yet? I think it's time we went back, otherwise those gannets will have eaten our share of the picnic as well as their own.'

'Oh, I'd almost forgotten the picnic,' Joy had said as Edward had helped her to her feet and they had begun to wade shorewards. ''Is the Imperial very grand, Edward? I know the reception hall must be huge because our voices had a sort of echo, and the lounge where we waited whilst Keith and Gillian fetched the hamper was big too. But what's it *like*? Never having been inside such a posh place before, I can't imagine it.'

'It is rather grand,' Edward had admitted. 'Potted palms and statues of flimsily dressed ladies bearing urns on their shoulders; you know the sort of thing.' As he spoke, he had been steering Joy up on to the dry sand and soon they had re-joined the other two.

'Thank goodness you've arrived,' Gillian had said. 'We're starving, aren't we, Keith?' She had reached up a hand to take her twin's and pulled Joy to sit on the very ledge of rock she still occupied. 'Do you want to get changed before we eat? I've already done so, but I don't mind helping you if you'd rather eat fully dressed.'

This, however, Joy had declined to do, loving the feel of sun and breeze on her body. She had felt amazingly free and amazingly hungry, and had chattered away to her companions as they devoured all the delicious things in the hamper. When at last they had eaten their fill, Gillian had patted Joy's hand to get her attention. 'You spent such ages in the sea, dearest Joy, that the afternoon is half over and we've still not gone up the Orme or walked along the pier. The coach leaves at half past six but we've time to take a tram up the Orme. Only everyone says that the view is best as the sun begins to sink, so if it's all the same to you we'll do the pier first.'

Joy had pulled a face. 'Would it ruin all your plans if you left me on the beach?' she had enquired hopefully. 'I promise not to move from this spot – it's well above where the tide could come in, isn't it? – and I'd love to go home with a tan, which I'm unlikely to get walking along the pier or catching a tram to the top of the Orme, because I suppose I should have to put my clothes and shoes back on.'

This time it had been Keith who answered her. 'You're right there; folk would think it very odd indeed if you went sightseeing in your swimsuit,' he had said. A hand had reached out and touched her costume, making Joy jump. 'Yes, it's still wet. Well, if you don't want to see the pier and the Orme . . . oh, hell, I'm so sorry, Joy. I keep forgetting.'

'Don't be sorry,' Joy had said quickly. 'I told you, it's nice when people forget.' She had then turned towards Gillian, sitting beside her. 'I know you worry about leaving me in strange places, but I've got my white stick, and, as I said, I shan't move.'

'I'll stay with you; I came for the sea and the sand so I don't mind missing out on the pier,' Edward had said, and Joy had thought she could hear a little wistfulness in his voice. Accordingly, she had turned on him sharply.

'Oh, for God's sake, Edward, stop behaving as if I were five years old and completely dependent on other

317

people. I don't suppose it will take the rest of the afternoon for you and the others to walk the length of the pier and back and I'll be perfectly happy here, honest to God I will.' She had leaned forward and fumbled with the lid of the hamper, opened it, and begun to poke the contents. 'There's still a packet of those delicious cakes with only one taken out, and some sandwiches . . .' she had picked the packet up and sniffed it, 'oh, ham and pickle – my favourite. I won't guarantee the food will still be around when you get back; perhaps that will encourage you not to be too long away.'

'Well, if you're sure . . .' Gillian had begun, and Joy had heard the uncertainty in her voice. 'If we just go to the pier and come straight back . . . why, we shan't be gone for more than twenty minutes. What can happen in twenty minutes?'

'A lot,' Edward had said grimly before Joy could reply. 'But if young Joy here really wants to sunbathe, and promises not to move away from this spot . . . well, I dare say she'll enjoy just being alone for a change.'

Thus it was that Joy now sat on the ledge of rock with a ham and pickle sandwich in one hand and a towel within reach of the other, lest the sunshine, magnified by salt water droplets, begin to burn, and her shoulders need to be covered.

'Lovely, loverly day,' Joy carolled beneath her breath as she finished off the sandwich and rummaged in the hamper for one of the little cakes. 'If I was lucky enough to live here, I'd come down to the beach every day, and find a friend who could teach me to swim properly, not just to doggy paddle. If I lived here . . .'

She ate the cake, dusted her hands and then smoothed

her hair back from her forehead, smiling to herself as she did so. She remembered Mr Dodman and the cap he always wore out of doors, so that when he removed it his brow was white at the top and mahogany brown further down. She did not wish to become two-tone as well as unable to see, so she slicked her fringe back from her face.

She was leaning back and enjoying the sunshine when something else occurred to her. If she left her dark glasses in place, then when she removed them she would look like a panda. Better to take them off now so that her whole face would be a beautiful golden brown, she thought hopefully. She was in the act of removing them and fumbling for her handbag, which contained her spectacle case, when a group of people surged past, talking and laughing. As their voices faded, Joy was jerked upright as if pulled by invisible strings. Someone was whistling a catchy little tune to which she could not give a name – as she had been unable to give it a name on both the previous occasions on which she had heard it. Joy jumped up, and without giving a single thought to the promises she had so eagerly made, set off in pursuit of the whistler.

But running on soft sand is never easy even for a sighted person, and it was not long before Joy stubbed her toe on what she assumed was a small rock, or a very large pebble, and gave a squeak of dismay. But even this could not stop her eager pursuit of the whistler. Her keen hearing had noted the fact that he had veered to the left, towards the sea, but no thought of possible danger so much as crossed her mind. She simply thought that hard, wet sand was a good deal easier to run on and followed doggedly in the whistler's wake.

It was not until she felt the first little wave splash up over her feet that the dangers of her situation struck her and she stopped running abruptly. Whatever was she doing? She had scattered promises like chaff in the wind, and was now behaving as though they were indeed chaff, and meant nothing. She put a hand to her side, suddenly aware that she was breathless and had no idea of her present position, save that she was on the very edge of the sea, that her stubbed toe was throbbing and that the whistling she had followed was fading into the distance, getting fainter with every moment.

She took a couple more steps in the direction she thought the whistler had taken, then stopped again, really frightened for the first time. She had believed she was walking along the tide line, yet her last step had brought the water halfway up to her knees. Telling herself that all she needed to do was veer to the right, she turned slightly in that direction, took another step and realised that she had somehow managed to get on to a rocky part of the shore; the very part where Edward had said earlier that they might find crabs, sea anemones and little fishes.

For a moment, terror threatened to overwhelm her. If she fell and banged her head on a rock she could drown, with half the holidaymakers on the beach looking on, never dreaming that she was in trouble. Joy stood very still. Even if she regained the safety of dry sand, she could walk straight past the spot she had abandoned and be lost once more.

But simply standing still had calmed her, she realised, so she continued to stand motionless, her face turned away from the sea, and her heart gradually ceased its mad hammering and began to beat normally once more. As it did so, the perspiration which had run down her neck and breasts began to cool, and she told herself that she was in no danger from the turning tide, because Keith had said the water never came right up to the promenade save in winter, and now it was summer, the sea was calm, and the wind was negligible. I was a fool to run after the whistler, she told herself. If I move very carefully and very, very slowly, at least I should be able, when I feel dry sand beneath my feet, to sit quietly down and wait for the others to return from the pier. The beach isn't going to get up and walk away, after all.

But right now, her main objective was to regain that beach, if possible, unhurt. Then she would simply sit down and wait. Considerably heartened by the thought, she moved one foot cautiously forward . . . and felt the roughness of a chunk of rock beneath her toes. Hastily, she replaced her foot in its former position, then bent over and felt around her. Big stones or small rocks . . . she supposed that if she simply stood where she was her friends would spot her and come to her rescue, but it would be a good deal less humiliating if she could reach the sand and sit down. She would tell Gillian that she had had a fancy to cool her feet in the briny but had ventured too far and got caught in the rocks.

She stood where she was for a moment longer, but her legs were growing tired so she descended to all fours, and nearly came to grief when her seeking hands found what must, she thought, be a rock pool and she plunged up to the elbows in water. Fighting an urge to burst into tears, she was about to try another direction when she heard someone splashing towards her and a voice said: 'You all right, chuck? Tide's on the turn and once the water covers them rocks you can be hurt bad, honest to God you can.' Hands seized her beneath her armpits and helped her to her feet and her rescuer said encouragingly: 'That's the ticket! Now tek hold of me mauly and we'll give them rocks a wide berth . . . there's quite a big one coming up . . .'

Joy began to ask just where the big rock was when she found it by the simple expedient of walking into it and would have fallen again but for her helper's quick grab. 'Good God, gal, are you blind? It's perishin' well big enough!'

'Yes, I'm blind,' Joy said wearily. 'I thought you'd guessed. I got amongst the rocks because I can't see 'em . . . so you see I'm very grateful.'

'You're blind? Dear God, queen, you shouldn't oughter be left alone on the beach! Anything could ha' happened! Where's your minder, then?'

'My friends have walked out along the pier. I was supposed to stay just where I was put, so if I'd done as I promised . . .' Joy said, trying not to sound offended at his reference to her 'minder'. As she spoke she felt firm sand under her feet and turned towards her rescuer. 'You are good! And don't blame my pals, because it was all my own fault. Now, can you see some towels and a hamper . . . shoes and things as well? Only if you can take me to the little camp we made on the shore they need never find out.'

'Too late,' her companion said. 'There's a girl . . .'

He stopped speaking as trembling hands seized Joy's and Gillian began to berate her and hug her all at the same time, whilst Joy gave up all pretence of being brave and self-confident and wept, taking her twin's proffered hanky and blowing her nose heartily.

Presently, however, she regained control and turned to her rescuer. 'This is my sister – my twin sister,' she explained. She turned back to Gillian. 'This gentleman saw I'd got amongst the rocks by mistake and rescued me. I don't know what might have happened if he'd not seen I was in trouble.' She held out her hand, and after a second's hesitation her rescuer grasped it. 'I'm so grateful, truly I am,' Joy said awkwardly. 'You might well have saved my life, because I kept thinking that if I fell and bashed my head . . .'

''S awright, queen,' the man said diffidently. 'Glad to have been of use.' He chuckled. 'Now off wi' you, because I reckon you've had a bad fright and need to sit down and recover yourself.' He waved aside Gillian's heartfelt thanks but could not resist telling her that in his opinion Joy should not have been left alone.

'Actually, she wasn't alone, though she thought she was,' Gillian said. 'I wasn't going to tell her, because I know she likes to be independent, but one of our party refused to leave her on her own on the beach. He stayed about ten yards away but unfortunately, what with the hot sun and the meal we'd just eaten, he fell asleep. He awoke to find her gone and was in a rare old state, so he rushed to find us, only we had no idea where she was either. Now he's quartering the beach . . .'

'Poor Edward – I take it it was Edward who stayed behind?' Joy interposed. She chuckled. 'We'd best go after him, Gillian; it wouldn't do to lose two people in one day.'

'That's right, missy, but get some clothes on because the sun's mortal hot,' her rescuer said. 'Oh, hang on – there's someone slogging along the beach towards us, coming from the direction of the pier; would it be your pal? Sandy hair and freckles?'

'That's him,' Gillian and Joy said in chorus, Gillian adding: 'And the dark-haired feller just behind him is Keith. I'm sure they'll be as grateful to you as we are.'

'Forget it,' Joy's rescuer said gruffly. 'And now I'd better be gettin' back to the missus or she'll think I've run away to sea.'

The twins repeated their thanks as the man's shuffling footsteps faded and the two boys joined them. Joy smiled in their direction and gave her sister's hand a convulsive squeeze. 'It was all my fault,' she said contritely. 'I was so stupid; a group of people passed me . . .' She told the story of her foolish flight as Gillian began to lead her towards their encampment on the rocks, assuring Edward as they went that no one could possibly blame him for Joy's mad behaviour.

As they walked, arm in arm, Joy felt something trickle down her legs; was it seawater or blood? She pulled at Gillian's hand and bent her head to look, and just for a split second she saw her own legs, scratched and bruised, with a thin trickle of blood running down her shin. She gasped, and started to tell Gillian that she could see, but then everything was blackness once more and Gillian was saying they would have to take her back to the hotel and get some sticking plasters before they all caught a tram to the top of the Great Orme.

*   *   *

As they sat on the grass at the summit of the Great Orme, Keith suggested that the three of them might like to visit Llandudno again over the August bank holiday weekend, but though they liked the idea neither Edward nor Joy felt that it was fair on Keith and Gillian.

'We could come again at the end of August or early September, just before your job here finishes,' Edward suggested. 'We'll have to see how we go on. Both Joy and I hope to be in reasonable jobs and earning a salary quite soon, so we should be able to afford another coach trip. Only next time, we'll provide the picnic.'

Keith pressed Gillian to come down on bank holiday Monday, but Gillian was oddly evasive. 'I'm not sure what I'll be doing,' she said. 'As you know, the Ocean Assurance Company employs me as holiday relief . . .'

'Oh, come on, Gilly,' Keith said impatiently. 'No insurance company would dream of expecting any employee to work on bank holiday Monday. It's different for me because the hotel will be packed to bursting and as busy as it's possible to be, but . . .'

'There you are, you see!' Gillian said triumphantly. 'Even if I *could* get down, I wouldn't see much of you, would I? It's no fun playing the machines on the pier by yourself, or buying fish and chips and sharing them with the seagulls because the friend you've come to see is working. If I could come on a Wednesday, of course . . . but Ocean Assurance wouldn't release me again, so I'm afraid we're doomed not to meet until your work here finishes.'

Keith pulled a face. 'And then I'll be getting ready to return to Cambridge and you'll be swotting for your Higher School Certificate,' he said in a disgruntled tone. 'Anyone would think we weren't going steady!'

'Well, we're not,' Gillian snapped. 'We're too young for that sort of commitment. I'm only seventeen and you're only two years older; either of us might meet someone else.'

'I shan't; meet anyone else, I mean,' Keith said quickly. 'You know how I feel about you, Gilly.'

'And *don't* call me Gilly; you know I hate it. Why, even my twin doesn't shorten my name,' Gillian said crossly. 'Don't start taking me for granted, Keith Bain.'

Keith began to mutter indignantly that he was only taking her for granted because that was how she treated him, but Joy felt she could not let Gillian forget that their lovely day had largely been possible only because of Keith. 'Shut up, *Gilly*,' she said brusquely. 'You're tired and irritable and don't mean a word you've said. Just you apologise to Keith, thank him for a lovely day, and tell me what I'm sitting here staring at.'

Edward, who had been very silent since Joy's experience on the beach, came over and sat down next to her. 'I'll tell you what we're looking at,' he said quietly. 'And I'll tell you how sorry I am . . .'

But Joy hushed him at once. 'If I've said it once I've said it a dozen times, it was all my own fault,' she reminded him. 'And before you say another word I'll tell you what I *think* I'm looking at.'

Edward laughed and squeezed her hand. 'You're a generous lass,' he said. 'Fire ahead, then.'

Joy began to speak in a hollow, echoing voice, the tone she had once heard a fortune-teller at the fair use. 'I see a wide expanse of ocean with tiny waves, and purple mountains in the background,' she said. 'I see fields of golden corn and gentle, sloping green meadows, dotted with sheep. I see a cliff edge and a blue sky, and warm yellow sunshine . . .'

'Not bad, but you've left out miles and miles of sand, ridged by the waves, and something else which you must have been hearing all day,' he said, and when Joy, after much thought, admitted herself baffled, he announced triumphantly: 'Seagulls, my dear little halfwit; they're everywhere, great strong wings taking them round and round the highest cliffs, and then they come down, all greedy yellow eyes and sharp beaks, to see if they can persuade us to part with sandwich crusts.'

'Oh, I wish I could feed them and stroke their lovely white backs,' Joy said longingly, and heard Edward chuckle.

'Their backs are dove grey; only their undersides are white,' he told her. 'And I'm not sure they'd appreciate being stroked.' She heard him rummaging in the picnic hamper, then felt some pieces of bread being pushed into her hand. 'Throw them one at a time, as high as you can, and I'll tell you whether you hit or miss. 'By the time you've run out of bread, we'll have to catch the very next tram to the town, because we don't want to miss the coach.'

'Couldn't we walk down?' Joy asked hopefully, but Gillian, overhearing, immediately vetoed the idea. 'It would take too long,' she assured her sister. 'Come on then, let's get going.' She turned her head and addressed Keith. 'I bet the hamper's as light as a feather now that we've eaten just about everything.'

'As light as a gull's feather,' Joy said. 'Oh, what a wonderful day this has been!'

*   *   *

327

Keith felt very alone when he saw the other three climbing aboard the coach and taking possession of the back seat. He had often envied Gillian her twin's companionship and now he felt a twinge of envy of Edward as well, because Gillian had told him that Billy and Doris Williams were the proud parents of five sons and a daughter.

Now, having spent a day with Edward as well as with Gillian's twin, Keith had begun to feel part of a real group, an enjoyable sensation which he hoped to repeat when they were all in Liverpool once more. He was standing on the bottom step of the coach, bidding farewell to his three friends, when the vehicle's engine roared into life and he stepped hastily back on to the paving stones. The noise of the engine drowned their words but he knew they were thanking him and saying goodbye as well as waving and, in Joy's case, blowing kisses. Keith laughed; it had seemed strange to begin with that she was exactly like the girl he planned to make his wife – oh, not for many years, but eventually – but it was extraordinary how quickly one could grow accustomed. They were an extremely pretty pair, too, though Joy did not seem aware of the fact, which made her easier company in a way than his beloved Gillian.

He knew that Gillian was academically very bright indeed and she had several times referred to her twin as being the more practical of the two, though he had seen no sign of this. Joy had done very well at Blinkers, coming out with a sheaf of diplomas, and she was well read, too, always quoting the classics; she must have memorised great chunks of Shakespeare if her conversation was any guide. Keith had felt uncomfortable in her presence at first, but very soon her liveliness and sense of humour had made him forget her disability, and by the time they had paddled in the sea and begun their picnic he had felt totally at ease with her and eager for her friendship.

Edward, too, was someone Keith wanted for a friend. The other fellow was older than he, though only by a few months, but they had got along very well. Edward was reading accountancy and Keith himself was reading medicine, so one might have been forgiven for thinking they had little in common, but this had not proved to be the case. Keith was fascinated by engines, as was Edward, and both were fans of Everton football club. Before they parted they had arranged to go to a match together when both were back in Liverpool, and Keith was already looking forward to introducing this new chap to his friends.

He waited until the coach was out of sight, then sighed and headed for the promenade once more. He would not be back on duty until the following day, but he decided he might as well take the hamper back to Mrs Hubbard and assure her that the contents had been truly appreciated by one and all.

As he walked, he wondered why Gillian's attitude towards him had suddenly become, if not antagonistic, definitely less loving. Without being conceited Keith considered that he was quite a catch, and had assumed that Gillian was aware of this. Yet today she had been rather offhand with him, not at all her usual appreciative self. If he were honest her twin had been the friendlier of the two. Odd! He knew himself too well to imagine that he could take on a blind girlfriend; he had no intention of being more than brotherly to young Joy. Besides, he had always been sports mad; he and Gillian played tennis together in the mixed doubles, and had won cups for their prowess. She did not swim but he meant to teach her, and like himself she excelled at most forms of sport. Joy, because of her disability, could scarcely indulge in any sporting activity. But what was more important was the fact that he had always thought he and Gillian would make a match of it one day, and now she had made him worry that she was cooling off.

If that was so, however, he knew he could easily find another girl, though he had no desire to do so. Perhaps he was only imagining that Gillian was no longer quite so fond; perhaps it was just the excitement of being in a strange town which had made her seem different. He would wait and see how things stood when they were all back in Liverpool.

Whistling a tune beneath his breath, Keith set off for the hotel.

Chapter Thirteen

Chalky went round to the Finnigans' house as soon as he had finished his breakfast. He went the back way, uncomfortably aware that he was not looking forward to the forthcoming interview. He knew Irene very well indeed, mainly because of the many times Alex had paired them off together, and though Irene had always put a good face on it Chalky knew she had not been pleased.

On previous occasions, however, there had been no question of Irene going anywhere with Alex, because he had always refused even Irene's most innocent suggestion that they spend time together. Outings to Sefton Park, trips on the ferry to New Brighton, a visit to the cinema had all been passed immediately on to Chalky, and though Irene affected complaisance Chalky knew that on each occasion he had been, if not actively resented, at least second best.

Now however, knocking on the Finnigans' back door, he was horribly aware that Irene might well have believed herself to have broken down Alex's resistance at last. This time the invitation to take a trip to the Isle of Man had come from Alex. True, it had been given because Irene had been unable to join the twins and Edward on their outing to Llandudno, but Chalky rather feared that this fact would have been pushed aside by Irene. He had seen her only once since Alex had issued the invitation and had noted both her triumph and her excitement, realising that the poor girl honestly thought that Alex had given in at last and had begun to take her passion for him seriously.

So when the back door shot open and Irene gave him a big smile and invited him in, Chalky entered the house with considerable trepidation. The kitchen was crowded with Finnigans large and small, and all of them were dressed ready to go out. 'Mornin', young Chalky,' Fred Finnigan said jovially. 'Ain't it a lovely mornin'? Seein' as how young Irene here is off on a pleasure trip, Mother and meself thought we'd take the kids to Seffy for the day. Mother's packed a picnic, Timmy's got a bag full of scraps for the ducks and Solly and meself have got half a dozen bottles of Corona, so we mean to have us dinners by the boating lake, and have a pot of tea and a bun at that there caff down by the water for us tea.'

Mrs Finnigan looked up from the bread she was buttering and grinned at Chalky. 'Want to join us, young feller?' she asked. 'I'm sure I've done enough grub for ten, so you're welcome to come along.'

Feeling extremely self-conscious, Chalky shook his head. 'No can do, Mrs F, I'm off to the Isle of Man,' he said. He turned to face Irene. 'I mentioned to the boss that I were at a loose end and he said I might as well go along, so I've got a ticket for the good old *Tulip*.'

There was a sudden stillness in the kitchen. Irene, already half into a light mackintosh, stood like a statue, one arm in the coat, the other grasping the second sleeve. '*What* did you say?' she said at last. 'You don't mean you're coming aboard the *Tulip* with Alex and me?'

'Well, yes,' Chalky said diffidently. He saw Irene's eyes widen and then narrow until she looked like an angry cat about to pounce, and broke into hurried speech. 'It's a free country, Irene. It were real kind of Mr Lawrence to suggest I might go along.'

Irene had been swelling with indignation, but at his words she seemed to see reason. 'Well, I can't stop you comin', but just you remember, Chalky, that two's company and three's a crowd. You can bloody well keep clear of Alex and meself.'

'Language, chuck,' Fred Finnigan said reprovingly. 'That weren't a very nice thing to say to your old friend Chalky. Besides, the *Tulip* must hold gettin' on for a hundred souls. Likely, young Chalky here will meet up wi' some pals once he's aboard and you won't so much as spy each other until you're disembarkin' at the end o' the day.'

'I suppose that's true,' Irene said grudgingly. She brightened. 'We're going to have our lunch in the *Tulip*'s dining room; a proper meal, not perishin' sandwiches. Alex said he couldn't be bothered to make a picnic when he'd just come off the night shift. I did offer . . .' she opened the back door as she spoke, bidding her family goodbye and actually smiling at Chalky as they turned into the jigger, ''cos I enjoy a picnic on a lovely day like this, but I'd rather have a proper meal, especially since I'll be sharing it with Alex.'

'You won't, because Mrs Clarke will probably make a picnic for all of us,' Chalky said thoughtlessly, and could have bitten his tongue out. Once Irene realised there would be four of them, she would also realise that the tête-à-tête she had planned with Chalky's sub-officer was unlikely to come to fruition, and react accordingly.

333

'Mrs Clarke will make a picnic,' Irene said slowly, giving undue emphasis, Chalky thought, to each word. Then she grabbed Chalky's shoulders and swung him round to face her so that they were almost nose to nose. Chalky was tall but Irene was only a couple of inches shorter, and looking into her eyes as comprehension dawned Chalky flinched back, reading the retribution there. 'I suppose the pair of you had it all planned,' she said bitterly, giving him a shake. 'I suppose Mrs Clarke is coming on the *Tulip*, and probably that horrible Dilly as well.' She was gripping Chalky's upper arms now so hard that his muscles squeaked and he guessed he would have bruises by morning. 'Go on, Chalky bloody White. Mrs Clarke is to be the fourth member of our party, isn't she? Well, I don't mean to go on making a fool of myself chasing a feller who invites me out and then asks a stupid fireman and a silly old woman as well so that we shan't be alone. He can stick his bloody trip where the monkey stuck its nuts, and you can tell him so from me.'

Chalky had freed himself from her grip, though not without difficulty, and now he began to expostulate, to say that it wasn't like that at all, she had completely misread the situation. 'And Dilly isn't coming, honest to God she isn't,' he added hastily. 'Alex thought, when he mentioned the trip to Mrs Clarke, that she does an awful lot for the Lawrence family and might appreciate—'

'Oh, and I suppose I do nothing!' Irene hissed. Her cheeks were flushed a deep pink and her eyes sparkled with fury, and Chalky thought he had never seen her look prettier. 'Well, you can go and tell your beloved Alex that I've got better things to do than chase round after him, and next time he wants someone to take Joy shopping, or to a job interview, he can count me out.'

She turned away and Chalky, genuinely shocked, grabbed her and twisted her round to face him. 'You nasty little bitch!' he said violently. 'Okay, I admit you help out with Joy from time to time, but you do no more than everyone else does, and if I were to tell Alex or any other member of the Brigade what you just said they'd not speak to you in a month of Sundays. Just you say you didn't mean it or I'll spread the word that you're nothing but a selfish little cat!'

Irene began to answer him hotly, but suddenly her resistance seemed to crumble and she began to sob in a helpless, frightened sort of way. She sounded so like the little girl Chalky remembered from when he had first joined Blue Watch that his heart melted. It wasn't her fault that she had fallen in love with the unattainable Alex. He, Chalky, might think that it was just puppy love, but he supposed that puppy love could be just as painful as the real sort.

He took the sobbing girl into his arms and when she turned her face up to his and began to wail that her heart was broken and she would never love anyone as she loved Alex, it seemed only natural to bend his head and kiss her tear-wet eyes and cheeks, and finally to home in on her quivering mouth. In all the time that he had been taking her to the cinema and squiring her to dances he had never kissed her, because, subconsciously or not, he had considered her Alex's property. But now she flung her arms round his neck and, still sobbing and hiccuping, began to respond.

That was why, when Mrs Clarke and Alex boarded

the *Tulip* later that morning with a carry-out for four, they climbed the gangway alone.

'I can't imagine what must have happened. Chalky left the station with me when our shift ended at nine, and said he was going to call at the Finnigans' as soon as he'd had his breakfast, but even if he changed his mind Irene was mad to come and I thought she wouldn't have missed it for anything,' Alex said as they stood by the rail, anxiously scanning the scurrying crowds below. 'But I don't intend to get off now we're aboard. If they can't manage to arrive before we sail, then it's their own fault if they're left behind.'

Mrs Clarke looked guilty. 'Oh, Mr Lawrence, I'm very much afraid it may be my fault,' she said apologetically. 'I know how fond of you young Irene is, and how she's been trying to get you alone now for months, if not years. The fact that you invited her to visit the Isle of Man and then added two more members to the party without so much as a word to her must have upset her. I know Irene is normally an even-tempered girl, but I've seen her lose control once or twice when things haven't gone her way and she can really get quite angry.'

'I believe you,' Alex said fervently. He remembered an occasion when Irene had dropped a well-buttered muffin on the floor and Dilly, seizing it, had dared to growl at her when she bent to retrieve it. The little dog had sailed across the kitchen and out of the back door on the toe of Irene's boot, and Irene had used unladylike language and slammed the door in Dilly's face when the pug, gulping down her booty, had tried to regain her favourite place beneath the kitchen table.

336

Alex grinned to himself, remembering. Mrs Clarke was right: Irene could indeed lose her temper with a vengeance when things were not going her way. But he hastened to reassure his old friend. 'Oh, nonsense, Mrs C! If it's anyone's fault it's mine, and I refuse to take responsibility for one rather spoilt little girl's cutting off her nose to spite her face, because that's what it amounts to.' The *Tulip* hooted her siren and began to move slowly away from the quayside, and Alex put his hand under Mrs Clarke's elbow to steer her towards the nearest companionway which, he knew, led down to the dining saloon where the staff were even now offering passengers cups of coffee or tea and some large and remarkably jammy doughnuts.

'Shouldn't we tell someone that we're two passengers short?' Mrs Clarke said uneasily as Alex settled her in a chair and prepared to join the queue for refreshments. 'Oh, I do feel bad about it, Mr Lawrence.'

'Nonsense,' Alex said again, but even more briskly this time. 'And isn't it about time that you stopped calling me Mr Lawrence and I stopped calling you Mrs Clarke? After all, we've known each other for a good many years now!'

'I don't always remember to call you Mr Lawrence,' his companion admitted rather shyly. 'And you some-times call me Auntie Clarke, as the children do. But I'd far rather you used my first name – Ada – and then I could call you Alex, as almost everyone else does.'

'Ada and Alex; they sound rather good together,' Alex said, and was immediately smitten with embarrassment. What on earth had possessed him to say that? But then he was asking her whether she would prefer tea or coffee, and how about a jam doughnut or a Belgian bun, all covered with thick white icing and scattered with chopped nuts? Ada – he must think of her as Ada in future, Alex reminded himself – said she would enjoy a cup of coffee but breakfast was too near a memory to allow her to eat even the tiniest doughnut, let alone the vast ones which she had seen being carried past by other voyagers.

Alex went below and presently came back with two cups of coffee and a plate of biscuits and the two of them settled down to their elevenses, Alex at least suddenly aware what a relief it was not to have to keep young Irene at arm's length all the time. Furthermore, Ada Clarke was clearly enjoying herself in a gentle, unassuming way, chatting about his children, her troubles with Dilly and her intention to adopt a skinny stray cat which had taken up its abode in the piles of equipment kept in the fire station.

'Oh, but she keeps the mice down,' Alex objected. 'Even rats steer clear of those sharp little claws. Find yourself another cat! We'll hang on to ours.'

'Oh aye? And what will she have to eat when mice and rats run out?' Ada Clarke said with spirit. 'Which of you will provide her with chopped liver, a nice slice of ham, or a bowl of milk? And how often does she sit on your lap and purr whilst you're knitting?'

They both laughed, and stretched out in the warm sunshine. How nice it was to lie here with no responsibility for anything or anyone, Alex thought drowsily, and said as much to his companion. How nice, how very nice it was . . .

And Alex was asleep.

* * *

By the time the passengers from the *Tulip* were disembarking at the Pier Head that evening, Ada felt she was an entirely different person from the woman who had climbed the gangway, eagerly anticipating a day out with a man she had long admired.

Being both kind and polite, she had pretended disappointment when Irene and Chalky had failed to put in an appearance, but in truth she had been rather pleased, though her pleasure had been tinged with apprehension. Suppose Alex had really intended to cement a relationship with Irene by giving her a day out? Suppose it had been Chalky's idea that she herself should come along as a sort of chaperon? And worst of all, suppose Alex had meant to take Irene to some beautiful secluded spot on the island, there to beg her to become his wife? Ada Clarke had heaved in a deep breath and scolded herself, though only in her mind. If Alex had wanted to have Irene to himself, he could easily have done so by not mentioning the voyage aboard the *Tulip* to anyone.

But Ada knew it was pointless to ask herself questions which were both irrelevant and unanswerable. Besides, she was well aware that Alex was embarrassed by Irene's all too obvious infatuation, and when the poor chap had fallen asleep even before the *Tulip* had passed the Mersey Bar she had sat quietly beside him and simply enjoyed looking at his sleeping face. He had not slept prettily, either. The wind had tossed his dark hair into a comical quiff, his mouth had hung open and very soon loud and porcine snores had issued forth.

Ada had smiled indulgently and driven off a small boy with a tin whistle, seeing at once that the child had intended to blow a sizeable blast straight into Alex's sleeping ear. She would have defended him against dragons or sea monsters had either threatened, and had been quite content to sit beside him and stare, in a way which would have been impossible in other circumstances, at his dear, familiar features.

When the *Tulip* had breasted the waves of Liverpool Bay, however, he had awoken, looked wildly around him, caught Ada's eye and pulled a rueful face. 'Sorry, my dear; how rude you must think me,' he had said apologetically. 'But Blue Watch was up most of the night, fighting a fire in a warehouse down by the docks.' He had stretched and yawned cavernously, then stood up. 'But I shan't fall asleep again; firemen only need a catnap, not the eight hours to which ordinary folk are accustomed. Now what can I get you: tea, coffee? How about a cake this time?'

When they had reached Douglas, Alex had asked a crew member where they should make for, and received a reply so comprehensive that he had blinked, reminding the man that this was a day trip and not, unfortunately, a week's holiday.

The man had grinned and scratched his head. 'I'm a local, see,' he had explained. 'There's no place like the island, nowhere wi' such grand views ... but since you've only the one day I'd advise you to tek a taxicab to one of our famous beauty spots, where you can eat your picnic and feast your eyes on the best view in the world. After that . . .'

And from that moment on, the day had gone like a dream, until it was time to return to the *Tulip* and prepare for the voyage back to Liverpool. Ada and Alex had settled themselves in deck chairs once more, saying little as they watched the sun descend into the sea in fiery splendour, whilst Ada told herself that it was proof of their friendship that they did not need to chatter but could remain contentedly silent.

'Well, Ada? What did you think of the Isle of Man?' Alex said now as the two of them descended the gangway at the Pier Head. He glanced at the clock tower, then at his watch. 'Goodness, doesn't time fly when you're having fun! I don't feel inclined to go all the way back home only to find myself having to turn round and retrace my steps in order to buy fish and chips.'

'I think you'd better count me out,' Ada said regretfully. 'You'll have had quite enough of me for one day and the twins will want to tell you how they got on. They won't want me cluttering up their kitchen.'

Alex sighed and took hold of her arm. 'You will come home with me and eat your share of the fish and chips,' he said firmly. 'I don't believe I need to tell you how much I've enjoyed our day out . . . surely it's natural that I don't want it to end.'

Ada Clarke snorted. 'You're afraid you'll find Irene hiding behind the kitchen door, rolling pin poised,' she said accusingly. 'You want me to protect you, but I'm afraid I can't possibly do so. Dilly has been alone since early this morning and has probably torn up a couple of cushions and reduced at least one chair to matchwood by now. She can be very nasty when she feels hard done by.'

'Right; I'll come home with you and escort you and Dilly back to our place,' Alex said. 'If the girls are home, the fish and chips will be keeping warm in the bake oven, and if they aren't home you can make a big pot of tea and feed Dilly anything you can find whilst I go down to the chippy for supplies.'

At this point the tram they wanted drew up alongside and they got aboard, though Ada was still protesting that there was no need for Alex to accompany her. 'I hadn't meant to come back with you, but I've just had a rather daunting thought,' she said as they settled on to a hard, slatted bench. 'You've obviously not remembered that you told Gillian to get fish and chips for seven.'

Alex clutched his forehead dramatically. 'Oh my God,' he moaned. 'I forgot! That just goes to prove we need not only yourself, but also Dilly. I bet she's a champion at getting outside two spare portions of fish and chips!'

Chapter Fourteen

It was midway through September by the time Joy found work. She had attended a dozen or so interviews, always accompanied by Gillian, Edward or her father, for though Mrs Clarke had offered to take her to one interview, and had in fact done so, she had been so nervous and ill at ease that Joy thought it would be best not to trouble the older woman again.

Despite her hopes, it had taken much longer than Joy had anticipated before she struck lucky, partly because at first she had only applied for secretarial work, knowing that her Pitman certificates proved that she was both fast and accurate on the typewriter. However, she soon realised that employers were put off by the fact that she was blind, so she had lowered her sights and decided to apply for other jobs.

Gillian had been back at school when an import/export firm called Wittard's had advertised for a switchboard operator and Joy had applied and been given an interview. Her father had been on call, so Joy had telephoned Edward at his uncle's farm and he had agreed at once to come back to Liverpool to escort her.

He had taken her to the large block of offices down by the docks, and had waited for her in reception whilst she had the interview, rejoicing with her when, flushed and excited, she had re-joined him. 'Got it!' she had

343

exclaimed. 'It's only part time to start with; three days a week whilst they train me to recognise which socket belongs to whom. The girl I'm replacing is partially sighted, so each socket has been numbered and you can feel the numbers below each hole because they're raised. They gave me a test, and though I fumbled at first the boss, Mr Murchison, said I'd passed with flying colours, so once they see I can cope it will become full time, which is nine to five Monday to Friday and nine to noon one Saturday a month.'

So now Joy was a switchboard operator with a large board on the wall before her, earphones upon her head and, on occasion, a queue of callers waiting to be connected. She enjoyed the work and liked her colleagues, and on this particular morning, as a brisk little wind blew off the Mersey, she set off for work at an especially early hour, since it would be the first time she had undertaken the journey alone.

Tapping briskly along the pavement, she knew when she reached the tram stop because, though she would have been hard pressed to explain why, she had noticed many times that a large number of people congregated together and standing motionless gave off a different sort of vibration, if you could call it that, from the vibration of people moving in one direction or another.

When she reached what she thought was the back of the queue, she cleared her throat and asked in a general way whether everyone was waiting for the 8.35 and if she had joined the tail of the queue and was not pushing in. The man behind whom she stood was beginning to answer when a voice called her name and Joy turned her head. 'Hey up, Joy, is you goin' to work? If so, you can

344

come along o' me; I dare say no one will mind if you skip a few bods so's we can travel together.'

'Oh, it's you, Ducky,' Joy said, a little disappointed that her solo trip was not to be, yet also slightly relieved. She would have had to enquire of someone the number of every tram which drew up alongside the queue. Ann Drake, nicknamed Ducky by common consent, also worked in Joy's building, as tea girl and messenger, with no qualifications other than a pair of sturdy legs to work the bicycle and a cheery disposition.

Joy moved up the queue until Ducky's hand slid into hers and Ducky's voice said in her ear: 'Mornin', Joy. Ain't it a nice one for October, eh? But why's you so early? I have to be at work betimes to take parcels in and sort the post, but you don't start until nine o'clock.'

Joy sighed. 'I decided it was high time I came to work by myself,' she explained. 'Usually, a neighbour or a pal sees me on to the tram and the conductor tells me when to get off and suggests that anyone bound for the Liver Building might give me a hand crossing roads and dodging lampposts. And I can't see the destination board, of course, so I'd have had to ask either someone in the queue or the conductor himself whether I was about to climb aboard the right tram. But honest to God, Ducky, I can't always depend on other people, and I'm getting to know the journey to work like the back of my hand, so today was to be a sort of test.'

'And I've bleedin' well ruined it all,' Ducky said, but she spoke without remorse, clearly not understanding how important independence became for someone who could not see so much as a flicker of light.

But now Ducky was helping her up the step and telling

the nearest seated passenger brusquely that if he were half the gent she thought he was he and his pal would perishin' well give up their seats to a couple of young ladies, one of whom was—

'Oh do shut up, Ducky; I don't need to see to strap-hang,' Joy hissed, thoroughly embarrassed, but the men had clearly taken Ducky's point, as Joy realised when she was pushed on to a seat still warm with recent occupancy, and felt Ducky slide into the one beside her. She began to remonstrate with the younger girl, but Ducky was having none of it.

'Think o' me as a total stranger, chuck,' she said. 'You know very well you'd have asked someone which tram were which, and whether it were safe to cross the road. Well, now you won't need to ask, 'cos I'm here to tell you. Or if you like I'll leave you stranded on the kerb and whizz into the office by meself.'

Joy couldn't help laughing. 'Oh all right, I give in; I really am grateful for your help, Ducky. Besides, I reckon there'll be plenty of opportunities to go it alone now that I'm working full time, though my sister's boyfriend will be back at university in a couple of weeks, so Gillian and I will start to go around together again. Of course she can't come to and from work with me because she's at St Hilda's, studying for her Higher, but I expect we'll spend our evenings together, and all day at weekends, of course.' As she spoke, Joy realised that she was not being strictly truthful. Of late, Gillian had made excuses even when she and Joy had both been free, and Joy thought rather sadly that it was a sign they were growing up. They still loved one another, that went without saying, but they had their own lives now, in a way that they had not done even when Joy had been at Blinkers. However, she had not even told Edward how she felt about this, so she had no intention of confiding in Ducky.

The two girls chatted idly until the tram reached their stop, when Ducky nearly caused an accident by dragging Joy bodily off the tram and into the crowd of men and women waiting to board. Joy bumped into a child who squawked indignantly, got tangled up with her own white stick and cursed Ducky roundly for impatience, but once again Ducky waved her words aside. 'It's awright for you, queen,' she said breathlessly, yanking at Joy's arm so hard that Joy dropped her stick for the second time. 'You don't have to be collectin' the keys from the night watchman and startin' on the post by eight o'clock, but I does. Oh, you've dropped your stick. I'll pick it up for you . . . no, don't bend down now, for God's sake!'

The warning came too late; Joy's head met that of someone else. Both grunted with shock, though not with pain, for their two heads had only grazed.

'I say, I'm extremely sorry, but it doesn't do to bend down without warning on a busy pavement,' a man's voice remarked ruefully as Joy straightened up, her stick in her hand.

She felt the man's shadow fall on her and took a step backwards. 'I should be the one to apologise, it was my fault . . .' she began, but got no further.

'Haven't I met you somewhere before?' the man said. 'You look familiar . . .'

Joy hesitated. Now that he mentioned it, she realised she had heard his voice before, though she could not put a name to it. She was about to say so when Ducky interrupted. 'Oh, shurrup, mister, that's the oldest chestnut on the tree,' the girl said with all her usual insouciance. 'She and meself work at the Liver Building, so we're always around this area.' She turned to Joy. 'Mustn't linger if I'm to be in work punctual like,' she said briskly. 'If you're lookin' to pick up a feller, this ain't the time nor the place. Come *on*, will you?'

The man with whom Joy had bumped heads laughed, albeit ruefully, and Joy could imagine him rubbing the sore spot as he turned away from them, whistling a tune beneath his breath and causing Joy to gasp and open her mouth to speak . . .

Ducky, however, heaved an impatient sigh and positively dragged her companion across the pavement. 'I wonder if he really knew you or if he were just tryin' it on,' she said conversationally as they walked. 'You can never tell with fellers.' She giggled. 'I mean, you'd never know where his hands were goin' till they got there.' She giggled again. 'I suppose you didn't reckernise his voice?'

'Well, I thought I did. What did he look like?' Joy asked, but Ducky's reply was unsatisfactory.

'Oh, he were just a feller, dark-haired and about thirty, though I'm not too good on age,' the girl said airily.

She continued to chatter but Joy no longer heard her. She was wondering whether it was the man who had rescued her from the bullies, or even Amy's partner from the Blinkers Christmas treat, but after her experience in Llandudno she did not try to follow, and let Ducky, scolding, lead her into Wittard's.

After three or four weeks Joy was thoroughly at home with her switchboard, and on occasion was called upon

348

to type out invoices and letters to customers. She did this by means of an object called a Dictaphone that recorded dictated memos for her to type out, and she was very soon as competent upon her Remington type-writer as she was with her switchboard.

When the Christmas holidays arrived and the twins spent more time together, Joy was uneasily aware that Gillian was either withholding something from her or was in some way unhappy, but questioning merely made her cross and defensive and no one else seemed to have noticed anything wrong.

But Joy very soon realised that she was not the only one being targeted by her sister; Gillian was not comfort-able in her relationship with her boyfriend, home from Cambridge for the vacation. She was never antagonistic to him, was often very sweet, but on other occasions she was offhand to the point of rudeness and Joy knew now she was not the only one who noticed. Keith had not said anything but Joy could tell from the tone of his voice that he too was uneasy, and one dark and icy cold evening, with Christmas almost upon them, Joy came tapping out of Wittard's, heading for the tram stop, when someone said her name and put a detaining hand on her arm.

'Joy? It's me, Keith. I happened to be in the area so I decided I might as well meet you out of work and take you home. Gillian's busy; she said she had to meet an old girlfriend to go Christmas shopping.' He took Joy's hand and tucked it into the crook of his elbow. 'She said I'd just be in the way and to amuse myself until six o'clock when she'd be back from shopping and I might share your evening meal.' He laughed a trifle bitterly. 'It

349

was a put-off; I'd have to be pretty dense not to realise that, but of course I went along with it. Well I would, wouldn't I? It's no secret that Gillian is the most important person in my life and I'd always planned that our future would be together. Look, would you mind if I took you to the nearest café, where we can talk in the warm?'

Joy hesitated. She knew just what Keith meant, but she did not know him terribly well and anyway her first loyalty would always be to her twin. However, she liked Keith and was sorry for him too, so she agreed that it might be pleasant to share a cup of tea and a bun at a café she knew quite near the tram stop. And soon the two of them were seated on opposite sides of a small table, with a pot of tea and a plate of buttered crumpets in front of them.

Once the waitress had left them Joy waited for Keith to speak, and when he failed to do so she raised her brows interrogatively. 'Well?' she said, rather truculently. 'What's this all about, Keith? If something's worrying you about your friendship with Gillian, she's the person you should be discussing it with, not me.'

'Oh, I know, I know,' Keith said hastily. 'But I can't discuss this with Gillian because – look, will you let me explain without interrupting? Only I've simply got to tell someone and I know you're good at keeping secrets.' He laughed rather bitterly. 'Gillian told me ages ago, when we first started getting serious, that she could confide in you without any qualms, knowing you'd never tell on her.'

'That's true,' Joy said, thinking that while that might once have been the case she was no longer in Gillian's confidence, though whether what her sister was keeping from her was something important or merely what you might call a Christmas secret she could not say. So she smiled apologetically at her companion before completing the sentence. 'That's true,' she said again, 'but if you want me to keep a secret from my twin, I'm telling you now I won't do it, or rather I can't.'

Opposite her she heard Keith sigh and then take a drink of his tea before speaking again. 'All right, if that's the way you feel I'll have to talk to someone else. But honestly, Joy, I know your sister very well and she wouldn't want what I was going to tell you to be bruited abroad. So it's your decision really; either I tell you and we keep it in the family, so to speak, or I tell someone else.' His hand reached out and patted Joy's. 'Well?'

Joy frowned. 'You've got me in a cleft stick,' she observed ruefully. 'I promise I won't tell a soul, then, so long as it won't hurt Gillian.'

'I wouldn't hurt Gillian for the world,' Keith said indignantly, and there was no doubting the sincerity in his tone. 'Dammit, I love the girl!'

'Sorry, sorry, sorry,' Joy said at once. 'Forget I spoke; it was a stupid thing to say. Fire ahead then.'

'Okay, here goes. I don't know if you've noticed, but several times since I got home I've suggested outings of one sort or another to your sister and she's been unable to come, having some sort of previous engagement . . .'

'What's wrong with that?' Joy said rather more sharply than she had intended. Goodness knows, she had suffered from the same treatment, but she could not bear to hear her twin criticised. 'Remember, Keith, you've been miles away for weeks and weeks; did you think Gillian would sit around waiting for you? She's a very popular girl and has heaps of friends.'

'Yes, yes, I appreciate all that,' Keith said quickly. 'I'm not suggesting for one moment that she should cast her old friends aside just because I'm home for Christmas. But today we'd agreed to go out together; a shopping expedition, lunch and then a visit to the cinema. I was really looking forward to it, especially as I meant to watch Gill very carefully . . . no, no, don't frown, I meant make a note of anything pretty she admired because I've not bought her gift yet and this seemed an ideal opportunity to find out what she would like . . . do you understand, Joy? As I said, I was really looking forward to it, arrived at your house ten minutes early . . . and Gillian answered the door, all dressed up to the nines but full of apologies, saying that she had just received a letter from an old friend announcing that she was coming into Liverpool this very day on a Christmas shopping trip and she wanted Gill to meet her at Lime Street, since she doesn't know the city at all well.'

'Oh dear,' Joy said in a hollow voice. 'Did she – did she give you the name of the person she was meeting?'

'Oh *please*; I'm not a complete idiot, you know,' Keith said reproachfully. 'Don't get angry with me, Joy, but I simply didn't believe her. First of all she couldn't meet my eyes and then she was talking far too loudly. And there was no sign of a letter . . . Well, anyway, I suggested I might go with her to meet this friend off the train and she said that she didn't know which train her friend meant to catch but would stay indoors to wait for a telephone call. She asked me very prettily if I could bring myself to put off the shopping trip we had planned until

352

tomorrow or the next day, and naturally I said that would be fine. I waited for her to invite me in, but she didn't do so. I won't say she shut the door in my face, but it was perilously like it.' He paused, and Joy could imagine his furrowed brow and hurt expression. For the first time she felt really angry with Gillian for causing such pain, but when she would have spoken Keith's hand came out and covered her own. 'No, no, let me finish. I walked up to the fire station feeling puzzled and hurt . . . dash it, I felt all the emotions one would expect. But I decided I'd have to have it out with Gillian the very next time we met, and was turning back to catch a tram to the city centre when your front door opened and Gillian came out.'

'I expect she'd decided to make her way to Lime Street after all,' Joy said rather wildly. 'Or perhaps her friend had rung the very moment you left the house . . .'

'I followed her,' Keith interrupted flatly. 'And you'll never guess where she went.'

Joy shook her head. 'I can't imagine,' she said truthfully. 'Go on, tell me.'

'Well, it was the weirdest thing,' Keith said, his tone puzzled. 'She hopped on a tram and as soon as she had settled herself downstairs on one of the front seats, I ran across the pavement and jumped aboard. I was sure she was going to meet someone and found myself praying it would be a girl. I won't go through all the intricacies of the journey, but we ended up in Rodney Street. It was just about lunchtime and there are no cafés or restaurants on Rodney Street, but apparently your sister was not interested in food. She simply strolled up and down that exceedingly long street for about an hour and then she dived down a side street. I'd been keeping well out of sight as you can imagine, which wasn't easy, but I'd turned up my coat collar, wrapped my scarf round the lower half of my face and didn't walk so much as slouch. The truth is, she glanced neither at me nor at any other passer-by, to the best of my knowledge. She seemed to be concentrating on the houses themselves and I could tell from the droop of her shoulders that she was becoming discouraged. Yet what had she expected? If she'd had a rendezvous, why on earth choose Rodney Street? As I said, there are no shops or cafés, just medical consultants and specialists. It really is a very boring street . . .' he chuckled suddenly, his voice lightening, 'as I can tell you, having spent the better part of the morning and early afternoon parading up and down it.' He sighed deeply. 'I know it was sneaky of me to follow her, but what else was I to do?' He reached across the table once more and took Joy's hand. 'What would you have done in my position? And can you explain her behaviour, because I'm damned if I can?'

'I dare say, in your shoes, I'd have done just what you did,' Joy said at length, after the silence between them had begun to stretch uncomfortably. 'As for her behaviour, there's only one person who can explain it, and that's my twin. If you think she was really meeting someone, then it's your right to ask why she lied. But I fear if you do so . . .'

'. . it might ruin our relationship,' Keith said miserably. 'Have you *no* idea why she told me such fibs? It would have been understandable had she met someone, but I'm very sure she didn't. Can't you find out for me, Joy? If the same thing happens again and you follow her . . .'

Joy, who had just taken a mouthful of tea, spluttered and fished a hanky out of her bag to mop up. 'Of course I can't! I can't *see* to follow anyone,' she said impatiently. 'And without giving away the fact that you did follow her and then confided in me, I can't possibly help.'

Once again, Keith's hand reached across the table, but this time it was to smooth down her cheek. 'I'm really sorry; you must think me a great fool,' he said penitently. 'The fact is, you don't *look* blind; you don't even act it most of the time. You've got so clever at disguising your disability that some folk don't realise the significance of the white stick and behave as though you can see. I do the same – treat you as I treat Gill.'

Joy laughed. 'I think you should rephrase that remark, since I've heard you and Gillian canoodling in the back yard before coming into the kitchen,' she said. 'But actually I'm really thrilled that you say you're not aware of my disability and I'll do my best to help you to find out just what is going on. But Gillian may guess that you know. Will that be all right?'

'Oh . . . but suppose she *is* meeting someone, and gives me the elbow?' Keith said. 'She can't want us to split up or she would have been honest . . . oh hell, what am I to do?'

'I don't want to say too much because it would only be conjecture, but if you ask me she's playing a – a very silly game,' Joy said carefully. 'Look, I promise to try to keep you out of it, and as soon as I have definite information I'll get in touch. Will that do?'

She felt her hand being seized and wrung heartily, then felt Keith's lips on her cheek and told him, with mock wrath, to 'Gerroff!'

355

Keith laughed and squeezed her hand. 'You're a sport, Joy Lawrence! If I can just keep my Gillian, I'll be grateful to you for the rest of my life,' he said breathlessly. 'And so far as I know, she was only out of my sight for about ten minutes; that was when she dived down the side street and I couldn't follow her because she would have spotted me, since that street was deserted.'

'When she came out of the side street, did she seem flushed or excited?' Joy asked curiously; she had not forgotten her twin's obvious exhilaration after her encounter with the young man in the grounds of the new cathedral. But surely that one encounter could have nothing to do with her twin's behaviour? She hated to think that Gillian might have been deceiving not only Keith but herself also, but it had to be faced. Gillian had never mentioned their trip to Rodney Street again, nor her meeting with the doctor's son, but now Joy remembered every detail of her twin's story. Would she tell lies and hang about the doctor's surgery just to see the chap once more? But Keith was drumming his fingers on the table, clearly thinking, so she repeated her question.

Though Keith gave the matter more thought, he was unable to answer her satisfactorily. 'She came out of the side street like a rocket and hurried off down the road at such a pace that it was all I could do to keep her in sight,' he said. 'In fact she turned on to Mount Pleasant and jumped aboard a tram before I could catch up, leaving me to follow on the next, which was at least seven or eight minutes behind the one that Gillian had caught. But if you and I are to find out what's going on we must arrange to meet on the quiet, because we don't want her getting suspicious.'

'Why not?' Joy said, smiling to herself. 'It might do her good to be just a touch jealous and to see that you are not always available. I gather you've agreed to a day out with her tomorrow? I think you ought to mention Rodney Street; just see what her reaction is.'

Keith laughed. 'Righty-ho, Miss Lawrence,' he said. 'And you've reminded me of something. I don't suppose you've ever met Paul Everett, who was in my class at school. He's one of Gillian's many admirers and he's got a kid brother, Stevie, who's just had his tonsils out. I'll tell Gillian that I met Paul and we took Stevie to see a doctor in Rodney Street and spotted her through the window of the waiting room, but when we came out she had disappeared.' He chuckled delightedly. 'Howzat!'

'Brilliant,' Joy said. 'See what she says when you tell your story and then we'll decide what to do next, if anything.'

Keith agreed that it might well do the trick. They caught the next tram and arrived home before Gillian, though Alex and Mrs Clarke were already in the kitchen, Alex laying the table and Mrs Clarke frying cold potatoes from the previous night and slicing onions into the sizzling fat. She turned and beamed at the pair of them, then said placidly that supper would not be long. 'Did you have a good shopping trip?' she asked. 'Oh, Gillian dear, did you buy Joy's present?'

'No!' Joy yelled, then began to giggle. 'Just because I came in with Keith doesn't make me Gillian!'

'Oh, Joy, I'm so sorry . . .' Mrs Clarke began just as the back door opened again and Gillian entered, already apologising for being late. She asked Joy if she'd had a good day at the office, came over and gave Keith a

357

quick kiss on the cheek, and then began to help in the preparation of the meal.

When they were all seated with plates of food before them, Keith plunged in. 'Went and met your sister out of work, seeing as how you were busy with your friend, and we came home together,' he said easily. 'Did you have a good shop, Gill? Oh, and I met Paul Everett. Do you remember him?'

'Of course,' Gillian said impatiently. 'He's got gingery hair. He's back from Oxford, I suppose?'

'That's right. He was taking his kid brother to see a doctor on Rodney Street.' Keith continued with his apocryphal story, his voice lacking conviction to Joy's ears, though she was sure no one else doubted his words. He finished his tale and must have turned to look at Gillian, seated beside him. 'Odd coincidence, wouldn't you say? I mean, there aren't many shops in Rodney Street . . .'

'Oh, my friend wanted to see how the new cathedral was getting on,' Gillian said airily. 'So we went there first. Any more spuds? We didn't have lunch so I'm starving.' She turned to her sister. 'What about you, Joy? If Keith met you out of work you must have done a bit of shopping. You were going to go halves with me over something a bit special for Dad . . .'

Hastily, Joy said she'd not got out of Wittard's until six o'clock and turned the conversation, observing half-admiringly that Gillian could certainly think on her feet. Because of her sister's quickness, she and Keith had not found out anything, though Alex suddenly cleared his throat uncomfortably a couple of times, making Joy wonder whether their father, too, had been aware of a certain atmosphere. Then he got up and served his daughter with more fried potatoes. 'When we've finished eating, why don't Auntie Clarke, Gillian, Keith and myself have a hand of cards, whilst Joy plays one of the books the Listening Library have sent?' he said. He turned to his younger daughter. 'Will that suit you, sweetheart?'

Joy smiled; once she would have enjoyed a game of cards, but now it was impossible, and anyway she loved listening to stories. 'That'll be fine, Dad,' she said. 'Only I'll get on with my knitting at the same time. I'm on the last sleeve, so if I'm lucky I'll finish it by Christmas.'

After that one occasion, Gillian made no attempt to sneak off and seemed to be her usual loving self and Joy thought, hopefully, that whatever her twin had been up to was clearly a thing of the past. Probably she had just wanted to glimpse the young Dr Slocombe again for her own satisfaction, and having ascertained that he was nothing special had resumed her relationship with Keith.

Christmas Day passed uneventfully, though it was bitterly cold. Keith and Edward, as well as various members of Blue Watch, were invited round on Boxing Day to help the family finish up the cold turkey, and after lunch they played childish games – Chinese whispers, musical chairs, charades and postman's knock – and had a grand high tea, the visitors gazing with awe at a table upon which Mrs Clarke's genius was displayed to great advantage. 'Auntie Clarke works miracles,' Joy assured everyone. 'Not only is she the best cook in the world, but she will go miles to buy an ingredient she needs if it's not available nearer at hand.'

Edward made it clear that he enjoyed being part of the Lawrences' extended family, helping Joy unobtrusively when she needed a hand, teasing her, laughing both at and with her, and proving himself to be, as always, her best and closest friend. And Irene and Chalky had clearly come to an understanding and only stopped holding hands, Gillian whispered to her twin, when they were putting food into their mouths.

Gillian herself and Keith stayed in the hall so long when playing postman's knock that Chalky made ribald suggestions, and all Keith's fears and uncertainties must surely have dissipated, for he emerged from the hallway, Edward told Joy, with an arm slung round Gillian's shoulders, a big grin on his face and lipstick on his chin. In fact a grand time was had by all and both Alex and Auntie Clarke were pleased that their efforts had been appreciated.

When Gillian and Joy went to bed that night Joy was eager to talk over their day and to remind Gillian how much she had enjoyed herself. 'I say, what do you think of this sledging expedition the boys are planning?' she said, pulling her nightie over her head. 'It'll have to be this coming weekend, and they say if we can get ten or a dozen people, then we can catch a bus to the nearest village and hike to Chalky's uncle's place, which is pretty remote. Chalky says the snow is deep and pretty well undisturbed there and it's quite hilly, so if we can find some sledges, or trays even, we should have a great time. Edward says on a good run a sledge can get up speed until it's going faster than a horse can gallop. Imagine that!'

Gillian gave a little squeak. 'I'd love it, if only it comes off,' she said enthusiastically. 'Keith's got a real sledge, big enough for two, and your Edward has a little wooden one that his dad made years ago. Several of Blue Watch want to come . . . if only it stays cold until the weekend!'

'I'm sure it will,' Joy said. 'I reckon sledging will be almost as much fun as ice skating, when you've got a first-rate partner of course. And Chalky's uncle says we can use his hill pasture not just for sledging, but for a sort of party. He says when they were kids they'd build a bonfire and bake spuds and apples in the embers. He says we can have flasks of tea – Chalky's Aunt Beth will provide them – and go back to the farmhouse afterwards for hot mince pies and punch. Oh, how I pray the snow lasts!'

And obligingly, the snow remained on the ground all the rest of the week, whilst the twins and their friends laid their plans for the trip.

'Though it will be later than we thought, since the chaps in Blue Watch say they can't get away much before three, and it'll be coming on dark by then,' Gillian said. The girls were in their room, sorting out their warmest clothing for the trip next day. 'Not that it matters, though, because there's a full moon, and we've all got torches.'

'True,' Joy said; she forbore to point out that moon or sun, she would be in her usual perpetual darkness, since her twin was well aware of the fact. 'Oh damn, my mittens have sprung a hole; how irritating! Have you seen the size of the basket of Welsh cakes Auntie Clarke has baked for us? Bags I not carry them.'

'Nor me,' Gillian said at once. 'The fellers can do the carrying; it's what men were made for!'

Joy laughed but protested. 'That's unfair! Keith and

Edward have done no end of work in setting this up – so has Chalky for that matter. And they'll be carrying their sledges, so perhaps you and I should cart the grub between us. I don't want to spoil the boys' evening by giving them a double load.'

'And you don't mind spoiling mine,' Gillian said sharply. 'Just because we're twins, everyone, including you, will think it my duty to dance attendance on you, see you aren't left out or ignored . . . not that you will be, because you're always the centre of attention and I'm—'

Joy blinked. Her twin had been chattering away happily and all of a sudden she was snapping and snarling! 'Hold on, Gillian,' she said, feeling her own annoyance begin to boil up. 'I'm sure someone will give me a hand with the basket. And if I'm such a nuisance then you'd better steer clear of me, because I *won't* be a burden, I bloody well won't!'

Chapter Fifteen

The sledging party met as arranged soon after three and stood on the icy pavement, rubbing their hands and stamping their feet until they were able to board the bus. Chalky seemed very excited over something, but simply said mysteriously that this was not just a new year but a new decade, and wasn't that a good enough reason to start a whole new chapter in one's life? He had been talking to Keith, but Joy, overhearing, said she agreed. 'I mean to startle you all in the course of 1950,' she announced. 'I think I'll leave Wittard's and join a circus as a trapeze artist or – or a lion tamer. A switchboard can get boring after a while.'

She had been thinking of her sight and her hope that it would soon return, but she did not mean to say anything to anyone of that particular secret hope. Instead, she turned to Chalky. 'What do you think? Would I suit spangled tights? Pink ones, with a little bolero top to show off my magnificent bosom?'

Due to the fact that Joy was slightly built, this remark caused much hilarity and Gillian reminded her twin how she had once thought being a fireman was the career she would enjoy most, and then others joined in, shouting and joking, suggesting a number of strange occupations whilst staring hopefully up the road in the direction from which the bus would come.

The group assembling on the pavement was now sixteen strong, since the younger members of Blue Watch had brought girlfriends along, and a good deal of teasing and flirting went on as the bus arrived and they began to take their seats. When the conductor saw the sledges and trays the boys were carrying he added to the fun by telling them that he wasn't a Pickford's van and didn't mean to go in for furniture removals, but since the bus was almost empty save for the sledging party, he allowed himself to be persuaded to pile most of the 'luggage' under the stairs whilst the rest was wedged around the seats.

'I just hope no perishin' inspector jumps aboard and asks me wharr I charge for such things,' he said, grinning to himself at the mere thought. Irene, clutching a bag of potatoes, offered him a piece of treacle toffee from another bag which Auntie Clarke had given her, and he took it and thanked her, commenting that if an inspector did appear he would say the lump in his cheek was a tooth abscess. 'I'll say the bleedin' agony caused me to overlook the extry luggage,' he said thickly. 'Oh, go on wi' you! Gerraboard and don't forget the last bus back to the city leaves Cutten's Corner at ten o'clock on the flamin' dot.'

'We won't forget,' Gillian said, jumping on to the platform and holding out a hand to Joy, only her twin was already being steered to a seat by the ever-faithful Edward. Gillian sometimes thought that her sister did not fully appreciate Edward, but in a way it was his own fault. He was always there when he was needed but should someone else come forward he would, so to speak, step back. Perhaps Gillian was the only person to notice

364

his rueful look as someone else caught Joy's attention and Edward became unnecessary, a part of the background. Sometimes she tried to make Joy realise what a grand person her old friend was, but usually decided to let well alone. Perhaps Edward was not the strong character Joy would need when she left the nest, as all young things must; perhaps they both realised it, though neither ever said so. And I've got my own life to lead, Gillian reminded herself; I shouldn't try to manoeuvre Joy in any direction. The choice of a life partner must be her twin's and hers alone.

Thinking the matter over now, as she settled in her seat beside Keith, Gillian realised that she had no idea whether Edward really had any feeling for her twin stronger than that of friendship. Whenever Gillian had tried to get Joy to consider him, Joy always replied laughingly that she loved Edward like a brother.

Now Gillian, staring at the backs of their heads, so close together, had to admit to herself that she did not know whether Edward and Joy had exchanged even the lightest of kisses. They held hands in the street, linked arms in a crowd, but Gillian knew that this meant nothing; anyone accompanying Joy anywhere would pretty well have to take her hand or her arm.

She remembered that she had seen them dancing together at a Christmas party and had felt tears come to her eyes as she watched her twin and Edward slowly circling the floor. Joy had seemed to nestle into Edward's embrace and he had held her with such tenderness that for a moment Gillian had felt a pang of envy and had honestly thought the couple must love one another, even if neither had as yet realised it. But then Edward had said something which had made her twin gasp, laugh and give him a push in the chest. As the music ended and they had moved off the dance floor, Joy had said loudly enough for Gillian to hear: 'You cheeky beggar! Don't you go getting ideas just because we dance well together!'

As soon as she had been able to do so, which was when they were queuing for their coats, Gillian had asked her sister just what Edward had said or done which had made her laugh and push him away. But Joy had only giggled again. 'He's daft, Edward, but he can always make me laugh,' was all she would vouchsafe.

Chalky's voice broke into Gillian's thoughts. He was standing at the front of the bus, his fair hair hidden beneath a blue woollen bobble hat, his duffel coat unfastened and his cheeks flushed. He had one hand on Irene's shoulder and had to raise his voice to be heard above the roaring of the bus's engine. 'Ladies and gents, although you're mainly gents being as how there's no such thing as a female firefighter,' he shouted. 'Next stop is ours, so you'd best get your things together. And while I'm on me feet, I'll tell you a bit of news what'll knock you for six. I've popped the question to young Irene here and she's agreed to give it a go, so next week we'll buy the ring and make it official like.'

There was a startled pause before the rest of the company began to shout congratulations. Gillian giggled and leaned closer to Keith to whisper in his ear. 'Trust Chalky to pick the worst possible moment for making an announcement,' she hissed. 'But I suppose he's so thrilled she's given in at last that he couldn't wait to tell everyone, just in case she changed her mind.'

Keith grinned at her. 'I reckon you're right,' he said. 'Chalky's been trying to get next to Irene ever since I met you. He's a really nice chap; I never could make out why Irene didn't grab him, but you women have your reasons, I suppose.'

'Oh, Keith, you must have noticed that Irene was always tagging round after our dad,' Gillian said. 'Of course Dad simply wasn't interested, and when he took Auntie Clarke to the Isle of Man the iron entered Irene's soul. She stopped thinking the sun shone out of Dad and began to appreciate Chalky.'

'Well, I'm glad for both of them, because I think they're well suited . . .' Keith began, just as some enterprising soul began to sing 'For he's a jolly good fellow' and the bus drew to a shuddering halt.

As Chalky and Irene passed him the conductor seized their hands, adding his own congratulations to those of the sledging party. 'But mind you arrive at this 'ere stop on time 'cos I dursen't wait more than five or ten minutes at the most,' he warned them. 'An' it's a helluva long walk from here to the city centre.'

Chalky, grinning from ear to ear and clutching Irene so possessively that she squeaked a protest, said that the conductor was not to worry; he would round up his party and have them down the lane and gathering at the bus stop well before ten o'clock. Then he stood on the platform, making sure that they left nothing behind.

As soon as everyone was ready he and Irene shepherded the party up the narrow lane that led to Ravensbrook Farm. The lane was steep and the bare branches of the trees which grew on top of the enclosing

367

banks met overhead, but because of the snow's capacity to reflect the moonlight no one strayed from the straight and narrow, or landed in the ditch. They reached the farm, where Chalky's uncle Ned and aunt Beth greeted them, and whilst Mrs White returned to her kitchen Mr White took them to the field which he had selected for their use. 'I've been piling up dead branches torn off by the last gale for a month or two, meaning to have a good big bonfire when the weather eased,' he said. 'But you'm welcome to set alight to it right away so's your spuds'll be baked by the time you've had enough of the sledging. Ronnie will bring you all up to the farm before you leave for the bus. The missus has baked mince pies and I'll be brewing up a bowl of punch . . . but there, I dare say Ronnie has told you all this, so I'll leave you to your sport.'

'Keith and me will start the fire going, so Joy and Edward can have first go on Keith's sledge because it's a proper one, big enough for them to share,' Gillian said quickly. She was uncomfortably aware that she had been poor company for her twin over the last couple of weeks, but she meant to make up for it by being truly sweet to Joy today and would start by letting her sister and Edward have first go on the big sledge. She looked around her and there was Joy, a smile lighting her countenance, one hand held loosely in Edward's. Gillian's heart missed a beat. Joy looked so happy and she, Gillian, was going to take that look off her sister's face . . . oh, dammit, she must not think like that, she must tell herself that Joy would be better off for some space about her . . . as she would herself . . .

'Right you are, Gillian.' It was Chalky speaking, and

Gillian turned to smile at him. 'I've got a can of paraffin if the wood's too damp to light without help, but have a go first. Here's a box of matches and some spills which Uncle uses to light his pipe.'

Resolutely, Gillian approached the enormous pile of dead wood, old newspapers and dry hay. 'Here we go,' she said cheerfully as she struck the first match. 'Baked potatoes, here we come!'

By the time the potatoes were cooked in the dying embers of the great bonfire, Joy was telling Edward that sledging was even more fun than ice skating. Keith, overhearing, said that in that case he claimed the credit, since Edward and Joy had had a good few goes on the big sledge, sitting together and screaming in unison. Edward, however, denied this, saying that when he and Joy had commandeered the round tin tray one of the chaps had provided, they had beaten all the speed records set by everyone else . . .

'And ended up arse over tip in a snowdrift,' Keith jeered. 'Now when I took dear little Joy for a ride on my wonderful sledge, we arrived at the bottom without turning over once.'

'And very boring it was too,' Joy whispered, her mouth very near Edward's ear. 'I like excitement, I do. I don't even mind slogging up the hill in order to come whizzing down. Oh, I wish today could go on for ever!'

'It isn't today any more, it's tonight,' Edward observed. 'And even if *you* could go on all night, my little plum, the rest of us want to get our teeth into those baked potatoes.' He looped an arm around her shoulders and guided her, she presumed, towards the farmhouse. 'Mind

369

you don't burn your mouth on the spud or you won't be able to enjoy Mrs White's mince pies.'

Joy was promising to be careful just as Gillian came up, demanding to know whether her twin had managed to escape serious injury when earlier in the evening she had seen her rocketing down the hillside and stopping only when she, her companion and their conveyance had met the hedge.

Joy laughed. 'I dare say I'll have a few bruises by morning,' she admitted. 'But so will everyone else. Irene came a cropper when Chalky decided he could steer round some fir tree or other; she told me her blood ran cold but I take it that the said blood remained in her veins since she was laughing when I saw her. But what about you, Gillian? I know Keith claims to be the safest sledger on the slopes, but surely he must have upset you at least once.'

Gillian chuckled. 'You make it sound as though getting thrown off a sledge is the greatest fun imaginable, and if you mean it, I can't say I agree. And Keith, bless him, didn't upset ours once. But each to his own, I suppose; and now it's time for mince pies and punch in the farm-house kitchen.' She had been addressing Joy, but turned her head to speak to Edward. 'Shall I take Joy up to the farm while you help Keith and Chalky and the other fellows to put out the fire?'

'No, that won't be necessary,' Edward said quickly. 'What are firemen for if not to put out fires? I dare say Chalky could douse the embers unaided, but the rest of Blue Watch will doubtless want to get in on the act and show off to all the pretty girls.'

Gillian sighed. 'I thought it would be nice to have a

word with my twin. Oh well, I'll go back and get Keith; he's getting the chaps to clean the snow off the sledges, otherwise they probably won't let us on the bus. I'll join you in a minute.'

Edward looped an arm round Joy's waist as they walked, saying as he did so: 'Better hang on to each other; it's no use pretending I can warn you of every obstacle in our path because the snow hides things. I wonder what your sister was going to say to you? Something she didn't want anyone else to hear, I'd guess.'

Joy sighed and rubbed her face against Edward's shoulder. 'I don't know. I know you won't tell anyone, Edward, but she's been really difficult for the last couple of weeks; ever since before Christmas, in fact. And yesterday she crowned it all by saying – no, I won't tell you because it wouldn't be fair. She lost her temper and said something I'm sure she didn't mean. It made me feel that she found me a confounded nuisance at times, so I told her she wasn't to come near me today.' She tightened her arm round Edward's waist for a moment. 'I knew I could rely on you to see I was safe and make sure I enjoyed myself, so if she tries to winkle me away from you, *please* don't let her!'

She turned towards him, a question trembling on her lips. She longed to ask him if he thought her a burden, if she had spoiled his fun, because she guessed he had not attempted the more dangerous runs whilst he was with her. But what was the point in asking the question when she knew what his answer would be? They had been bezzies since shortly after their first meeting and she knew Edward would have died rather than let her down, would never admit she was a responsibility even if she was one which secretly he would be glad to shed.

'Well? I can see you're dying to ask me something, so get it off your chest before we reach the kitchen,' Edward said. 'It's not far now, I should say about twenty paces, so you'd better get a move on.'

'Oh, it was nothing much,' Joy said vaguely. 'It's a bit mean of me actually, but I was going to ask you to be sure to sit next to me in the bus. I know Gillian, and she's quite likely to try to get me to herself for the journey home, and I'm still cross with her. If she wants to apologise she can jolly well do so when we're back in our own home, getting ready for bed.'

'Miss Lawrence, you are a minx,' Edward said gravely. 'But I'm damned if I see why I should give up my place beside the prettiest girl on the bus just so her twin can say she's sorry.'

Joy heard the sounds of excited chatter, muted by the closed door, as Edward drew her gently to a halt, heard the sounds intensify with the opening of the door. 'In you go; no steps, march straight ahead and the table's right in front of you. I'll pull out a chair and sit you down, but first I'll help you out of that coat or you won't . . .'

'. . . feel the benefit when you go outside again,' they finished in chorus and Joy let Edward unwind her scarf, pull off her woolly hat and take off her coat, then settled herself on what she realised was a ladder-backed kitchen chair, whilst her hostess folded her chilly hands round a mug of something hot and told her that the plate before her held two mince pies and to bite into them with care, since 'they's only just out of oven, my duck'.

Joy thanked her politely and carried the mug to her mouth. She expected tea or coffee but her first sip told her that it was the punch and she took a cautious swallow. 'That'll warm the cockles of your heart,' Edward's voice said in her ear. 'Shove up; there aren't enough chairs to go round so you can jolly well share. I say, this punch has quite a punch, ha ha ha. It's all right for me; us blokes are used to strong drink, but namby-pamby little girls like you will probably end up under the table after half a glass.'

'You cheeky beast,' Joy said wrathfully. She pinched Edward's arm but moved up so that they could share the chair. Then she bit into a mince pie and gasped. 'Hot is an understatement, but so is delicious! Oh, Edward, isn't this fun?'

It had been around half past eight, Edward told her, when they had entered the kitchen and at quarter past nine Chalky began to marshal his troops for the return journey. They tumbled out of the kitchen into the snow-covered yard, shouting back their gratitude to the Whites in somewhat slurred accents. 'There isn't a cloud in the sky and the moon's at the full, so provided you hang on to me and neither of us slip, we should reach the bus in safety,' Edward said. 'Have you enjoyed yourself, queen?'

'Oh, so much!' Joy breathed. She could feel a dampness on her lips and cheeks and guessed that it was her breath steaming out into the frosty air. 'Tell me about it, Edward.'

Nothing loth, Edward described the scene. 'The sky is full of stars, and, as I've already said, it's a full moon,' he said dreamily. 'We are just entering the lane, everyone talking and laughing, as you can hear, and there's quite a lot of kissing and cuddling going on. The lane slopes down and at this level there are no banks – they come later – but there are plenty of trees which look wonderful against the moon. Can you smell the snow, queen? And the pine needles?'

'Yes, I smell the snow and the pine needles; and I remember how moonlight leaches colour so that everything becomes black and white,' Joy said. She cuddled Edward's hand in both of hers. 'You make me remember the things I once saw with my own eyes, kind Edward.'

To her surprise, Edward promptly freed his hand and gave her a very small admonitory shove. 'Don't call me that; I'm not kind,' he said sharply, then slid his arm round her waist and sighed. 'Sorry, sorry, I shouldn't have said that. It's just I couldn't help thinking that for two pins you'd have said you love me like a brother.' He drew her to a halt. 'We've reached Cutten's Corner in good time; the bus will be here in a few minutes and our lovely party will be over.'

Chalky's voice rose above the rest. 'Five more minutes and we'll be climbing aboard that nice warm bus! In the meantime, why doesn't everyone follow my example and give the lady of their choice a kiss and a hug?'

'Good idea; only why limit it to one lady when there are so many of us to choose from?' Irene cried. 'Wharrabout playin' postman's knock in the snow, eh? C'mon, fellers, make the most of it 'cos this may be your last chance to snog the prettiest gals in Liverpool.'

'You're drunk,' someone shouted; Joy thought it was Keith, but could not be sure. She hung grimly on to Edward's arm, but he laughed and sat her down on the bench which had been erected to identify the bus stop, first brushing the loose snow away. Then he detached himself from her hold. 'Can't insult the newly betrothed,' he said gaily. 'Just going to give the lady a kiss; shan't be a mo, chuck!'

Joy expected to remain alone on her seat until the bus arrived, but it was not to be. Within seconds of Edward's leaving her, she found herself being grabbed and kissed, sometimes gently, sometimes not. She could smell the alcohol on the lads' breaths and tried to push them away, giggling, but her pushes were half-hearted, for once more she was feeling the sheer bliss of belonging to the normal world, of being kissed and cuddled because she was a pretty girl, and not merely from kindness.

It was not until she heard the roar of the bus's engine approaching – from a distance, for sound travels far on a cold and snowy night – that she stood up, knowing Edward must be near, because he would never let her down. She bent to pick up her handbag, and as she straightened someone caught her in his arms and this time there was no doubt about the kiss. It began gently enough, then deepened and strengthened until she was giddy with pleasure, though this was mixed with a little apprehension. Could one have a baby from a kiss? She did not think so, but could not ask anyone without giving away the fact that she was so ignorant. The boy, whoever he was, broke away, presumably scared off by the approach of Edward, who said interrogatively: 'Joy? The bus is here, queen. Are you going to sit wi' your sister, or . . .'

'I'm sitting with you, whether you like it or not,' Joy said. 'I told you earlier . . .'

'Right,' Edward said. He seized her arm. 'Three paces, then the step up, turn to your left and take your place on the first seat; I told the conductor to keep it vacant for you.' He laughed as he helped Joy to negotiate the step. 'Your sister is sitting right at the front, with Keith of course, so she must have anticipated that you'd not want to swap partners at this stage. And besides, look what twerps me and Keith would look, sitting together on the love bus with all the crumpet surrounding us.'

Joy agreed, and the bus jerked into motion as the last passenger climbed aboard. Joy rested her head against Edward's shoulder. 'Oh, I'm so tired – and so happy! Did you kiss all the pretty girls, Edward? I bet poor old Keith didn't dare.'

'I didn't do badly for a green-eyed student with carroty hair and a squint,' Edward said, and then a thought seemed to strike him. 'I suppose Gillian has described me to you many a time? Only I've changed quite a bit since I was a pupil at the Bold Street school.'

Joy was so surprised that she jerked upright. How odd that Edward of all people should ask that particular question! But she answered it honestly: 'No, she's never said a word. Oh, when you first started walking me to school, she said – well, that you were a bit of a weed. Then when I came back from the LSB, you said you had spots, freckles and a squint. Were you joking, then? Are you really dark-haired, blue-eyed and irresistible?'

Edward laughed. 'I'm whatever you want me to be,' he said. 'Aren't I the lucky one, then? One day, a golden-haired Greek god, the next a dead ringer for John Gregson or Kenneth More.'

'Oh, shut up, you,' Joy said, settling herself comfortably against his shoulder once more. 'You didn't ask me whether I was kissed. But of course you must know I was because it was your voice asking me if I was ready to leave which made the last fellow stop. I suppose – I suppose you didn't notice who it was?'

'Haven't a clue,' Edward said cheerfully. 'Everyone looks the same by moonlight, especially when they're all wrapped up in coats and scarves and hats. Why? Was it nice?'

'Very nice. This has been the happiest day of my life,' Joy said sleepily. 'I hope I didn't spoil it for you, Edward.'

'Spoil it? You made it,' Edward said, though Joy thought he was merely being kind, despite what he had said earlier. Presently, they both fell asleep and had to be roused when the bus reached their stop.

Despite her protests – and Gillian's – that the Lawrence twins were quite capable of making their way to their own home, Edward and Keith insisted upon accompanying them to their very door. In fact it was quite a good thing, because when they entered the kitchen Alex was sitting on one of the fireside chairs, his eyes on the clock above the mantel, and Auntie Clarke, already coated and hatted, was fastening Dilly's lead to her smart red collar. As the four of them entered, the older woman turned and beamed at them. 'I don't need to ask if you had a good time; one look at your pink cheeks and bright eyes tells its own story,' she said. 'And you're just in time to stop Alex here sending out a search party.' She bustled over to the back door, dragging a reluctant and growling Dilly behind her. 'You're quite capable of making yourselves a mug of cocoa and a jam butty, so I'll leave you to it.'

There was a chorus of goodnights and then Gillian hurried over to the stove, giving her father a pat on the head in passing. 'Dear old Dad,' she said affectionately. 'Did *you* have a nice evening? I know you meant to take Auntie Clarke to the flicks.'

'We had a grand time, thanks, queen, but I'm bushed,' her father said. He turned to Keith and Edward. 'I don't want to hurry you, chaps, especially as tomorrow's Sunday and we can all have a lie-in, but I for one am pretty well whacked, so if you want jam butties you'd better start cutting them whilst Gillian makes the cocoa.'

The boys did not remove their coats, and said good-night politely as Alex, yawning widely, headed for the stairs. 'Glad you had a grand time,' he called over his shoulder, 'and don't regard what Auntie Clarke said. I wasn't a bit worried – well, only a bit – but now I'll hit the hay. See you in the morning.'

He disappeared, and the boys refused both cocoa and butties and made for the back door. Edward had a ten-minute walk and Keith would have to catch a tram, but they replied cheerfully to the girls' farewells that they would probably be around in the morning to talk over their party.

When the door had closed behind them, Gillian gave an exaggerated sigh and threw herself into one of the fireside chairs. 'Thank God they've gone,' she said devoutly. 'I'm fond of them both, but I need to talk to you.'

'Oh really?' Joy said, with more than a touch of sarcasm. 'I thought I was just a burden, but it appears I have my uses, few though they are.'

'Aren't you touchy?' Gillian said, and Joy imagined she heard a sneer in her voice. 'Well, be like that; I'm off to bed.'

'Go then, see if I care,' Joy shouted. 'I don't need any help from you, Gillian Lawrence.'

'Oh no?' Gillian shrieked. 'Well, we'll see! Damn your eyes!'

As Gillian disappeared Joy heard the kettle begin to boil and turned off the gas, then made herself a hot drink. She was still shaking with rage and was determined not to go up to bed herself until her sister was soundly sleeping. If she did, the quarrel would escalate and she didn't want that after such a lovely day.

When an hour had passed she crept up the stairs and into the bedroom. Gillian was just a hump beneath the covers and Joy undressed as quietly as she could and slid into bed, heaving the blankets up over her shoulders. By golly, it had been a grand evening, something really different; she would not let Gillian spoil it for her. She snuggled down; everyone wanted to do it again, though once the cold snap broke . . .

Exhausted as much by the argument as by the sledging, Joy slept at last.

Joy awoke and lay on her back, wondering when the alarm would go off. Then she remembered it was Sunday and she could have perhaps as much as an extra hour in bed. She turned on her side and snuggled her head into the pillow, trying to go back to sleep. Suddenly, she realised, in the way one does, that the room was empty save for herself. Was it later than she had thought? Sighing, she swung her legs out of bed, wincing as the chill on the linoleum made itself felt, then padded across the room, heading for the bathroom. Gillian must be in there, either spending a penny or washing; she would be able to tell her sister what time it was and whether she should get up.

Joy crossed the small landing and put a hand out towards the doorknob, then realised that the door was open and the bathroom was empty. Lord, it must be later than she had thought! Yet when she returned to her bedroom she realised that the Sunday sounds to which she had grown accustomed were missing. Normally, the pavements rang with the footsteps of people hurrying to church and bells sounding at different times from various places of worship, but now all was quiet.

She had been about to get back into bed, but now she hesitated. If it was really, really early, say five o'clock, then why on earth was Gillian not in her bed? Had she arranged to meet Keith for an expedition into the country? It was possible; Gillian and Keith sometimes went off by themselves to visit friends, or so they said. But she did not think any such arrangements had been made last night. Certainly Keith had said 'see you tomorrow', but that meant little. Had he had an early start in mind, he would have reminded Gillian of the fact, knowing how fond she was of her bed.

Joy hesitated for a moment outside Alex's door, but he was sound asleep; in fact he was snoring. It would be most unfair to wake him. But having ascertained that it was certainly not yet eight o'clock, the time the family usually rose on a Sunday, she returned to her room and began hastily to dress. It took ages, for her fingers were slippery with perspiration and her heart was pounding most unpleasantly. Something was wrong! Oh, why hadn't she realised that Gillian was being nasty to her because she was unhappy? For now, insensibly almost,

380

Joy had reached the conclusion not only that her sister was not in the house, but that she had gone off on some private business of her own.

As soon as she was respectable, therefore, she went downstairs, checked each room – they were all empty – and then returned to the upstairs landing and banged on her father's door. 'Dad, I'm sorry to wake you . . .'

He groaned and stirred, then sat up. 'Gillian? Is anything the matter? Is your sister all right? It's the middle of the night . . . well, quarter to six anyway, which is the middle of the night on a Sunday.' He was getting out of bed as he spoke, and Joy knew he was putting on his dressing gown and scuffing his feet into his old carpet slippers. 'There must be something, or you wouldn't have roused me so early.'

'I am my sister,' Joy said confusedly. 'That's to say it's Gillian who's disappeared. Oh, Dad, I don't know what to think!'

'Disappeared, pet?' Alex said, his voice sounding faintly amused. He came past her and headed for the stairs. 'I expect she's got up early for some reason and gone off with Keith. There'll be a note . . .'

They reached the hall, crossed it and entered the kitchen. Joy heard the light click on and her father reach for something on the table, saying cheerfully as he did so: 'I told you she'd leave us a note, telling us where she's gone and when she'll be back. I wonder why it's in an envelope, though?'

Joy heard the envelope being slit open and the sheets within withdrawn before she said quietly: 'Have you ever known Gillian go anywhere without telling me? I haven't. But what does the letter say?'

There was a short pause, and when Alex answered his tone was no longer cheerful; in fact, he sounded thoroughly puzzled. 'She says she's arranged to stay with the Dodmans, in Devon, for a few days. They've invited her often and now she feels the time is ripe.' He reached out and patted Joy's cheek. 'Darling, she says she loves you – and me, too – but is beginning to feel desperate to get away. What with Christmas, and Keith pestering her to get engaged even before she takes her Higher, she feels she needs time on her own to sort her feelings out. She promises to come back in a week or so . . .'

'But what about school?' Joy asked. 'Term starts in a few days.'

'Oh, she'll be back before then,' Alex said with a confidence Joy was sure he did not feel. He swung round and took her hand and she imagined she could feel his anxiety coming down his arm and through his hand into hers, like an electric shock. She was tempted to remind him that her twin was self-confident, clever and had two perfectly good eyes. Why should he worry about Gillian just because she had gone off in such a heedless, impulsive way? But then Alex seemed to recollect himself. 'Are you telling me, Joy, that she's left without so much as a word to you?' he asked incredulously. 'And without so much as a spare pair of nylons? I think we'd better go up to your room and see if you can tell me what's missing.'

Half an hour later, father and daughter sat at the kitchen table with a teapot and a plate of bread and butter before them, though neither attempted to eat or drink. They now knew that Gillian must have planned her flight well in advance, for she had packed a

Gladstone bag with all that she felt she would need during her absence.

Joy had bitten back her annoyance upon discovering that her twin had taken not only her own belongings, but also some of Joy's. 'She's pinched my new grey corduroys and the cherry red sweater Auntie Clarke made me,' she had said crossly. 'And she's left me her disgusting old flannel and taken my nice new one, as well as the little shoe-cleaning kit which Edward gave me for Christmas. I do hope that she's not snitched my wellies, because she takes a size smaller than I do and if I have to cram my feet into hers I'll be crippled as well as blind.'

However, Joy's wellies were discovered to be safe, and now Alex was getting down to the serious business of trying to discover some reason for Gillian's flight. 'You know her better than anyone, pet,' he told Joy. 'Are you absolutely sure that she said nothing of this in a casual sort of way over the last few days? Has she had a letter – oh, of course you couldn't possibly know if she'd received a letter and chosen not to tell you. But she might have mentioned the Dodmans. Have you any idea why she could have gone?'

There was a short pause before Joy replied, and when she did so she chose her words carefully. 'To tell you the truth, Dad, she and I had a bit of a barney on Friday night. She was complaining that I was a – a heavy responsibility, and saying that everyone expected her to keep an eye on me – as if I were a burden, you know. I got angry, I'm afraid, and said some things I didn't mean.'

'I did hear raised voices, but I didn't pay much attention,' Alex said. 'But if Gillian said those things she would have been joking, surely? She's never so much as hinted that she isn't delighted to go about with you. Why should she be? You're identical twins.'

'Oh, Dady, cast your mind back!' Joy interrupted. 'Before my accident, she was always saying that she hated being an identical twin and wanted to be regarded as a person in her own right. I'm not blaming her,' she added quickly, 'but I've thought quite often lately that she still sometimes resents our – our twinnishness.'

She expected her father to disagree, and was pleasantly surprised when he said thoughtfully: 'I know what you mean. Whilst you were at Blinkers, Gillian was free as a bird to do whatever she liked, whenever she liked. To tell you the truth, Auntie Clarke told me a couple of times that I should curb Gillian or she would become thoroughly selfish. I didn't really know what she meant, but now I suppose I do. She thought that whenever your sister announced – she never asked – that she was off somewhere, perhaps for a couple of days at the weekend tramping through the Welsh hills with a group of girlfriends, I should have asked for more details. It never occurred to me that she might be telling an untruth, but . . .'

'Gillian would never tell you a lie, Dad,' Joy said at once, then realised that she had leapt to her twin's defence without a thought. If she had given the matter consideration, she would probably have responded quite differently, but now was the time for little white lies, not for the starkness of the whole truth and nothing but the truth.

Alex leaned across the table and pushed a slice of bread and butter into Joy's hand. 'You must eat something,' he said coaxingly. 'I'm sure we're worrying for no reason; it's like brides before a wedding, nerves and so on.'

'But as we've already said, she'll have to come back in a few days because of school,' Joy observed. 'She won't risk losing valuable lesson time, because she really is serious about being the first Lawrence to go to university. She wants to go to Cambridge, like Keith, and I believe only the cream of the crop get to go there.'

Alex let out his breath in a long whistle of relief and Joy could imagine how the frown had lifted from his forehead as a smile lit his dark eyes and curved his mouth. 'Oh, darling, you're right, of course. She won't want to miss school, though I suppose a couple of days wouldn't make much difference. But now I want you to think hard. Has Gillian said anything, anything at all, about going off without a word to anyone? We would have been delighted to give her a little holiday, wouldn't we, Joy? I don't see why she couldn't tell us straight out. You could have gone with her, though work might have made it difficult . . .'

'Impossible, you mean,' Joy said ruefully. 'I'm not due for any time off until I've been at Wittard's for six months. But if Gillian wants to be alone to think, she wouldn't want me with her. It's a pity neither the Dodmans nor the Goodys are on the phone but Gillian's an adult, Dad, and extremely capable, even though she's not of age. I can tell you, she'll be furious if we try to interfere. We know she's safe with the dear Dodmans, so I really think we must grit our teeth and let well alone.'

The opening of the back door cut across her words and he and Joy turned towards the person who entered, well wrapped up against the bitter cold but immediately identifiable by the snuffling pug which barged in ahead of her.

'Say nothing . . .' Alex was beginning in an urgent whisper, but Joy shook a reproving head.

'Not sensible, Dad,' she hissed. 'Everyone's got to know; better say we agreed that Gillian needed a little holiday before beginning the spring term.' She raised her voice. 'I mean, Keith and Edward will be round later, and even if I could bring myself to lie to Keith, I could never do so to Edward. Why, with Gillian flying off in a temper I shall need dear Edward more than ever!'

'What's that?' Mrs Clarke said, bending to unclip Dilly's lead and propelling the fat little dog towards her favourite nook by the stove. 'What's Madam up to this time? She's been edgy for the best part of a week, complaining that she was scarcely able to leave the house without someone demanding to know where she was going.'

'Auntie Clarke, you're incredible,' Joy said, meaning every word. 'There's me and Dad wondering why Gillian should have decided to take off without a word to anyone, and you knew things weren't right all along.'

'I'm ashamed of myself,' Alex began, but was shushed at once by Mrs Clarke.

'The onlooker sees most of the game,' she said placidly. 'Gone off, has she? Well, I can't say I'm surprised.'

Gillian sat in the train which was taking her away from Liverpool and contemplated her past and her future. She had begun to plot as soon as young Dr Slocombe had told her he was off to take up an advantageous position as registrar at the Barnstaple infirmary. 'Don't you wish you could come with me?' he had said, giving her the benefit of his slow, meaningful smile. 'But there's no chance of that, of course, the way you feel. Indeed, it might be best if we said our goodbyes now, because I'm leaving next Saturday.'

Gillian had tried to display indifference, though she suspected she had made a poor job of it, telling him airily that next Saturday was the date fixed for the sledging party. 'So I shan't even be able to see you off,' she had told him. 'Never mind. I shall miss you, though . . .'

They had been meeting in the coach house at the back of the doctors' surgery whenever she could get away, exchanging delicious, wicked kisses and some rather heavy petting, so by the time the sledging party had been mooted she was deep in his thrall. It was odd really, because she was sure she did not love him, was indeed half afraid of him, but she was fascinated by his experienced lovemaking. If she went down to Devon for a couple of days he might expect her to share his bed, but she had no intention of so doing; it would simply be delightful to walk openly down the street, hand in hand, acknowledging their relationship. Maybe she might even discover that she did love him, that her fear was all part of that love; if so she would consider a more permanent relationship, though he had never suggested it.

However, she found she could not ruin her friends' pleasure by absconding on the day of the sledging party, so she decided not to tell Jason Slocombe that she meant to join him and laid her plans accordingly.

The train began to slow as it approached a small station and Gillian glanced at her wristwatch. They would have found her letter by now; probably they would be discussing it, deciding that Gillian had fled because she had been mean to her sister. She had engineered the row with her twin regretfully, for she knew Joy would be upset, but she told herself that it was just one of those things. She had to have a reason for her flight and could not tell anyone the truth, but at least she had left them an explanatory letter of sorts. Hopefully, by the time they managed to contact the Dodmans she would have arrived there and thought up some story that would satisfy the old couple and even soothe the worried breasts of her father and sister. Of course if she changed her mind and decided to dump Keith and take up with Jason Slocombe properly, there would be a great deal of difficult explanation to be done, but in her heart she knew that 'taking up' was a two-edged sword. Jason, the mature, experienced doctor, would not want to 'take up' with a girl of her age, who had no earning capacity to speak of.

The train slid to a stop at the platform and the porter hurried alongside, beginning to bawl out the name of the station. Gillian opened the magazine which lay on her lap and began to leaf through the pages. Presently she would be arriving in Barnstaple, finding accommodation, booking herself in for bed and breakfast . . . and her little holiday would begin!

Gillian descended from the train when it reached Barnstaple in a flurry of snow, alight with excited anticipation. She went straight to the infirmary and asked for Dr Slocombe, but to her disappointment the receptionist knew no one of that name either attached to the infirmary or about to take up a position there. Gillian explained that the young doctor, Jason Slocombe, had been in practice with his father, Dr Richard Slocombe, but had been offered a post – or so she believed – at this very hospital and was due to start work here the very next day.

The receptionist was charming and helpful. She summoned nurses and doctors and questioned them about a mysterious Dr Jason Slocombe who had told this young lady he had accepted a job as registrar in this very hospital. Unfortunately, though they racked their brains, no member of staff had so much as heard of a Dr Slocombe, either in their own area or in a neighbouring one. It was only when Gillian suddenly recognised both pity and embarrassment in their eyes that she realised she was making a fool of herself.

Jason was not here, never had been here, had no intention of coming here. If she had accompanied him as he had at first suggested, he would probably have told her that he would not start work until after she had left for Liverpool once more.

She left the infirmary as the snow eased, with many expressions of gratitude, and on impulse went down to the station, where she learned some indisputable facts. An elderly porter remembered the arrival the previous day of a handsome young fellow who had asked him to recommend a lodging. 'Cheap and cheerful,' the young man had said. 'I'm starting work here as chauffeur at Huntingdon Hall, but the job doesn't begin till Monday, so I'll need a roof over my head for tonight and tomorrow night too.'

The porter had recommended his sister-in-law, whose house was only a hundred yards from the station, and as he had heaved up the young man's suitcase had noticed the name upon the label. Jason Crawford, the label had said, c/o Mr Driscoll, Huntingdon Hall, Barnstaple, Devon.

So Jason wasn't even a doctor, but a chauffeur! What a stupid, blind fool I've been, Gillian told herself, thanking the porter in a choked voice and setting off in the direction in which he had pointed. Not that she had the slightest intention of calling on Jason . . .

'Hello there! So you decided to come after all; welcome to Barnstaple, my dear. I take it you've just descended from the train now pulling out of the station?'

It was Jason, urbane and smiling, in a white shirt and dark overcoat, a few snowflakes scattered on his shoulders. He was as immaculate as though he really were a doctor going off to visit his new hospital, and not a confidence trickster who had practised his wiles upon an innocent girl a dozen years younger than himself.

Gillian jumped and felt her heart give a tremendous leap, but replied as coolly as possible. 'Oh, it's you, Jason. Yes, I came after all, but you'll be relieved to know I shan't be staying. I am on my way to visit relatives and when the train stopped at Barnstaple I remembered you were starting work here . . . as a chauffeur, I believe?'

There was an infinitesimal pause before Jason's mobile brows shot upwards and he grinned lopsidedly. 'Well, well, well! Quite the little detective, aren't you? I admit I exaggerated the position I should hold at the infirmary, but . . .'

'Don't bother with any more inventions, Jason; I've been to the infirmary and very soon realised that you'd lied to me from the word go,' Gillian said wearily. 'You were Dr Slocombe's chauffeur, weren't you? You had the flat above the surgery and acted as security when you weren't driving the doctor. In fact you were a general handyman, emptying the dustbins, cleaning the car and brushing down the yard, right?' Light suddenly dawned. 'Why, it was *you* that my sister met on the train, not Dr Slocombe, and you were telling her a pack of lies when you pretended to be the doctor! I don't understand why you did it, because she had nothing you wanted . . . why, if she'd taken you up on your suggestion that she should visit Dr Slocombe's surgery you'd have been properly in the cart.'

Her companion grinned. 'So she *was* your sister, that kid in the train! I'd not realised . . . but you're right, my impersonation added a spice of danger to a rather mundane existence. Mine, that is, not your sister's. What's wrong with that? I wasn't hurting anyone, if that's what you think.'

Gillian laughed. 'Of course it's what I think, you stupid, conceited little man! You made a fool of me all right, but I'm wise to you now. I suppose Dr Slocombe found out that you had been using his name and dismissed you.'

'I left,' Jason Crawford said stiffly. Gillian watched as a tide of red crept up his neck and invaded his face, and realised that the words to which he objected must have been 'conceited little man'. It had flicked him on the raw, for she guessed no one had ever called him that before. He took a step towards her, retribution flaming in his suddenly narrowed eyes, but before she could turn away to run from him for the second time a fat little woman in a floral apron came panting along the pavement and seized his arm. 'Oh, Mr Crawford, sir, there's a Dr

Slocombe on the phone for you, something about a reference,' she said breathlessly. 'Can you come?'

Gillian had the satisfaction of seeing her adversary's
face go the colour of a Wensleydale cheese. Sweat had
broken out on his forehead, and with one last glare at
Gillian he turned and followed the woman who had
accosted him. Gillian realised she had been holding her
breath and let it go in a long whistle of relief, then set
out once more in the direction of the station.

Chapter Sixteen

Gillian had not doubted that she would be welcomed with open arms by the Dodmans, but their unfeigned delight was balm to her pride. She arrived in the early evening, having splashed out on a taxi from Barnstaple station, and when she paid the driver and approached the once well-known front door she feared for a moment that there was no one at home, for no light showed. However, just as she raised her hand to knock a light bloomed in the sitting-room window, and she remembered Mrs Dodman's little economies, which included not lighting the lamps until it was almost too dark to see one's hand before one's face, and handing out one's bedroom candle with the injunction to snuff it if there was moonlight enough.

So Gillian completed the movement and knocked with the familiar dah, dah, dee, dah, dah which she and her sister had always used on the rare occasions when they had come to the front door. She would have gone to the back, where the door opened straight into the kitchen, but because she had not written to warn of her arrival she felt it would be an intrusion. And now she could hear shuffling footsteps approaching the front door and remembered, rather guiltily, how they had teased Mr Dodman when he had said front doors were only used for weddings and funerals.

There was a grating of bolts, long unused, being drawn back and then a quavering voice spoke. 'Who be that? If you're after my hubby, he be here all right. He's been shootin' rabbits; still got his gun cocked and ready.'

Gillian giggled, but sobered up at once. 'It's all right, Mrs D, it's only me, Gillian. I meant to write and tell you I would be coming . . .'

The rest of her sentence was drowned as the bolts screeched back and the hinges groaned a protest as the door was pushed open. Gillian moved forward but was forestalled by Mrs Dodman, still clutching the lamp. She gathered her unexpected guest up in a hard hug, exclaiming tearfully: 'Oh, Gilly, Gilly, Gilly, 'bain't this the best surprise anyone could have? Come in, come in! My, how you've growed, my lover.' She pulled Gillian into the tiny sitting room, then looked past her, holding the lamp high and peering out into the gathering dusk. 'But where's my little Joy? Joy? Don't ee hide from me.'

Hastily, Gillian interrupted. 'Oh, Mrs D, I'm so sorry but Joy isn't here. The fact is I was supposed to be visiting friends in Barnstaple, only when I got there they were called away. I had meant to come on here to see you after spending a couple of days with my pals, but I was going to warn you by letter or telegram first. Only as it happens there simply wasn't time. As soon as I arrived they had to leave, so I decided to come straight to you.' She laughed. 'It never occurred to me for one moment that you might not be here.'

Mrs Dodman laughed too, then shivered. ''Tes mortal cold in here, my lover,' she observed, and Gillian saw her breath puff out like steam from a railway engine. 'Best you come wi' I into the kitchen where 'tes warm, for the stove don't never go out so the kettle's hoppin' on the hob. We'll have a nice cup of tea and tell each other all our news.'

Following her hostess into the cosy kitchen, Gillian was presently sitting on one of the creaky wooden chairs with a cup of tea before her and a plate of shortbread awaiting her attention. For a moment, sheer pleasure brought tears to her eyes. The mingled smells of the oil which fuelled the lamp, the scent of the bowl of hyacinths on the windowsill and those other, indefinable but well-remembered smells of the Dodmans' kitchen brought nostalgia and a longing for the old days winging back. Then she shook herself; this was no time for indulging in reminiscences. She was going to need all her wits about her if she was to keep her visit to Jason Crawford a secret.

But Mrs Dodman was gazing at her with bright-eyed curiosity and Gillian decided delaying tactics were required. 'Oh, Mrs Dodman, I really don't want to have to tell everything twice,' she said apologetically. 'What time will Mr Dodman be home?'

The old lady glanced at the clock on the mantel. 'It 'bain't his turn for the milkin' so he'll be back in half an hour,' she said, pushing the plate of shortbread towards her guest. 'Help thyself; 'tes a long cold way from Barnstaple to here, as I should know since Mrs Goody and meself stand a market there from time to time.'

By the time Mr Dodman returned, Gillian knew exactly what she was going to say. She had decided to tell the Dodmans that she and Joy had quarrelled. 'I was horrible to her, and I think it was because we are too close,' she said. 'When she was at the London School for the Blind she was only home at holiday times, but now she's home

395

all the time. She takes it for granted that I will go everywhere with her and do everything for her, in fact have
no life of my own, and it was beginning to get me down.'

'That don't sound much like the little Joy we knew . . .'
Mr Dodman began doubtfully, but Gillian shook her
head at him.

'She doesn't realise that she relies on me so heavily,'
she explained. 'And when I try to tell her, she either
laughs and says it's my imagination or takes the huff
and accuses me of no longer loving her. So I felt it would
benefit us both to have some time apart. I knew, though,
that if I said I was coming to see you Joy would have
insisted on accompanying me, which was the last thing
I wanted.' She gazed wryly from face to face. 'Did I do
wrong?'

'Yes, I reckon you did,' Mr Dodman said. 'If you want
the wood without the bark, I reckon you've prettied up
what happened so as to make yourself look better. You
always were a one for stories; now let's have the truth.'

Gillian tried to smother a giggle but failed. 'Well,
maybe what I told you wasn't entirely true,' she admitted.
'But Joy *is* too reliant on me, and anyway she's in work
now and couldn't have got away.'

'That's more like it,' Mr Dodman said sagely. 'But what
about these young fellers you and Joy mention in your
letters? What about them, eh?'

Gillian sighed. She might have known that there was
no sense in trying to pull the wool over Mr Dodman's
eyes, though his wife was far more gullible. 'Keith, d'you
mean? And Edward? They're nice young fellows, but . . .
look, I'll tell you what really happened if you'll swear
on the Bible never to tell a living soul.'

Mr Dodman grunted but his wife said eagerly: 'I'll fetch the Holy Book and we'll put our hands on it.'

'We shall do no such thing; that's blasphemy, that is,' Mr Dodman said sharply. 'We'll just promise not to tell.' He turned to Gillian. 'Will that suit your ladyship?'

Gillian agreed that it would, and began her sorry tale; she no longer thought of it as anything but that. 'Well, Joy was travelling home from London on the train when a strange man got into her compartment . . .'

Gillian finished her story with her discovery that Jason Crawford was most certainly not a doctor but a chauffeur and that he was also a confidence trickster, since he had called himself Dr Jason Slocombe and claimed that the real Dr Slocombe was his father.

'But what did he get out of it, my handsome?' Mrs Dodman said anxiously. 'Don't say ee gave way to him!'

Gillian felt a tide of colour flood her face. 'No I did not, thank God,' she said devoutly and then, seeing Mr Dodman's eyes fixed thoughtfully upon her face, added: 'I'm not such a fool as that! Oh, I admit I went to Barnstaple knowing that he might try it on, but I never would have let him.' Mr Dodman's eyes were still fixed on her face and she said crossly: 'I'll swear on the Bible that it never got as far as – as that, if you like.'

'That won't be necessary,' Mr Dodman said gruffly, whilst his wife nodded furiously and then shook her head, not sure which of these gestures was applicable. Mr Dodman turned to his wife. 'My, I'm so hungry my belly thinks my throat has been cut. Serve up that rabbit stew, Mother; if I don't get fed soon my nose will dive across the kitchen straight into that big old saucepan and help itself.'

Mrs Dodman complied, and as they ate the delicious rabbit stew the three of them worked out a story, part truth, part fantasy, which would satisfy the Lawrences. ''Tis very wrong to lie to one's family, but 'tis almost as wrong, sometimes, to tell the whole truth,' Mr Dodman said, whilst his wife nodded agreement.

'Since you've done nothin' to be ashamed of, the full truth could only worry poor Mr Alex, to say nothin' of our little Joy,' she said. 'What a good thing you came straight on here after you'd visited that infirmary. If you leave Barnstaple out of it altogether, you won't have to tell a single lie.'

Gillian thought it over and found to her relief that Mrs Dodman had hit the nail on the head. And at Mr Dodman's suggestion, as soon as supper was over Gillian borrowed his old bicycle and set off for the village, armed with a good handful of pennies. As soon as she was connected, the receiver was snatched up and Joy's voice, high with worry, gabbled out their number and then said anxiously: 'Gillian? Is that you? Oh, darling Gillian, we've been so worried!'

'Yes, it's me. I'm so sorry I worried you,' Gillian said. She was not surprised that Joy had known it was her on the other end of the telephone – they were twins, after all – but found she was dismayed by the distress in her sister's voice. 'I suppose I should have phoned earlier, but I had to summon up all my courage because it was a rotten thing to do to go off and leave you with no real explanation. Only I knew you would know I'd be safe with the Dodmans . . .'

The receiver was snatched from Joy's hand and Alex's voice came down the wire. 'Gillian? You wretched, thoughtless young devil, how dared you worry us so! Joy kept saying she knew you were all right, but you've had everyone worried stiff. Keith was frantic, kept talking about some feller called Rodney who as far as I could gather he thought might have whisked you away.' He chuckled. 'To South America, I presume; the white slave trade, you know. If the Goodys and the Dodmans were on the telephone we could have made sure you'd arrived safely, but we still can't understand why you went off so – so furtively. You didn't even tell Joy, and you tell her most things . . .'

Gillian began to mumble that she had had her reasons, then came out with the half-truth which she and the Dodmans had decided on. 'I knew Joy couldn't possibly take time off from Wittard's to come with me and to be honest, Daddy, I didn't want her. I wanted to be alone to think. Joy and I could have rushed down one Saturday and returned on the Sunday, but that wasn't what I needed. Can you understand?'

'No, not really,' Alex said after the briefest of pauses. 'I take it you mean to return before term starts? If not, you'll have to explain to your teachers yourself, because I don't intend to do so.'

Gillian sighed. 'I'll be back in less than a week, so no one need explain anything to anyone else,' she said. 'And now I simply must get back to the Dodmans because I've only got five pennies left and I'm deathly tired. Put Joy back on so I can say I'm sorry I worried her and then I'll climb aboard Mr Dodman's old bicycle and get back to the cottage.'

Joy's voice came down the wire. 'Gillian? What a beast you are to worry us so! But I forgive you, darling twin, because I understand more than you think . . .'

Gillian was about to reply when the operator's voice cut in. 'Have you finished, caller? There are others waiting for this line, but if you wish to continue to talk please place another shilling in the slot.'

'Haven't got another shilling. Goodbye!' Gillian shrieked and replaced her receiver with a thump.

I might have guessed Joy would begin to put two and two together, and she knows me so well that she could make four, she told herself, emerging from the stuffy kiosk and taking deep lungfuls of the icy air. It had not snowed on her bike ride into the village and now, looking up at a black sky spangled with stars, she thought that it would remain cloudless and therefore snowless until morning.

As she mounted the bicycle, her thoughts went back to the time she and Joy had spent here as children. How they had loved everything about it! In a big city, when peacetime brought street lighting back to even the tiniest alleys, one seldom noticed the stars, but out here they blazed as they had done in biblical times.

Pedalling with care, Gillian decided to write a long and apologetic letter to her twin, and then settled down to the journey home. As she rode, she found herself singing:

> *We three kings of Orient are;*
> *Bearing gifts we traverse afar*
> *Field and fountain, moor and mountain,*
> *Following yonder star . . .*

She bounced on the bicycle's ancient leather saddle and realised suddenly that she had seldom felt happier;

not, in fact, since she had lived here as of right rather than as a guest. Recklessly she speeded up, ignoring the ruts and the iced-over puddles. She was young Gillian Lawrence again, making her way home after a trip to the shops for something Mrs Dodman needed. She glanced into the bicycle basket, almost expecting to see groceries, then smiled to herself. Tomorrow she would go into the village and visit Mrs Bailey's little shop. She would buy aniseed balls and liquorice sticks, both great favourites with the Dodmans, if her sweet coupons would stretch that far; if not, it would have to be pipe tobacco for Mr Dodman and a packet of the little iced cakes his wife loved. Pedalling hard, she broke into song once more:

> *O star of wonder, star of night,*
> *Star with royal beauty bright . . .*

* * *

When Gillian awoke on the third day of her visit to the Dodmans, she knew at once that her carefully laid plans were about to go awry, and seldom had she felt more pleased over the prospect of such a disruption. Sitting up on one elbow she tweaked the curtain back and breathed a porthole in the frosted pane, though she had little doubt of what she would see. Snow! Not the sort of snow which could be brushed aside – ha ha – but the sort which trapped people in their homes and might take a whole family the best part of a day to dig themselves out of. It must have been snowing all night, and certainly it was snowing still; big flakes were being whirled almost horizontally by the wind, but even so the branches of the trees were white with it, and Gillian knew that the lane which led in one direction to the Goodys' farmhouse and in the other to the village would already be almost impassable, for the banks on either side – sweet with primroses, violets and wild strawberries at other times of year – would have filled up with snow as a cup fills with milk.

This made her remember that possibly Mr Dodman might be on early milking today; if so, she should get up at once since he would need all the help he could get to reach the lane, let alone to traverse it. She got out of bed, cringing as warm feet touched cold floorboards. She had not packed a dressing gown, having taken only essentials when she had fled from her home, but reached for her trusty duffel coat, slipping her arms into the sleeves and doing up the toggles before she shot her feet into her brogues and set off for the stairs. The warmth coming up from the kitchen – for the staircase led directly into that room – was delicious and Gillian fairly scampered down the rest of the treads to be met by big smiles from her hosts, both seated at the kitchen table as though snow was nothing out of the ordinary.

'Marnin', maid. Hast come to help dig we out?' Mrs Dodman said cheerfully. 'We'm heard the weather forecast; 'tes likely we'll be snowed in for a day or so, but you won't mind that. Father is on early milking, but Mr Goody knows we 'baint as young as we used to be so he'll send Alfie and Mick up to help clear a way through.'

Mr Dodman nodded confirmation, then stared hard at his guest. 'Are you'm dressed under that coat?' he asked suspiciously. 'If not, you'd best get upstairs again.

Mother's made the porridge and brewed the tea, so you and myself can dig a way across the yard as soon as you're decent and you've had some grub to line your stomach.'

'Right,' Gillian said briskly, turning on her heel and beginning to mount the wooden stairs she had just descended. As she reached her own room and began to dress, she thought guiltily that at home she would have brought hot water up and given herself a good wash. But that could come later, after she and Mr Dodman, ably assisted by Alfie and Mick, had fought their way through to the shippon and the cows waiting patiently to be milked.

Later, relaxing in the kitchen again and seeing the flakes continuing to whirl past the window, Gillian thought that she really should try to reach the village so that she could warn her father and sister that she might not be able to return as planned, but she knew it wasn't really necessary. Joy would hear on the wireless that the snow had descended over places like Exmoor, that the ponies were being brought into shelter or at least fed with bales of hay, and would guess that her twin's leaving would be held up, perhaps for several days. And since Mr Goody had agreed that whilst the severe weather lasted he would not expect his 'best cowman' (his very words) to fight his way to the farm each day, Gillian was not the only one to suddenly find herself enjoying a little holiday.

And enjoying was the word. Somehow, in the un-demanding company of the two old people, Gillian began to see that though she had honestly believed she had told the Dodmans the whole truth, she had only told them half, chiefly because the other half was so deeply buried in her subconscious that it had taken time, quiet and a good deal of self-examination before she had begun to accept that there was more to her running away than even she had realised.

Little remarks, often coming from Mrs Dodman, had helped. On one day, when Gillian had battled into the village and returned triumphant with flour, sugar, margarine and sultanas, Mrs Dodman had remarked as she unloaded the goods: 'Once it would have been young Joy who went off after me messages, as you children used to call errands. I used to think you were a bit jealous of young Joy . . . well you were, there's no denyin'.' She had shot a beady, bright-eyed glance at Gillian, who was staring at her round-eyed, and chuckled. 'Oh aye, lover, I dare say now you'm ashamed, but I reckon you're still a bit envious like . . .'

Gillian had begun to protest hotly, to point out that her sister was blind, almost entirely dependent on others, but Mrs Dodman, though she cackled, had shaken her head. 'Envy and jealousy bain't 'xactly the same, my little love, and as mortals we'm all at their marcy, so to say. You bain't jealous of Joy, but I reckon, from odd remarks you've dropped, that you envy the way people love your sister. Oh, I don't doubt you've a heap of pals and are headin' for a great future, but there's a sweetness and generosity in Joy which makes her loved wherever she goes, and she don't have to make no effort, it comes nat'ral. Know what I mean?'

Poor Gillian would have liked to deny it, to say that Mrs Dodman's imagination was running away with her, but her innate honesty forbade it. Instead, she began to think hard and eventually of course to realise that her old friend was right. She did envy Joy her ease with people, was definitely envious of the care and affection their father lavished on her twin, and though she would not have exchanged sight for lack of it she was now aware that in a deeply buried part of her mind she blamed herself, as the elder twin, for not grabbing her sister and pulling her back into the room so that the window crashed harmlessly back into place, injuring no one.

And the best part of this was, she thought now, that confession can go hand in hand with absolution. As she admitted these things to the Dodmans she was aware that they understood, did not condemn her, even admired her honesty. And this filled her with such overwhelming relief that she longed to spend the rest of her life in the little cottage, even though she also longed for the new Gillian to return home so that Alex and Joy could appreciate the change.

Whilst the bad weather continued Gillian revelled in the company of her two old friends, and when at last it cleared she packed her belongings and bade them goodbye with many tears and much gratitude. 'You don't know what you've done for me, the pair of you,' she said as they stood on the station platform waiting for the train which would take her, she felt, from one home to another. 'You've made me see things clearly for the first time. I'm so very grateful . . . and I mean to come back in the summer holidays, if that's all right by you. And this time' – the pang of previously unrecognised jealousy shot through her and was quickly dismissed – 'this time I'll bring Joy, I promise.'

* * *

All the way home in the train Gillian had been buoyed up by a feeling of righteousness; she was going to tell Joy everything, and once she had done that she would tell an expurgated version to her father, perhaps even drop a hint or two to Auntie Clarke, because that lady spent almost as much time in their house as in her own.

But as the train neared Liverpool the first tiny seeds of doubt began to make themselves felt. Suppose Joy was so angry with her that she would not listen, would not believe that her sister had changed, that the quarrel had been manufactured? After all, it was a lot for anyone to take on board. She had left her home more than two weeks previously thinking, she now realised, only of herself. She had intended to have some sort of affair with Jason, though she had told herself she did not mean to let it go too far. But when she had tried to explain that to Mrs Dodman, that wise old person had clucked disapprovingly. 'Don't this feller have no mind of his own?' she had enquired. 'What might have happened between the pair of you would have been as much his choice as yours. Don't ee realise that, maid?'

Gillian had seen that Mrs Dodman, as usual, had hit the nail on the head, but had clung stubbornly to the belief that she would have come to her senses before things had got out of hand.

'Liverpool Lime Street!'

The porter's voice had Gillian hopping up and dragging her bag from the rack. It was Saturday, so Joy would not be working, but Gillian had not mentioned which train she would be catching. She had had to make several changes, and had not wanted either her twin or Alex to waste a perfectly good day hanging about the station, so she climbed down without looking round and headed for the street.

'Gillian? Over here!'

Gillian jumped and looked wildly about her, so keen to see her twin that she missed her completely and was accordingly nearly bowled over by Joy's impetuous hug. 'Darling, darling twin! Oh, I was sure you'd arrive around now . . . Edward brought me down to the station but he pointed you out – your general direction, that is – and then went off. Dear Edward, he's so tactful!'

'And boring,' Gillian said before she could stop herself, and could have bitten her tongue out. This was the sort of remark that she had made too often, not consciously meaning to denigrate her twin's friends yet managing to do so with odd snide comments. She felt Joy withdraw a little, saw her sister's mouth tighten, and burst into speech. 'Joy, I'm so sorry; what a dreadful thing to say! You couldn't have a better friend than Edward; he's totally reliable and always willing to help in any way he can.'

'And boring,' Joy said regretfully. 'But then I'm pretty boring myself.' She gave herself a little shake and tucked her hand into Gillian's arm. 'Edward's just a friend, you know; I'm not planning to spend the rest of my life with him or anything like that. Oh, Gillian, it's so good to have you back! I know you've only been gone a couple of weeks, but I've not had a single flash of sight in all that time. Odd, isn't it? But probably it was just because I was anxious about you.'

'Well, you needn't be anxious any more,' Gillian said, laughing. 'We're just approaching the end of the tram queue so we might as well join it, because judging by its length there's one due any minute.'

'Right,' Joy said. 'Dad's on Watch and Mrs Clarke has gone up to the church hall to help with the Scouts' jumble sale, so we'll have the house to ourselves for a bit.'

As they joined the end of the queue, Gillian stood her bag down for a moment and took both her twin's hands in a warm clasp. 'D'you know, Joy, as the train got near Liverpool I began to wonder if you could ever find it in your heart to forgive me for inventing that quarrel so that I had a reason for running away. I actually imagined you'd give me the cold shoulder and refuse to speak to me. I should have known better; you've always been so generous and loving.'

Gillian had dropped her voice to a whisper but Joy spoke normally. 'How could you be so daft! Sisters fall out and have rows; even twins can get a cob on from time to time. But we never mean it and never will. So now, Gillian, you can tell me why you ran off. Don't pretend you just went to visit the Dodmans, because once you'd admitted that the barney was your own invention it's clear even to boring old me that you must have had some much more interesting reason for bobbying off. And I'll guess it had something to do with that young doctor—'

'Hush,' Gillian hissed, suddenly certain that every person in the queue was listening with great interest to their conversation. 'You're right, of course, but we can't discuss it now. Wait until we're home. If Auntie Clarke and Dad are still out, as you say, I can tell you exactly what happened to me and you can tell me what everyone here thinks. Did you tell Keith I was all right before he went back to Cambridge?'

Joy nodded. 'Yes, of course, and he accepted my

explanation that we'd had a disagreement and you'd gone flouncing off to Devon without a murmur.' She grinned. 'I won't say Keith's boring, because it isn't true, but he's certainly not the suspicious kind.'

'I thank God for it,' Gillian said devoutly. 'Oh, Joy, I've been such a fool . . . but I won't say any more until we're somewhere slightly less public.'

In the event, both girls' stories were soon told and Joy was triumphant when her sister revealed that Jason was a confidence trickster and not a doctor at all. 'So he wasn't even Dr Slocombe's son, but his chauffeur! He fooled us both, didn't he?'

Gillian nodded. 'Only of course you would probably have guessed he wasn't a doctor if you had been able to see his face when he tried to get pally with you on the train.'

'But *you* saw his face, though admittedly not on the train, and you never guessed he wasn't a doctor,' Joy pointed out. 'I don't think that seeing or not seeing, in this instance at least, makes any difference. So it wasn't his father – I mean Dr Slocombe – on the train either?'

'No, it was Jason. But I hope it's taught me a lesson; I'll never be so perishin' gullible again,' Gillian said. They were sitting in the kitchen, munching toast and warming their hands round mugs of tea, for although there was no snow in Liverpool it was very cold. 'And now let's put it all behind us. I'll go back to St Hilda's – I wrote to tell the head that I was snowed up and would be late back – and you're already back at Wittard's, of course. I'm quite looking forward to seeing old Keith, but I suppose I won't do so until his Easter vac.' She sighed and stretched. 'I wrote to him from the farm, but Mrs

Dodman thinks I should tell him that I'm too young to be going steady with anyone. After all, when I go to college I'll meet heaps of young men and I don't want to feel guilty every time I smile at one of them.'

'Then you ought to tell Keith to back off a bit,' Joy observed. 'If you explain . . .'

'I'm sick and tired of explanations,' Gillian said. 'He's not my perishin' keeper. And now let's decide exactly how much to tell Dad and Auntie Clarke.'

That night, with all the telling over, Joy lay on her back in her bed, listening to Gillian's snuffling snores and the familiar sounds floating up both from the street outside and from their kitchen below, where Alex and Auntie Clarke were having a last mug of tea before Auntie Clarke went home.

Gillian's story had been placidly accepted, though she had had to employ some fairly nifty footwork in order to avoid mentioning the episode in Barnstaple. The twins had decided that the quarrel would have to be a sufficient reason for Gillian's flight, so had exaggerated the bad feeling between the two of them. Alex had pulled a rueful face – he hated to admit that his daughters were capable of such bitter feuding – but Joy had sensed that Auntie Clarke knew more than she was prepared to admit and hoped that her dear old friend would manage to satisfy Alex that the quarrel, though violent, was now over and forgotten.

As soon as I can, Joy planned drowsily as sleep began to overtake her, I'll have a word with Auntie Clarke. Dad would be terribly worried and upset to know that Gillian was taken in by that wicked Jason Crawford, but Auntie

Clarke's a woman and understands such things. She's always been against Gillian tying herself down, as she puts it, before she even goes to university. She'd probably say that the Jason business has taught Gillian a valuable lesson – if she knew about it, that is. Only I suspect she's twigged that there was more to Gillian's running away than either of us cared to explain.

Joy turned her head towards the window, pulled back the curtain a little way, and rested the palm of her hand on the pane. The glass was cold, but not frosted, and by leaning forward and pressing her cheek against it she could just hear the gentle sound of falling rain. She smiled to herself. Spring was just round the corner, she and her twin were back together again, and all was right with their world.

Joy slept.

Chapter Seventeen

By the time summer arrived Joy and Gillian had almost forgotten the 'Jason episode', as they called it. Gillian was working far more wholeheartedly than ever before in order to gain her Higher School Certificate, whilst Joy was well regarded at Wittard's. She had made several friends, and Ducky, who had served her six months as tea girl and messenger, had been promoted to the most junior member of the typing pool, which meant that she no longer had to arrive early. The two girls had formed the habit of meeting at the tram stop nearest Joy's home and travelling to work together.

For all her flighty ways, Ducky was proving to be not only a good friend but also sensible and helpful. She understood Joy's needs and went out of her way to be around when necessary, though, as Joy told Gillian, she did this as unobtrusively as Edward.

Standing by the tram stop now, waiting for her, Joy thought back to an occasion a few weeks earlier when she and Gillian had taken Mrs Clarke out one weekend. They had gone ostensibly to admire the floods of daffodils and other spring flowers in the park, but really to explain more fully to Mrs Clarke what had happened when Gillian had run away from home. 'I think it's only fair, because she's been as good as a mother to us,' Joy had said. 'I suppose you really ought to 'fess up to Dad as well, but I think we'll let Auntie Clarke decide how much he should know.'

Mrs Clarke had nodded wisely when the story had been told. 'No point in worrying Alex,' she had said serenely. 'Not since it came to nothing. In fact, my dears, the person who should be told is Keith.' She had turned rather a stern look upon Gillian, the first such look the older twin had received from that good lady. 'Have you examined your feelings for Keith? You're eighteen now, love – your mother was married to your father at eighteen, and expecting you. So you're not too young to decide how you feel.'

'I've told him everything,' Gillian had said quietly, and Joy had turned quickly away so that her twin should not read her surprise. 'I explained that the business with Jason was just a sort of super-crush, or pash, or whatever you like to call it. I told him that it had made me realise that it was him I loved.'

They had been in the park café, sipping a welcome coffee, and Joy had turned her head towards where she knew her sister was sitting. 'You never told *me* Keith knew,' she had said reproachfully. 'I thought we told each other everything!'

'Now that's where you're wrong, Miss Know-all,' Gillian had said rather sharply. 'I didn't intend to tell you, Auntie Clarke, but you sort of lulled me into it. And I'm not sorry, that I told, I mean, because you'd have noticed sooner or later that I've stopped pushing Keith away when he gets lovey-dovey. He still wants to get engaged, but I don't want to do that until I've got my degree. It's not that I'm doubtful any longer, because I'm sure Keith is the man for me, but—'

413

'I've always said you shouldn't be tied down until you've seen a bit more of life,' Mrs Clarke had interposed. Joy had heard the click as the older woman replaced her cup in her saucer and the rustle as she stood up. 'I take it I am now in possession of *all* the facts and not just half? Very well then; you promised to take me on the boating lake, so we'd best go down there and hire something large and comfortable.'

Right now, however, Joy heard the clatter of a tram approaching and guessed that the tap-tapping of someone's shoes as they flew along the pavement would almost certainly be Ducky. Blessed with an easy-going mother and four or five younger brothers and sisters, Ducky was in the habit of helping her parent to get the younger ones ready for school, so was always in a rush.

'Made it!' Joy heard Ducky's breathless voice in her ear, even as her friend's hand tucked itself confidently into Joy's own. 'Gosh, it were a rush this morning! Emmy could only find one sock, Freddie spilt porridge all down his clean shirt and I burnt the first batch of toast to a cinder. Still an' all, I made it.' The queue began to shuffle forward and Ducky gave Joy's hand a pinch. 'Here's your pal Edward, very red in the face; looks as though he's been running. Does he want this tram? I've give him a wave, so he's comin' to join us . . . Mornin', Edward!'

'Good morning, ladies,' Edward said breathlessly; clearly Ducky's guess had been right, Joy thought, as she echoed her friend's greeting. 'Joy, are you doing anything in your lunch hour? Only we need to talk.'

'Ooh, what about? Anything exciting?' Joy asked hopefully. 'I won't ask if you mean to buy me lunch because Auntie Clarke made Cornish pasties last night, so I've got one of them, an apple and a couple of ginger snaps.'

Edward laughed. 'Mine's corned beef sandwiches and brown sauce and I've got an apple an' all,' he said. 'We'll take 'em down to the Mersey – the tide will be out – and watch the kids mudlarking whilst we eat. I'll watch, I mean, and tell you if they find anything interesting.'

'Sounds fun; reckon I'll come along an' all,' Ducky said cheekily.

Edward began to protest as they climbed aboard the tram, but Joy grabbed his shoulder, felt up his neck and plonked a hand across his mouth. 'She was only joking, you twit,' she said reprovingly. 'Today's Friday, which is her canteen day, isn't it, Ducky?'

Ducky squeezed between them, strap-hanging as they were, and giggled. ''S right, only kiddin',' she agreed cheerfully. 'Why's your face so red, Edward? Ooh, that reminds me, I promised me mam I'd buy half a pound of tomatoes so she can make a salad for tonight's supper.'

'Are you trying to say my face is the colour of a tomato . . . ?' Edward stopped speaking as the tram ground to a halt at the next stop, and the conductor began to push his passengers as hard as he could in order to get a further half-dozen people aboard. 'You all right, Joy? Keep a good hold of that strap and I'll keep a good hold of you.'

'I'm fine, if a trifle squashed,' Joy assured him as the tram lurched into motion. 'It's poor Ducky who gets trampled underfoot 'cos she's so little . . .'

'I am not – little I mean,' Ducky squeaked. 'It's only because your mate Edward here is a great overgrown beanpole that I seem little. Last time I measured meself I were five foot four.'

'You? Five foot four? Four foot five perhaps,' Edward said, just as the tram stopped again with a jerk which caused several passengers to crash into one another and complain vociferously.

'I were in a cattle truck on the Burma railway during the war and I swear this is as bad,' one passenger shouted. He turned to address the conductor. 'The only difference is you ain't a little fiend, like what the perishin' Japs are.'

There was a general laugh as people began to fight their way off the tram against the tide of incoming passengers, and the conductor grinned sheepishly when someone pointed to a sign giving the number of standing passengers allowed. 'Awright, awright; but if I stuck to them rules you'd none of you be in work on time,' he pointed out righteously. He reached up and tinged the bell. 'Hold very tight, please, ladies and gents.'

With a little more room, Joy tried to move away from Edward, but he was having none of it. 'Stop wriggling,' he ordered. 'We get off at the next stop so this will be my last chance of a cuddle before you go your way and I go mine.'

Joy giggled. 'Trams are not the place for cuddling,' she said reprovingly. 'However, if you're set on it, you might give Ducky the odd squeeze. She's had a tough morning and could do with a show of affection.'

Edward was beginning to respond when the tram stopped once more and a number of passengers, including Joy, Ducky and Edward, surged off the vehicle and on to the pavement. Joy felt the breeze from the Mersey caress her face and turned impulsively to Edward. 'It's a lovely day, isn't it? I can feel the sunshine, and the breeze too. Wouldn't it be nice to go into the country tomorrow, if the weather stays good? Or we could go to New Brighton; oh, do say we can, Edward! Gillian's off somewhere with Keith, but if you were free . . . oh, was that what you were going to suggest when we meet at lunchtime? I do hope so.'

Edward laughed. 'Well, maybe something similar,' he said cheerfully, drawing her to a halt as they reached her office block. 'It's exciting . . . but I don't mean to say any more. I'll pick you up here at half past twelve, and don't forget to bring your grub. I'll buy you a cup of tea, though, before we part.'

All through the morning, Joy wondered what delightful treat Edward was planning. She had sensed his excitement, felt it running through her like an electric shock when he had put his arms round her in the tram.

She was just thinking that it would never be half past twelve when she felt a hand on her shoulder. 'Off with you, queen! I'll take good care of your switchboard, you can be sure of that. Enjoy your lunch and be back by half past one,' a cheerful voice said in her ear.

Joy turned towards the girl who had spoken. 'Thanks, Myra. I hope the weather will stay fine for me,' she said. She stood up and heard the other girl slide into her seat. 'Don't worry, I'll be back in plenty of time. I've got a carry-out so shan't be queueing for a seat in Lyons or Fuller's.'

She hurried out of the building, not bothering to use her stick, and was no sooner through the double doors than a familiar voice hailed her and a hand took hers. 'On time, as usual. Come on, let's get ourselves a seat where we can't be overheard.'

'Secrets?' Joy said hopefully. 'Oh, Edward, I do love secrets.'

'Well, not exactly . . . here's a good place to sit,' he said, and pressed Joy gently down on what she realised was a painted wooden bench; she could feel the bubbles in the paintwork where the sun had raised blisters. 'Ready?'

Joy hugged herself, then fished her lunch packet out of her handbag and began to undo the greaseproof paper in which the food had been wrapped. 'Carry on. Want a bit of my pasty?' she asked, speaking rather thickly through a mouthful.

'Later,' Edward said. 'Listen, queen; do you remember the summer before you went to Blinkers when you and I didn't meet in the holidays because I was working for my uncle Meirion on a farm outside Denbigh? And I went last summer as well, but for a much shorter time?'

'He's the one who broke his leg, isn't he? You've mentioned him several times, but of course not having actually met them—'

Edward interrupted her. 'Well, we can soon remedy that. If you're agreeable, we could go there this very weekend. The thing is, queen, Uncle Meirion and Auntie Myfanwy have no kids of their own, and Uncle Meirion has made me an incredible offer. I guess he knows I find accountancy pretty boring, and he says if I'll give up my place at university and my holiday job and work full time on the farm, he'll leave it to me in his will. But even better, he means to make me a partner once I've proved my worth. That shouldn't take long, because I don't mind telling you, sweetheart, that I'm a good deal better at farming than accounting. So I'm going to leave university.'

418

There was an appreciable pause before Joy spoke. 'Of course I can quite see that it's a wonderful opportunity,' she said at last, 'but oh, Edward, I shall miss you dreadfully. Not because you're such a tremendous help to me, I hope I'm not that selfish, but because you're my best friend, the person I love most next to Dad and Gillian. In fact, I can't imagine life without you, but of course that's downright silly. You weren't with me at the LSB, and I managed to survive the time, so I'm sure I'll very soon learn to manage without you. I expect you'll come back to Liverpool sometimes . . .'

'But you won't have to learn to manage without me,' Edward said eagerly. 'You're eighteen years old and I'm twenty, exactly the same ages as your parents were when they married.' He leaned across and took both her hands in his. 'Darling Joy, I explained the situation to my uncle and aunt and they are willing – no, eager – for me to bring a wife with me to Cae Madog farm. Poor Auntie Fan – that's what I call her – has terrible arthritis and would be glad of a hand around the house.'

Joy frowned. Could she be hearing right? He was talking as though the whole thing was cut and dried, yet there had certainly never been any mention of marriage between them. Surely he should not have told his relatives that he was contemplating such a huge step without consulting me first, she thought angrily. But Edward was speaking again. 'Darling Joy, I know it's all a bit sudden; I haven't even told you how very much I love you, but can't you see, this is a chance in a thousand and I've simply got to take it, or regret it for the rest of my life.'

'Oh, I quite see, but I'm afraid I'd be pretty useless on a farm,' Joy said coolly. 'Have you forgotten I'm blind,

419

or did your aunt and uncle say it didn't matter? Honestly, Edward, of all the daft ideas! I earn a good salary from Wittard's and I manage pretty well with the house-keeping, though I admit Auntie Clarke gives me a lot of help. What's more, I don't want to be separated from Gillian by miles and miles.'

'But sweetheart, you know very well that Gillian means to marry Keith and go happily off to be a doctor's wife as soon as he qualifies,' Edward said, and Joy could hear the desperation in his voice.

She was sorry for it, but was still suffering from a sense of annoyance because he had not thought to even hint at any of this until the chips were down and a deci-sion had to be made. 'Oh, I know that Gillian and Keith will marry and move away,' Joy said impatiently. 'But that's been planned well in advance, wouldn't you say? Keith's been talking about it ever since he and Gillian got serious, whereas you seem to have planned my future without a word to me.'

'You're right. I'm a thoughtless, selfish fool,' Edward said humbly. 'It's just that when my uncle's letter arrived this morning, my first thought was that I couldn't bear to be parted from you. So I rang him and explained and he said at once that as my wife you would be very welcome. I'm sorry, I do realise I did it the wrong way round and should have put it to you first, but I thought – I thought . . .'

'You thought that poor old Joy would be glad to do anything to secure her future,' she said bitterly. 'You thought I'd jump at getting any husband, like a trout at a fly. But just because I can't see doesn't mean I'm desperate for marriage.' She turned angrily towards where Edward was sitting next to her. 'So far as I can make out, marriage is just a trap and I'd be better off single.'

'You're misunderstanding me, Joy,' Edward said, sounding both hurt and puzzled. 'What's the matter with you? You've never spoken to me like this before. Most girls would think a proposal of marriage a compliment . . .'

'Oh, most girls might, but I'm not like most girls, so the answer's no,' Joy snapped. 'You've been a good friend to me, Edward, but I couldn't possibly marry you. You see, I'm already in love in a sort of way. Do you remember when those girls tried to beat me up and I was rescued by a fellow who heard my shouts?'

Edward listened whilst she described the whistlers – or rather whistler, for she had always secretly believed that it was the same person on each occasion. When she had finished, he was silent for a few moments, wondering what to say. He hated to disillusion her, but it had to be done. 'Oh, sweetheart, a whistle is just about the most anonymous sound that anyone can make. Of course, all your whistlers *might* have been the same person, but do you think it's likely, given that you heard them in London and Llandudno as well as Liverpool? What's more, it could have been a woman – had you thought of that?'

'No,' Joy said sulkily, after a pause. 'But there is another reason for my not marrying and going away from Gillian, not yet. I've been having these brief moments, sightings I call them, when I can see for a flash of time just as clearly as I did before the accident. Well, you were with us by the boating lake when I had the most recent one. And I'm pretty sure it means my eyes are beginning to work properly again. The thing is, it's only when I'm with Gillian that I get these sightings. I'm sure they will improve and happen more often, and they probably don't depend upon Gillian's presence, but I need to be near her for the time being. It's a secret from everyone else, including Dad, and I want to be certain before I talk of it. Oh, I would so love to be able to see again, to see the man I mean to marry, whether it's you, the whistler, or someone else altogether. Can you understand that?'

'Ye-es,' Edward said slowly after a moment. 'But suppose I told you it's possible that those – those sightings were caused by something quite different? Weren't really your eyes seeing at all? After what happened at the boating lake I talked it over with Gillian and she agrees with me . . .'

Joy felt herself begin to bristle. 'So you've discussed me with my sister, as well as your aunt and uncle?' she said, keeping her voice level with difficulty. 'And Gillian told you I'd had other moments when I could see? And the pair of you decided I was making it up – wishful thinking, it's called – so I might as well marry you, squint, wooden leg and all?' She jumped to her feet and brandished her stick, scattering her food and not caring a jot. 'Well, you're both bloody well wrong, do you hear me? I *have* had flashes of being able to see, and they *will* get closer and closer until I can see just as well as you or bloody Gillian! And now bugger off and don't ever come back, because I'm going back to Wittard's now and I don't need you or anyone else to show me the way!'

Edward jumped to his feet, then very slowly he sat down again, watching Joy's slender, upright back disappear into the distance. What a dreadful mess he'd made of everything! He didn't blame Joy for turning down an offer of marriage which had not only been made clumsily, but had come out of the blue. In all his previous dealings with Joy, he had been careful never to let her know how he felt. He knew how important it was that she should know he loved her for herself, was neither sorry for her nor pitied her. In fact he had loved her ever since he had started accompanying her to school, though in those days he had not realised it. Why in God's name had he not told her so? But the situation was a difficult one; to speak of love to a girl who had had no experience of other men and could not see his face seemed unfair to say the least. And of course it had been madness first to discuss the matter with his aunt and uncle and then to admit that he had talked about her so-called 'sightings' with her sister. The odd thing was that neither Edward himself, nor Gillian, had seen the fatal flaw in Joy's most recent 'sighting' at first, not until she had described the scene in great detail to the pair of them as they had hurried home, Gillian on her left and Edward on her right.

They had taken a boat out on the lake so that Joy could display her rowing skill to Edward, but the boat had sprung a leak and Edward had grabbed the oars from her and made hastily for the bank. The three of them had been standing on the bank, the girls wringing out the skirts of their summer dresses, when Joy had stopped doing that in order to clutch the arm of each. 'I saw it!' she had said, her voice high with excitement. 'I saw the lake, and you, Edward, and Gillian in her best blue gingham dress . . . it's gone again, but I did see it, honest to God.'

Neither of her companions had spoken for a moment, Edward too startled to say anything and Gillian giving him a worried glance before breaking into hasty speech. 'Oh, Joy, how wonderful! But we can't stand here in wet dresses, even though it's a lovely sunny day. We'd best get back home and change.'

They had set off for Old Gadwall Street and it was not until Joy was upstairs cleaning up that Edward had managed to get Gillian to himself and they were able to discuss what had happened, and the discrepancy that had struck them on the way home. For now they both believed that Joy's 'sightings' were not what they seemed. Gillian's dress that day was sunshine yellow; it was Joy who had worn blue gingham.

'I don't understand it,' Gillian had whispered as she and Edward laid the table for tea. 'But I think it's something to do with being a twin, a sort of thought transference, only in pictures. Thinking back, it's only happened two or three times, and on each occasion something pretty dramatic was taking place. The first one was on the platform at Lime Street, when Daddy said I wasn't there and then Joy must have sensed that I was, and thought she'd actually seen me. We do sense each other's presence. The second time was on the beach at Llandudno, when she'd been lost and heard someone whistling . . . and then saw her own legs, scratched and bruised and sandy. Only she thought it was *her* seeing them, whereas really it was me, running over to take her hand and lead her back to the others. Thought transference, in other words – twins can do that sometimes.'

'And the third time was just now,' Edward had volunteered, nodding. 'Because the boat was filling up with water and I was trying to get us ashore . . . it *was* quite dramatic, come to think, and it seems to be dramatic events which poor Joy thinks she actually sees. Now we know different, however, what do we tell Joy?'

'Not the truth, not yet,' Gillian had said decidedly. 'Poor darling, she sets so much store on those "sightings". It would break her heart to know she wasn't seeing with her real eyes, but only with her mind's eye. Leave it to me, Edward. I'll find the right moment.'

But she had not done so, Edward thought ruefully now. And he had gone and put his great foot right in it, and ruined Joy's day. But never mind, he'd make it up to her, take her to Cae Madog and help her to see everything – the cows in the meadow, the sheep on the hill, the poultry clucking round the yard, even the ducks on the pond. He just knew she would love it, for hadn't she loved everything about the Dodmans and life on a Devonshire farm? All he had to do was explain . . . He had best pluck up his courage and go round to Wittard's and ask if he could have a word with Joy.

He arrived in reception and was immediately recognised by the young lady behind the desk. Before he could frame his request, however, she spoke, her voice plaintive. 'Where's Joy? She should have been back half an hour ago, but there's no sign of her yet. We thought she were wi' you.'

'She's not,' Edward said briefly. His mind raced as he sought for an acceptable explanation. 'She wasn't feeling too well, so if she's not here I expect she's gone home.'

'Oh, ah; there's a lot of it about,' the receptionist said, but she was speaking to Edward's back. He was already heading for Old Gadwall Street.

As he hurried along he realised that for the first time he was rather dreading entering the Lawrence kitchen, which would be full of people, including Joy. Their first meeting after the quarrel was bound to be difficult, but he hoped he might persuade her to go for a walk. If he managed to, he would apologise all over again and somehow make things right, though as yet he had no idea how. He wished he could consult Gillian, but that was plainly impossible since neither Gillian nor Keith was any longer in Liverpool. Keith had taken up his old summer job at the Imperial Hotel a couple of days before and Gillian was working there too, waiting on the guests at mealtimes.

Edward smiled to himself as he walked up the familiar road. Joy had been so envious, poor kid, wishing half a dozen times a day that she, too, could be a waitress. 'They get lovely tips and really good meals as well, and quite a lot of time off,' she had told Edward wistfully. 'I like Llandudno, especially the beach; if I were lucky old Gillian I'd spend all my spare time swimming in the sea, exploring the rock pools and building sandcastles.'

She had laughed at herself and Edward had laughed with her. 'You're a real baby,' he had said affectionately. 'The staff at these big hotels get hardly any time off in the summer, so you'd find yourself swimming in the sea and building sandcastles at midnight when you ought to be sleeping.'

Joy had shrugged. 'It wouldn't make any difference, would it, since to me it's as dark at noon as it is at midnight; still, I take your point.' She had chuckled, her mouth curving into the sweet, wistful smile he knew and loved so well. 'So I shan't be a waitress after all. Never mind, Edward, you can think up some other nice career which I would like. Wittard's and the switchboard are beginning to get me down.'

If only I'd spoken then, Edward thought sadly, making his way along the crowded pavement. Why didn't I tell her about Uncle's farm and how she would enjoy living there? Only of course his uncle hadn't made the offer then.

He entered No. 77 by the back door, as he always did, and though there were indeed several people in the room, none of them was Joy. Mrs Clarke was at the sink, cleaning lettuces and new potatoes, Irene was sitting at the table with her little brother in her arms, feeding him spoonfuls of what looked like grey goo, though Irene referred to it as groats, and Chalky was putting away the crockery and cutlery he had just dried up. They all turned as Edward entered the room. 'Hello 'ello 'ello,' Chalky said breezily. 'Hey, ain't some people lucky dogs then! Here it is, nigh on two o'clock and you aren't slavin' over a hot desk. What's up?'

'Nothing. Everything,' Edward said comprehensively. 'Anyone seen Joy? Where's Alex?'

Mrs Clarke turned away from the sink. 'Alex has gone shopping; I offered to go with him but he said not to bother.' She beamed at Edward. 'If you want to know the truth, he's gone along to the coach station to buy tickets for Llandudno. Joy's not working this weekend so Alex thought we might all go down and have a day at the seaside.'

'Oh. Llandudno. Right,' Edward said. He started to back out of the room, then stopped, turning to Chalky. 'What are you doing here?'

'We was invited to lunch by this good lady,' Chalky said, jerking a thumb at Mrs Clarke. 'I expect Alex will get you a ticket an' all if you rush off to the coach station before he's parted with his dosh.'

Edward was halfway down the street, retracing his steps, when a tram rattled up behind him. He glanced at the destination board: *Lime Street Station*, it read. Edward did not hesitate. He jumped aboard the vehicle whilst it was still moving, earning a sharp reproof from the conductor, and sank into a seat. It had suddenly occurred to him that the last place his Joy would go would be to Llandudno. She had been furious to learn that he and Gillian had discussed her mysterious 'sightings', so Llandudno, since the town contained Gillian, would be somewhere she would avoid like the plague.

In the back of his mind, a much likelier destination was struggling to come to the fore. If he sat quietly on the tram and let his mind go where it would, he was pretty sure he would be able to find Joy before any harm befell her. Suddenly it struck him: she would do as her sister had done, though for a very different reason. She would head for the Dodmans' cottage, where she had been so happy, and that must be where he himself would go. It would be difficult, because he only had the haziest idea of precisely where the cottage was, but he knew that Barnstaple was the nearest railway station.

The tram rattled along at a good pace, though it was not fast enough for Edward. If only he could reach her before she bought her ticket, before she boarded a train, then he was sure his earnest protestations and apologies would be enough to bring her to her senses. No, that was not right; it was he who must come to his senses, not she. She had been right to object to the way he had behaved. He had scorned her rather touching faith in the whistler and had then compounded his faults by starting to cast doubts over her ability to see. However, he was prepared to crawl, to eat humble pie until it came out of his ears, to promise the unpromisable – that he would never ask her to marry him again – if only she would return and be his good friend once more.

The tram came to rest outside the station and Edward managed, by being most ungentlemanly, to be the first person off. He charged across the pavement, under the arch and into the concourse. A porter went by, trundling a noisy metal cage packed with suitcases, and Edward grabbed his arm. 'Have you seen a girl, quite young – well, very young – carrying a white stick and wearing . . .' Oh dammit, what had she been wearing? He had never taken much notice of clothes and saw Joy, in his mind's eye, first in blue, then in yellow, then in pink.

But the porter was eyeing him up and down. 'Blind girl?' he asked knowledgeably. 'No luggage, just a red shoulder bag and a white stick? I took her to the train, I did. Platform three; gorra ticket? Can't go on the platform without—'

But Edward was already running towards the ticket office. Fortunately the queue was a short one and presently, heart hammering, Edward was asking for a platform ticket.

The uniformed man behind the glass sighed and reached under the desk, giving Edward a baleful look as he did so. 'That'll be a penny,' he said wearily. 'Last of the big spenders, ain't you?'

He pushed the pink ticket towards Edward, who grabbed it and looked round for Platform 3, found it and ran over, and was about to hand his ticket to the waiting ticket collector when he realised that there was no train drawn up alongside the platform. 'Hang on a minute,' he said as the man held out a grimy hand. 'Where's the train?'

The man tilted his cap to the back of his head and scratched his thinning grey hair. 'If you mean the 3.05, it left five minutes ago,' he said laconically. 'Next one's in an hour.'

Edward's heart descended into his boots, but all was not yet lost. There were other platforms, other trains; he only had one porter's word for it that his little darling had been heading for Platform 3. Edward set off at a smart pace towards Platforms 1 and 2.

Joy arrived at Barnstaple station after what felt like days of travelling instead of hours. She was hot, weary and tear-stained, for when she had telephoned home after a mere couple of hours of travel it was to find the line engaged. She had tried again and again, which was how she had come to miss a connection, and in the end had given up, realising that either there was a fault on the line or someone had knocked the receiver off its hook.

Oddly enough, once she had accepted that she could not get in touch with her father she became far less anxious. No use fretting over what could not be helped, and angry though she had been with Edward, she found herself thinking quite calmly that he would guess where she had gone and reassure Alex.

Right now, however, the guard who had taken care of her on the train hailed a porter. 'The young lady needs a taxi,' he said. 'Tell the driver to see her safely to her destination . . .' He coughed, clearly embarrassed by what he was about to say. 'She can't see so good,' he ended feebly.

Joy laughed when the porter took her arm. 'That's one way of putting it,' she said cheerfully. 'In fact I'm blind as a bat. But once we reach Millers Lane I can direct the driver if he's unsure whose house is which because I was evacuated there during the war and know it well.'

'Right you are,' the porter said. Joy could hear that he was an elderly man and local, since he spoke with the familiar Devonshire burr. He led her out of the station and over to the taxi rank, hesitated, and then took her, she assumed, to the head of whatever queue there was. 'Evenin', Mr Charley,' he said. 'Any objection if I puts this young lady into the next cab?'

Joy guessed there was a good deal of nodding and winking and gesturing to her white stick going on, but though she always claimed that she did not want to use her disability to get special treatment she was too tired and too anxious to reach her destination to quibble. 'Here we are then,' the porter said jovially at last. He opened the car door and helped her inside, addressing the driver with mock ferocity. 'You take good care of this young lady, Bert. She'll give you the address she wants.' He turned to Joy. 'I know 'tes Millers Lane, but are you wanting the Goodys, or one of the cottages?'

Joy leaned forward and addressed the driver in ringing tones. 'Oh, the Dodmans' cottage, please.'

'I knows it,' the man said gruffly. 'Here we go then.'

It was a fair journey out to Millers Lane; Joy, who had walked it often, reckoned it must be about five miles and tried to chat to the driver, but it appeared he was a man of few words. When they reached Millers Lane, however, she learned the reason for his apparent surliness. 'I've got to pick up a regular fare who works nights at one o' they big factories down by the river. It won't do to be late acause they have to clock on,' he explained, slowing as the car began to negotiate the ridges of the untarmacked lane.

'Oh I say, I'm awfully sorry,' Joy said guiltily. Poor man; he had obviously felt he could not refuse to take a fare who was blind. However, she assured him that once he reached the Dodmans' cottage she could manage the short path to the front door and he would not need to leave the car to help her.

'That's rare good of you, miss,' the man said gratefully. He stopped the car and left the engine running while Joy opened the door and jumped out. 'Are you sure you'll be all right?'

'Of course, I'll be fine,' she said happily. Journey's end at last, she was telling herself as she fished the fare out of her purse, added a tip, handed it to the driver and turned to open the Dodmans' small front gate. She heard the car roar off and smiled to herself; the Dodmans would hear the engine and be alerted to the fact that they had a visitor.

Before she had raised her hand to knock she heard a second engine and realised that another vehicle was approaching. Funny! Millers Lane led nowhere – well, it led to the two farm cottages and to the Goodys' farm itself, but it was a dead end – so probably someone had turned into the lane in error.

Still, it was no concern of hers. She knocked. The strange car drew up outside the cottage, then the driver

432

began the manoeuvre which Joy had expected. Yes, someone had driven into Millers Lane by accident, had realised their mistake and was turning round.

Odd, though, that no one had yet answered the door. To be sure, it was late; she had arrived at the station after ten o'clock. But the Dodmans, though early risers, rarely sought their beds before ten or eleven o'clock, and would come down to answer the door from sheer curiosity if nothing else. Joy heaved a deep sigh and knocked again, more loudly this time. She was tempted to simply lift the latch and walk inside, but suppose the Dodmans thought she was a burglar? Mr Dodman had an ancient shotgun . . . No, perhaps simply walking in would not be the sensible thing to do.

Joy stood there, gnawing her lip. Then she was struck by a sudden thought: it was Friday! Once a month, on a Friday, the Dodmans went into the village to a whist drive. Joy cursed. Of course it was just her luck to decide to come calling on whist drive night! What was more, if the Dodmans were at the whist drive they might have chosen to lock the doors. You could never tell; sometimes they did and sometimes they didn't. She put her hand out towards the latch, hesitated, then swung round. Footsteps, the click of the gate, more footsteps.

Suddenly Joy was petrified, too frightened to scream, with nowhere to run and no idea who was approaching. She raised her stick in what she hoped was a threatening manner. 'Who's that?' she managed in a small, shaking voice before a familiar voice spoke her name, familiar arms came round her and she found herself nestling into Edward's embrace; fear and anger swamped in an enormous wave of relief and love.

433

'Edward! How on earth . . . ? I don't understand. I've never told you, where the Dodmans live or anything; but oh, Edward, I'm so pleased it's you! The Dodmans are out and I was beginning to feel so frightened.'

Edward rocked her gently in his arms, resting his chin on the top of her head. Then he must have looked around him and seen the bench which stood just inside the Dodmans' porch. 'Here, let's sit down whilst I explain and apologise all over again.'

Joy laughed. 'Oh, Edward, it's *me* that should be apologising,' she assured him. 'You're my oldest friend, yet I fell out with you and flew off in a temper because you told me the truth. The awful thing is I knew it was the truth, only of course it was a sort of dream and sometimes dreams are even more precious than reality.'

They had sat down side by side on the bench, but suddenly Joy threw her arms round Edward's neck, pulled his head down to hers and began to kiss his face with quick little kisses. 'Oh, Edward, I really do love you. Not better than I love Dad and Gillian, but differently. And if you still want to get married, it's what I want as well.'

Edward gave a deep, contented sigh and lifted her on to his lap. 'Of course I want to get married,' he said huskily. 'Oh, Joy, this is the happiest moment of my life! I took a chance that you were on your way to Devon, as I was pretty sure you were too cross with Gillian to go to Llandudno, and I made my way to Lime Street where I missed you by the skin of my teeth. Fortunately for me, however, you were aboard what they call a stopping train and the one I caught was an express. I actually saw you getting on the second train, but at that stage I simply dared not approach you – remember, you'd told me to bugger off and never come back.'

Joy moaned. 'And you thought I *meant* it? Well, of course I did at the time because I was in a rage, but it didn't last. Anyway, what happened next?'

'Well, when my train stopped at a station, I waited for yours to arrive, checked that you were still aboard, and simply got on myself. Of course by then I knew your destination would be Barnstaple, but you'd never mentioned the Dodmans' address and I was terrified, having followed you so far, of losing you. When you were taken to the head of the taxi queue I very nearly asked if I could share your cab, but whilst I was still dithering your chap drove off.

'Then I'm afraid I behaved very badly. I jumped the queue, hailed the taxi which was just drawing alongside the rank, waved a pound note under the driver's nose and shouted, "Follow that cab!" I'm sure he thought I was a lunatic until I explained that the cab in front contained the girl I meant to marry and then he was a real sport, quite a racing driver in fact. He swerved round corners, cut red lights and generally behaved like a driver in a gangster movie, but I didn't care. I was so keen not to lose you that if he'd refused to take me, I believe I'd have run all the way!'

Joy chuckled. 'What an exciting day we've both had,' she said sleepily. 'Is it very dark, Edward? Can you see how nice the Dodmans' cottage is? Has the moon risen?'

Edward gave her a squeeze and kissed the side of her face. 'The moon is at the full and lighting up everything: the cottage, the garden, the trees, even the lane. Although it's quite a different time of year, and a very different place, I can't help remembering our sledging party, because that was the first time I kissed you.'

Joy drew in a deep breath and released it in a long sigh. 'So it *was* you,' she murmured. She had been nestling in his arms, almost purring with contentment, but now she pulled away and turned to face him. 'You know I said I was hoping for a miracle? Well, it felt like a miracle when you suddenly appeared just now. And when you said I wasn't really seeing with my own eyes I tried not to believe you, even though in my heart I knew you were speaking the truth. I'll never see again, no matter how long I may live.' She nestled into his arms once more, and when she spoke, it was dreamily. 'I'll never see the stars shining up there in the black night sky, but when I'm in your arms, Edward, I'm almost sure I can hear them singing.'

ALSO AVAILABLE IN ARROW

The Lost Days of Summer

Katie Flynn

Nell Whitaker is fifteen when war breaks out and, despite her protests, her mother sends her to live with her Auntie Kath on a remote farm in Anglesey. Life on the farm is hard, and Nell is lonely after living in the busy heart of Liverpool all her life. Only her friendship with young farmhand Bryn makes life bearable. But when he leaves to join the merchant navy, Nell is alone again, with only the promise of his return to keep her spirits up.

But Bryn's ship is sunk, and Bryn is reported drowned, leaving Nell heartbroken. Determined to bury her grief in hard work, Nell finds herself growing closer to Auntie Kath, whose harsh attitude hides a kind heart. Despite their new closeness, however, she dare not question her aunt about the mysterious photograph of a young soldier she discovers in the attic.

As time passes, the women learn to help each other through the rigours of war. And when Nell meets Bryn's friend Hywel, she begins to believe that she, too, may find love . . .

arrow books

A Mistletoe Kiss

Katie Flynn

It was only a mistletoe kiss, Miss Preece told herself, stepping out into the icy December evening and locking the library doors behind her. A mistletoe kiss means nothing, everyone knows that; but this did not quench the warm glow inside her.

Hetty Gilbert is a canal child with no permanent address, so when she needs to join the library, she cannot do so. Miss Preece dislikes children, but Hetty's longing for books touches a chord and she stretches the rules to allow the girl to read on the premises.

Soon, Hetty's chief desire is to become a librarian like her friend. But with war on the horizon, their lives will never be the same. In 1939 Hetty joins in the war effort, for her knowledge of canal boats is desperately needed, whilst Miss Preece can only sit and listen to the dangers her young friend faces, knowing she herself can do nothing to help.

But her chance will come, and with it the meaning behind that fragile mistletoe kiss . . .

You are my Sunshine

Katie Flynn
Writing as Judith Saxton

Kay Duffield's fiancee is about to leave the country, and her own duty with the WAAF is imminent when she becomes a bride. The precious few days she spends with her new husband are quickly forgotten once she starts work as a balloon operator, trained for the heavy work in order to release more men to fight.

There she makes friends with shy Emily Bevan, who has left her parents' hill farm in Wales for the first time; down-to-earth Biddy Bachelor, fresh from the horrors of the Liverpool bombing, and spirited Jo Stewart, the rebel among them, whose disregard for authority looks set to land them all in trouble.

arrow books

WILD THING

Also by Philip Norman

Fiction
Slip on a Fat Lady
Plumridge
Wild Thing (short stories)
The Skaters' Waltz
Words of Love (a novella and stories)
Everyone's Gone to the Moon
The Avocado Fool

Biography and journalism
Shout! The True Story of the Beatles
The Stones
The Road Goes On For Ever
Tilt the Hourglass and Begin Again
Your Walrus Hurt the One You Love
Awful Moments
Pieces of Hate
Elton (reissued as Sir Elton)
The Life and Good Times of the Rolling Stones
Days in the Life: John Lennon Remembered.
The Age of Parody
Buddy: The Biography
John Lennon: The Life
Mick Jagger
Paul McCartney: The Biography
Slowhand: The Life and Music of Eric Clapton

Autobiography
Babycham Night: A Boyhood at the End of the Pier.

Plays and musicals
Words of Love
The Man That Got Away
This is Elvis: Viva Las Vegas
Laughter in the Rain: The Neil Sedaka Story

WILD THING

Also by Philip Norman

Fiction
Slip on a Fat Lady
Plumridge
Wild Thing (short stories)
The Skaters' Waltz
Words of Love (a novella and stories)
Everyone's Gone to the Moon
The Avocado Fool

Biography and journalism
Shout! The True Story of the Beatles
The Stones
The Road Goes On For Ever
Tilt the Hourglass and Begin Again
Your Walrus Hurt the One You Love
Awful Moments
Pieces of Hate
Elton (reissued as Sir Elton)
The Life and Good Times of the Rolling Stones
Days in the Life: John Lennon Remembered.
The Age of Parody
Buddy: The Biography
John Lennon: The Life
Mick Jagger
Paul McCartney: The Biography
Slowhand: The Life and Music of Eric Clapton

Autobiography
Babycham Night: A Boyhood at the End of the Pier.

Plays and musicals
Words of Love
The Man That Got Away
This is Elvis: Viva Las Vegas
Laughter in the Rain: The Neil Sedaka Story